Acclaim for
VIVID

"I was swept away in the magical world of *Vivid*. This rich fantasy is bursting with romance, mystery, and characters both dark and delightful. Strikingly original, *Vivid* is a story that you'll remember long after you close the book."

— JESSICA ARNOLD, author of *The Looking Glass* and *The Lingering Grace*

"Ashley Bustamante's *Vivid* is as rich and colorful as its title suggests. The land of Magus blooms to life from page one, drawing you into an addictive world of irresistible—and forbidden—magic. I simply couldn't put it down. Readers will swoon over this fantastical debut."

— SARA ELLA, award-winning author of the Unblemished trilogy, *Coral*, and *The Wonderland Trials*

"*Vivid* is exactly the magical read I was looking for! It's an exquisite story with unforgettable characters, and I cannot wait for more in this series!"

— S.D. GRIMM, author of the Children of the Blood Moon series and *A Dragon by Any Other Name*

"Captivating. Ashley Bustamante expertly draws the reader into the Magus world where Red and Blue magic thrive and Yellow magic is outlawed. *Vivid* felt like reading a fresh new take on a dystopian society and something akin to *The Story Peddler*'s magic. If that isn't enough, the relationship between Ava and Elm kept me flipping pages for more."

— CANDICE PEDRAZA YAMNITZ, author of *Unbetrothed*

VIVID

ASHLEY BUSTAMANTE

COLOR THEORY | BOOK ONE

Published by Enclave Publishing, an imprint of Oasis Family Media

Phoenix, Arizona, USA.
www.enclavepublishing.com

ISBN: 978-1-62184-230-9 (hardback)
ISBN: 978-1-62184-232-3 (printed softcover)
ISBN: 978-1-62184-231-6 (ebook)

Cover design by Emilie Haney, www.eahcreative.com
Typesetting by Jamie Foley, www.JamieFoley.com

Printed in the United States of America.

To Chris,

who has made my world more vivid

from the moment we met.

1

HOW DO YOU KEEP A MENTALIST OUT
of your head?

How do you evict them when they creep in and seize
control? When the words out of your mouth no longer belong
to you? When your will is torn away?

I shiver and rub my arms, trying to warm away the
goosebumps rippling over my skin. My skirt does absolutely
nothing to help with the cold or with the pine needles poking
my legs. Stupid, impractical uniform.

I readjust—cross-legged feels somewhat better than being
on my knees. The branches of the oak tree above me stretch
out as if to clutch me nearer in a protective way rather than
threatening. The oak is so alien here among the pines, but it's
my favorite spot. Nobody comes here.

In front of me, a cluster of hefty books details the specifics
of Augmentor capabilities and Red magic. The small notebook
in my lap, where I scrawl out ideas, successes, and failures, is
ready to be decorated with discoveries. I survey the textbooks
once more, smoothing the pages down with my fingertips as a
light breeze stirs them to life:

> *Red magic deals with the body. Strength, agility,*
> *and healing are among the core components of Red*
> *magic . . .*

*Any admirable Red uses their power to protect.
Healing is one of the greatest skills an Augmentor
possesses . . .*

*Focus on your body. Imagine yourself growing
stronger. If you start to feel heat, hold onto that
warmth . . .*

Red magic, like any magic, can be dangerous . . .
Don't let yourself be distracted . . .
Don't try anything unusual without guidance . . .
Don't practice new abilities alone . . .

The cautionary words blur together, a deluge of red flags
and flashing lights. What would Selene think if she knew I was
out here trying something like this? On the one hand, as my
mentor, she might rebuke my reckless behavior. On the other
hand, as head Benefactor, she would encourage any efforts
to protect Augmentors and Shapers, wouldn't she? If we can
safeguard our own minds, we will never have to worry about
Yellow magic and Mentalists again.

You don't have to worry about Mentalists now, says the
sneering voice of self-doubt in my head. *The Benefactors make
sure of that. What use are you to the Benefactors?*

True, I've never met a Mentalist, much less seen one in
action. I can't remember the last time I even heard about a
mind-control incident on the news. But it doesn't hurt to be
prepared. An ounce of prevention . . .

So how do I prevent it? As an Augmentor, with power
and command of my body, I should be able to gain power
over my mind. Nobody's allowed in there but me. If I'm
correct, this will revolutionize the world of magic. Combined
with Selene's advances in biology, the results could be even
more widespread. We will have protection. Peace of mind.
Security of mind.

If I don't die.

I reject the thought and take a steadying breath. A

sudden but gentle heat courses through my chest as I begin a strengthening spell. The sensation is welcome, and it's near impossible to resist the temptation of letting it spread. I direct the energy on my brain, drawing all the warmth to one focal point—instead of letting the power fully encompass me as the spell typically calls for.

Nothing. Another failure?

A distinctive warmth reaches my head, like a beam of sunlight. My heart palpitates with anticipation, but I can't let excitement drive away whatever this is. The heat and pressure build. My head twinges in a steady, uncomfortable pulse. I keep going.

A surge of power erupts beneath me like an electric shock. My head snaps backward, jerking my now-fearful eyes wide open. In an instant, the magic flow cuts off, leaving nothing but a dull, unsettling quiver. Lights rupture behind my eyes, and a ferocious pain rips at my skull. I clutch my head and keel over, gasping and moaning on the cold forest floor.

The pain dulls. I open my eyes to a curtain of coppery hair and sweep several tangled strands out of my face. An uncontrolled shiver runs through me.

What *was* that?

Still shaking, I struggle to my feet and brush dry pine needles from my school uniform. My feet are asleep, and I stomp my boots on the mushy earth a few times to bring back the feeling. My wary eyes survey the area. Nothing looks out of place, but the relentless pounding continues in my head. I could use a healing spell, but I don't dare. Who knows what will happen to me if I try using magic again so quickly?

Maybe the books are right—this is reckless. I could die out here, and nobody would know what happened. The thought chills me more than the November air. Perhaps I should listen to the warnings in my textbooks and give my theory a rest until I'm more prepared. Try again some other time.

Time.

Hurriedly, I check my watch. I have an aptitude test, and the last thing I need is to explain tardiness to Selene. But the once-smooth face of my watch is now fractured and jagged. I stare at it, perplexed. Did I land on it, or was this another side effect of the magic? Or someone else's magic? I can't think. I need to get out of here.

I start off but come to an abrupt halt, remembering my books scattered at the base of the tree. I turn back, but perhaps a little too fast, because I crash headlong into something, or rather, someone.

A disoriented moment passes before my eyes lock on a young man—perhaps in his early twenties—in a dark gray jumpsuit. His own eyes carry a frenzied look, like some demented animal. I take in his pale and unkempt figure with snarled, overgrown hair and a gaunt face sporting a layer of stubble. He snaps into an immediate defensive stance, and I jump back in alarm. His wild eyes dart quickly over my uniform, and something about him relaxes.

"You attend Prism, yes?"

"Yes," I say, unable to keep a small note of hesitation out of my voice.

"What direction is it?"

"That way," I point. "Not far from here."

"Delightful." He tips his head at me. "A word of advice, Miss Student. Be more discerning of what you reveal to strangers." I'm startled as he flicks me between the eyebrows. "And tell no one you've seen me." He then takes off at a full run—in the exact opposite direction of the school.

"What in the . . ." I watch him disappear into the trees, trying to process what just happened, but my head gives another throb, reminding me of more pressing matters. I go back to my books and heave them into my bag. Were they always this heavy?

I hurry down the path to the academy, still rickety and disoriented from my experimentation in the woods and the strange encounter with the disheveled young man. Part of me feels I should report it to a Benefactor, but another part calmly reasons that thought away. He didn't hurt me, and he clearly wanted nothing to do with the school, so there is likely no urgency in mentioning it.

I look up at the sky and immediately regret it as another wave of dizziness overtakes me. The sky flickers—just barely perceivable—the only evidence of the magical barrier that keeps us safe from the toxic outer world.

Once I arrive outside the large wrought iron gates to the school grounds, I stop and comb through my hair with my fingers and smooth out my clothes. A few overlooked grains of forest soil pepper my red skirt, and I do my best to rub them away. I have to get it together. I hastily remove my broken watch and tuck it inside my bag, not wanting to answer questions if it were noticed. My bag seems slightly less stuffed than usual. What's missing? Oh no. My notebook. I turn wearily toward the forest, but the thought of returning there, feeling like I do—and with all my books—is torture. Nobody will see it. I'll get it later.

It takes an absurd amount of effort to push open the gate and only slightly less to open the large glass doors leading into the school. My body feels wrong, like I'm lacking substance somehow. Each step against the silvery marble floors feels unsteady and disorienting.

I try to ground myself by focusing on reality and the things I know for certain: I'm Ava Locke. I'm seventeen years old. I'm not bleeding. My bones don't feel broken. Mind still intact. I'm okay, right?

I could see Dr. Iris—Prism's resident Healer—as a precaution, but that would mean explaining how I ignored all the safety rules they teach us from day one.

I'm fine.

There are stories, though. The ones about Augmentors who did dangerous things and ended up hurt on the inside. They didn't know until it was too late. Not until their bones puffed into dust or their organs split open.

Fine. I'll give it ten minutes. If nothing improves, I'll visit the Healer's office. "Walk it off," I tell myself, ambling in the direction of the locker rooms so I can change into athletic gear for the aptitude test.

Down the main corridor, a gaggle of male Red-magic students peacock for a group of Red and Blue girls on the sofa and lounge chairs. I'm surprised to see them together. Separation of magic types tends to happen organically at Prism because many of our classes have to be split by color. Friendships naturally form with those we see most. Well, naturally for those who have room for the distraction. My studies leave little time for anything else.

I pause to watch as the boys take turns lifting various pieces of furniture with the girls—squealing and giggling—still sitting on top. A pretty, dark-skinned Shaper I recognize from one of my Elite classes watches nearby.

She rolls her eyes. "Any Augmentor could do that." She glances over, noticing me. "Hey, Ava, come show them."

It shouldn't be surprising that she knows me—many students recognize me as Selene's mentee. Nevertheless, the acknowledgement catches me off guard and fills me with embarrassment because I can't remember her name. Natalie? No, Nikki. I think it's Nikki.

They're all staring at me, waiting for a response.

"Oh, I don't think we're supposed to . . ." It's a predictably dull reply, but I still don't trust myself to use more magic.

"No biggie if you don't want to." Nikki—or was it Natalie—shrugs. "I just wanted to show these guys they're no big deal."

"I have to get ready for an aptitude test. Sorry," I mumble, wishing I could stay. As I retreat, I pass under an archway with the inscription All Questions Will Be Answered. It is the creed of the Benefactors and one of the reasons I hope to unite with them; transparency in leadership is admirable. This reminder lifts my spirits. Someday I'll be working with Selene and the other Benefactors to answer all the questions in the land of Magus. No more need for secrets in the forest.

A smell stings my nose the instant I enter the test room—a harsh scent with a hint of citrus. Cleaning chemicals. Now, the question is, did they clean up vomit or blood? The first-year aptitude tests were in this room last hour, so it had to be one or the other. Mishaps abound in that group.

As though confirming my suspicions of calamity, Dr. Iris leans against the far wall of the classroom. The tight line of her lips and the way her hair hangs loose from its braid in distressed strands betrays any attempt at composure. Her skin beads with moisture, causing her glasses to inch down her nose. Likely, she has already remedied multiple accidents today. We anticipate injuries during aptitude tests, especially for students in their final year, and a Healer is always on hand in case of anything severe. Hopefully I won't need her services today.

"How bad was it?" I ask.

Dr. Iris merely shakes her head. "Bad enough."

"Good morning, Dr. Iris. Ava." The voice behind me reverberates in the near emptiness of the room, not unfriendly, but authoritative. Selene stands tall and is all business, her hair pulled into a no-nonsense ponytail.

"Good morning," I greet Selene quickly, masking my

apprehension. I'm eager to show her my skills in the hope that she'll return even a fraction of the admiration I have for her, but I still feel just a bit off. Why did I think it was a good idea to mess around before a test?

Selene slings her satchel onto the teacher's desk and rifles through it as she asks Dr. Iris, "Any severe incidents I should be aware of?"

"I'll brief you once you're settled."

"Thank you." Selene pulls a chart from her bag. Today's name pairings for the aptitude test. I want to reach out and grab it from her hands but will myself to wait until she posts it on the wall. She glances at me. "Would you like to know who you're testing against?" She knows me too well.

"Yes, please."

"Blake Woods. Can you handle that?"

Blake Woods—a Blue Shaper, and a far-too-familiar face. His parents are my legal guardians during school breaks, so he's practically my brother. Can I treat a match with him the same as any other?

"It won't change how I fight." Maybe if I say it, I'll believe it.

Selene studies my face, and I shrink under her perceptive stare, fearing my anxiety shows. Unacceptable weakness. "You realize the other students—and your instructors—will compare you no matter your connection. He's your competition first and foremost. Don't forget that."

I nod. Selene always challenges me to consider every angle. I never thought of my relationship with Blake as a hurdle . . . but here we are. We're both Elite students, and while I'm top rank, he's not far behind. What does it mean for my future if I can't fight him objectively?

Selene fastens the chart to the bulletin board. "I look forward to viewing your accomplishments, Ava." She joins Dr. Iris, and the two begin a murmured conversation about last-hour's events.

Students trickle into the room, pausing to view the chart, and then line up along the wall beside me like a row of obedient ducklings. Like me, everyone is decked out in athletic shirts of their respective magic colors and black tactical pants. The air booms with sudden boisterous laughter as Blake enters with a group of companions. As they stop to view the name pairings, one of our classmates elbows Blake. "You're up against Ava? She'll destroy you."

"She knows your fighting style. It'll be fun to see you get squashed," another student goads.

Blake rolls his eyes at his friend and flashes a light grin in my direction. He turns to Selene. "Do we get a lifeline today?"

There are two large baskets of kickballs—one containing red and the other blue—against the wall closest to Selene. Our instructors sometimes allow one "lifeline" in our respective magic color to give us something besides our gemstone pendants to draw power from.

"One lifeline," Selene responds and returns to her conversation.

I toy with the tear-shaped pendant around my neck, wondering whether the lifeline is a blessing or a curse. On the one hand, it means a chance for extra power if needed—stones behave as an amplifier for our magic, but we can only reach a certain "volume" without an extra power source. On the other hand, it means more strategizing, and I know Selene will be judging that too.

At eight a.m. sharp, Selene does a quick visual inventory of the room. She scrutinizes me for just a moment. Though she tries to appear unbiased, she fails to conceal the reflection of pride in her eyes. This should be comforting, but it only adds weight to my desire to please her.

She delivers instructions to the group. "Today's matches will be ten minutes. School pendants and one lifeline are allowed. Drawing from any other objects will mean immediate disqualification and a failing grade. Non-life-threatening injuries are permitted."

So, I'm allowed to hurt Blake. Will I do that if it comes down to it? Will he? Does Selene expect that of me?

Selene picks up a clipboard and pen for taking notes and nods her head toward the center of the room. "Ava and Blake, you're up."

Blake steps forward without a second's hesitation. He's of average build, but he's handsome. He takes his place on the floor, cocks his head to the side with a confident smile, and directs his attention to the blue basket. One of the balls floats free from the rest and makes its way to Blake's hands. Foolish. I've told him before he should save his energy for the test instead of wasting it on bravado, but Blake is Blake.

I step out of line, hoping to show the same level of confidence he exudes, and grab a red ball from the basket before meeting Blake in the center. We place the balls on the ground—it doesn't matter where they are at this point, as long as we can access them when needed. Blake extends a hand toward me, and we shake.

"Well, this should be fun. Good luck," he says brightly.

How can he be so casual in the face of pressure? I'm sure I can feel the cloud of Selene's judgment on my every move. "Let's take this seriously, okay?"

He looks a little surprised, as though he truly expected playful sparring. But Selene made it clear the stakes are high with Blake as my competitor, creating an even greater desire for me to come out on top.

As we move to opposite ends of the room, I plan my approach, utilizing each second of time before the test starts. My mind habitually singles out red objects everywhere as potential power sources, even though that isn't an option for this match. I focus on the space we have to work with. The desks have been pushed against the walls to make more room for us and might provide cover if needed. I could easily strengthen myself enough to throw one at Blake, but then that may hurt him too much. Maybe—

"You may begin," says Selene, abruptly ending my time to strategize.

I focus on my body. My muscles. My skin. As an Augmentor drawing on Red magic, I use powers of the body. Strength, healing, agility.

A pair of scissors flying toward me catches me off guard. Shapers manipulate and control objects in the space around them, and Blake is ready to fight. I must have spooked him when he realized I wasn't here to play.

Warmth from my magic spreads through me, but before I complete my strengthening spell, Blake strikes. The sharp points of the scissors slash into my arm, and I hear a unanimous gasp from our observing classmates.

I flinch, but strive to hold my spell. "So, you *are* taking this seriously."

"You started it."

If he isn't showing me any grace due to our ties, there's no sense in holding back. As my body grows stronger, the pain from my wound dissipates, and I feel reborn. The effects from this morning have also vanished. Blake hasn't abandoned the idea of the scissors, and I see a metallic flash when they pull back, as if held by a phantom hand, and move forward to strike again. I snatch them out of the air, throwing them hard across the room. Propelled by the extra force of my strengthening spell, they dig several inches into the wall.

"Have fun getting those out," I say, hoping to throw him off balance.

"It's not a competition, you know," he says through gritted teeth, mentally struggling to free the scissors. "We get an individual score on skill, even if we don't pummel each other."

I'm all too aware of Selene silently watching our every move. "It's *always* a competition." Doesn't he realize that?

While Blake grasps for a new tactic, I tend to the injury on my arm. I direct all my attention to the damaged area, envisioning the cut pulling closed and my skin fusing together. A bright heat surrounds the gash, followed by a strange prickling sensation. The wound begins to close, and within a matter of seconds, my body is once again unscathed. I know Blake won't waste time on those scissors forever. Anticipating his next move, I immediately begin another strengthening spell.

With his object manipulation, Blake can propel things at me from a distance. I don't have that luxury. My power lies within my body, and I can't do much without getting close to him.

I advance on him but change course rapidly as a heavy book targets my face, followed quickly by a stapler. As I duck away, a particularly malicious steel protractor skims the top of my head.

"You're not getting even an inch closer," Blake taunts as he continues to hurl various objects at me. My agility spells quicken my reflexes enough to dodge these objects, but each rapid movement requires more effort. At this rate, he'll wear me out. Do I dare use my lifeline this soon in the match? We're caught in a loop of throwing and dodging. If I don't think of something fast, my test time will pass with virtually nothing accomplished that would impress Selene.

I shriek as my pendant flies off my neck without warning, and I scramble to grab it before it gets away, clutching it securely in my hands.

"That's dirty," I shout. I hear roars of agreement from our classmates. Our powers are nearly obsolete without another source to draw on, which is why every magic user worth their salt wears a stone of some kind—a power source that never fades, though there are limits to its power.

"It's always a competition," Blake mocks, though his smirk doesn't reach his eyes, which seem to offer an apology.

Still, he went there. I pull power from my pendant carefully, in spurts. With each object Blake sends my way, I send it back to him with a punch of my Red-powered fist. He isn't as fast as I am, and it doesn't take long before he gets clipped by the very objects he tries to hit me with.

I cuff an unfortunate textbook with a particularly zealous blow, and the spine cracks, sending its pages flying. I gasp and jerk my head toward Selene, my eyes wide. "Sorry!" A ruined book is a tragedy.

She clears her throat loudly, and I snap my attention back to Blake. In my moment of distraction, he changed tactics. His body is still, but his expression is intense. Curious, I divert my eyes to his lifeline. As expected, the vibrant blue of the ball rapidly fades to gray as Blake pulls its color away to amplify his magic. He's gambling everything on this play. Another book flies at my head, but stops abruptly and floats toward the center of the room. Pencils, papers, chalk, erasers, and a barrage of other school supplies all shoot in the direction of the book and branch out.

I don't know what Blake has planned, but this could be my one opening. After taking a moment to catch my breath, I build my strength and speed and sprint toward him. The sudden blur of a huge object causes me to change course and flit out of the way as it blocks my path.

It takes a moment to fully process the oddity before me—an amalgamation of classroom tools forming a giant, lumbering spider. Unsteady and unpredictable. Blake breaks out in a sweat with the effort it takes to control his hodgepodge of a creation and keep it assembled. The spider throws one of its legs down in front of me, forbidding any progression closer to Blake.

Surprisingly swift, the spider swings another of its

composite legs at me, and I leap to avoid it. I miss the brunt of the blow, but it still manages to clip my ankle. My heavy boots aren't enough to spare me from the pain. Taking time to stop and heal could be my undoing, so I work through the discomfort. The spider flails its limbs again and again, missing each time, but only just. It's clear that without putting some space between us, I don't stand a chance of beating it.

Rolling underneath the desks against the wall, I crawl as far back as the space allows, silently praying Selene hasn't noticed the fear my expression surely exposes.

Meanwhile, Blake struggles to maneuver his formation. It requires much more precision to go after me in my tight hiding place than it did to swat at me out in the open. This buys me the time I need to build my vigor once more.

My body feels like a live wire. The amount of power I can draw from my pendant reaches its plateau. With luck, it will be just enough . . . but I'm not the type to rely on luck. My eyes scan for my lifeline, but I can't get a visual on it from my hidden position. I'm not sure if I can focus enough to draw on it without risking accidentally pulling from another red object. Drat!

Sensing movement from the spider again, I heave out from under the desks as it smashes into them. I glance away from the spider just long enough to search for that precious red ball. There. Across the room. I focus on it and pull hard for its power, then make a fierce dash through the spider's legs, directing myself beneath its center. With all the force I can muster, I spring upward and smash into the creature's core. It bursts apart, but instead of the satisfying explosion I expected, it seems to be moving in slow motion. I don't believe it . . . Blake is trying to piece everything back together. But his moves are sloppy. He's blindly pulling objects in every direction and has lost all control.

And then I catch a glint—those scissors have finally come

loose from the wall and are now headed right toward Blake's face at high speed. I use a burst of agility to land in front of Blake and throw my arm up, sending the scissors flying in the opposite direction. Blake at last gives out, and the remaining floating objects fall. We exchange a quick look, his eyes quizzical. I don't even want to see what expression might be on Selene's face.

"Time," says Selene. "Very resourceful, Blake. That's one of the most interesting creations I have ever seen. Ava," she adds, as an afterthought, "your speed is good."

I should be watching and learning as the rest of the class goes through their aptitude tests, but an anxious tempest undulates inside me. Selene's words had an obvious undercurrent of disappointment. Should I have been more aggressive? What can I offer beyond skill? All Benefactors are skilled—that's how they get to be Benefactors to begin with—so proficiency alone isn't enough. Unlike me, Blake is personable and has many friends, and his parents are already prominent Benefactors. If he chooses to be a Benefactor himself, he will progress rapidly to the top. But was I just supposed to let those scissors hit him?

When class ends, I assist my classmates in the obligatory task of cleaning up drained lifelines and putting the room back in order. As we work, a Benefactor enters the room, making a beeline for Selene, and whispers in her ear. Selene's eyes widen, and they both exit at a brisk pace. Shoot. I was hoping to catch her before she left. I need to explain myself. I avoid Blake's gaze as I toss the last ball in the "to be recolored" basket and chase through the doorway after her.

2

SELENE IS AT THE END OF THE HALLWAY,
still talking rapidly with the other Benefactor. She looks . . .
angry? Worried? The Benefactor leaves, rushing down the left
corridor. An urgent student issue, perhaps? Whatever the case,
I don't want to lose my window. Selene is already headed down
the right corridor, and I run to catch up, mentally rehearsing
what I want to say.

The main job of the Benefactors is to protect, so of course I
would want to help Blake. That's reasonable, right?

"Selene," I say as I approach, "About my test—"

"Ava, now is *not* the time—"

Commotion sounds from the next hallway. Through the
babble of voices, I'm able to make out bits and pieces:

"In the sky! Do you see it?"

"What does it say?"

"It's yellow!"

I stiffen for a moment before bolting to the nearest window.
Crying *yellow* in Magus is the equivalent of yelling *bomb* or
fire. Yellow, the power source of mind-controlling Mentalists,
is forbidden.

Several other students try to get to the window now, and
I stubbornly hold my ground. Floating in the sky above the
school are four wispy words, in blinding yellow:

See you soon! —Elm

"Stand aside," Selene pushes through the students, and her face contorts with fury as she reads the message in the sky.

Another Benefactor sprints down the hall, red faced and out of breath.

"Selene, did you—"

"Of course I saw it," she shouts back. "That idiot!"

The students stare in surprise. We have never seen her lose her cool before.

As if remembering she has an audience, Selene takes a breath, steadies herself, and turns to the red-faced Benefactor.

I strain to hear her over the thunder of excited students.

"Obviously, we have no choice but to inform the students now. We need to make sure no further damage is done. Please, call an emergency assembly in the auditorium."

Selene raises her voice. "Quiet, please, everyone! All questions will be answered. You are all to report immediately to the main auditorium. No detours, please."

I take one last glance at the strange message in the sky before joining the now-fearful crowd of students.

The congested auditorium reverberates with discussion. Students crowd every seat on the floor, sporting either red or blue school uniforms. The walls of the room match, each alternating between the two colors. This is the one place in the school that lacks elegance, choosing instead to promote unabashed school spirit. The teachers stand at various points around the perimeter to confirm order and safety, ensuring all students are securely in their seats. Everyone, regardless of location, stares at the podium at the front of the auditorium, waiting. After a few minutes, Selene enters with two other Benefactors beside her—a man and a woman. The man seems familiar to me with his graying goatee, bulbous nose, and prominent eyebrows, but I can't quite place him. I do not recognize the woman. Something about her pale blue eyes and white-blonde hair makes me think of winter. If a snowflake ever became human, I imagine it would look like her. All three faces are unreadable. No doubt they are trying to present a calm demeanor to the student body. Through the uncertainty, I feel a brief twinge of longing, wishing I could be there with them.

Selene steps forward, and the loud chatter quiets to hushed murmurs, then silence. Selene's grave voice—amplified by a strengthening spell—echoes through the room. "We, the Benefactors, are charged with the safety and well-being of the entire world of Magus, most especially the students of Prism Academy. Therefore, it is our duty to inform you of a new danger among us."

The murmurs start up again, but the teachers cut everyone off with a thunderous "shh."

Selene continues. "I'm sorry to report the discovery of a rogue Mentalist."

Selene holds an egg-shaped device in her hand—a viewdrop—and clicks a button, causing an image of a man to flicker into view on the wall in front of us. He wears a gray outfit that reminds me of a magician. Not a true magician, but one of the illusionists from hundreds of years ago, before Magus was known to the world. The ensemble consists of a clean-cut gray suit, cloak, and top hat. Pale yellow lines his cloak, and he wears a vest and tie of the same color. His style of dress isn't entirely unusual for Magus. Fashion became progressively flashier over time as magic-users sought to make a name for themselves. His face has a sinister smirk. It's hard to make out details due to the shadow cast from his hat, but something about the features holds a vague familiarity.

Selene speaks over the picture's display. "This is Elm Ridley—a very powerful and very dangerous Yellow magic-user—a Mentalist. We are taking the highest precautions to make sure our students are safe and that Elm cannot harm you. However, should any of you spot him or notice anything suspicious, you are to report it to a Benefactor immediately. Do not speak to him. Do not engage him. Remember that Mentalists are able to manipulate the mind and use the lowest forms of cunning and deception." The image of Elm disappears, and Selene addresses us again. "As a friendly reminder, the color yellow is banned. Yellow clothing, objects, or anything of the sort, is strictly forbidden. Students breaking this rule must be reported immediately, and appropriate action will be taken. This is especially important now, with Elm on the loose. Any yellow object can serve to strengthen his power. The odds of catching Elm are higher in our favor if his power is limited. We expect and appreciate your cooperation in this matter."

The auditorium explodes into disarray, every student wondering about these new developments. A voice comes over the loudspeaker, barely audible above the chaos. "Attention, students. Classes will resume as normal. Please report to your classrooms."

Perhaps more than all else, the Benefactors like to maintain order. Disruptions in routine must be kept to a minimum. It's probably easier for them to keep an eye on us in class, anyway. The students release a collective moan of disappointment and begrudgingly file out of the auditorium, but the speculative rumblings continue.

I linger behind as students shuffle past me. *Tell her. Tell her. Tell her.* My conscience nags at me. We were told to report anything suspicious, and the encounter in the woods definitely falls under the odd category.

Selene makes her way to exit the auditorium, the other two Benefactors in tow. They speak with one another, grim looks etched on each of their faces. I shouldn't put it off.

Selene notices me as I approach, and I open my mouth to tell her about my encounter, but something compels me to stop, and I can't get the words out. Telling her suddenly doesn't seem so urgent. I stay silent, and instead she speaks. "Since we won't have lessons today, I have a job for you."

My heartbeat quickens in eager anticipation, any thought of speaking to her gone. Am I finally being allowed more responsibility? Maybe Selene wasn't as disappointed in my aptitude test as I thought.

Selene holds out a sheet of paper with a picture of Elm and the word WANTED in bold letters. Someone altered the yellow on Elm's clothing to a neutral gray in accordance with the ban on the color. "I need you to make copies of this and distribute them in and around the school."

Making copies. How anticlimactic. As a ward of the school, I'm given a small allowance; in exchange, I do student-worker tasks like this from time to time. Not exactly high-status work. It's amazing how such a small thing can shatter my hopes so completely.

I take the sheet of paper from her, and she must sense my crestfallen mood because her voice is gentle, "I know it may not seem important, but the sooner we get a lead on Elm, the better. Increased student awareness is vital to this cause. Sometimes, the small things make all the difference."

"Of course," I reply, still stifling disappointment. "I'll take care of it.

The keys to the battered supply room door nearly fall from my hands when I jump at the sight of the figure inside.

"Sorry to spook you, Ava. I'm just finishing up. Selene asked me to hurry down and make sure this was ready to go."

I smile in relief at Mr. Dawson—a Shaper, and the instructor of the Blue-Magic Application class—who recharges the copier's stone every few weeks.

"Take your time," I say.

Blue magic powers many of the devices on Magus when possible, as it enables us to do things we couldn't do with electricity alone. The copy machine is a perfect example. What used to merely print copies on pieces of paper can now physically duplicate plant-based physical objects.

Mr. Dawson removes his hands from the large blue stone set into the left side of the smooth, polished rectangle of the copier. "There we are. Let's give it a test run." Mr. Dawson places the flyer I hand him onto the copier's surface. I punch a quantity into the keypad, and the machine glows.

Mr. Dawson eyes the criminal's face on the growing stack of flyers, brow furrowed.

"Who exactly is Elm?" I ask. Judging by Elm's message in the sky, he has a lot of nerve, but that's all I know.

He shakes his head. "I haven't heard anything about a Mentalist in years. I was beginning to think they didn't exist anymore."

I consider this. I thought the Mentalists were all . . . where, exactly? I search my brain, digging deep, but I can't produce any memory of hearing about where they went.

"Ah, I'm running late to my own class," says Mr. Dawson, excusing himself. "Take care of yourself, Ava."

The door clicks shut behind him, and the repetitive sounds of the copy machine allow my mind to meander. *Where did you come from?* I stare at Elm's multiplying picture. While studying his face, it strikes me why he seems familiar: The man in the woods. Could it be? No, surely not. They look completely different. The person in the picture seems older. Not so haggard. Besides, if I had bumped into Elm, I probably wouldn't still be here—if he's as dangerous as the Benefactors say he is. There's no need to sensationalize things because of an escaped criminal. *That's right,* says the voice in my mind. *Nothing to worry about.*

The machine notifies me with a cheerful chime that it has finished. I gather the large stack of papers in my arms, flick off the lights, and make sure the door is locked securely.

As I navigate the school, leaving pictures of Elm in high-traffic areas, I notice a large number of Benefactors present in the corridors. They are glancing about, speaking in intense whispers, and gesturing nervously. They must be looking for ways to safeguard the school. Usually, the Benefactors don't release details of these measures to students—it isn't necessary to know how they keep us safe, only that they do. I hurry along, so they don't think I'm spying. It's important that I stay in their good graces, especially now that I'm in my final year.

After thoroughly papering the inside of the school, I move onto the grounds. Not a trace remains of the writing in the sky. Did it disappear on its own, or did the Benefactors manage to make it vanish somehow? I can still see it burned clearly in my mind, and it seems to appear in front of my eyes everywhere I look. Up in the clouds. In the trees. Near the forest.

The forest . . .

My notebook is still there. Would it be problematic if Elm came across it? My name is written in it. I know little about how Yellow magic and mind control work—what if something as simple as that could give him access to my thoughts? But besides that, the Benefactors are sure to be patrolling the area. If they find my notebook, they will have questions for me, and I'm bound to let the whole story out. What would Selene say if she learned I was practicing untested magic in the forest alone? Not good.

I set off toward my forested study spot. As a precaution, I place flyers on random trees and light posts along the path as I go, so I'll have an excuse if someone sees me.

As I prepare to place the last flyer near the cusp of the forest, I catch a flash of something out of the corner of my eye. A bright glint of . . . yellow? I whirl toward the source and stand still, eyes darting. My body begins strengthening itself, bracing to fight or run, or whatever might be required. But there is nothing within the forest except the shadows of the trees. My heart pounds, and I stay frozen for a minute or two more.

I don't see anything.

I turn back toward the tree I was placing the flyer on but stop myself. Instead, I spastically stuff the last paper into my school bag and take off at a full run toward the school, casting one last uneasy glance back at the forest. Forget the notebook. I'll deal with the consequences.

The words *See you soon!* play across my mind, powering my escape.

3

I GRIND THROUGH MY LAST CLASS OF
the day like a restless child. As a rule, school receives my full
attention, but today the library beckons like a siren's song.
The other students are equally fidgety, which tells me I'm not
the only one bursting with questions and curiosity . . . and a
touch of fear. This morning's announcement was a minefield,
detonating waves of excitement and leaving the student body
shaken in its wake. But, regardless of what we might otherwise
wish to be doing, we still have to get over the hump of classes.

Today's final hump is intermediate healing. In previous
lessons, we healed minor wounds such as paper cuts and small
scratches. Now, we're moving on to slightly bigger and deeper
wounds. Of course, we can't heal injuries that don't exist.

"Can't we just cut you instead?" a student asks.

The rest of the class releases nervous laughter, and our
healing instructor, Mr. Blythe, shakes his head.

"It takes a much higher level of skill to use Red magic on
someone else," he says. "Healers go through years of training
to perfect it. Deal with it."

We all stare uneasily at the sharp blades placed in front of
us. The blades might look innocent if we didn't know what
we had to do with them. Mr. Blythe takes his own knife and
demonstrates the safest place on his palm to cut.

"You don't want to risk doing damage to tendons or muscles, or it will be much more difficult to heal. Don't go more than about two millimeters deep." He hardly flinches as the blade grazes his skin, leaving a blossoming streak of red. I cringe along with the rest of the students.

Dr. Iris stands by in case someone acts carelessly. And, from what I hear about this lesson, someone usually does. Perhaps this is why she looks so guarded. Every now and then, she nudges her dark glasses up on her pointed nose.

Mr. Blythe delivers a few more instructions and tips, and then he turns us loose. The class erupts into awkward giggles and squeaks of pain as we slice into our flesh. Only in a healing class would this sort of mutilation ever be condoned. I take a deep breath, knowing hesitation won't make it any easier. A quick, searing sting and then relief as I start my healing spell.

Mr. Blythe walks by my desk, observing my clean skin. "Aren't you going to get started, Ms. Locke?"

"I already did it." Ick. Is he going to make me do it again?

"Once more, if you don't mind," he says.

Drat.

My skin takes another swift slice, and I heal just as quickly.

"Very good!" Mr. Blythe remarks. "You have the hang of this."

"I've practiced this with Selene," I explain.

"Why don't you see if you can help anyone else out? Sarah looks like she could use a hand."

He gestures toward one of my classmates sitting quietly at her desk and staring in fixation at the instrument before her. She hasn't attempted a single cut. My heart fills with sympathy, recalling my first healing lesson. It took significant encouragement from Selene before I worked up the nerve to do it. I can imagine how Sarah feels, dreading the sensation of the knife and the trickle of fresh, warm blood.

"Hey," I say, approaching her. "Need some help?"

"I don't think I can do this," she says, looking nauseated.

"It's not that bad. It only stings a little, and it heals up pretty quickly."

She continues staring at the blade on the desk. "I really don't do well with blood."

I attempt my best encouraging smile. "That's why this is a great skill to learn. Next time you get a cut, you can make the blood disappear that much quicker."

She frowns, unconvinced, then asks, "Do you think maybe you could do the cutting? I think that would be easier for me than doing it myself. Then I can just focus on the healing part."

I give a nervous laugh. "If you think it will help." I don't want to, but we can't pass the class without this lesson, so I feel compelled to do what I can for her.

Sarah holds out her hand and squeezes her eyes shut tight. She tenses as I swiftly draw the blade across her skin, but otherwise she doesn't react.

"The worst is over," I say cheerfully. "Now, concentrate on your hand. Wait until you start to feel heat, then imagine it moving outward."

She opens her eyes and looks at the shallow cut. The color drains rapidly from her face. Maybe this was a mistake.

"Oh no. Oh no," she mutters.

"It's okay," I say, hoping my words might reassure her. "Start healing now."

Breathing heavily, she closes her eyes. "Focus on my hand."

I watch, expecting to see the cut diminishing, but instead it grows larger.

"Um . . . Sarah?"

She opens her eyes and sees the enlarged wound, which now flows more steadily with blood. She panics.

"Oh no. How do I stop it?" Her voice is pitched.

Something is odd. The bright red blood on her hand

gradually dulls in color, becoming muted like an old photograph. It takes me a second to realize what's happening.

"No, stop! You shouldn't drain power from your own blood!" Normally, magic-users can't draw on body parts or liquids. Augmentors and blood are the one exception, likely because Red magic-users are so connected to the body. Doing this is perilous, as blood becomes useless once lacking its color.

"I feel dizzy," Sarah says. The sight of her blood is confounding her so much she just continues to suck it dry of pigment. At this rate, she'll do permanent damage.

I rush to Dr. Iris, who has just finished healing the hand of another student. When I explain the situation, she immediately hurries to the now passed-out Sarah. Finding the wound through the gush of fading blood, Dr. Iris thrusts her hands over the cut. She begins a healing spell under the encompassing eyes of students and Mr. Blythe, all of whom now convene around Sarah's desk. The cut is gone in an instant—the work of a pro—and Dr. Iris keeps her attention on Sarah. A soft red glow works outward from Sarah's hand to the rest of her body as Dr. Iris repairs the damage from the depleted blood.

After a few moments, Sarah lazily opens her eyes, and we heave a collective sigh. Mr. Blythe helps her up, shooing students away and talking to her softly to explain her mistake.

Dr. Iris's face relaxes but almost immediately pinches in irritation. "This is exactly why I didn't think it was a good idea to do this lesson today. The students are too wired from this morning."

"Will Sarah be okay?" I ask.

"Oh, she'll be fine. She's not the first Red student to draw from her own blood instead of healing. We caught it fast enough. She'll just need to take it easy while her blood filters through her system."

Mr. Blythe tries to bring us back to our assignment, but for all the good it does him, he might as well be communicating with a pile of rocks. As Dr. Iris said, Elm's escape already has us too worked up. Add a classroom calamity on top of that, and the room is in chaos. Mr. Blythe dismisses us early, which suits me fine. I move resolutely to the library to find as many books as I can on Yellow magic.

I float in a wavering, vast space. Soft colors distort and shimmer all around me, a pearlescent ripple in varying shades of blue, purple, and silver. I reach out to touch them, but my hand slips into empty air. As I drift in circles, trying to make sense of it all, a round, swirling vortex opens up a short way ahead of me, smoky and white. I fixate on it and take a step, which is an odd sensation since my feet can't seem to find solid ground. As I approach the vortex, a figure jumps out of it, and I leap back in surprise. He turns in my direction.

It's Elm.

My senses light on fire, yet I can't react. He considers me for a moment, winks, and then vanishes into another swirling mass as quickly as he arrived.

I blink my eyelashes, slowly awakening. My alarm hasn't gone off yet, so I cocoon myself in the cozy, burgundy covers of my twin bed, thinking about the dream. Well, I guess it isn't remarkable that I would dream about Elm. I saw his face on those wanted posters all day. I spent hours at the library trying to learn something about him. About Mentalists.

I lie awake in bed for a while, lingering on the dream and replaying it in my mind, unwilling to let it slip away from memory the way dreams often do. When I at last hear muffled sounds of other students waking in the rooms that share a wall with mine, I drag myself up to get ready for the day.

At breakfast, my lack of sleep makes me sluggish as I scan the dining choices.

"Eggs today. Wow," someone says.

My stomach churns as I rest my eyes on the tray of scrambled eggs. Gray, colorless mush. They are not the fluffy, appetizing yellow I recall from my childhood. Eggs, like other yellow foods, now go through a color-draining process before landing on tables or in grocery stores. Yellow foods are strictly regulated, and it's against the law to produce them independently. I haven't ever adjusted to the unappealing color and milder taste of these altered foods, particularly since Augmentors tend to be more sensitive to taste and smell. The color-draining process also makes yellow foods significantly more expensive. Whoever added eggs to the menu today probably thought they were giving us a treat. I skip the eggs and pile my plate with toast.

I seat myself at a table occupied by a group of students, but I'm not actually sitting *with* them. Maybe I'll have closer relationships with my colleagues once I'm a Benefactor. Surely there will be time for friends when I'm not constantly studying?

"I heard Elm is part demon."

My ears perk up at Elm's name, and I slow my eating to eavesdrop. There's no way Elm is actually part demon, but I'm curious to hear any spreading rumors. Any information, even hearsay, is interesting to me at this point.

"They say he takes control of people's minds and drives them insane."

"Why would they keep us in school when someone that dangerous is loose?"

"Seriously. I was hoping to at least get out of some homework."

I want to join the discussion and mention that being here, with the Benefactors, is likely the safest place we could be at the moment. It wouldn't make sense to send students anywhere else. But before I can work up the courage, the conversation moves forward, and I continue to listen in silence to their wild rumors and stories.

Get it together, Ava. Your elective class is supposed to be fun.

Even as I tell myself this, I fantasize about skipping class in order to research in the library. The intrigue of Yellow magic is strong, and I keep hoping to come across new information, some lost grain of enlightenment that I haven't yet sifted through. Because I can't bring myself to skip even an elective class, however, I attempt to make the most of it.

At Selene's recommendation, my elective is Blue-Magic Application. She believes a Benefactor should be well-rounded in their knowledge of magic types because they will represent more than their own. Without the ability to use Blue magic myself, I'm here merely as an observer.

I move to my usual spot near the back of the classroom and set my bag on the desk to prepare. It's easier to linger in the background, scribbling notes while the other students participate. A chair scuffs across the floor as Blake takes his usual spot in the desk next to me.

"Morning!"

"Hey." I try not to feel down when I see him. We haven't spoken since the aptitude test, and my pride is still wounded from Selene's response. It's not Blake's fault, so I know I should be more positive around him.

I retrieve my notebook and pencil and set my bag on the

ground, harder than I intended. My breath catches as my forgotten watch tumbles out onto the classroom floor, its broken face glittering in the light.

"What happened here?" Blake asks, reaching down and carefully picking up the watch.

"I slipped."

Blake sets the watch on his desk, examining it. He steals a quick look at me and runs his fingers through his dark hair. Then, he holds the watch in his hands, and his expression grows serious. He turns red, and I recognize that same intense concentration he displayed during the aptitude test. The broken watch surface bubbles and undulates, encompassed by a gentle blue glow. Suddenly it's whole again.

Blake grins and displays the watch with a smile. "Good as new."

"Wow, thanks," I say, fastening the watch around my wrist and marveling at its now-flawless surface. I have studied enough about Blue-magic theories to know that was not easy. "It's no wonder Selene is impressed by you."

He must catch the undercurrent in my words. "Hey, don't sweat the test. You're still number one."

"But I don't stand out. I can master the basics, but I—"

"Don't go stress-monster on me now," he says, cutting me off with a grin. "You're such a perfectionist."

Stress-monster was a game we used to play as kids. When I got too overwhelmed from studying, Blake would assemble small "monsters" out of objects for me to practice strength moves on. He's always been good at helping me calm down.

I smile back at him. "Thank you."

"Anytime." He adds, "My friends are wondering why you don't come hang out with us anymore."

How do I answer that? I remember that last time I joined them—a gaggle of students crammed into Blake's dorm room, playing board games. Selene later scolded me for wasting my time and reminded me not everyone can be a Benefactor. *He's your competition.* Her warning from the aptitude test flashes through my mind again.

"I just don't have time these days," I avoid his eyes.

Blake looks like he has more he wants to say, but our teacher, Mr. Dawson, enters the room. I can feel Blake's gaze lingering on me for another moment before turning to the front of the class.

4

"YOU ARE A PERSISTENT ONE, AREN'T YOU?"

"I just want to know who you are."

We face each other, Elm and I, albeit with several feet of distance between us. I'm afraid to step any closer in case he retreats again.

Elm gives a short laugh. "Who I am? That's a question I cannot answer for you, my dear. I'm afraid I don't yet know the answer myself. But perhaps someday we'll both know."

I inch closer, but he puts his cane sharply between us and jumps back, adding, "Besides, it doesn't matter because you're not going to remember any of this in the morning." Without another word, he vanishes into the portal.

I awaken, frowning. It is morning and I do remember. Vividly. And who does he think he is, telling me what I will and won't remember? I repeat his words in my mind, obsessing over the details and feeling senseless for being so bothered by a dream.

This is my fifth night in a row dreaming about Elm. When it happened twice, I called it a coincidence. Three nights, and I chalked it up to obsession. But now, I'm starting to wonder what it means. Maybe it doesn't mean anything. Maybe the idea of him occupies my mind to the extent that I can't envision anything else.

Or it could be something worse. Something that started that day in the woods.

I shiver and push the thought aside.

Elm's words play on repeat in my mind several hours after waking up and going to class. *I'm afraid I don't yet know the answer myself. But perhaps someday, we'll both know.*

"Ava, can you recommend a good book on healing theories?"

I start. How long have I been spaced out? The question brings me back to the library, where my classmates sit at the surrounding tables, discussing different subjects with one another. We're supposed to be picking topics for theory essays, and now Sarah stares at me expectantly with wide brown eyes.

"Oh, healing," I say quickly. "I think that would be a great topic for you. *Healing Crimson* by Amelia Trost is a good one. I'll help you find it."

Sarah follows me to the reference section of the library, and I do my best to stay on track. I'm still out of sorts, and my thoughts threaten to slip away again. As I skim the books by author, a title catches my eye: *The Mystery of Dreams* by Austin Trosen. I freeze, and my hand hovers over the book. I almost take it but remember why I'm here to begin with. Quickly, I find the book by Trost and hand it to Sarah.

"Here you go. There's a lot of great information in this one."

"Thanks so much," she says, excitement coating her voice. "Is there a particular section I should focus on?"

I'm sure there is, but I can barely remember what's in that book while I'm so distracted. "Just . . . start at the beginning," I say. "It's all good. And you don't have to wait for me. I'm going to browse here for a bit."

"Okay. See you back at the table."

I grasp the book on dreams as soon as she's out of sight and scan through the pages. I'm not sure what I'm looking for, but I hope I'll know when I find it. Maybe there's a connection between dreams and Yellow magic, or maybe I'm desperate to find anything at all that can explain what is happening to me now. Something to tell me dreams are just dreams and I have nothing to be afraid of

After a few minutes of surveying pages, my mind spins. This isn't going anywhere. I can't start without a specific objective. I slip the book under my arm and locate one of the library catalog devices.

The titles I find while scrolling through the long list of books on dreams sound interesting but not very useful. Most of it is information from centuries ago, regarding interpretation. Nothing recent. I'm not even sure what to search for. Recurring dreams. Lucid dreams. Dream retention. Nothing quite fits.

What I'm having aren't recurring dreams: they are different every time but always in the same place and with the same person. I guess they must be lucid dreams because I'm aware of myself and in control of what I'm doing. But I certainly have no say over what Elm does. And I don't have any problems with retention after I wake up. I'm even more confused now than when I started.

I jump at the light touch on my shoulder.

"Sorry, I didn't mean to startle you," Sarah says. "Class is leaving now."

Time escaped me again. "Okay. I'll catch up." I log off and return *The Mystery of Dreams* to its shelf, already knowing I'll be back searching for more answers at the first-available opportunity.

The colors swirl around me, but I'm unmoving against their backdrop. I wait, still and silent, as though even a breath could shatter this delicate space. I'm not moving from this spot until I get some sort of answer or resolution.

A month now. A month straight of dreaming about Elm. I'm past pretending this is normal. The dreams never last long and always happen in the same setting. Sometimes Elm speaks, but not a lot, and always in that formal tone. He doesn't answer my questions. He doesn't linger. I can't get closer than a few feet from him before he disappears. The dreams are vivid, too real for comfort. How is it that I can recall them as easily as the memory of a visit with a friend?

By now, every detail of Elm's appearance is tattooed into my memory, such as his curly, dirty-blond hair and the firm structure of his face. The first time I saw his picture at the emergency assembly, I took in the basics of his outfit—the gray suit, hat, and cloak, accented with yellow. But now I know the shoulders of his cloak boast embroidery in delicate, swirling patterns. His vest and tie have a faint paisley texture. His sleeves each sport a yellow gemstone cufflink. He carries a cane, intricately carved out of a rich, warm-colored wood, with a row of yellow stone inlays in the hilt. How did he come by these? Gems are rare and precious. Whenever they're found, they are set aside to give to new students or power technology, and usually only the wealthy can have something other than the pendant the Benefactors give us when entering school. Aside from that, each extra gem must be registered and documented. This ideally prevents others from abusing their increase of power. With so many stones, Elm would have a fair amount of power at his disposal even with the ban on yellow.

In spite of all these, he doesn't wear the typical tear-shaped pendant given to all magic students in their first year of school. He should have one . . . unless he never went to school. Or perhaps the Benefactors took it from him before his imprisonment. Of course, with all of the other stones he has on him, he wouldn't need the extra pendant for a boost in power . . . if he were real. Perhaps the real Elm has a pendant.

I sense a presence and turn toward it, my mind awake with anticipation.

Face-to-face again with my familiar haunt. The portal appears as it always does, and I'm about to call out to him before he can evade me once more, but he turns and looks my way unbidden. Rather than retreating, he floats toward me. I'm not afraid of him. He is a familiar part of the landscape now, and he can't hurt me here inside my delusions. Yes. Just a dream. I know that. I *know* it. Yet, I hope he might reveal something new. I want to know more. I crave it.

He's only inches away now, and he furrows his brow. He stops and examines me thoroughly. Now, he's an active observer, acutely surveying me in a way he hasn't ever done before. His eyes are intelligent and intrusive, but I'm no less bold in my observations.

We are two equally prying parties, searching for something more to satiate our ever-growing curiosity. I stare into his hazel eyes, so clear to me for the first time as they reflect the pastel light around us.

Then he turns to run.

"No!" This can't happen again. I use an agility spell and race to grab his arm, strengthening my grip on his sleeve. His eyes widen in shock. A puff of smoke appears around us, and by the time my vision clears again, Elm is gone.

5

MY EYES SLOWLY OPEN, AND THE SOFT glow of dawn lights my window. The world is silent and still. Considering the few hours of sleep I had, I should feel exhausted, but I'm wide awake, motionless, except for the wild thumping of my heart. My mind is a blank, blurred canvas. I'm unaware of the passage of time, even as the light grows brighter outside. My alarm pierces the silence, and its shrillness shocks me back into reality. I force myself out of bed.

It feels like I'm somehow in the wrong place. But my room is unchanged—twin bed with burgundy bedding. Matching curtains on the window. Wall-to-wall bookshelves, filled to bursting. A desk, covered in papers and school supplies, with a large rectangular mirror above it. But it doesn't feel right. Nothing does.

That dream. What was that? I stare at my fingertips and can clearly feel the rough slip of his sleeve pulling from my grasp.

Everything has a logical explanation. Could pure obsession fuel a dream like that? Something that was so tangible? And why does it feel so disappointing that he got away? He's still on the loose out there somewhere. Maybe I could . . .

No. He's the number-one enemy of Magus. I, of all people, should put as much distance from this as I can and be content to let the Benefactors handle it—at least until I'm one of them. I gave up everything for that. I was taught by my mentors to shun social events and companionship in favor of learning. I can't fall victim to these hero fantasies and blow my chance. I just can't.

I need to see Selene immediately.

I make it to Selene's office as fast as the crowded halls allow and give the door a soft knock. I hear shuffling from inside, and the heavy wooden door creaks open. Selene looks only mildly surprised to see me.

"Ah, Ava. What can I do for you?"

"Can I ask you about some things?"

"Of course. Come right in." She motions me inside and shuts the door. As busy as she is, I can usually count on Selene making time for me.

Selene's office is sterile: bare wooden walls, perfect stacks of papers, and tall filing cabinets and cupboards. It's just like Selene, neat and orderly, no room for nonsense.

Now that I'm here, I'm not quite sure how to start. Normally, I'm at ease talking to her about anything. But somehow, I feel I'm breaching a forbidden subject, and I'm aware information on Elm's disappearance has been intentionally withheld. What will happen if I tell her about the dreams? Will they put me under surveillance?

I fidget and begin with a broader focus. "Can you tell me . . . about Yellow magic?" If she would just answer some of my questions, maybe that would help.

Her response is nothing but calm. "There are lots of books that talk about magic types in the library. Have you done research yet?" Selene has always encouraged me to seek answers on my own before asking others, believing self-exploration enhances learning.

"I have, but they don't say much. I can find whole textbooks covering theories of Red and Blue magic, but never more than a paragraph or two about Yellow."

Her face tightens ever so slightly. "There is no need for us to have more information about Yellow magic. It is forbidden. That should be enough for you."

"I know, but I think if we all understand it better, it could lead to Elm's capture sooner."

She purses her lips. "So, you're preoccupied with him as well? Ava, I know you are naturally curious, but I think the less you know about it the better. The whole student body has been abuzz ever since the announcement was made."

I don't like where this conversation is going. "But the Benefactors want us to be vigilant, right?"

"Of course. But you don't need to know everything about *him* in order to do that. You and the other students simply need to keep your eyes open and report anything strange to someone equipped to handle it."

"But I'm on track to become a Benefactor after I graduate," I protest. "Don't you think I have a right to more information?" Now, I've done exactly what I didn't want to do—pushed my luck.

"Ava," Selene says sternly. "Your parents died defending you and the people of Magus from the likes of Elm. Or have you forgotten that? Why do you feel the need to meddle in something they gave their lives to protect you from?"

"That's all the more reason for me to learn more," I insist, fighting to keep my voice even through the pain at her mention of my parents. "How can I protect myself—or anyone else for that matter—if I don't even know what I'm up against? My parents would have wanted me to be prepared. I'm sure of it."

"If you're becoming a Benefactor to honor your parents,"

Selene's voice is cold, "you won't do them any favors if you die before you make it that far. Mentalists kill. Until you are ready, it is my duty to protect you in any way that I can, and right now, that means keeping you as far away from Yellow magic as possible. I owe your parents that much, and I'm frankly disappointed that you don't comprehend that."

A shadow of shame and sorrow crosses me. I don't remember my parents well, as I was only five when they died. The few memories I have left are covered in clouds of forgetfulness. I'm one of many orphaned children, taken in by the school after The Canary War—the war against the Yellows. While I'm unfamiliar with the details, I know many lives were lost during that time.

"You're right. I'm sorry."

Selene reaches across her large wooden desk and gently takes my hands, breaking from her mentor role to the maternal role I see on rare occasions. "All questions will be answered, but not yet. When it's the right time, you will learn everything you need to know. But now is simply not that time."

"I want to know what you know." My voice sounds whinier than I intend, and I cringe.

Selene smiles. "You want to know everything, which is not necessarily a bad quality. Believe me, it's not that I want to keep you in the dark. But you are still a student, and I have to keep you safe and treat you the same as the other students. Being in charge doesn't mean I can do whatever I want." She releases my hands. "Before too long, we can work together, and you'll be privy to everything. I know it's hard, but be patient. You're not quite ready yet." Her demeanor becomes more serious as she studies my face. "Now, is there something more you want to tell me?"

"What?" I ask, caught off guard.

She eyes me intently. "The librarian told me you have been looking up a lot of books on dreams lately."

"You asked her about me?" I keep my voice calm, as though I'm asking out of mild curiosity rather than panic. Has Selene been spying on me? Why would she do that?

"I have been inquiring as to your general well-being." She watches me closely. "Some of your teachers have asked if you are well. They say you have been distracted, and I can see they're right."

She pauses, waiting for me to explain myself, but I can think of nothing to say.

"Ava, you would tell me if something strange were happening to you, wouldn't you?"

"Of course." Why am I holding back? I can trust Selene, can't I? I have always been open with her. But now I hesitate.

"Are you sure? Nothing unusual is going on?"

"No."

Selene changes tactics. "Why the sudden fascination with dreams?"

What answer can I possibly give her? What wouldn't raise suspicion and cause her to ask more questions? "They're interesting," I say. "I think the sort of dreams people have reveal a lot about them." What do dreams about chasing down Elm reveal about me?

She gives me a long, hard look, and at last, accepts my answer, or at least accepts that she isn't getting anything more out of me. "Well, yes, dreams certainly can be interesting. But I hope you'll tell me if there is anything more to it than curiosity."

I nod, knowing there's no way I can tell her what's happening. I can't explain to her that I dream of Elm every night. I can't tell her that, even now, I wish I were asleep instead of awake.

I walk through the halls at Prism, and students stare at me and whisper. Is there something wrong with me? I look down and see that I'm not wearing my normal school uniform. Although I'm wearing the same white dress shirt and fitted charcoal jacket, my red skirt has been replaced by a yellow one. My pendant is also yellow—a beacon of guilt.

"Somebody call a Benefactor!" a student shouts.

"No," I cry. "This is a mistake." I run down the hall to escape their accusing eyes and round a corner, bumping right into Selene. I frantically try to cover myself, ashamed. But that treacherous yellow on my clothing only glares brighter.

"Traitor," Selene hisses.

"I'm not a traitor."

"Oh really?" She holds up Elm's wanted poster, but the image shifts, and the face on the poster does not belong to Elm. It is soft-featured and round, sporting wide blue eyes and long copper hair. It's me.

Benefactors appear out of nowhere, grabbing my limbs.

"Stop, please! This isn't my fault."

I open my eyes. Just a dream—or a nightmare. I'm in the safety of my own room. My uniform rests where I left it on the floor last night, still red. I haven't betrayed anyone. I'm not on a vigilante mission to find Elm against Selene's wishes.

Elm. I didn't dream about him last night. That's good, isn't it? Maybe I'm done with all of this and can get back on track to being Prism's top student. No more dreaming about someone I should put out of my head. No more keeping shameful secrets from Selene.

The nights go on, and Elm remains absent from my dreams. Instead of relief, I feel something else, something I never expected—I want it back.

That flighty excitement of having mysteries at my fingertips. The thrill of seeing the one who has remained secret for so long. The possibility of doing something *real* for Magus— something important. And now that I've had some separation to clear my mind, it seems more and more likely that Elm and the person I bumped into in the woods are the same.

True, the Elm in my dreams looks to be in much better shape than the man I saw, but it's the eyes. I can't forget the eyes. Of course, when I think logically, I know I haven't ever met the real Elm, and I'm projecting memories of the man in the woods to the Elm from my dreams. Still, I wish I could get one more look.

Each night, I do things I think might bid him back. I stare at his picture until I fall asleep. I repeat his name over and over in my head and sometimes out loud. But he is never there. This maddening development only strengthens my obsession. It feels like some sort of abandonment, which is crazy. I'm going crazy.

I need an intervention or at least a distraction, but there is never enough to do. Lately, as part of my student-worker duties, I have been cleaning and organizing the supply closets in the classrooms after school hours; however, I have already run the gamut of frequently used classrooms. The last area on my list is an old wing of the school that's rarely occupied.

I haul my bucket of cleaning supplies to the old wing and go down the hall to the farthest classroom. Stepping inside,

I nudge my shoulder against the light switch, but the light doesn't come on. Besides that, the room is stuffy, as though it's no longer being air-conditioned. They must not turn the power on through this wing of the school anymore.

I set down my supplies, so I can let in some air. Dust and cobwebs float by in a filthy puff as I pull aside heavy, faded green curtains and pry at the window's latch. It squeaks and grinds against its frame, and it lifts crookedly. I jiggle it around until it's as straight as I can get it. As soon as I let go, it creeps shut again. I search and find a cracked wooden ruler in one of the drawers on a weathered teacher's desk, which works well enough to keep it propped up.

"There." The room feels better with the breeze stirring through it and a little bit of natural light coming in.

The closet here hasn't been cleaned, or even opened, for quite some time. The door sticks when I pull, and I have to tug hard several times before it finally gives way. I sneeze as dust tickles my nose.

Inside is a disaster. Supplies and books lie in cluttered heaps on the floor and the shelving. Cobwebs decorate every nook. The smell of dust and old paper is strong.

I might as well get to it.

I grab a timeworn chair from one of the student desks and cautiously test my weight before positioning myself to examine items on the top shelf. As I pull an old dictionary free, another heavy book thuds at my feet. The spine cracks as it lands, and several pages fall out.

"Oh no," I moan, bending down to salvage what I can. I hate to see books destroyed, especially old ones with so much character. Its pages are crinkled and off-color, and the picture on the cover shows its age with fading and fissures. I examine the title: *Magus: A History of the Magic Continent*. I know this book. In fact, the new edition sits on a shelf in my room even now. I wonder what might have changed since this edition was written. Gingerly, I flip the book open to a random page and begin to read.

> *Years of mystery surround Magus, which formed in an area of the North Atlantic Ocean once known as the Bermuda Triangle.*
>
> *Over time, magic-users began to leave Magus and travel to other continents. Across a period of several decades, magic-users populated the gene pool all over the world. Initially, non-magic-users were afraid of the magic-users, fearing that they would be seen as a weaker population and preyed upon. But it was soon discovered that magic-users could only use magic on other magic-users. Thus, the two groups were able to coexist peacefully. However, other continents were not able to sustain magic in the way that Magus was, and magic-users' powers would fade after time spent off their continent. For this reason, many of the people who left Magus returned to keep their abilities intact, only venturing to the world outside for short amounts of time to visit loved ones.*

I stop reading, brow furrowed. I remember this passage from my own book, but it's different. My book doesn't say that the people of Magus visited other continents—even for short amounts of time. It only says that the world outside of Magus became unstable and unable to sustain life. This book must be older than I thought.

As I check for a publication date inside the tattered cover, the lights come on in the classroom, jolting me out of my search. A wooden clatter precedes the sound of the window slamming shut.

"Who's here?" I call, dashing out from the closet and

letting the book fall—again. But the room appears empty. Maybe just the wind?

But that doesn't explain how the lights turned on.

Goosebumps run up my arms. Someone had to have been here—maybe is here still. I scan the room for red objects in case I need a power source in a pinch.

I cry out as a shrill wail pierces the silence in the old room. It takes me a moment to realize what I hear is the warning alarm, which means Elm was sighted nearby.

A wave of excitement hits me. Where is he? How close is he? Are we safe? I try to recall what the protocol is and where to go. At the very least, I shouldn't be alone in this wing of the school. My first thought is to find Selene, but then our recent conversation comes to mind. I need to blend into the hallways in the height of chaos, or else a Benefactor or teacher might stuff me inside a classroom to wait it out. I leave everything behind and sprint for the main corridor.

Students fill the halls, crowding the windows—likely hoping to catch a glimpse of Elm. I don't bother fighting through the mob because I doubt he'll be hanging around in plain sight. Still, the alarms haven't stopped. He has to be near the grounds somewhere.

I scurry through the school like a ravenous animal in search of food. No sign of Elm. No sign of anything unusual. That is until I turn a corner and spy the door to the supply room opened up a sliver. If I wasn't so used to making sure that door was secure, I might not have noticed. In a time of heightened security, it's odd that anyone could make such a thoughtless mistake. I check to my left. Then to my right. Convinced nobody will notice, I tiptoe down the hall toward the room.

The faint sound of someone whistling meets my ears. I crack the door open wider and suppress a gasp as my heart travels to my throat.

Right in front of me is the one who has frequented my dreams and teased my curiosity for weeks now.

Elm.

The disheveled, curly hair. The gray magician's getup with the pale yellow lined cloak and vest. His top hat. His cane rests against the counter, which I guess must be for style. He doesn't need it for physical support. He looks out of place among the neatly organized boxes and office supplies. He's tall. Almost a foot taller than me. It feels surreal, seeing him this way, precisely as he appeared in my dreams. I hardly have time to wrap my head around this before I take my attention off of his person long enough to notice what he's doing. He churns out copy after copy of bright yellow flowers, and the sight dazzles my eyes. I'm certain I have never seen so much yellow in my entire life. Each time a new bundle of copied flowers appears, he adds more to the copier's surface, further multiplying the end result.

He hasn't seen me yet, which leaves a precious window of time to get one of the Benefactors as quickly as possible. So why can't I get my feet to move? My senses all scream there is danger, but I want to stay. I want him to look up and see me and give me no choice but confrontation.

He seems so calm and non-threatening, in sharp contrast to the wanted posters that make him look sinister. And he's younger than I thought. Seeing him now, he can't be more than two or three years older than me. Here, he looks pleasant. He's filled out since that day in the woods.

I should turn him in to the Benefactors right now. I would receive honor and status. If anything can get me on a faster track to becoming a head Benefactor, this is it. The idea is deliciously tempting.

But even if I turn Elm over to Selene, is that a guarantee I'll get answers, or will I still have to wait until I achieve Benefactor status? Instead, I have the source of my questions right in front of me—a treasure trove of firsthand information. In spite of Selene's warnings, I believe I can protect people better if I'm more informed.

How dangerous can he really be? There have been no reports of him attacking people since his escape. He hasn't ever hurt me. *In your dreams, Ava,* I remind myself. I struggle with that distinction, especially now that he stands before me, a perfect doppelgänger of the one in those very dreams. And if I turn away now, I might never get a chance to learn more. Benefactors and teachers all around me could come to my defense if things get bad. And his magic will be limited inside the walls of the school without sources to draw on. Surely he can't harm me here. This is the best opportunity for learning about this mysterious rebel. Maybe my only opportunity.

I enter the room and shut the door. Elm looks up and surveys me, and I stand as still as he does, his eyes darting up and down, almost as though he's mirroring my feelings of disbelief. I don't dare move as I wait for him to react. And then he sticks his tongue out at me and resumes copying the flowers.

My mouth drops open. What kind of response is that? He continues to ignore me as I approach. Why isn't he saying or doing anything?

Does he plan to evade me in reality the way he did in my dreams? The thought infuriates me, and I can't stand it anymore. He will not dismiss me as though I'm not even worthy of his consideration.

I let go of all caution and address him outright. "What do you think you're doing?"

There. That forces his attention. He looks up at me, surprise on his face, and then he returns to his task, brow now furrowed.

Insatiable curiosity and indignation embolden me. "Are you just going to keep ignoring me?"

At last he fixes his eyes on me. "Sorry, can you see me?"

"Yes." I'm not sure what puzzles me more—the familiarity of his voice or the oddness of his question.

"Well, what an interesting little freak you are."

"I'm not a freak," I object, angry at his nerve.

"Nobody else can see me, strange one. And I do plan to keep it that way."

Strange one? I'm not so strange. And he's not as smart as he thinks he is. "Obviously, somebody saw you, or that alarm wouldn't be going off." I block his way to the door, but he heads toward it anyway with a smile.

"They saw me momentarily, yes, because I wanted to be seen. Believe it or not, it's easier for me to sneak into the school that way. If people are looking for one specific thing—like me, for example—they tend to miss the odd little details. Those looking for the visible man pay no mind to the invisible one."

He gives me a pat on the head and moves past me to the door, as I stand there flabbergasted. Just as he reaches for the handle, he stops and turns back toward me slowly. The calculating expression on his face makes me question my decision to catch his attention.

"Miss . . . Ava, was it?"

"I never mentioned my name," I say, wary. How did he know?

He gives an over-exaggerated bow. "Why, there was never a need. Everyone, even the infamous Elm, knows of Miss Ava. Leading student of the school. Selene's little pet." A sudden glimmer of something ravenous enters his eyes, like a wolf coming across an unexpected, delicious prey. "Yes . . . Selene's pet." Just as suddenly as it came, the shadow passes, and his face resumes its previous jovial nature.

"Well, my day just became substantially more interesting. I've decided you're going to help me, Miss Ava." He walks briskly back past me again and grabs a large box from the bookcase against the wall, unceremoniously emptying it of its contents.

He begins stuffing yellow flowers inside. "Help me fill this, will you?"

His pretension is unreal. Does he really think he can just come in here and boss me around? And help him put everyone in danger? No way. "What makes you think you can decide that?"

"What makes you think you can decide otherwise?"

The hairs on the back of my neck stand up. *Mind control, Ava. Don't you remember? That's his specialty. What are you doing?*

He gives an unexpected chuckle. "Don't look so grim. You're still here, so I assume you're hoping to get something out of this rendezvous. That, my dear, is why you are going to help me. Am I wrong? Come now, we should hurry this up a bit."

Well, he's not wrong, but I also should have thought this through more carefully. Hesitantly, I pluck a flower from the countertop, examining it and trying to steady the shaking in my hands. It has been so long since I've held an actual yellow object that I can hardly believe it's real. And considering my present company, I don't trust that it's harmless either. Beyond that, what will happen if I refuse to help him? Sudden visions of becoming a prisoner in my own body as Elm pilots my mind compel me to play his game—at least until I can find an out. Like it or not, I'm in. With adrenaline, fear, and just a shade of odd excitement, I join Elm in stuffing the flowers into the container.

"Excellent." Elm surveys the box, now brimming with tightly packed flowers. "That should do for now. Can you carry it?"

He can't be serious. "Walk down the hall with a box full of yellow flowers? That's not going unnoticed by anyone. Especially right now."

"Hmm. That's a valid point." He pauses, regarding me, and then asks, "How tall are you? Five feet?"

"I'm five-foot-three," I respond, irritated.

"And how much do you weigh? Surely not an ounce over one hundred fifty."

I stare at him, aghast. "Excuse me? I'm not anywhere even near one hundred fifty. I'm only—" I'm not about to reveal my actual weight to him, and I can see by the look on his face that he was only fishing for a reaction.

He smiles. "Not going to share? No matter. I'm fairly good at guessing."

Looking me over one last time, he grabs his cane from its resting place and gives it a sharp flick. My ears ring with a popping sound, and at once I feel the strange sensation of my school attire growing around me. Folds of fabric billow out, and any remaining trace of my uniform vanishes into a sunshine-yellow dress that falls just past my knees. It is ruffled and girlish, covered in ribbons and lace. I look like a yellow doily, only more ridiculous.

I turn around and tug at the dress, disbelieving, "Explain how this makes me less noticeable?"

He stifles a laugh behind his hand. "Oh, you have the most ridiculous expression on your face. Don't fret. It suits you."

I don't understand this magic or the intention behind it. What if this is only the first step in his process of control?

"No," I say, feeling panic creep into my chest. "Get this thing off me."

"Calm yourself. This isn't just any dress. When you wear it, I'm the only one who can see or hear you. Which is a shame, really. I hate to waste your charm on me."

"That's all it does?" My voice wavers, though I try to keep it steady.

"That's all?" He scoffs. "I should think that is more than enough. More than the other dresses in your wardrobe, I would imagine. Or . . ." He tips his head. "Are you perhaps wondering if I could control you with it? Don't worry. There will be no need for such a production if I choose to do that. The box, please."

His words send another chill through me. Still battling my flight instincts, I ask, "Won't everyone just see a box floating down the hall?"

"The box will be invisible, too, as long as you or I are holding it. I wouldn't drop it, though. That might cause a stir. Actually, do drop it. It sounds like fun."

Is this all just a joke to him? I weigh the options before me. What if I drop the box? Everyone will see it. The Benefactors will be alerted. Can I escape?

But he has nothing left to lose. He has a power source within the school. We could all become his puppets. I need to get him far from the school. Away from victims. Then I'll get out of this . . . somehow.

"After you, m'lady," he says, opening the door for me and gesturing out into the corridor.

I shift uncomfortably, wishing there was some way to get him out of here without first going into the halls of the school, surrounded by students, while he now has a source of power to draw from. Blake always said my curiosity would be my downfall someday. He is probably right, and I shouldn't have been stupid enough to drag everyone around me into it, too.

"What's the matter?"

I fish for an excuse that I'm comfortable voicing to him. "I can't really be invisible. You'll get me in trouble." Or you're going to destroy us all.

"It's perfectly safe. Trust me."

My eyes scan the area with Prism's students scattered about. Something in my face must have revealed my fears.

"Ah. I have no intention of harming anyone, if that's your concern. I simply want to be on my way."

"Why do you need me for that?"

"We're wasting time, Miss Ava. And I don't think you're in a position to be questioning me." He rips a nearby wanted poster off the wall and waves it at me, with a sideways grin. "Don't forget, I'm apparently a very dangerous fellow."

He knows I'm afraid of him. But somehow, I believe him when he says he just wants to get out of the school. I inhale deeply. "You're sure nobody will see me?"

"Not a soul."

I frown at him, still skeptical, but take a few steps into the busy hallway where most students remain glued to the windows. The chatter is so loud by this point that I wonder if anyone would even hear me if I screamed.

"Here, let me show you how this works." Without warning, Elm takes his cane and taps three students behind their knees. They fall in a crumpled heap to the ground.

"What are you doing?" I cry. "You said you wouldn't hurt anyone!"

The students struggle to their feet, baffled.

"They're not hurt, see?" Elm seems more cheerful now and continues down the hall, humming and twirling his cane behind his back.

I focus on not tripping as I carry the oversized box. Why do *I* have to carry this thing? It's not heavy, but it's awkward.

It would be much easier for someone of his height. "You want to take this?"

"Oh, no. You're doing marvelously." He looks at me as I eye my fellow students with concern.

"They're fine. It's all in good fun. What's the point of being invisible if you can't enjoy yourself a little?"

We continue down the hallway, which seems to stretch for miles as Elm continues to prod a student here, toss a book down there. In all my years of school, I have never caused an ounce of trouble. Never played a single prank. Now I'm walking down the hall doing absolutely nothing as Mr. Wanted himself harasses students for fun. I'm officially the worst. At this point, the most I can do is be grateful he's only fooling around and get him out of the school before he decides to do some real damage.

Elm tips my face upward with the crook of his cane. "Keep your chin up. You'll miss the best part."

"Best part?" I croak.

He smiles deviously at something in front of us. There, in the center of the hallway, stands a glass monument, intended as a shining emblem of our school pride. A sparkling-blue gem rests in the petals of a deep red rose as a symbol of our two schools of magic. Elm snaps his fingers, and out of nowhere, a large yellow ball appears, floating in midair. He angles the straight end of his cane toward it, closing one eye.

"Oh no. No!"

But it's too late. He thrusts the cane against the ball and sends it careening into the monument. At first there is nothing but a dull *tink* sound. And then the whole monument explodes into glittering shards of glass. The air fills with screams of surprised students and commotion. With a swift motion, Elm picks me up—along with the box—and dashes out the doors into the fading sunlight.

"Put me down," I command.

"Can't do that yet," he says jubilantly as he runs. "Unless, of course, you'd prefer to be visible again."

I keep my mouth shut and clutch the box tighter, stewing. I can't let anyone see me like *this* and he knows it. We head toward the forest, and it isn't until we are nestled well into the trees that he releases me. I drop the box angrily to the ground, scattering yellow blooms across the forest floor.

"Aw. Just a bit too late," he says with mock sadness. "That would have been so much more exciting at Prism."

"Give me my uniform," I say, voice trembling. "You got what you wanted. I'm going back." *Please let me go.*

"Emerging from the forest during all this commotion when you ought to have been in school? A bit inadvisable, but it's your choice," he says, seemingly oblivious to my distress. He blows a yellow blossom from his palm, and it lands in my hair. I pluck it out in frustration and plop down on the ground. I'm at my limit.

"Oh, don't be that way. You can keep the dress. It's a gift."

"As if I even want it," I grumble.

"Look, wear it back to the school. You can go back unnoticed. Once you're tucked away snug and safe in your room, you can change out of it. Your uniform will appear. No harm done."

"That easy, eh?" I say.

"That easy."

I get to my feet and look up in surprise as I hear the soft thud of hooves in the distance.

"I do believe," says Elm, "my ride is here."

"You have a horse?"

"No."

Confused, I watch as a wild stallion tears through the trees. We have several of them in the area, and something has badly spooked this one. Its eyes are white and bulging, its mouth slathered with foam. I cover my eyes as Elm steps directly into its path. But when I don't hear the sickening sounds of collision I expected, I peek through my fingers. Elm's cane emits a soft yellow glow, and the horse has stopped in its tracks. Elm is gazing into the horse's eyes, and the creature begins to relax, its breath becoming soft and slow.

I stare at him. "How did—"

He raises his hand. "Another time. You'd best get back before someone notices you're gone."

He hastily scoops what he can of my rage-scattered

blossoms into the box, and hoists himself onto the horse's back, securing the box firmly in front of him. He takes off his hat and gives me a little bow. "My dear, thank you for your service. Goodbye, Miss Ava. For now."

Then he gives the horse a pat and a nod, and they gallop away, leaving me in a daze behind them.

6

DILEMMA.

This is the word spinning through my mind as I return to Prism, still trying to grasp what just happened.

I remember once reading about a large bird called a rhea that was hunted long ago for its beautiful feathers. It was easy to kill because of its tendency to run in circles when frightened, making it simple to shoot. Right now, my mind is the rhea, running in circles and waiting for the bullet of reason to bring it to a halt. I just fraternized with the most-wanted person in Magus. I devoted myself to the cause of the Benefactors but assisted the very one we are fighting against. What in the world was I thinking?

Before I know it, I'm at Prism's gates. I almost forget that sneakiness is unnecessary since the dress still conceals me. But maybe it's some kind of trick. Perhaps the dress only works when Elm is nearby, and this is just more of the mischief he enjoys so much. I slip inside the gates and approach the main entrance, noting the silence of the alarms. Students chatter on the steps outside, and nobody notices me. They look excited, some of them frightened. No doubt they are preoccupied with thoughts of Elm.

Welcome to the club.

For the moment, it looks as though I'm safe. As I enter

the main hallway, I do a double take. The monument to the school is there, polished and completely whole. Impossible. I saw it shatter with my own eyes. And yet, there it is, still in one piece. The Benefactors surrounding the area appear just as puzzled as I am.

"And you're sure you saw it break?" a Benefactor asks a small group of students nearby.

"I'm positive," a girl in a blue uniform replies. "The pieces flew everywhere."

A boy speaks up. "But then after a few minutes, all the broken glass was gone, and the monument was back."

Two Benefactors give each other a look, and one of them quietly murmurs, "An illusion."

Is that all it was? A clever illusion to make us believe the monument had shattered? How is that possible when it was so real? More than that, why wouldn't he just break it? If he's actually the criminal the Benefactors paint him as, he wouldn't think twice about committing such a disrespectful act of vandalism. And why use his magic for that instead of controlling us all? I can't figure out his motivation.

The instant I reach my room and lock the door, I'm exhausted. A tremor starts in my lips, and soon I'm trembling from head to toe.

Dilemma. Dilemma. Dilemma. Round and round and round.

I helped Elm today with who knows what. I have secrets. *Real* secrets. Secrets that could ruin my entire future if revealed.

I'm terrified of seeing him again. But the perplexing part—the part that my customarily logical mind can't work out—is that I'm even more terrified of *not*. Fear. Exhilaration. Danger. Adventure. I somehow want all of it. I want to see Elm again.

I sink to the floor and pass out.

I jolt awake. It's morning? I'm still in the yellow dress. More importantly, my first class started twenty minutes ago.

"No, no, noooo!" I jump up and struggle with the dainty clasps on the back of the dress. I have never, never been late to a class. Just as Elm promised, my school clothes appear as soon as I remove the dress. Thank goodness, at least, for that. Thinking only of my academics, I fling open the door to my room and tear through the dormitories and down the hallway to the learning wing.

I open the classroom door as quietly as possible to avoid a disruption. No sooner have I turned to tiptoe to my desk than the entire class lets out a gasp. My face reddens. I know my record is flawless, but my first time showing up late can't be that big of a deal, can it? Should I have brushed my hair or something before coming?

My instructor, Mr. Lansley, stares at me as though I just swallowed somebody. "Miss Locke! Have you lost your mind?" The whole class whispers and points, and I start to wonder if this is some terrible joke. Nobody gets this much grief for tardiness.

"I-I'm sorry." I scramble for an explanation. "I just—"

"She's wearing yellow," someone blurts.

"What? No, I'm . . ." But as I look down, the evidence of guilt manifests. Around my neck, where my red charm normally hangs, is a shining yellow pendant. An astonished scream bursts from my lips, and I grasp the pendant with the intention of throwing it to the ground, but it doesn't come off.

Do something, do something, do something. My world

freezes as I'm seized with panic, and only one solution comes to my frantic mind: *Run.*

Flight instincts kick in hard, and I bolt from the room, leaving behind a scene of shouting and confusion. I summon an agility spell so I can run faster, but without my pendant, I can't pull as much speed as I normally would. I don't want this. I don't want any of this. But it's my own fault, of course. How could I have been stupid enough to assume I could have a brush with Elm without consequences? I hasten back to my dormitory, wondering how long I have before the Benefactors show up at my door. Grunting, I tug at the necklace as hard as I can, but it won't budge. My neck feels raw from the useless strain of my trying to remove it.

"Okay, think," I pant. "How do I get this off?" I try a few Red spells. One for strength. One for healing. One for flexibility. Nothing works. I guess I didn't expect it to, but it's all I know. I flip myself upside down, hanging off my bed and vainly hoping that the necklace might simply slip off. The pendant remains firmly in place on my neck like some horrifying yellow parasite. Outside my door, I hear the thud of footsteps rapidly approaching.

This is it. I'm done for. A lifetime of hard work and devotion, ruined because of this yellow pariah strangling my neck. Destroyed because I sought to answer the question "Who is Elm?" Well, I still don't know who he is, but I hate him.

"I hate Elm!" I scream, desperate tears in my eyes, thinking maybe if the world believed my words, I could be redeemed. A popping sound immediately follows my yell, causing my body to jump in alarm. As I tumble from my bed, the pendant disappears, and the yellow dress once again adorns me. I pull at its gathers and folds, wide-eyed and disbelieving. A moment later, the door to my room flings open. Three Benefactors stand there with Selene among them, and every one of them looks edgy. I stare at them, wholly exposed.

"She's not here. Don't waste your time," Selene says firmly. "Split up so we can cover more ground. We need to find her immediately. Even now, we might be too late."

My stomach churns. Selene has never looked that afraid, at least, not when I'm involved. While the dress gave me a temporary escape, I know I'm in enormous trouble when she finds me. No . . . oh no. Elm has me trapped. I know nothing about Yellow magic and have no choice now but to seek him out. No choice but to plead with him to release me from whatever hold this is. I don't like it, but I don't know what else to do.

Wasting no time, I clatter through the halls and out of the school. But where exactly am I going? I know I have to find Elm but can't even fathom where to look. Even the Benefactors haven't been able to track him down. How can I? With nothing else to go on, I run toward the forest in the direction he rode off yesterday.

"Elm!" I call over and over. "Elm, where are you?" My desperation turns to anger, which grows with each minute that passes until my insides are red hot and seething.

I have no idea where I am.

The trees are dense, and nothing looks familiar. In my frenzied attempts to find Elm, I didn't pay attention to where I was going. I stand alone in the eerie quiet of the forest, and it's easy to believe the looming trees want to swallow me up. My blind anger sizzles into fear. There are miles of forest, and it all looks the same.

"Okay," I whisper to myself. "Don't panic. It's going to be fine." I retrace my footprints, but the foliage on the forest floor is so thick that I soon lose them.

Close to tears, I release a groan. I have gone so long without causing trouble, and now everything is falling apart so quickly. One weak brick to crumble my entire foundation.

"All because of that stupid necklace!" My choking voice echoes through the trees, and I hear a huff behind me.

"Stupid? Really? I didn't think it was that bad."

Elm leans against a tree a few yards away, and a tumultuous mix of relief and contempt fills me at the sight of him. Narrowing my eyes, I give him what I hope is a piercing look while trying to hide the tremor in my voice. "How long have you been there?"

"I've been following you for quite a while, actually."

If I weren't dependent on him to free me from this situation, I would kill him right now. How hard would it be to use a strengthening spell to drive him into the earth? Or send him reeling into that tree? Oblivious to my thoughts, he just smiles.

I approach him with resolve and do my best to stare him in the eyes. Standing on my tiptoes still can't quite get me to his level. Why is he so blasted tall? "Enough games. Your necklace is going to get me expelled. Or locked up."

"Mmm, but you can always become invisible if it's troublesome to you. The necklace conceals the dress. Don't you think having that lovely yellow dress in your room would be much more conspicuous?"

"So, my options are either be invisible or flaunt the forbidden color all around school grounds?"

Elm casually snaps his fingers, and with another pop, I'm back in my school clothes. He removes the necklace from my neck with his cane and dangles it in front of me with smug satisfaction. "I didn't plan on keeping it stuck on you forever. I simply needed to give you a reason to come back."

"What is that supposed to mean?"

"The Benefactors put a nasty spell in place to keep me from interacting with their students. I can't approach anyone—they have to come to me. And so, Miss Ava, I needed to give you a reason to come to me."

He told me he triggered those alarms on purpose . . . of

course. He wanted everyone looking for him so he could approach whomever he wanted. "So this was your plan from the beginning?" I knew I couldn't have escaped him that easily. He's conniving. Of course he never had any intention of letting me walk away.

"Oh, yes. And you played along like a champ." He taps the pendant with his cane, and it transforms into a silver, heart-shaped locket. "A little less incriminating, yes? Just don't unlatch it for anyone." He snaps it open to reveal a yellow gemstone inside. "You're quite clever, though, Miss Ava. You figured out how to turn it back into the dress without any assistance from me."

The inadequacy I now feel is humiliating. "I have no idea how I did that." I'm not sure how else to ask him about the locket's secret without admitting this to him.

"A movement and a keyword," he says. "You simply have to say my name while holding the pendant upside down in your hands." He looks pleased with himself. "I'm curious, in what context were you calling me?"

"I wasn't calling you. I was saying I hate you."

"Well, I suppose that works too. Ah, you might also be wanting this back." He reaches into his suit-coat pocket and produces my red pendant. I might have known he has slippery hands to go with his slimy agenda. I wordlessly snatch the pendant from him.

The necklace fiasco is temporarily resolved, but I'm not going to be able to go back to school—at least not without a harsh interrogation. And probably imprisonment.

"What am I supposed to do now?" The words are out before I can stop myself.

"Are you waiting for instructions from me?"

"Absolutely not. I'm not your lackey."

"Oh, you're not?"

I answer him with a scathing look.

He smiles. "Of course you're not, Miss Ava. But we do need each other. Doubtless, you wonder what you are supposed to do now that the whole school has seen you sporting a lovely necklace in the forbidden color?"

"Yes. That."

"Well, the Benefactors will probably have a lot of questions for you."

"Yes." I almost roll my eyes at the obvious.

"And a punishment, no doubt. There's sure to be punishment."

"Oh, you think?" I snap. He is still in good humor, despite my obvious displeasure. He seems to actually be enjoying this. He knows he holds all the leverage while I have none.

He rests a hand on my shoulder in reassurance, and I start at his touch. "You need not worry, Miss Ava. I'll take care of everything."

"How can you do that?" I ask, shrugging his hand off.

"Oh, you'll see. It might take a day or two before things are fully resolved, but it will be all right. For now, you simply have to trust me."

"I'm not so sure I can do that."

"Try," he says simply.

At this point, I don't see what my options are. I can trust him and go back to Prism, or live out the rest of my life in exile. Neither option is appealing, but if there is a small chance I can continue at Prism, then I guess I should take it.

Elm holds the locket out for me, and I take it reluctantly. I turn it in my hands and murmur, "Elm." The locket pops and turns into the dress again.

"There now," he says. "Easy."

"So I'm just supposed to walk up to school like nothing happened?"

"I don't think it matters how you walk up to the school. You're going to create a fuss either way."

"But what do I say?"

"Say anything you'd like. I would appreciate it if you don't mention me, but of course, you may say whatever you wish. You have your will . . . now, at least."

My blood turns to ice. "What do you mean 'now'?"

"Ah, well, when we first met, you may recall I requested you not tell anyone you saw me. Forgive me, but that was more than a simple request."

My breath catches. He already put me under his control? Is that why I could never bring myself to tell Selene about him? I stare at him, horrified, and to my surprise, he looks . . . worried? Ashamed?

He holds up his hands in supplication. "Consider my situation. I had just escaped, half-mad, and you were the first person I ran into. I didn't know where I was or who I could trust. I dare say you would have done the same. But, the suggestion is now removed."

"So if I wanted to, I could turn you in right now?" Why would he give me back my will at such risk to himself? My guard slips slightly.

Elm shrugs. "If that's really what you want, Miss Ava."

"Miss Ava, Miss Ava," I mimic. "Why is it always 'Miss Ava' with you?"

"I can't afford to be too informal with you. People would think me a scoundrel, Miss Ava."

I raise my eyebrows. Surely he can't expect me to buy that.

"Oh, fear not," he says. "A few years from now, after you've joined the ranks of your dear Benefactors, everyone will call you Ava."

Ah. So that's the reason. He won't call me simply "Ava" because of my connection to the Benefactors. We refer to all Benefactors only by their first names rather than formal or grandiose titles. They believe it instills the idea that they are members of the public, like anyone else. He must not like the association.

I cross my arms and tip my head, studying him. "Obviously, you don't like the idea of my becoming one of them someday."

"I dislike the idea of you uniting yourself with someone who doesn't have your best interests at heart." He draws a smoky yellow heart in front of my face with his cane. I swipe it away.

"Of course they have my best interests at heart. They keep us safe. All of us. And Selene basically raised me."

"Yes, raised you to be an academy robot," he says dryly. "Tell me, did she encourage you to have friends? To have a life?"

He touches a nerve. "She just wants me to do well. She cares about my success."

He smirks. "She doesn't care about you. If she did, she would want you to have experiences along with your knowledge. Instead, all she wants is someone she can train to do her bidding. No reason for you to have a social life for that."

I get defensive, refusing to admit that he could be right. "She never said I couldn't have friends. That was . . . my choice." It sounds pathetic when I say it. What kind of person chooses not to have friends?

"But she never encouraged it either. I'm curious, do you think anyone who truly cared about you would want you to devote the entirety of your life to one cause and then to die alone?" He draws another heart in the air and then slashes through it, emphasizing his point.

I hadn't thought about that. What do I plan to do with myself? My goal all along has been to become a Benefactor. But at some point, I'll want more than that, right? A family. Friends. I can't expect that to magically happen if I don't meet people.

He has unearthed worries I'm not yet ready to think about. I push past him toward what I believe is the path back to Prism.

"Oh, dear. You probably don't want to go that way if you don't feel like spending the night in the trees."

I stop and wordlessly turn in another direction.

"Well, you would eventually get there down that route, I suppose."

I glare at him. "Will you just tell me the right way?"

He grabs me lightly by the shoulders and turns me a few steps to my left. "Keep walking straight this way until you see a clearer path. You'll be able to follow that back to your dear school."

"Thank you." I grumble back over my shoulder to him, "You'd better not be lying to me about fixing this."

I hear the slightest laugh in his voice as he replies, "Dear Miss Ava, *I* would never lie to you."

Once I'm back in my room, tiny strings of panic thread through me. I know eventually I'll have to take off the dress and become visible again. I'll have to face Selene and the other Benefactors. What explanation can I give for wearing a yellow necklace? Maybe my best option is just to tell the truth or at least some semblance of it. I could say I woke up with it and couldn't take it off. That will work, won't it? And that could be my saving grace. Naturally, they will draw the conclusion that Elm is involved, but it won't be me saying it. The cat will be out of the bag and the burden off my shoulders. The Benefactors will see me as the unsuspecting victim and help me out of this predicament. Keep me safe.

But then, of course, they will go looking for him. They may capture him, and I will most likely never see him again. This bothers me more than it should. I have no reason to feel protective of him. And yet, I don't want to put him in danger. He's irritating, for sure. Arrogant. But he doesn't seem to be dangerous.

No, I cannot rationalize this. He doesn't seem dangerous, but he's a Yellow. Deception is their specialty. He already used his powers on me once—that I know of. My stomach churns again thinking about it. Even more unsettling, he obviously has plans for me. He intended to lure me back to him from the beginning. And now, I don't have a choice but to rely on him. I played right into his hand.

I remove the dress again, and in its place, resting delicately around my neck, along with my school pendant, is the harmless-looking locket Elm created. I hold my breath and lift it over my head. I expect it to get stuck at the last second, but it comes right off. So Elm was honest with me about this, at least. I play with the chain of the locket for a moment, contemplating it before I stuff it to the back of my dresser drawer. He doesn't have bad taste.

Annoyed at myself, I shove the thought away. Good taste in jewelry doesn't make up for . . . whatever he did. The Benefactors didn't lock him up for nothing.

I should not see him again. As soon as the pendant issue is resolved, I will tell Selene and remove myself from the situation. If this meeting with Elm continues, it's only a matter of time before someone discovers me. And then I'll lose everything I have worked so tirelessly for. That is, assuming everything isn't already lost.

It's useless to delay the inevitable. If my chances of being a Benefactor are destroyed, waiting won't change that. I brace myself for an ambush as I step into the hallway, but I'm alone. A quick look at my watch tells me afternoon classes are still in session but should be ending shortly. I pick up my pace. It's better if I turn myself in before the halls fill up.

And then the bell rings, mocking me. Too late.

I prepare for some kind of outcry, knowing the story of an Elite student wearing yellow must have circulated by now. I put my head down and walk swiftly, hoping to blend into the crowd.

A moment later, I hear the dreaded declaration I anticipated. "Yellow!"

I flinch and turn toward the source as though expecting to be run through with a dagger, but the owner of the condemning voice isn't looking at me. She's gazing outside. The students all flock around the windows, and increasing numbers of bewildered exclamations burst through the halls. I force myself between them for a look and can't prevent my mouth from gaping.

Scattered all over the school grounds are yellow flowers. The same yellow flowers I helped Elm duplicate. A rush of livid heat flushes my cheeks. That . . . idiot. Was this his plan? Create another ridiculous diversion, so people will forget about me? If anything, this only made my situation worse. I show up, wearing yellow, and then yellow flowers appear. This will make everyone think I'm responsible. Of course, I *am* responsible.

The intercom comes on. "All students please report back to your classrooms immediately. This is a safety measure. All students please report back to your classrooms immediately."

In the midst of scurrying students, a firm hand lands on my shoulder.

"Selene," I say in surprise. Her eyes are dark.

"Come with me. Now."

A shadow of dread fills me. She keeps her arm on my shoulder, steering me through the crowded hallway back toward her office. I get the impression she's afraid I'll try to get away. Her suspicion isn't altogether wrong. Running seems like a great alternative at the moment.

I recoil as we get to her office, and she shuts the door. She doesn't slam it, but somehow the sound is ominous, like a death sentence.

"Take a seat," she says sharply.

I obey.

"I suppose you saw the flowers outside?"

"I did." I maintain eye contact. The last thing I want to do now is appear nervous or guilty.

"And did you have anything to do with that?"

"No." I hope I didn't answer too quickly. "I don't know anything about where to find yellow flowers."

She watches her office window, eyes narrowed. "And I suppose you have a *very* good explanation for that yellow necklace? And where you disappeared to?"

I freeze. I want to say something, but the story I thought up earlier now sounds like a terrible excuse. My throat seems to have closed up.

"Ava," she says in a deadly voice. "Have you seen Elm?"

I shiver. "Of course not. No. Well, I mean, aside from his posters. And at the assembly. I haven't seen him anywhere else. I—" I'm rambling.

"I need answers. If you have seen him, we can make it right. But I need to know. I can't protect you if you aren't honest with me." Her voice loses some of its edge, and her expression turns to one of pleading. "You could never disappoint me if you would just tell me the truth."

Who am I kidding? Elm isn't going to fix this. Any moment now, he'll execute whatever plan he was cooking up. I should inform Selene immediately, assuming he was telling the truth about allowing me to do that.

"I saw him," I say. Wow. I guess he *was* honest about that part. "Right after he escaped."

Her eyes turn fearful, and she studies me more seriously. "Were you hurt?"

"No." He didn't seem interested in hurting me.

"I need you to tell me everything. We can't waste a moment."

She leans in close and looks me dead in the eye. "Where did you last . . . see . . ."

Her voice trails off, and she gets a glazed look, like someone turned on a fog machine behind her eyes.

"Selene?" She doesn't respond, staring forward in a strange daze. For a moment, I panic. "Selene?" I wave my hand in front of her face.

She remains unresponsive. I should find Dr. Iris. I spring from my seat, but on my way to the door, I catch a fleeting glance of something out the window. I stop short, realizing that the bright yellow flowers are fading. Someone is drawing on them, and there is only one person it could be.

Selene blinks a few times, and I hurry back to my seat and sit as straight and still as possible as she appears lucid again. "As I was saying, Ava. It's not a good example for our top student to be late or skip classes, so try not to let that happen again."

"I . . . what?"

"Haven't you heard a word I've been saying? Goodness child, where is your head?"

"Oh . . . I'm sorry. I just haven't been sleeping much lately. I'm so worried about doing well. I'll try to do better."

Selene relaxes. "Well, don't overdo it. We need you at your best. Go ahead and take the rest of the afternoon off, but I expect you in class as usual tomorrow."

"I'll be there."

My chest and lungs come to life as I leave Selene's office, allowing me to breathe again. Elm used a memory spell. He must have. And judging by the way he had to drain all of those flowers, he must have altered the memories of everyone in Prism. He would have to make anyone who saw the yellow pendant forget about it, as well as making everyone forget they saw the yellow flowers. He could easily have made me forget, too, but my memory is still clear. I get the unsettling confirmation this means he isn't done with me. But he did tell me the truth.

When I turn on the light in my room, I release a startled squeal. There, written on the mirror in my favorite lipstick is the message:

*if I were you,
I'd clean up the flowers.* ♥

Apparently, he also found the copy of his wanted poster I had stashed away because it's taped to the mirror with little hearts drawn around it. I yank it down and crumple it up, embarrassment ballooning inside my chest. And fury. He was in my room. And now he wants me to go clean up after him.

I clench my fists. My eye actually twitches. The worst part is he has a point. If I don't clean up the drained flowers, the Benefactors will eventually see them and know someone was drawing power. A lot of power.

I rummage in my drawer for the locket and panic when it doesn't turn up. Where is it? I put it there less than an hour ago. My eyes dart around the room and find it dangling from my bedpost, as though waiting for me. So he was in my drawers, too. I snatch up the necklace, loathing that I now have to speak his name.

"Elm," I hiss through clenched teeth. The locket faithfully transforms. Somehow this still surprises me.

Once safely cloaked in the dress, I grab my school bag and whisk out of my room with a desperate hope that nobody sees my mirror before I get a chance to clean it. The flowers in plain view of everyone are more pressing.

I work quickly, stuffing the colorless flowers into my bag at the fastest pace I can manage, relieved that students are in their classrooms and the grounds are empty. Many of the flowers have already started to dry out, and they crumble under my touch, making my task more tedious. I stop periodically and give myself an agility boost to increase my speed. No room for dawdling.

I manage to clean the last of the blossoms seconds before students populate the halls and grounds again, my bag stuffed to bursting with withered flowers. I'm exhausted, but my job isn't done. I trek a half mile into the forest, to a stream, and empty my bag of its contents. A layer of gray powder remains, covering the inside. Looking down, I realize I'm also coated in it, and I spend a moment dusting off, then washing my hands clean in the icy water.

Chilled and sore, I make my way back to Prism. Despite my initial hesitation, I'm now relieved I have Elm's dress to hide me and won't have to explain my haggard appearance. Any hopes of collapsing on my bed once back in my room flicker away at the vision of my mirror, still tainted by Elm's message. For the next hour, I scrub away the sticky, smudgy lipstick. He could easily have written his message on a piece of paper. I have notebooks and writing utensils all around my room in plain sight. Even if they weren't in plain sight, he certainly didn't mind nosing around for the locket, so why not find a pen? What a jerk.

Memories erased, flowers disposed of, mirror scrubbed. Everything is taken care of.

If I'm lucky, I will never have to deal with Elm again.

7

"AVA! JUST THE PERSON I WANTED TO SEE.
We're running low on some supplies. Would you mind running
to the city? I'll give you a permission card."

It's almost impossible to conceal my irritation. Ever since
the incident with Elm a week ago, Selene insists on giving me
a multitude of tasks. She can't possibly remember—after Elm's
memory spell—but it's almost as though she's punishing me.
Maybe she's just trying to keep me distracted. I'm sure she's
doing it for my well-being, but I don't like forceful redirection.

"Sure, I can go," I say, obedient in spite of my feelings.

She hands me Prism's purchasing card, along with a list
of supplies and the permission card students are given when
travelling off school grounds outside of designated free days.
"Thank you. Will you need anyone to go with you?"

For a moment, I consider this, wondering if it's safe to go
out alone when I'm on Elm's radar. But I haven't seen or heard
anything from him since the flowers.

"No, I'll be fine. Thank you."

The weather is clear as I leave the school grounds. I squint
into the bright yellow sun and wonder briefly if a Mentalist
could draw from it if we were closer. Proximity is required for
us to draw on objects, so of course the sun is impossible to
use as a magic source. I have heard many Shapers attempt to

find ways to draw power from the sky. I stare into its vast blue, trying to imagine it drained to gray.

I step lightly down the cobblestone path from the school, which curves left half a mile to the hover-cart station, ignoring the Benefactors that have been a permanent part of the landscape since Elm's appearance.

Travel is mostly provided by small, white, enclosed carts that hover about a foot off the ground and travel along a lighted blue path. They are yet another invention powered by Blue magic. With blue stones lining the bottom of each cart, the carts are unmanned, and when they start to run low on power, they dock at stations where Shapers recharge them.

Thankfully, when the next cart arrives, it has enough charge to get me into the city without extra stops. I step on board and program in my destination, using the touch screen at the front of the vehicle. The cart requests ID, and I scan my student identification.

The screen displays PERMISSION TO TRAVEL? I scan my permission card, and a happy chime confirms my clearance. The smooth purr of the cart begins, and I'm on my way. The hum is soothing, and the scenery is comforting in its familiarity.

Now and then, I imagine flickers of yellow whizzing by, but I know that's impossible. The Benefactors are especially diligent about high-traffic areas, such as the hover-cart paths. Naturally occurring yellow objects are more and more rare, thanks to Red magic-assisted biological manipulation, and anything that falls through the cracks is quickly eliminated when spotted. Still, Elm managed to find that flower somewhere.

I can't keep my mind off him for long. His mannerisms and his voice. His insistence on calling me "Miss." Even the first time we met.

Miss Student.

Is that why he got me further involved? Did I make myself his target by bumping into him that day? And the way he flicked me between the eyebrows . . . what if that was what gave him access to my mind? Oh, how I wish I understood Yellow magic.

The small bump of the cart as it docks at the city station shakes me from my thoughts. I step onto the clean white platform to direct myself through the bustle of the city, now on higher alert than before. Violet City is one of the largest hubs in all of Magus. The name is appropriate, as the city is a sea of red and blue. Many shops cater to either Red or Blue magic-users and decorate in their respective colors.

I feel overwhelmed and out of place in the city. It's such a change from Prism's orderly environment with everyone dressed in uniforms. Here, people are free to dress according to their own eccentric styles. Magic-users sport a wide range of clothing and styles. In every direction, my view fills with capes and cloaks, frilly dresses, decorative chains, glitter, and an array of garish patterns. Hair dyed in shocking shades of red or blue.

In spite of the liberties taken with fashion, it's rare to see a Red magic-user wearing blue or vice versa. Most people say they color code this way as a precaution—if they needed to use a great deal of power in an emergency, they could draw on their clothing for extra strength. But we can't pretend it isn't also to separate and define ourselves; we grow proud of our magic type and want others to know exactly who we are.

"Hey, settle a bet for me!" a woman loudly hails me from the door of a cute, boutique-style shop. "Which Colorstick brand is better quality? Pigmentia or Undertone?" She holds up two blue Colorsticks of vibrant wax, which can be purchased as temporary power sources, and waves them in my direction.

"Oh, I wouldn't know." Apart from being somewhat expensive to buy a quality brand, it's illegal to sell Colorsticks to minors.

Another woman appears in the doorway and bops the first

over the head with a red Colorstick. "Like she would know. She's a kid."

"Just need to get the best in case that guy shows up. What's his name? Elmer?"

"Elm," the second woman says with a magnificent eye roll. "Heaven help you if he shows up on your doorstep."

Before they can drag me into it further, I tiptoe away as they argue.

It's not just those two thinking about the escaped Mentalist. Elm's face smirks at me from the corner of every sidewalk. His wanted posters decorate the city. I stop to examine one on a rustic lamp post, unable to escape my fascination for him and the power he holds even here.

"Scary, isn't he?"

I turn and come face-to-face with a craggy old man sporting an iridescent blue cloak.

"Oh," I reply. "I guess so." Of all my feelings for the mysterious Mentalist so far, fear takes a backseat to intrigue.

"I could help you out. Teach you some defense." His smile has too many teeth, and he gestures toward a rickety, wooden carnival cart with the words "Defend Yourself!" painted on the side. The cart sticks out oddly, parked on the gravel road in front of a row of sleek, high-end retail shops.

I'm hesitant to get my hopes up. So far, everything relating to Elm or Yellow magic leads down an endless rabbit hole, and this man hardly looks like a reputable source. Still, it can't hurt to ask. "You know how to defend against Yellow magic?"

"Course I do. Fought 'em for years."

"Not to be disrespectful," I say, "but you're a Shaper. There's not much you could teach me, since we don't practice the same magic."

"My brother's a Red," he says. "We work together."

An equally aged man pokes his head out of the side window on the cart and waves at me. He wears a cloak similar to his brother's, in glittering crimson. "We'll give you a great price, young lady!"

"What exactly do you know about Mentalists?" I ask casually.

"Well," says Red, "they deal with illusions and the mind."

"They get inside your head," says Blue.

"Everyone knows that. What else can you tell me about them?" I prod.

They look at each other uncomfortably—at a loss for words. Blue finally says, "Well, that's the gist of it, really. But we sure can teach you how to defend yourself. We're the experts."

I smile at them and shake my head. "Maybe another time." Either they are worried about the implications of giving a student unnecessary information, or they don't know anything more than I do.

But someone in this city has to know more. I remember hearing Blake's parents discuss their duties as Benefactors, often having to shut down operations on . . . what was it . . . Chrysanthemum Street?

I walk past tall square buildings of glass and steel, azure and ruby posters blanketing every window. The sidewalk opens up into a brick-paved courtyard, and the center has what I hoped for—a city directory. I tap the map on the large screen and scan for Chrysanthemum Street. Before zooming in on the map for a more precise location, I take a quick look around and can't help but notice the Benefactors. They are hard to miss in their black uniforms, which stand out strikingly amongst the blue and red. Some of them talk to each other in low, muted tones, while others merely stand still, their eyes sharply surveying the area like birds of prey. I have never seen so many of them in the city before, and it's no wonder the two brothers would hesitate to talk to an underage magic-user about forbidden subjects. Fortunately, the Benefactors couldn't care less about a student staring at a directory.

Once I'm sure I know my way, I set out, winding into more

obscure parts of the city. The Benefactors aren't as thick down these twists and turns of concrete and crumbling brick— probably more focused on highly populated areas, where they think Elm will look for victims.

The air smells stale and smoggy, and the structures become more sandy brown and less red and blue as efforts to decorate dwindle. A shifty-looking man in a dusty blue jacket meanders down . . . Chrysanthemum Street. Here goes nothing. I wait a moment to give plenty of distance between us before heading the same direction.

Before long, I find myself in the middle of a large square. The buildings here are run-down, many of them abandoned. The square, not to be wasted, now serves mainly as a space for street vendors to sell their wares. My attention turns to a tiny shop with broken windows, nearly every inch covered in posters of Elm. These are different from the ones I saw earlier—less professional in appearance, and rather than the *wanted* inscription, they have the words WHO IS ELM? above his picture. I step closer and notice smaller print below the photo: "Do you feel safe? Do you think the Benefactors are telling us enough? Demand answers. Demand them now. Hold the Benefactors to their word."

I shouldn't be here. I shouldn't be reading this. *Look somewhere else.* Anywhere else.

I swivel to see a building with the peeling words on the window: Dr. Thompson, MD Traditional Practice. The building has a giant PERMANENTLY CLOSED sign on the front. While sad, it's not surprising. Traditional medicine is a dying art on Magus since healing spells are much more efficient. However, some Shapers want to be doctors, and traditional medicine is their only option. Others believe we should still teach traditional methods in case magic ever disappears. But even with those reasons, it's hard to convince people to go under the knife when a few minutes with a Healer will have them up and walking again. As far as I know, Dr. Thompson was the last traditional doctor in Violet City. Before long, I don't know if any will remain on Magus.

What was it like before magic, when people weren't automatically expected to fill an occupation based on their magic-type? I look around the mostly abandoned shopping square and imagine for a moment what it would have looked like in another time, when anyone could be anything. Maybe the buildings would be bustling with life instead of serving as a courtyard for street vendors.

It's clear the two brothers I encountered aren't the only ones hoping to use fear as a means of making extra money. The city vendors sell all sorts of trinkets, claiming their items fend off Yellow magic: pendants boasting the ability to boost spells to five times their normal power, charms said to scare off Mentalists, and special clothing promising to protect from any Yellow spell. I doubt any of them work.

When we have so little information available to us on this banned magic type, how are any of us truly supposed to protect ourselves? Even more puzzling is that all this excitement and activity is the result of Elm's escape. If he's really that dangerous, why am I still okay?

"No school today, hon?" A woman with short scarlet hair startles me out of my thoughts. She leans over her shop cart, watching me with interest.

"D-Done for the day," I stammer quickly. "I'm on an errand."

She raises her eyebrows. "Around here? We don't see many students in these parts." Her eyes scan the area, and then she adds in a softer voice, "It's okay. You're here for protection, right?" Before I can respond, she holds up a glittering white pendant. "White magic," she whispers. "You and your friends can use this."

"White magic?" I ask, intrigued.

The murmur of vendors fades unnervingly fast, and the woman's eyes flicker with fear before she quickly tucks the pendant away in the pocket of her red jacket. I turn and see the source of her unease—two Benefactors just entered the square. Oh no. What if they tell Selene I'm here?

"You can buy your school things in there, hon," the woman says loudly, pointing at one of the few open shops in the square. "I'm sorry. I'm out of pencils for you today."

Nodding, I hurry inside, my heart in overdrive.

Like everything else in this area of the city, the small shop is in need of care, but it does carry the basics. I wander the aisles three times, barely conscious of what I'm looking for.

Stop.

Breathe.

I go down my list of items, focusing on filling my shopping basket only with what the list demands. It isn't until I get to the checkout counter that something else catches my interest.

A bright orange magazine—probably colored that way because it was legally as close as they could get to yellow—has the words *Who is Elm?* in bold lettering on the cover. Just like the posters. It displays the same smirking wanted poster picture of Elm under the title. Curious, I take the magazine and flip through it. It's mostly advertisements, but I'm anxious to get to the meat of it.

"Are you getting that, too?" the cashier asks as he rings up my last item.

I look quickly around the shop to make sure nobody I know is around. I'm not sure why, but I feel guilty for even looking at the magazine.

"Yes, I'm getting this," I say. "But ring it up separately, please."

I pay for the items for Prism with the purchasing card and use my own currency card for the magazine. The cashier hands me a large paper bag, full of school supplies, and gives me the magazine, which I swiftly stuff into my messenger bag.

I continue surveying my surroundings as I leave the shop, paranoid, as though I'm carrying illegal paraphernalia. But that's stupid. If stores sell the magazine in checkout lines, it must not contain anything incriminating . . . even in this part of the city. Yet, I can't help but feel Selene wouldn't like me coming back to Prism with it after her warnings to put Yellow magic out of my mind.

As I leave the shop, I immediately notice the absence of the Benefactors, and with them, the posters on the vandalized building. Somehow, this is a relief. I feel the eyes of the scarlet-haired woman on me again, and I consider approaching to ask about the pendant. But I think I have played with fire enough for today and don't have the energy to listen to what is most likely a snake-oil pitch anyway. I resist the urge to make eye contact with her and instead head toward more familiar parts of the city to catch a hover cart back to the school.

The magazine wickedly taunts me as I ride the hover cart back to Prism. All I can think about is returning to my room and reading it in total privacy. I track down Selene once back at the school and stiffly hand her the purchasing card and supplies.

"Find everything?" she asks, relieving me of the hefty bag.

"Yes," I squeak. She raises her eyebrows at me, and I clear my throat loudly. "Sorry, just need some water."

Like a thief, I steal away to my room, locking the door and shutting the curtains on my window tightly. Eagerly, I remove the magazine from my bag and sift through the pages for the cover story.

Who is Elm?

Yellow magic has been completely banned in Magus for more

than a decade. In fact, even the color yellow is forbidden and is not found anywhere on Magus . . . until now. A gray cloak with yellow lining. A yellow vest and a dapper top hat. Who is the mysterious Mentalist who has been haunting Magus? Where did he come from? What are his plans?

Mentalists are known for powers of the mind. They specialize in illusion. This falls outside of the realm of both Blue and Red magic, which deal with physical objects and the body. The Benefactors have worked tirelessly to keep the citizens of Magus safe from the harmful influence of Yellow magic. However, their best efforts are in danger of upheaval.

Elm is on the loose and at large. We have been warned that this man is highly dangerous and should be apprehended at all costs.

What do the citizens of Magus think of the mysterious criminal called Elm?

"Well, I wouldn't mind if he put me under a spell, if you know what I mean," laughs one female Shaper.

"He's so attractive," says an Augmentor. "I know I shouldn't be saying that, but he is."

Is this roguish Yellow devil out to steal the hearts of the ladies of Magus? Careful, girls! This bad boy is bad news.

Disappointed, I throw the magazine down. Nothing but a bunch of tabloid garbage. I guess I shouldn't be surprised. If I'm not finding new information anywhere else, why would a trashy newsstand publication tell me anything useful? All I got from it was that apparently females of Magus find him handsome. A good-looking bad boy. I stare at his picture again.

I suppose he is a little good-looking.

Blushing and embarrassed, I shove the magazine under my pillow.

8

I GROAN AND STUMBLE OUT OF BED.
My eyes protest, feeling like small pebbles in my sockets. I
rub them and yawn. My head hurts, and my every movement
drags. I turn quickly away from the flash of myself I catch in
my bedroom mirror; I look as though I haven't slept for a year.

I keep waiting for something to trigger Selene's memory
of the yellow necklace and flowers, but everything seems
normal. Elm did a thorough job, and while this is a relief,
it's also unsettling. Now that I have a sense of what Yellow
magic can do, I wonder how much of what I know is real. I
didn't recognize the first time Elm used his powers on me.
Would I notice if he did again? This is all the more reason
to stay away from him. And yet, if I'm honest with myself, I
also know part of my restlessness is because I want Elm to
come back for me. This curiosity and thirst for information is
insatiable, and I can't ignore the feeling that Elm could give
me the answers I need.

As is typically the case these days, I'm awake much earlier
than I need to be. The extra free time is a burden. It's more
space in the day that I have to fill. More time to think and
formulate questions without answers. More frustration. More
mystery. More time to feed my unhealthy obsession with
wanted criminals.

I decide to spend my time before class getting some magic practice in. I don't know what I should practice and I hardly care, but I have to do something busy until my school schedule begins for the day. Anything.

The designated practice area at Prism consists of a spacious hallway broken off into several rooms with thick plexiglass walls. A Benefactor is always patrolling to be sure nothing goes awry. Today it's a young man I haven't seen before. He looks a little older than I am, and I guess he is probably just starting. This could be me in a year or two. My heart leaps at the thought.

The first room in the hallway is full of random objects students can use for training: wooden boards, punching bags, stuffed animals, metal rods, cloth, foam cushions, and whatever else people decided to put there. There is also a sign-out desk, where we can borrow stones. We may only use these in the practice area. I usually work without extra stones, as I like to mimic testing situations where we have nothing to use but our pendants.

After selecting a few heavy wooden boards and figuring out how to balance them in my arms, I go to the room farthest down the hall. It gives me a false sense of privacy. I get self-conscious when I'm training and prefer to be in an area fewer people will pass by.

I step into the room and let the glass door swing shut. Padded gray floors help keep injuries to a minimum. The walls, though thick, are not soundproof, and all around me, I hear the din of practicing students: thuds, loud cracks, squeaks, occasional grunts of pain, laughter, exclamations of accomplishment.

As always, I start with an agility spell as a warm-up. Selene taught me this, explaining it helps stimulate the mind and keep one sharp. The energy from the spell shoots through me like a rubber band. It's easy to feel jittery when using an agility spell.

Your heart rate quickens; you feel hyper alert. The last thing
you want to do is hold still. Accuracy is difficult when you can
move so fast. I zip several times around the room, feeling the
air glide over my skin as I move. Now I'm awake. I grab one
of the wooden boards and place it in the center of the room.

The beginnings of a strengthening spell create a strange
feeling at first. Every cell within me vibrates with power, like
a temperamental bomb. The slightest touch could make it go
off. This is why we have to practice controlling that energy and
releasing it when we're ready. I feel a jolt as the spell reaches
its peak, and then I race headlong, pounding into the board.
It shatters, and I shield my eyes from the splintering wood.

"Careful in there," the monitoring Benefactor warns. "You
should use eye protection if you're going to keep doing that."

"Sorry," I call. I had almost forgotten he was there.

I stare at the remaining wooden boards, unsure of how to
continue. Normally, I would come here with a goal in mind,
knowing that I wanted to improve some skill or another.
But this time, I just need some sort of release. It would be
satisfying to keep smashing boards, but it wouldn't accomplish
much, and since I forgot to bring any eye protection with me,
it would likely get me in trouble.

I move another board to the center and think about that
day in the forest when I practiced alone. Something happened
there, though I don't know what. A little voice within me warns
not to practice my theories with so many people watching, but
I'm also so tired of doing nothing. I let warmth move through
me and gradually ease that warmth to my head, and then I
focus all my concentration on the board. I hold onto the energy
for what feels like an eternity, until I can't bear it anymore.

I stop, panting, and feel a cold sweat on my forehead. My
body shakes, weakened from the strain of whatever it was I
was trying to do. The board remains unscathed, and I release
an exasperated sigh. How can I feel so exhausted and yield

no result? But then, I don't know what I expected. It's not as
though I was performing any actual spell, at least, not one I'm
familiar with. It shouldn't surprise me that nothing happened.

But an eerie feeling slithers through me as I realize the
normal sounds of practicing students have all stopped. I look
quickly around, and through the glass of my practice room, I
see the students in the rooms nearest me clutching their heads.
Only then do I realize my own head is throbbing.

The young Benefactor rushes to the end of the hallway. "Is
everyone okay here?"

Students nods with unease, many still massaging their heads.

"I called Selene," he says, "but I need you all to stay put until
she gets here."

I kneel down in the doorway of the practice room, suddenly
too overwhelmed to stand. Now that I've noticed my head,
it won't stop aching. A few moments later, Selene enters the
practice wing with Dr. Iris at her side. They visit each of the
rooms one by one, asking questions as Dr. Iris examines
students and performs healing spells. I'm dying to know what
this is all about.

At last they reach me. "Selene, what is going on?" The
question bursts from me.

Her face is somber. "It seems suspiciously like Yellow magic."

Yellow magic? But then that means . . .

"Elm?" I ask loudly.

"Keep your voice down," Selene reprimands. "But it looks
that way, yes. We have a better chance of searching for him if
everyone isn't anxious and alarmed. So I advise you to be silent."

"I'm sorry," I mumble.

"It doesn't matter. I assume you can't tell me anything
different from the other students?"

"No. My head just suddenly started hurting."

"I can take it from here," Dr. Iris breaks in. "You should go,
Selene. You have other things to attend to."

"Can I go with you?" I ask.

"Certainly not." Her blunt words sting. "I'm sorry, Ava, but this isn't your place yet. It will come with time." She gives my shoulder a quick squeeze and then hurries back down the corridor.

"Well then," Dr. Iris kneels beside me and presses her fingertips to my temples. "Let's take care of that head."

Her touch is light and cool and soothing against the pulsating ache. After a moment, I feel a gentle heat. A warm wave of relief spreads through my skull, and soon the ache disappears entirely. I breathe a relaxed sigh.

"There," she says, smiling. But something seems to be bothering her, and there is a contrived aspect to her smile. She stands and tucks a stray strand of hair behind her ear, sighing. "I think that's everyone. I'm going to go see if I'm needed anywhere else." As an afterthought, she says, "Ava, I know you're curious about this, but please don't cause any trouble. Just stay with the other students until the all-clear is given. It's more complicated than you realize. Take care."

She exits briskly, and I'm left wondering what could have caused that look of uncertainty in her eyes.

"They really didn't find anything?"

"Nothing," replies Selene. "Which I suppose I should count as a good thing—we don't want Elm around students. But it means he evaded us again."

Initially, I was grateful my lessons with Selene hadn't been canceled as a result of this morning's incident; I had hoped to get some insider information. Now, I can see it's more of the same. At least we're doing our lesson outside today. It feels good to be out on the grounds—free from walls—although I can't stop my eyes from wandering to the forest.

Selene reaches into her bag and produces several bright blue-and-white-striped orbs about the size of a tennis ball. Target balls, powered by blue magic. She tosses them into the air, and they hover in place. She brings out the module that controls the targets. With it, she can control the speed and movement patterns.

"Let's work on honing your accuracy some more," Selene says. "I want to see just how quick you can go."

I don't want to do agility exercises right now. I want something new. Haven't I been fast enough? Her one compliment for me during the aptitude test was that my "speed was good," so why are we working on it now?

She hits a button on the controller and the target balls move at a moderate speed, flying in random patterns around me. My fists connect with each target without any trouble. Each target freezes in mid-air after I hit. When every target is frozen, Selene resets and starts them again, faster this time. Once again, I hit the targets without difficulty. Selene increases the speed.

This. *Hit*. Is. *Hit*. Boring. *Hit*.

I wonder what it would be like practicing magic with Elm. I miss.

"We'll start this round again," Selene says, stopping the targets. "Get them all the first time."

Breathe. Refocus. I hit the targets. Now Selene increases the speed significantly, the balls blurring before me. I swing. *Miss*. Swing. *Miss*.

"It looks like we've finally reached your limits. We'll work toward this." She freezes the targets again. "I want you to think—how do you solve this? What do you do if you can't even see your mark clearly?"

Just tell me how to be better, and I'll do it. I'm not in the mood for this. Why does everything have to be a question? Why can't she just tell me? But I know this frustration is about more than this. It's about always feeling left in the dark and working toward a goal that doesn't seem as fulfilling as it once was. Not when I know there's more to be found.

Selene is still waiting for an answer.

"I can't just make my fists faster," I say. "I have to react faster. I have to predict."

"Good." Selene nods with approval. "I'll start again, a little slower this time."

At once, a small yellow bird appears in front of one of the targets. I stare, freezing.

"What's the matter?" Selene must not be seeing what I see . . . which means this is an illusion. One just for me. An unexpected thrill runs through me.

"I'm fine," I say. "Just trying to stay focused."

The targets begin moving again, and this time I can see the yellow blur of the bird. I swing. *Hit.* The bird moves. *Hit.* Again. *Hit.*

"I'm impressed," Selene says, and I hear the genuine pride in her voice. "Let's see if you can be faster."

But now, even with the bird, it's impossible to track the targets. I stand firm, searching for a solution. Think.

Selene is about to dial the targets down again.

"Wait," I say.

She crosses her arms, waiting in interest. I can't disappoint her again. If I want to track the targets, I can speed up my body, but I need to speed up my mind, too. I have to be able to process what's happening before me. I think again to that day in the forest—I focused a strengthening spell on my mind . . . could I do it with agility, too?

At once it feels like the world is in slow motion. I can see the targets and the bird, which is now looking me dead in the eye. I'm isolated, just me, the targets, the bird, and the steady sound of my breathing. One by one I slam into the targets again, stunned to see them all frozen a moment later.

The world speeds up again.

"Well," Selene remarks, "your determination once again paid off. Nicely done. I'm proud to be your mentor."

I smile, giddy at my success, but the feeling is short-lived. The yellow bird flits in circles around my head. I fight to keep composed.

Selene gathers her bag. "I have to hurry back. Shall we go together?"

"I'm going to stay out here and study for a bit," I say. Nothing unusual about that. Selene knows I've preferred to work outside, ever since I was little.

I keep my arms pinned to my sides to avoid the feathered pest, now chirping loudly. It pauses to jerk its head in the direction of the forest. I'm at war with myself, knowing that following the bird is following danger, but also knowing answers live where those wings lead. *Ignore. Ignore. Ignore.*

Several popping sounds nearly shatter my facade, but I manage to maintain composure as the bird multiplies into six. They shoot forward and encircle my head like a bad cartoon joke, flapping and warbling.

"Thank you for the lesson," I say, hoping this prompts a quicker exit.

"Thank you for your hard work," is Selene's reply. I almost don't hear her over the noise. "We'll talk soon."

When Selene enters the school, I force myself to count to ten in my head—slowly—to make sure. The instant I hit ten, I spring down the forest path, forcing my hands to avoid swatting at the birds. I don't want to look like a lunatic, batting at things nobody else can see. They dance around my head, a strange twittering carousel, every now and then causing me to stop as one swoops down in front of me.

It doesn't take long to find Elm. He waits for me just inside the forest.

"Lovely day, isn't it, Miss Ava?"

I'm not prepared for the anticipation that overtakes me when I see him. This is not the proper response. I should be afraid. I shouldn't even be here. But because it's too late for that, I decide I at least need to appear angry. *Don't show him anything else.*

"Call off your birds," I demand.

He widens his eyes, as though surprised. "My birds? What makes you assume they're mine?"

I stare at him incredulously. It's hard to tell over the clamor of my feathered entourage, but I think I hear him chuckle. At the least, he's definitely smiling.

In an instant, the birds are gone. My ears still ring from their noise.

"What was the point of that?" I ask. "Why did you help me with my lesson?"

"The lesson seemed a bit dull, don't you think? I wanted to make it more interesting for you."

Why were you paying that much attention to me? How did you know I was having a lesson at all? How did you know I was bored? I want to ask him these questions, but instead, I ask, "But why interfere at all?"

"I needed to get you back to me. I thought I would have seen you again by now."

An inkling of caution peeks around the corners of my mind, reminding me that Elm has a plan—or plans—which somehow involves me. "What reason would I have to see you again? After the mess you got me into last time, I hoped we were finished." Not entirely true.

He approaches me and rests his arm on my head. "Ah, but I also got you out of the mess, didn't I? Wasted those flowers on you too. A pity. I was saving them for something else."

"Oh, I'm so sorry to inconvenience you," I say, shoving off his arm. "But don't worry. It won't happen again." I'm simultaneously aching to know what he planned and happy to never find out.

I turn, preparing to head back to the school, when he says, "I'm sorry if the birds upset you. I was troubled when I didn't hear from you and simply wanted to be certain everything had turned out all right."

I pause for an instant, but then I remember he's a Mentalist—a master of manipulation—and the Benefactors are out to get him. He's not the sort of person who would truly be concerned about someone like me. If anything, he would only be worried about his plans going awry.

"Well," I say, "it turned out fine. Thanks for that, I guess." I'm about to make a quick retreat, but once more, curious feelings creep in and dampen my desire to leave. "What were you doing at the school today?"

The surprise on his face looks genuine. "I wasn't at your dear school. Near it, yes, but not inside."

He must think I'm stupid. "There was an incident today. The Benefactors think Yellow magic was involved."

"They would think that, wouldn't they?" He chuckles. "Well, as much as I would have enjoyed seeing them run amok, I'm afraid I had no part in any such mischief."

We stare each other down for a minute, and I evaluate whether it's worth it to keep arguing. He changes the subject before I can pursue it further.

"Tell me, Miss Ava, do you make a habit of wandering out to the woods on your own? And do your Benefactor friends know about it?"

It strikes me all of a sudden how isolated we are. Of course I don't tell people when I leave school grounds—who would I tell? And nobody thinks to question me as Selene's mentee. Nobody knows I'm here. Not a soul.

"I have class," I lie, turning briskly away from him. "So I'm leaving. I probably won't see you again."

"You probably will!" he calls after me, engulfing me with another wave of unease as I retreat.

Another four days pass without seeing Elm, and I'm proud of that. Though curiosity and the allure of Yellow magic continue to gnaw like acid, I smother the feelings. The Benefactors will catch Elm eventually, and it will be as though none of this happened. That thought leaves me with an odd emptiness, which I shake away. As long as I gorge myself on distractions, it will be fine.

Fortunately, distractions are readily available today. Elite students have the unique opportunity to attend color-initiation ceremonies at Prism's junior academy, The Bright Academy, which I've looked forward to for a long time. Students enter Bright at age five, and at their initiation ceremonies, they learn their predisposed magic type. I haven't been to an initiation ceremony since my own twelve years ago.

A thrill of nostalgia overtakes me as Selene and I enter the initiation room. It looks just as I remember, and the iridescent cubes, which reveal a person's magic type, sit on pedestals at the center of the dimly lit space. The walls, the floor, and the pedestals are all white, which makes the shock of colored light from the cubes all the more dazzling when it happens. I remember my own ceremony in this very room, though the memory is foggy.

By the time I entered Bright, Yellow magic no longer existed in the curriculum, so only two cubes were present, like now. The red cube lit up almost instantly, and in my mind,

I see my parents glowing with pride, no doubt happy I was in the same class of magic as them. Selene told me she knew in that moment I would be a strong student, and this was why she decided to take me under her wing as her pupil.

Perhaps this is one of the reasons the initiation ceremonies mean so much to me—it's one of my last remaining memories of my parents, and it's the first time I met Selene.

Already in the room is another Benefactor, dressed in ceremonial robes rather than the black uniform. I recognize him as the man with the bulbous nose who appeared with Selene on the day Elm escaped. He looks deflated in his red robes, and his face is weary.

"Ava, I would like you to meet Jace," Selene says. "One of our best. He's usually hard at work behind-the-scenes, but I like him to come with me to the initiations. He has been traveling, so I'm glad he was able to make it back for today."

"Nice to meet you, Jace," I say, holding out my hand.

He shakes his head and smiles dismissively. "Sorry, but I've got a bit of a cold. Just haven't had the time to see a Healer yet."

How curious that an accomplished Augmentor—a Benefactor—would need to see a healer for a cold. Typically Augmentors at that skill level can heal small personal ailments themselves. But I couldn't ask about it without being rude.

The door to the initiation room opens, and a timid child steps inside, followed by his parents. He wears a white outfit, which is customary for these ceremonies. It symbolizes the blank slate children are before they discover their color. The boy looks nervous, his large brown eyes wide with anxiety. Selene and I greet him with reassuring smiles.

"Welcome to Bright," says Selene graciously. "As you know, today determines what type of magic you will study. Your power is already inside of you—we just need to reveal it. Focus your mind on the cubes, and the rest will happen naturally."

The boy steps forward, his parents standing tall in pride

for their son. He stares at the cubes. At first, nothing happens. But then a burst of light beams from the blue cube. The boy's face breaks into a relieved smile, and Selene steps forward and presents him with a blue pendant.

"Just like his dad," says the boy's father proudly.

The mother gently elbows him. "Well, let's hope his study habits are more like his mom's."

The child and his parents exit the room, already discussing plans for the future. After they go, I watch student after student find their color and leave elated, surrounded by loved ones. It's impossible not to share the buzz of their enthusiasm. I grin as a little girl bounces into the room, nothing but smiles. Her parents laugh at her excitement. Selene gives her the same brief introduction, and the girl focuses on the cubes.

Nothing. The girl's smile fades into a look of worried concentration. A minute or two passes, and she breaks into a sweat, her little face turning pink with effort. Her parents look at each other, eyes filled with concern.

Finally, Selene approaches and rests her hand gently on the girl's shoulder, shaking her head, face sad. Tears come instantly to the child's eyes, and my heart shatters. The rest of the room is deadly silent, making her breaking sobs even more prominent.

On rare occasions like this, a child cannot make a cube light up. These children are Mentalists. They can't attend Bright or Prism, as there is nothing they can learn there. A student who isn't permitted to use their magic is useless at a magic academy. From what I hear, these students end up in training for lower-level jobs in society. Selene explained this to me in the past, so pragmatically that I never questioned it. But now, seeing it played out before me . . .

Selene speaks in a solemn tone to the parents, who try desperately to comfort their child. "If you would, please go with Jace. He will go over your options with you. She won't be left without a place in the world."

The parents and the wailing child leave with Jace to discuss the child's fate, and I'm shaken. This is wrong.

"Will she be okay, Selene?"

"She has a hard road ahead, but she'll be fine. Magus has a place for everyone."

Except for Mentalists. We pretend they don't exist.

The air between us is heavy and uncomfortable as Selene and I travel on a secured hover cart back to Prism. I can't come up with anything to say that won't get me in trouble.

"You're bothered by what happened with the one girl, aren't you?" Selene finally says.

I nod, embarrassed at my transparency, but relieved I don't have to conceal my feelings anymore. "I feel so sad for her." Angry and indignant might be a better description.

"It's difficult," Selene agrees. "But you understand why it needs to be this way, don't you? Yellow magic puts our entire world at risk. Can you think of anything more terrible than losing your mind? Losing your free will and the very essence of the things that make you who you are?"

"I understand . . ."

"But?"

"But, were all Mentalists in the past really bad by nature? Couldn't we have just found a way to combat the bad ones?"

Selene looks at me. "You would think so, but imagine how difficult that becomes when you can't even determine who's being controlled and who isn't. You don't know who's on your side, and it becomes too easy for criminals to hide under illusions of good behavior. And I'm sorry to say the good ones were few. It was in their nature to use their powers to their advantage, and I suppose you can't blame them. As humans, we tend to look out for ourselves." Her tone brightens somewhat as she adds, "But, this is exactly why I do what I do, and it's what my biological studies involve. If we're lucky, we'll find a way to eliminate Yellow magic from the gene pool altogether, and no one will have to worry about losing their place . . . or their mind. We're already seeing fewer and fewer Mentalist children. You want to help with that work, don't you, Ava?"

"Yes," I say, although I'm not sure if I do right now. By restricting Magus to only two types of magic, I can't help but feel we're losing so much more than we understand.

When we return to Prism, I still can't stop thinking about the initiation ceremony. I haven't ever questioned treatment of the Yellows before. I assumed the ban on Yellow magic was for the greater good. But what about before the ban? Mentalists existed. What happened to them all?

I can think of one person who might have answers.

Today has taken an unexpected turn. The very thing I expected to distract me from Elm instead pushes me right to him. Can I really do this again? Every time I tell myself "no more," I somehow end up drawn back to the possibilities of the knowledge he holds. Just as he wants, I'm sure. But I don't care.

Back in my room, I dig through my drawers for the locket. *All questions will be answered,* one way or another.

9

HOW DID HE KNOW?

The vivid yellow butterfly sways in front of my face, beckoning. How did Elm know I would be searching for him today? Or is he always waiting? Watching like an alligator, still and silent, until I swim within reach of his jaws?

The butterfly dances past me, flicking its wings toward the trees, and I stop, watching it. It will take me to Elm, but that's about the only thing I can put on my list of certainties. Yet, I know myself too well. This isn't going away. This will never go away until I find satisfactory answers. If I don't follow the butterfly today, it will be tomorrow. It will be a week from now. Years, if that's what it takes. What's the point of waiting for the sword to fall?

Light from the trees casts strange patterns over the winged insect as I follow, but it isn't hard to keep track of its gaudy color among the greens and browns. After an extensive kaleidoscope of pine needles and foliage, the butterfly finally comes to rest on the arm of a figure behind a tree. My fluttering escort dissolves, and Elm emerges.

"Why, Miss Ava. I wasn't sure if I would see you again. To what do I owe the pleasure?"

I'm not sure what to tell him. Or perhaps I don't know what I *should* tell him. How would he feel about what I just saw at the color-initiation ceremony? "I want to learn more about Mentalists. And what you can do." Might as well cut to the chase.

"Ah. A hazardous request, don't you think? Especially for a future Benefactor." The way he studies me makes me uneasy. I know my connection to the Benefactors must be appealing to him for whatever his plans are. "Tell me, why this sudden attraction to the forbidden?"

"Just . . . curiosity." I won't give him the satisfaction of knowing I'm starting to question everything I've been taught. No way.

"Careful, Miss Ava. Rumor has it curiosity is deadly for certain creatures. But I will gladly meet your request if it's truly what you want." He extends his arm out to me. "Come this way, my curious kitten. I'll show you a few things."

I hesitate. This is too easy. What if it's a trick? Does he need physical contact to take control of my mind? "I'm totally capable of walking on my own."

"Are you sure? The forest is twisted, and it would be unfortunate if you lost your way." He pays attention to my every move, as though waiting for me to make the wrong one. I'm afraid of what might happen if I deny his requests, but I stick to my guns.

"I'm sure."

"As you wish. But do stay close."

As we travel through the forest, I wonder for a moment if Elm conjured a bunch of his butterflies in my stomach. I know I'm doing something brainless, but I can't seem to stop myself from walking forward down this road of mysteries. Bit by bit, I'm losing all the inhibitions that kept me safe until now.

Elm seems cheerful again, as usual, and at complete ease. He knows this place, like a trained animal through a maze. Each step is automatic for him, but I am in the dark. The fluttering of my nerves increases as we move deeper and deeper into the forest. I have never traveled this far in before, and we have taken so many turns that getting back without his guidance will be impossible. And I'm inherently edgy in Elm's company. I observe his every move, but as I do, my restlessness gives way to fascination. He moves with a strange grace, like something . . . well, like out of a dream. It's mesmerizing, and my already-feeble attempts at memorizing our route dissipate in my over-attentiveness to him. Are all Mentalists this way?

The silence as we travel has me aching to ask him questions. The opportunity hasn't ever presented itself until now. *Did you know about my dreams? Why did they stop? Are you planning to kill me out here?* The silence continues, and I subtly try to put a little more distance between us.

We come to a sudden halt when we reach a large sinkhole, filled with dead pine needles, moss, and crumbling logs. Several bugs scuttle and crawl through the rot, and the dank smell of decay cuts through the fresh forest air. Because of the sinkhole's size, I assume we'll have to figure out the best way around it.

"Ladies first." Elm gestures with a slight bow.

"You want me to go . . . *inside*?" He can't be serious.

"Don't you like it?"

A look at his amused expression tells me he's teasing again. Of course he realizes how unpleasant this spot looks. Of course we're going to go around.

"There's no need to be anxious, Miss Ava. Simply go inside."

"You've got to be joking."

"Often I am, yes," he admits. "But not this time. Now, if you'll please continue." He motions again for me to go forward.

"Is there . . . some kind of trick to it?" My mind goes to wild places. He's going to kill me and bury me here. He's going to hide me in the decay. Is there anything red around here for me to draw from if I have to fight him?

"Well, I'll tell you. Just step a little closer to the edge. No, closer still."

He waits expectantly until I walk as far as I dare go. If I move another centimeter forward, I'll fall. I'm still waiting for him to laugh and say he's just having fun with me, but he merely says, "Now, look down."

As I do so, Elm taps the back of my legs with his cane. With a scream, I lose my balance and plunge straight into the hole. I expect to feel the spongy crunch of rotting forest and scuttling creatures all over my skin, but instead I feel cool, solid ground. Upon opening my eyes, I'm met with what looks like a small cave. Elm stands next to me.

"There! That wasn't so terrible, was it?" He extends a hand to help me to my feet.

I ignore his assistance and pull myself up. "You! You—you . . ." I can't think of a strong enough word for what he is. This was an awful idea, if nothing else for the simple fact that Elm enjoys playing jokes. However, he catches on that I'm upset.

He lowers his extended arm slowly. "My apologies. I suppose I should have given you some sort of warning."

"Or I should have just known better." I glare. But I'm curious. "What was that? Some kind of portal?"

"Oh, no. This cave has been here for centuries. I merely camouflaged the entrance. I think I succeeded in making it wonderfully unappealing."

I have to admit it was clever. No sane human being would willingly enter that den of danger and filth.

"Is this where you live?"

"For now, yes. Someday, perhaps, I could build a lovely hermit's hut and live all alone . . . if your Benefactor friends would even let me get by with that much."

Why does that make me feel guilty? I'm not responsible for the choices he made in life. It's not my fault he's on the run.

The entrance of the cave dimly lights the space around us. I can see the forest outside, and I suppose Elm doesn't have any reason to mask the outside world from inside. I wonder how he has managed living here; the whole space can't be more than twenty feet wide. I survey him, and he certainly doesn't look like he's been living in a tiny crevice.

"Shall I show you around my place?"

"I think I have the gist of it." Surely he's joking again?

"On the contrary, Miss Ava. We haven't even scratched the surface. Close your eyes and I'll show you."

I'm not sure I trust him enough to take my eyes off him, but so far, he hasn't harmed me. He easily could have by now, if that were his plan. A moment after closing my eyes, his fingers slip into mine, and he pulls me gently forward. Now I *really* hope touch isn't required for his powers. We walk several feet, my stomach doing tiny somersaults, and confusion sets in. Even taking into account my disorientation from not being able to see, we should definitely have run into a wall by now. Instead, we keep walking. Is he playing another joke and just leading me around in circles?

Finally, we stop. The subtle light beyond my eyelids gives me the sense we are in a brighter room than before.

"You may open your eyes, Miss Ava."

Intrigued, I obey, and I gasp. Somehow, the cave evolved into a beautiful landscape. Green grass stretches out before me like a meadow. Flowers of every color—even yellow—surround me with a sweet perfume. A large willow tree stands as though beckoning someone to rest under its swaying branches, and I wonder how such a thing could possibly be here. Butterflies, like the one I saw earlier, flutter through the air, as do yellow birds. These, I make a point of ignoring, not wanting to encourage another winged parade around my head. Several yards ahead of me, a waterfall cascades off the rock wall of the cave down into a pool clear enough to see straight to its stony bottom.

All of this is in the midst of stalactites and stalagmites, which are the only things that hint at our cavernous location. Strangely, the cave is lit up, and I search for the source. I find it above me, in the form of several glowing spheres of light.

"How is this possible?" I ask, gazing around with wide eyes.

"You wanted to know what Yellow magic could do."

"So this is all an illusion?"

He nods. "Most of it, yes. The waterfall is real, and the cave formations, of course. But I had to do something to make this place more tolerable. And I can't have company without showing off a bit."

It's hard to process. Every inch looks so realistic, and it's difficult to grasp the sheer amount of power it must take to maintain such an illusion. Even with the extra stones Elm has, I'm not sure how he's doing it.

"Where did all of this come from? The room we were in before was so small."

"A false wall. It's simply an extra security measure. If someone falls into the sinkhole by accident, they will hopefully see a tiny underground cave and feel it isn't worth exploring. In reality, this cave goes on for miles."

"I like what you've done with the place." I'm surprised I feel so lighthearted.

"I'm glad it pleases you. Here, look, the garden is real." He leads me to a corner of the cave where plants grow in tidy rows.

"How do they grow without sunlight?"

He gestures toward the glowing spheres. "Artificial sun. It took me awhile to get it right, but now it's nearly as good as the real thing."

So he's an inventor as well. I wonder how long it took him to perfect something like this. But more than that, how does he keep it up? "This must have to run almost nonstop to grow plants," I say, voicing my thoughts. "How do you power it all?"

He tilts his head. "Mmm . . . I'm not quite ready to reveal that much to you yet. We've only just met. I can't give away my best secrets."

That's no answer. And it only creates more questions to keep me awake at night. But perhaps I can persuade him to tell me next time.

Great. I shake my head at myself. I'm already planning for next time.

As I continue to absorb the scene around me, I notice a small pile of books near the base of the willow tree. Curious as to what Elm would be reading, I walk over to examine them. My heart leaps as I read the cover of one of the books: *The Art of Yellow Magic, Volume One.*

I gasp and open it, practically drooling. Just as I'm about to start reading, the book is tugged from my grasp and snapped shut.

"Whoopsie," says Elm. "Can't have you reading that."

"But why? What do you care?"

"What kind of person would I be if I allowed a student to view such putrid contraband?"

For a wild moment, I consider using an agility spell and just taking it back from him. But there's so little I know about him and about Yellow magic that I'm not sure how he might lash out if I attempt it. "But . . . can't I read just a little? Please?" I'm not above begging.

He scrunches up his face in an exaggerated gesture, as though considering it is painfully hard. "Well, maaaaybe. I'll need to think on it. Perhaps, if you come back again, I'll let you take a peek. I have more than this one, even."

Again, I recognize him pulling on my strings, contriving ways to get me coming back. I don't like it, and yet the thought of having books on Yellow magic at my disposal gives me a dizzy thrill.

"We'll see," I say coolly. As I reach for another one of the books under the tree, a very familiar notebook catches my eye. "Hey! This is mine!"

"Ah, of course. I should have known," Elm remarks. "Only Prism's top student would take such tireless notes."

I narrow my eyes at him and point to the inside cover of the notebook. "That and the fact that my name is written on the inside."

"Well, don't be mad at me. If I find trinkets in the middle of the forest, I assume they are unwanted."

I know where he got it. It was left at the base of the oak tree on the day he escaped, and I never made it back there.

"You may have your scribbles back if you like, Miss Ava."

"They're not scribbles," I inform him. "They're important notes on—"

He smirks. "Combatting the evils of Yellow? Your Benefactors would love it. They seem to have an interesting view of history."

"Oh, I get it. Because they don't portray Yellows in the most flattering light, it's inaccurate. Is that it?"

He sidesteps my question with another one. "It seems a little excessive, don't you think, to ban an entire color?"

"Not really," I stare. "Not when it's a measure taken to make sure people don't lose their will." That's what I keep saying. That's what Selene keeps saying.

"Yellow magic is only one of many ways to deprive a person of their will, Miss Ava. Those who want to do so wouldn't need our help."

"That's true," I agree, hesitant. "But Yellow magic makes it easier. And that's why we have the Benefactors to keep us safe."

"And so Miss Ava is out to defend all of Magus from the likes of me."

This is an uncomfortable subject to breach with him. I feel guilty somehow, like being caught talking badly about someone when they're standing right behind you. "Well, I'm not a Benefactor yet."

"But you could have a lot of influence someday," he muses. "Being such a good student. Selene's obedient pet." He directs his gaze at me. "You could perhaps get the ban on Yellow lifted someday—with the proper persuasion."

The way he contemplates me makes me uneasy. He's not wrong. If I play my cards right, I will have influence as a Benefactor. Maybe that has been his goal all along—to convince me to trust him and then use me to bring Yellows back to power. Coming here with him, especially alone, was a mistake. Never mind the danger to myself—I could be putting our whole world in jeopardy.

"I need to go back now," I say, keeping my voice as composed as I can manage with so many warning bells ringing through my mind.

He tilts his head at me again. "So soon? Very well. I shall take you back."

He agrees too easily. "No . . . I can get back just fine." I turn toward the entrance of the cave. Truthfully, I'm not sure how I'm going to find my way to Prism, but it's unsafe to go with him.

He moves in front of me. "You couldn't possibly find your way back on your own."

"I have a good memory." I jut my chin out in defiance. "I don't need your help." I push past him and run from the cave. I look over my shoulder, expecting to see him following me, but he isn't there. Nervously, I continue, hoping my bluff doesn't come back to haunt me. I'm honestly not sure where I'm going.

After a long stretch of walking, the light turns orange in the trees, and the details of the forest fade into silhouettes. I quicken my pace. The last thing I want is to be in the forest alone when it gets dark. Surely I'm getting close to Prism by now?

But I'm not close to anything familiar. I can't see the tall white pillars of the school or the path that leads to the hover carts. I can barely even see the sky. Dense trees and shadows obstruct my view at every turn. I wish Blake were here. He's always been good at finding his way. Going somewhere once is usually enough for him to remember forever.

I halt as I hear a noise in the brush behind me. Something moves through the trees. Something large. The sounds of breaking twigs and heavy footfalls tell me this is no squirrel. I turn cautiously to find out what it is. It takes my mind a moment to process the dark shadow before me in the dissipating light.

A bear.

I hold back a scream, and my chest constricts. The bear appears to be looking right at me, but maybe it hasn't noticed me yet. Or maybe it simply doesn't care. My first thought is to use an agility spell and run from it, but I have no idea where I am. I couldn't just flee blindly into the dark. Perhaps my safest bet is to stay put and wait for it to pass. If I use a strengthening spell, I can be ready to take it on if I need to. I begin the spell, gearing myself up for what may come.

The bear charges. I fall backward, landing hard on the ground, my spell cut off. The bear paws at me, and I cry out and shield my head with my arms, pushing back at the same time. This hampers its blow, and I struggle to my feet. The bear attacks again, knocking me back to the ground and grazing me with its claws. It's much stronger and faster than I expected, not allowing me a chance to fully strengthen myself. I'm done for. Somewhere in the back of my terrified mind, I process more faint, frenzied rustling nearby.

A figure springs in front of me, and just as suddenly, the bear clambers to a stop and moves in the other direction. It crashes through the trees in its haste to escape. Breathing heavily, the figure turns toward me with disapproving eyes.

"It's fortunate I decided to follow you in spite of your

protests," Elm says. "Not that I ever had any intention of leaving you alone out here to begin with."

I try to slow my breathing, but it's useless. I want to say something to him, but I can only shake my head. What sort of illusion did he concoct to make the bear flee like that? He reaches out and helps me to my feet. "For being Prism's best student, you're not very bright."

I glare at him but can't come up with a counter argument. He has a valid point; wandering around at dusk alone in the forest is never considered wise, especially if you don't know where you're going.

"Are you hurt?" he asks, his voice gentle.

"No," I say. "I'm okay."

"Good." His tone changes. "Now, can we stop this nonsense? Do allow me to escort you back."

I nod reluctantly and gaze at the forest floor, humiliated and defeated. Like it or not, I have no choice but to follow him now.

I stay close to him as we move through the forest. Any sound makes me jump, and I imagine dangerous beasts in every shadow. Really, what was I thinking? Even if I don't trust Elm, my chances alone out here aren't much better.

"Thank you, Elm," I say to him at last.

"You can thank me best by not doing anything like that again."

As we travel, I can see he's angry. He walks stiffly, a contrast from his usual grace. Yet somehow, he still manages to move soundlessly. And why wouldn't he be upset? I essentially chose the dangers of the forest over him. It's not as though he doesn't realize it. I should apologize to him, but I'm too proud to do so. He's still a criminal, after all, and already admitted to using his power on me once. He can't blame me for not trusting him.

After a long, tense walk, we reach the forest's edge, and

I can see the lights glowing in the windows of Prism. I have never been happier to see them.

"I'll be fine from here," I say. "If you get any closer, you might trigger that alarm again."

"I doubt that." He still seems mildly irritated, but more relaxed now. "As I said, they only saw me last time because I wanted to be seen. But if it makes you feel better, I will go no farther."

"I don't think they're as oblivious as you think." I leave it at that to avoid an argument. "Anyway . . . thank you again for today."

I start to turn away from him but find myself wavering. Even after the scare in the forest, my mind has room to wander back to the mysterious illusions he created in the cave and his lingering tease of letting me see his Yellow-magic books if I return. "Um . . . if I wanted to see you again—and I'm not saying I do—how do I find you? Obviously, I'm not good at navigating the forest on my own."

"Just head down the forest path and wait. I'm sure we'll bump into each other eventually if you seek me. And after enough visits, I have no doubt you'll learn the way to the cave."

"We'll see," I say, uncomfortable that he seems to think this will be a common occurrence. "I may never come back."

"My curious Miss Ava, I think you'll find it hard to stay away."

It's a challenge maintaining a passive expression while I look at Selene's weary face. Her voice carries a slight hoarse quality to it that manifests when she's tired, and her agitation is obvious in the way she snaps out review points from our last lesson. I was already nervous about seeing her, due to my surreptitious meeting with Elm. I keep expecting her to halt our lessons and tell me to drop the act because she knows everything. Her obvious bad mood does nothing to make me feel more at ease.

"Should I come back another day?" I ask timidly.

"No, no." She sighs. "It's all this Elm business. It's bad enough that we can't track him down, but worse when we don't know whose head he's getting into."

"You think he's getting inside people's heads?" I ask. "Like . . . who?"

"Oh, it could be anyone. You never know. I'm sure he'd target anyone he felt he could manipulate in some way."

I have to wonder if that's how he feels about me—just someone he can manipulate. Still, he hasn't asked anything of me or tried to harm me. Yet.

"Anyway," Selene says, "enough of that. What else would you like to focus on today?"

I'm not sure how to answer. At the moment, I'm tired of Red magic. I wish she could teach me about Yellow. All she can show me now with strength, healing, and agility are different degrees of each. What I saw in the cave with Elm was unlike anything else I have seen or experienced.

What about the White magic mentioned by the woman in the square? Is that forbidden, too? Is it even real? But if I ask about that, I'll have to explain where I heard about it. I had no good reason to be on Chrysanthemum Street that day.

Selene is waiting for my answer. "Where did your ambition go? I can't help but notice you're not progressing as quickly as you used to."

"The work is harder."

"But it's at your level. The difficulty shouldn't make a difference if your dedication remains the same."

I have no response to that.

"Have you been spending more time with Blake? More idle chatter with your classmates?"

"Am I not allowed to have friends?" The question comes out more biting than I meant it to. "Why would spending time with Blake be a bad thing?"

Selene raises her eyebrows but considers for a moment before speaking. "What do you suppose would happen to this school if Mentalists came back to power?"

What would happen to Prism? I never thought about that. It's easy to think of the school as impenetrable with Selene and the other Benefactors here.

She takes my silence as an invitation to continue. "You would lose your home. We would return to war. I want nothing more than to see you happy and successful, working toward a safer future. Does your social life take priority over that?"

"But Blake and his family took me in . . ."

"Yes, because I asked them to. Do you think they will still keep you around once you are no longer a student?"

The words slap me. Would his family discard me so easily? But I suppose they did take me in initially as an obligation to the head Benefactor.

"You're in your final year. This is your last chance to show what you are capable of. Don't assume you're a shoo-in for a Benefactor position simply because you are my student. I wish it were that simple, but it's not."

She's right. My parents are dead. I have no ties. My whole life I have worked for this so I can fight for the future my parents never had. If I can't become a Benefactor, I lose everything I have left. So why does the goal now feel so hollow?

"I guess let's focus on healing again today," I say, wanting only to move this lesson forward, past the pain of her words. "I'm sure I could be much faster with more practice."

The same inkling of non-fulfillment pervades throughout the remainder of my classes. Every lesson feels like I've heard it before. Normally, I take pride in being ahead of the game, but now I'm bored. I would rather know how many minutes have ticked away on the clock than the appropriate number of seconds to extend a strengthening spell. My mind keeps wandering back to the forest.

To the cave.

The more I think about Yellow magic, the more disappointed I am that Prism no longer teaches it. It would add a completely new dimension to the school. Even if the practice of Yellow magic is forbidden, what harm is there in learning about it?

And there is someone living in a cave in the forest who might teach me.

When the bell rings in my final class, I'm first to the door.

"Ava!"

I'm already in the hallway and have to stop abruptly to see who called me. "Oh, hi, Blake." We haven't talked since the day in class he fixed my watch, and with Selene's words still fresh in my mind, I'm not in a mood to face him now.

He grins. "You're hard to track down these days. I can't ever catch you when class ends."

"I've been busy," I say, hoping he won't ask with what. We stare at each other uncomfortably for a moment. I search for a way to make my exit without hurting his feelings or causing suspicion. I'm about to say something when he speaks.

"Listen, I've been meaning to ask you for a while, do you think we could go together into the city on our next free day?"

His invitation catches me by surprise, and I must be taking too long to answer because he adds, "If you don't want to, that's fine. I just thought it might be fun. I mean, I know we haven't hung out as much lately . . . but why couldn't we?"

Because Selene says we can't. Because your family only looks after me because they have to. Because I want to hang out with a Mentalist and learn about Yellow magic and don't want you involved and at risk. So many reasons, and I can't say any of them to him. Instead I say whatever I think will get rid of him quickest in this moment: "It sounds great."

"Really?"

"Yeah. But right now, I have to get going. We'll plan soon, okay? I'll see you later." I begin walking again, only to find him falling in step beside me.

"Where are you headed next?" he asks. "I'll walk you there."

"Oh, no, you don't have to do that . . ."

He smiles. "It's fine. I don't have anything else to do."

I'm not sure how to turn him down more forcefully. The last thing I want to do is hurt him, but I can't drag him into my messes either.

We continue out onto the grounds, and I slow my step, weighing out ideas to lose him. My first thought is to tell him I have to use the bathroom, but the possibility of him going with me there embarrasses me too much to follow through.

Blake interrupts my scheming. "I never got a chance to tell you how impressed I was with you during that aptitude test," he says. "You're really good."

"You too," I reply and then smile slyly, "even though you barely practice."

"And you always practice too much."

We reach the gate. I shouldn't have come here with him.

I should have walked somewhere else and returned after he left. But I don't have a good excuse to turn back. I attempt to dismiss him. "Well, I'm going to go study now. I'll see you later."

"Where? The woods?"

"It's . . . quiet," I say sheepishly. "And the fresh air helps me focus."

He glances toward the forest and frowns. "That seems a little dangerous, going there by yourself, don't you think? Especially with that creepy Yellow guy on the loose."

I feel a slight prickle of anger at his description of Elm and grow defensive. "I can take care of myself. I've been doing this for years."

"I don't know . . . it just seems risky to be alone. I could come with you. I have some reading of my own to do, and I wouldn't bother you."

"Listen, Blake," I begin, "it's nothing personal, but I would rather be alone. I don't study well with other people around."

"Yeah . . . I guess I knew that." He hesitates, likely recalling the times I shooed him from my room in favor of books. "But you don't have to go to the forest for that, right? Why not just go to your room where it's safe?"

"Because I need the fresh air?" I can't mask my tone this time. This is getting uncomfortable. I could deny his request more adamantly, but I'm starting to fear that Blake will tell someone I've been going to the forest. Prism's students aren't explicitly forbidden from doing so, but I'm not very public about it either. Would the Benefactors catch wind of it and tell me it isn't safe to go there anymore?

And then I see Blake's face. He has that same glazed-over look Selene had that day Elm altered everyone's memories. He looks at me, his expression confused. He frowns a little and then says dismissively, "Well, I guess if you're okay, I'll head back to the school. I have a lot of reading to do. We'll go to the city soon. See ya!"

I don't know if I'm more relieved or alarmed.

After taking a moment to be sure nobody else is watching, I grab the locket out of my school bag and become invisible. Now at least nobody can bother me.

When I arrive at the forest's edge, Elm is already there. I'm not sure how I feel about the fact that he had already been waiting close by. I'm again skeptical about my dealings with him after seeing what happened to Blake. Now I know he doesn't need any physical contact to act. "You shouldn't just use your magic on people on a whim if you can help it."

"Oh, you caught onto that?" He leans against a tall pine and looks toward the treetops casually. "Boyfriend of yours?"

"I spend breaks with his family, so we're sort of friends," I tell him. "He's another Elite student. But don't change the subject."

Elm seems a little agitated. "I only did it to assist you. The fool can't take a hint."

"He's not a fool. He was just being friendly. What did you do to him?"

"I simply planted a suggestion in his mind. Made him feel that at the moment his studies were more urgent and prodded him into leaving you alone. For now, at least."

"Well, next time let me handle it," I say. "Getting inside people's heads is why Mentalists got into trouble in the first place."

He gives a wry, condescending smile. "Whatever you say, Miss Ava."

I cross my arms. "Look, if you keep doing things like that, I don't know if I can trust you."

"I never claimed I could be trusted."

My heart rate increases with the slightest tremor of fear. I'm reminded I'm dealing with the most dangerous man in Magus.

"As I have said, Miss Ava, you are free to do as you wish. If you don't want to be here, you may go whenever you please."

I look back toward the school, where I have combed through nearly every inch of the library. I have absorbed every lecture, aced every test. I have received praise from Selene and from my professors. And, in spite of all that, I know nothing. My knowledge is limited, and there are things Prism cannot— or will not—tell me. The idea of turning back now, with so much new information at my fingertips, feels confining.

"I want to stay," I concede.

He smiles at me mischievously. "And so, Miss Ava, the rebel begins her first lesson on forbidden magic."

"Don't make me change my mind."

"Oh, I wouldn't dream of it. If I wanted to change your mind, I have much more efficient ways of doing so."

I can't tell if he's joking or not, but I sure hope he is.

He leads me again into the forest until we arrive outside of a large meadow where a herd of wild horses grazes. The area is quiet, aside from the occasional snorts and stomps from the horses.

"Lesson one," says Elm. "You've seen this trick before. Follow me and be as quiet as you can."

We walk toward the clearing, and I wince as twigs and sticks crack loudly under my feet. Elm obviously has a lot more experience sneaking around than I do—he doesn't make a sound.

"Go ahead and walk toward them, Miss Ava."

"Won't they run?" I don't have personal experience, but I'm pretty sure starting a stampede isn't safe.

"Maybe." He tries to keep his face somber, but his eyes give away his amusement.

My mind fills with visions of being trampled by wild horses, but I assume if Elm wanted me dead, he could think of more creative ways. I walk timidly into the meadow. At first the horses don't notice me, but all at once, the earth rumbles to life. Thousands of thundering hooves take off into the surrounding trees. I scream and crouch down, throwing my hands over my head. I begin a frenzied strengthening spell, hoping I can hold up against the force of a hoof if it comes to that. My eyes remain clenched shut, and I'm too afraid of what I'll see if I open them.

The galloping sound of the horses grows fainter, replacing the vibrations around me with the echo of cracking branches as the horses push their way through the trees. Cautiously, I open my eyes, and as the dust clears, the murky silhouette of a large shape stands just ahead. One of the horses stares at me expectantly as I pull to my feet on shaking legs. I don't dare make any sudden moves.

"It's all right," Elm says softly. "You can pet him."

I remain frozen and silent.

"Are you afraid, Miss Ava?"

I'm too petrified to speak.

Elm comes to my side and leans down to look me in the eyes. He rests a reassuring hand on my shoulder. "You were never in any danger, Miss Ava. I would never let any harm come to you."

I relax a bit. His words are soothing, and the horse isn't alarmed by his presence.

"Here," Elm says, gently taking my hand in his. He leads me forward and guides my hand carefully to the velvety muzzle of the creature. Its warm breath tickles my skin. My face breaks into a smile, and I softly stroke the side of the horse's face.

"How did you do this?" I ask, now confident enough to break my silence.

"Mentalists have the ability to manipulate feelings. I made him feel calmness and curiosity rather than fear."

Calm and curious. Much like how I'm feeling now that my nerves have relaxed. *No.* I refuse to believe he's inside my head.

"Do you want to go for a ride?" he asks.

"You're sure it's safe?"

"Have I lied to you yet?"

I honestly don't know the answer to that. But I decide to trust him, at least in this. He jumps onto the horse's back and reaches out to help me up. I awkwardly manage to sit in front of him—the poofy yellow dress makes everything more difficult.

"No reins on this thing," he says once I'm situated. "So I'm going to hold onto you, and you'll hold tightly—very tightly— onto the horse's mane. Tell me if you feel like you can't, though as an Augmentor, I suspect you're up to the task."

I nod but am beginning to worry that this is a bad idea. He wraps his arms securely around my waist, and my heart rate picks up.

"Ready?" he asks.

"I guess as ready as I'll ever be."

The horse starts off at an easy trot, and I concentrate on gripping its coarse mane. After a few minutes, I settle into the jostle of the ride and my nerves relax. "This isn't so bad. I think I'm getting the hang of it."

"Are you ready for some real fun, then?"

"That depends on your definition of fun."

"Don't ease your hold, Miss Ava."

The horse bolts into a full gallop, and I shriek, clutching the mane with vicelike fingers. The wind whips by us as we bounce up and down.

"Are you watching, Miss Ava?"

When did I close my eyes? When I dare to look, the world rushes past us as the horse gallops around the clearing, a racing smear of greens and browns. I gain confidence that I won't fall, and giddiness overtakes me. I savor the wind through my hair and the smell of forest. The steady movement of the horse beneath us and the blur of trees and grass. I chance looking upward, and with the vast blue around me while I'm in motion, it almost feels like flying. I'm used to high-speed agility spells, but this is a whole different kind of exhilaration.

Elm has the horse take us back to the forest's edge, and I'm a little disappointed as we stop. I could easily have continued. Elm slides off the horse's back and helps navigate me and my ridiculous dress safely to the ground.

"Thanks for the ride," I say, patting the horse's neck. Only now do I notice how tired my arms feel and the ache in my fingers.

"Step away a little. I'm setting him free."

We move back a distance, and the horse thrashes its head, awakening from its trance. It disappears rapidly into the forest to find the rest of its herd.

I'm breathless and euphoric as we walk back toward Prism's gate. "That was incredible," I say. "I haven't done anything like that since . . . well, ever."

"I'm glad you enjoyed it." He smiles warmly at me. I become overly focused on removing a scrap of a leaf from my hair, avoiding his gaze.

"Well, I suppose this is goodbye," he says as we reach the gate.

I'm not sure what makes me do it—perhaps I'm just drunk on the moment—but on an impulse, I stand up on my tiptoes and steal his hat. I put it coyly on my own head. For once, he's the one who looks surprised.

"I'm keeping this for a while," I give it a pat. "So I have an excuse to come back."

He smiles and pulls the hat down over my eyes. "Keep it forever. It looks good on you. And you never need an excuse to see me again. You are welcome whenever you like."

Once I'm in my room, my mind is a racing blur—like the movement of the horse. I have never had an experience like today's. I spend most of my time with my nose in a book. Has it been worth it? True, I am the top student at Prism, and I'm almost certain to become a Benefactor—the most coveted occupation in Magus. But what have I sacrificed to get here? I don't have friends. I don't have experiences. I have knowledge with nothing worthwhile to apply it to. It's no wonder I do so well in school—it's all I ever do. Today there was life in me. More than there has been in a long, long time. I catch a glimpse of myself in the mirror as I'm removing Elm's hat, and I hardly recognize myself. My hair falls in a mess around a glowing face with eyes shining bright in elation.

I sprawl out on my bed and close my eyes, drinking in the memory and wanting to relive and savor every second of it. I can almost feel the wind in my hair and the steady motion of the horse beneath me. Elm's arms around me . . . his warm scent . . .

I sit up, my face hot and my heart fluttering. I try to shake the memory away. "Careful, Ava," I whisper. And yet, even as I give myself cautious warnings, I'm already making plans to see him again. *I simply have to be objective,* I tell myself. This is for the sake of learning and information and nothing more. If I keep getting to know him and making him trust me, he's bound to slip up and reveal something of his plans eventually. I'll see him again. Of course I will. But I won't let my guard down, and I'll use anything I learn to my advantage.

It's a tactic. That's all it is.

10

FOR THE FIRST TIME IN MY MEMORY,

Saturday is exciting. No classes—a full day to spend however, wherever, and with whomever I please. What should I wear? Normally, because we don't wear our uniforms over the weekend, I would just throw on something quick and comfortable for studying or practicing, but I suddenly feel more conscious of how I look. I pick out my favorite red tunic from my dresser and pair it with dark gray boots and leggings. As an afterthought, I remove Elm's locket from the drawer and put it on. Somehow, it completes my outfit. I hum to myself as I brush my hair, wondering when I last felt this light.

I take swift, eager steps down the path to the forest, anticipating more excitement today. But upon arriving at the forest's edge, Elm is nowhere to be found. I guess I can't expect him to be here every time, but he has always seemed to be around before, almost like he has some way of sensing my presence. Well, I'll wait for him this time.

I lean against a tree, ticking off the minutes in my head. Five minutes. Ten minutes. Thirty. Eventually I sit, fidgeting impatiently. An hour passes.

I hear the thunder of hooves and turn, expecting to see him, but it's just a few stragglers from the herd passing through.

I have almost made up my mind to go back to the school

when I hear a rustle close by. Elm appears from behind a cluster of pine trees.

"Finally! I've been waiting for—"

I stop at the pained expression on his face. The right sleeve of his suit jacket is slashed and stained a dark, wet crimson.

My mouth drops open. "What happened?" I rush to his side and gently take hold of his injured arm. "Here, let me try to heal you."

His eyes dart around. "Not here, Miss Ava. We need to get to the cave."

I pay strict attention to the twists and turns of the forest this time, hoping that in the future I'll be able to find the way on my own. At the same time, I fretfully watch him. He doesn't say anything, and I can tell his wound is agonizing. I desperately hope that I'll manage to help him in some way. I can handle most basic injuries to my own body, but it takes a skill level higher than mine to heal severe wounds on others. Healers go through years of training to get it right. I have managed to heal small scratches on other people, but there's so much blood. I need to get a better look. Hopefully it's not as bad as it appears. And what on earth happened? What—or who—did this?

As we arrive at the sinkhole and make our way into the cave, some of the illusions flicker and fade. Eventually, only the spheres of light remain, and the rest of Elm's illusions die away.

"Sorry," Elm says with a grimace. "I'd like to make this nicer for you, but—"

"Don't worry about that. It's not important."

I make Elm sit over by the waterfall, so I can clean his wounds. He removes his cloak and lays it on top of a large rock. He winces as I help him remove his suit jacket. His white shirt sleeve, like his jacket, is saturated with blood. I tear the damaged cloth away to get a better look and cringe.

The wound is deep. I think I might see bone, but I'm not sure. I have to look away and fight through the dizziness seeping in.

"You don't need to do this, Miss Ava. You are under no obligation."

I bite my lip and take a deep breath. "No, it's okay. I just . . . can't look at it for too long." This is so much worse than small slices in healing class. I rest my hands on his arm as close as I dare get to the wound, afraid of causing him more pain.

"Are you sure you know enough to not kill me?" he jokes with a strained smile.

I try to hide that I'm not entirely confident in my abilities. "Well, I don't think you'll die, but this might hurt."

"I trust you, Miss Ava."

I focus my energy on him, and the warmth starts in my fingertips. It flows through me, and I imagine it moving through Elm, pulling together his wound. I work at it for several minutes, my face breaking out in a sweat. Eventually, I can't continue anymore, and I pull my hands away from him, panting lightly. My arms feel sore, as though I've been working out for hours.

"I'm sorry," I say, exhaustion weakening my voice. "That's the best I can do."

He touches my cheek. "You have done well, Miss Ava. Thank you. The bleeding seems to have stopped, and the pain isn't as intense." He gets to his feet, leaving my cheek with the current of his touch.

"Do you want to tell me how that happened?"

At first he doesn't answer. He merely removes his vest and lays it on top of his cloak. I turn quickly away as he unfastens the buttons on his shirt, hoping the heat in my cheeks isn't as visible as it feels. I find myself suddenly weighing the pros and cons of sneaking a peek and the endless teasing I would endure if he caught me. The light splash of water a moment later tells me he must be washing the dried blood off his arm.

Finally, he speaks. "I was trying to destroy some devices put in place by the Benefactors. Apparently, they have security measures. I ended up on the wrong end of a body-tearing spell."

"A body-tearing spell?"

"Red magic," he eyes me. "Miss Ava—the Elite student—hasn't heard of such a spell?"

I blink, caught off guard. "No. I didn't know Red spells could cause injuries like that. We only learn about strength and healing. Things that help people—not hurt them."

"I suppose that doesn't surprise me."

It's hard to imagine the Benefactors, who keep peace in the land, utilizing spells that could do that kind of damage. It's easily justified as self-defense, so it shouldn't bother me as much as it does. We're allowed to defend, aren't we? Elm was trying to do something he shouldn't have been doing, after all.

"What kind of device were you trying to break?" I ask.

He seems unsure of whether or not to answer my question. "Something that would . . . get in my way. That's all I can tell you for now."

Once more, I'm reminded that I'm dealing with an enemy. A Mentalist. Whatever he was doing can't have been good. And yet, I can't help but feel horrified that he was hurt.

"By the way, Miss Ava," he says. "You look lovely today. The locket suits you."

My heartbeat thuds. How to respond to that?

"However," he continues, "please try not to come out to the forest again unless you are invisible. It's better if you're not seen."

"Oh," I say self-consciously. "I guess you're right." I'm still sitting with my back to him, unsure whether he's dressed again.

Neither of us says anything for a while. I sit with my knees curled to my chest, and my eyes fixed forward. Anything I could say now would be awkward.

"I hate to ask anything else of you today, Miss Ava, but could you assist me once more?"

Hesitantly, I turn to see him holding a strip of cloth torn from his shirt. Well, obviously the wound needs to be wrapped. Even if I couldn't fully heal him, I can help with that much.

"Hold your arm out," I instruct, taking the cloth from him. *All business, Ava,* I tell myself over and over, even as my fingers fumble. They might as well be webbed.

He dresses again and examines the tear in his clothing and then picks up his cane. He gives the torn area a tap, and his clothes are whole again. I blink in surprise.

"How do you do that?" I ask.

"It's just a trick. An illusion. They're still damaged, but now nobody knows it but me. A temporary solution, but I hate to appear in disarray."

I curiously touch the area on his arm where the tear was. I can feel that the cloth is ripped, but the clothes look whole.

"Let's consider that your lesson for today, Miss Ava," he says. "Things are not always as they appear. Whole to the eye but broken in reality."

"Such as?"

"I suspect you'll discover that in time. That time isn't now."

He's just like Selene. It's never time.

"Does this mean you're taking me back?" I ask, sensing the tone of dismissal in his voice.

"For today, yes. I'll escort you back, but please use the locket."

I wouldn't have expected the day to end with me sulking in my room. Before we parted, Elm asked me not to come and see him again for a few days. He said he needed time to recover and to think about some things. What if he decides he doesn't want me around anymore? Well, that would be for the better, wouldn't it? I shouldn't be spending time with him to begin with.

Aside from being upset at the idea that he may not want me around anymore, I'm also concerned about his well-being. For some reason, I never thought of him as capable of sustaining an injury. He has been almost mythical to me. Now that I've seen his flesh tear like anyone else's, I can't help but worry. I try to believe that he can sufficiently care for himself and doesn't need me around.

Well, I can sit and pout or try to make the best of today and be more productive in the library. It will be just like any other Saturday, which I have always been content with before, right? Besides, I'm curious about that body-tearing spell. We haven't ever been taught ways to use our magic that involve inflicting pain on others directly.

Since this could be vital self-defense, I wonder why this information has been withheld. Shapers can easily use objects to injure others, such as what Blake did with the scissors during our aptitude test. Something like that is unavoidable. However, the skills Augmentors are taught seem to be mostly on the protective side. We can use strength to our advantage to deliver a blow, but that involves combat skill, as well. If we were ever under direct attack, wouldn't it be useful to have the option of a longer-range force if needed?

At the same time, part of me is afraid of that type of spell. It's hard for me to imagine intentionally using my magic to injure someone. Healing and growing stronger is one thing, but a spell like body-tearing blatantly has no other purpose than to cause harm. Maybe even kill. The thought makes me shudder. Still, I believe wholeheartedly that the Benefactors wouldn't use magic like that unless it was to protect something. Or someone.

What was Elm trying to do that provoked such a powerful spell?

After about an hour passes, a definite trend presents itself in the books I'm reading. Everything that involves combat spells paints Augmentors and Shapers as peace-loving pacifists. Mentalists, though the information is vague and limited, are portrayed as the aggressors. It all feels one-sided. Does life work that way? Is any group of people all good or all bad?

Elm doesn't seem all bad. He doesn't appear to do anything on the offensive unless he needs to. Why is that? Why are . . . why does . . .

My thoughts grow murky. I know I was thinking hard about something, but it's starting to slip away. I grasp for it, but a little voice in the back of my head says, *You don't need to know this. It's not important. Just let it go.*

When I leave the library, overcome by sudden exhaustion, I have a nagging feeling something was bothering me, but I don't know what it was. I search the corners of my mind for an answer, but I come up short. It's like waking up from a dream and remembering it vividly at first, but the details quickly slip away until I remember nothing. Was it the body-tearing spell? What am I missing?

I give up. It will come back to me eventually, when I'm not trying so hard.

As I wander back to my room, I think I see a flash of yellow out of the corner of my eye. I whip around, but there is only a black half sphere on the ceiling—one of the school's security cameras. I stare at it for a moment, as though expecting it to change, but I'm not quite sure what I'm waiting for. It isn't until some students come around the corner that I move along, afraid of what they'll think of my staring at a camera.

Back in my room, I'm restless once again. This is becoming the norm for me.

Three days. Then I will see Elm again.

"Ava, are you okay?"

I startle out of my stupor and nod. "Sorry, Blake. I'm fine. Just a little tired." We're currently traveling to the city together for our free day, seated in a two-passenger hover cart. If I'm not going to see Elm until tomorrow anyway, now is as good a time as any to spend the promised time with Blake.

Much of the ride has been quiet. It feels strange to be sitting here like this with him, and I can't think of what to talk about. I watch the scenery streak by us. Every time I want to open my mouth, Selene's words come back to me. *You're just their obligation. He's your competition.*

"Hey . . . Ava," Blake breaks the silence. "I have wanted to talk to you for a while now."

Here it comes. He's going to ask why I'm never around anymore. Why we stopped talking like we used to.

"I wanted to tell you I'm really sorry that I cut you during the aptitude test."

I'm so taken aback that I don't have a response for him right away. This isn't at all what I expected. Nobody apologizes for slights during aptitude tests unless it was something severe.

He continues, "I didn't really want to hurt you, but I wanted to get a good score. And I had to give you a chance to do well, too. I knew you'd be okay with a healing spell. Someone had to attack first to get the match going."

"It's fine, Blake," I say. "I know why you did it. Everyone expects aptitude tests to be that way."

I have no trouble accepting his apology—there was no need for him to apologize in the first place. But something is bothering me. This is something I have thought about before. Something I have considered in the past. But I can't quite place it.

The cart docks in the city and not a moment too soon. I've decided I'm the worst conversationalist ever.

"So what do you want to do?" Blake asks.

"I'm up for anything. Did you have a suggestion?"

"Well, I do have a few errands to run if you don't mind coming with me. But before that, I thought we could play a few rounds of Zap Blaster."

Zap Blaster. Well, that's another thing I wasn't expecting. I haven't played Zap Blaster since I was a child.

Each player wears three circular devices: a small one on each wrist, which are their own magic color, and one larger one on their chest, which is the color of their opponent. The devices on our wrists deliver an amplified burst of magic in the direction we send it, with the goal being to hit the target on our opponent. Each time we hit the target, it grows a little brighter. The first player to fully light their opponent's target is the winner of that round.

We walk through the shopping area. I still see the occasional wanted poster, and I make a point of looking anywhere but at them. Finally we reach the large game center, featuring a handful of vintage arcade games, where Zap Blaster is the main attraction.

As we approach the sign-in desk, Blake asks, "Three rounds?"

"Sounds good."

He grins and addresses the woman monitoring the sign-in desk. "Three rounds, please." I have to admit his obvious elation is a little endearing.

The woman shuffles around behind the counter and pulls out two white bodysuits, one accented in wide red stripes down the sides and the other with blue. We wear these bodysuits during the game to protect us from any stray bursts of magic.

"I think these should fit just fine." She slides the suits across the counter to Blake and me, along with red and blue targets and amplifiers. "And you're in luck—we're not busy today, so you don't have to wait for an arena."

As I zip into my suit in the women's changing room, I start to feel inexplicably nervous. This game involves a degree of skill. What if Blake defeats me all three rounds? Or worse, what if he goes easy on me? What if Selene's right and I can't seriously compete against him? I have to prove her wrong.

Blake is already waiting when I step into the dimly lit game room. It's large and filled with ramps and platforms as well as various stationary objects to hide behind. If this were a normal match, I would have no problem using an agility spell to avoid him and defeat him in no time. But in this game, the amplifiers absorb and fire all of our energy, so we can't use normal spells. It's all about focus, aim, and defense.

At opposite ends of the room, there are squares, painted on the floor in neon orange, big enough for one person to stand in. We begin in these.

"Ready?" Blake asks.

"Ready."

An electronic voice chirps, "Ready . . . GO!" and the game is on.

I immediately hit Blake's target with a tiny burst of energy. His target is just perceptively brighter. Blake looks startled but then grins again.

"Okay, I see how it is. You want a serious match." He fires back at me, but I duck behind a pillar and start charging up. I knew my first shot wasn't going to do much without any time to charge up my magic, but the goal was to send a message and get the first shot in. Besides, that extra little bit could push me over the edge when I need it.

Once I'm fully charged, I peek cautiously out from the pillar, making sure my target is still shielded. I hold my wrists ready in front of me to shoot if needed. I don't see Blake now, and I guess he must be hiding behind one of the other objects on the opposite side of the room. I stay still, crouched and ready, scanning for signs of movement.

I hear a noise behind me but am a split second too late as I turn, and Blake fires, hitting my target straight on. The target shines blue, already almost at its full brightness. I fire back at him, but he dodges, and I shoot too far right, only just nicking his target. It increases in brightness, but not enough to satisfy me.

I advance on him at a full run. He retreats, periodically firing back at me. I'm able to dodge the majority of his shots, but one finally connects. A series of dings and chimes goes off, and my target flashes.

"Round one goes to Player Two," the automated voice announces. "Return to your starting positions."

That tight, panicked feeling settles into my chest. He's good. Even better than I expected. And he has started off in the lead. If he wins one more round, I lose.

I grit my teeth as we return to our starting positions. Of course he would be better at this than I am. He probably does this all the time. I don't play games. It was silly of me to think I could compete.

"Are you okay?" he calls across the room.

"Fine," I snap, and instantly feel bad. He has no idea of my inward battles.

"Players at your ready. Next round begins in thirty seconds."

Okay. So Blake is good. But I'm skilled, too, and I'm an Augmentor. Even if I can't use my normal spells here, I'm used to agility and speed. I can do this. I just need to slow down and think.

As soon as the voice command gives the signal, I rush

toward higher ground, scrambling up one of the ramps to the highest platform. There's no way Blake can have an advantage over me from up here. He is on my tail, but I have been charging up my amplifiers this whole time. I turn and shoot, hitting the target on his chest squarely in the center. It bursts into red. Yes!

Now, I'm secure on the platform, and he's below me. There is nowhere he can run that I won't be able to get a good shot at him. All I need is for him to turn around.

I duck and peer through the metal railing on the platform. Blake hides behind a large rectangle with his back to me. A few feet to the right of him, I see a mirror. Now I have an idea of how I can catch him off guard. I shoot toward the mirror, and my red blast of energy reflects off it. Just as I suspected, Blake jerks in that direction. I have a clear shot at his target and fire. The bells and whistles start again.

"Round two goes to Player One."

I smile, relieved, as we return to our starting positions. I've still got it.

"Nice job," he says. "That was pretty sneaky with the mirror."

"You're good yourself," I say, tension easing.

"Players on your marks."

Last round. I just need to beat him again, and then I win.

The signal is given, and Blake charges straight at me. I am completely unprepared since he didn't start forward so aggressively in the previous rounds. I dodge him and shoot. I don't expect to hit his target, and so the faint flash of red is a welcome surprise.

"Oh," I say. But in that brief moment, he fires back, getting a much better shot than mine. My blue target is now several levels brighter.

I go all out. I twist and duck and dodge and run with all the strength and speed I have, firing shots whenever I see an opening. I'm merciless. Blake looks overwhelmed, and within five minutes the bells chime for their final time.

"Round three, Player One. Game, Player One."

I turn to face Blake, trying to remain composed, though I feel like dancing inside. I can beat him at some things. "Good game."

"I sometimes think you don't like me very much," he pants.

The statement startles me. "Why?"

"Because this is more than a game to you. You act like it's personal."

Ouch. Guilt again. "I like to do my best."

He laughs. "But this isn't an aptitude test. This is supposed to be fun."

"I won," I say, smiling wryly. "So it's fun." Isn't that how it's supposed to be?

He shakes his head and laughs. "If you say so. Let's go to the cafe and cool off a bit. Then if you're up for it, I want a rematch."

The cafe is fairly quiet today, except for the buzz of news in the background. I try to pace myself as I sip my cherry soda, but I really am thirsty after playing so aggressively. Blake doesn't bother holding back—he just chugs. Why can't I relax like that?

"Blake," I say, "I'm sorry."

"For beating me? I don't care about that."

I shake my head. "For being so serious about it."

He shrugs. "You've always been competitive. Though I did hope you'd relax a little."

"I know. I'll try harder."

"The idea is for you to try *less* hard."

"Ha, ha."

" . . . suspected to be the work of none other than Elm—"

I manage to catch my drink before it spills as I whip around. My ears tune to the large projection playing the news in the lounge. A reporter interviews a solemn-faced Benefactor.

"We've been tracking Elm for a while now, and we think

we're onto him," the Benefactor says. "After Saturday's break-in, security measures have been heightened."

"What break-in?" I ask out loud.

Blake answers—I momentarily forgot I'm with him—"You haven't heard? They've been showing it all over the news. Someone tried to hack into the Benefactors' database two days ago. They're pretty sure it was that crazy Yellow."

Hacking into their database . . . what was he doing? "But they haven't caught him yet?" I ask, attempting only faint interest.

"No. I bet they will, though. He can't outrun the Benefactors forever. Hey, are you okay? You look pale."

"I—no, actually. I'm not feeling well. I think I overdid it in Zap Blaster. Do you mind if we call it a day?"

"Oh, okay," he says, concerned. "Do you want me to take you to a Healer?"

I shake my head and gather up my things. "I just need some rest, I think."

We finish off our sodas and swipe our currency cards on the table's designated tip box. Blake holds the door for me as we leave.

"You said you had some more errands to run in town, right?" I say. "I can go back alone. I don't mind."

He looks hesitant. "I don't want to send you back alone if you don't feel well."

I smile in what I hope is a reassuring manner. "I'm fine, I promise. It would be silly for you to have to come back when you're already here."

"Well . . . okay then. But I'll at least walk you to the station."

Forget waiting until tomorrow; I need to see Elm now. I have
to know what his plans are. The moment my cart is back at
the station near Prism, I duck around a corner when nobody
is looking and grasp the locket in my hands, twisting it upside
down. These days I always have it around my neck. I whisper
Elm's name and disappear out toward the forest as soon as I'm
in the familiar yellow dress.

I run and don't stop until I get to the forest's edge. Then,
frustrated, I realize that he isn't going to be here. We weren't
supposed to meet today. It's likely he'll be in the cave, though.

I make my way hurriedly through the trees and brush,
tripping a few times. I felt certain I was going the right way
when I started, but now everything looks the same. Haven't I
passed this tree before? Haven't I seen this rock?

I stop and take several breaths to calm myself. Think,
Ava. I close my eyes and concentrate on remembering my last
visit the cave—surely something still remains. All at once, the
way shimmers into existence, forming pictures in my mind. I
know exactly where I am. I can't explain how this happens,
and for the moment, I don't care. I continue forward until at
last I reach the sinkhole. I walk through the illusion wall and
stop cold.

The bright yellow light doesn't illuminate as it did before.
Aside from the faint sunlight streaming from the mouth of the
cave, it's dark. Do I dare move forward? I'm afraid of what I'll
find. I came for answers, but I did leave him injured. Maybe it
was worse than I thought.

"Elm?" I call with uncertainty. I hear nothing but the echo

of my own voice. Horrible thoughts flash through my mind. His wound must have worsened, and now he's in bad shape. Or maybe the Benefactors found him. He could be captured. He could be . . .

I'm about to bolt into the darkness when I hear a voice behind me.

"Miss Ava?"

My emotions spin as Elm enters the cave. Relief that he's all right. Anger at what he might have done. What he might be planning.

"I'm surprised to see you here. I wasn't expecting you until tomorrow."

I work past my tangled emotions to find words. "I had to warn you." Yes, let's go with that. He's not going to tell me anything if I go straight into accusations.

"Warn me?"

"They were talking about you on the news. They know you tried to hack into their system, and they said they're onto you."

"Of course they would say that," he says nonchalantly. "What else are they going to say?"

"You're not worried?"

"No more than usual. If they knew how to find me, they'd have nabbed me already. But it doesn't look good on their part to have a near break-in to their system and admit that they don't have so much as a lead."

"Oh."

"You are far too loyal to me, Miss Ava. But I thank you."

Loyalty . . . I don't know who I'm loyal to anymore.

Elm looks around. "Shall we turn on the lights?" He gives a flick of his cane, and the glowing spheres light up. One by one his illusions come to life until his beautiful world is fully operational again.

"Now that your mind is at ease, shall I escort you back?"

"Do I have to go back now?"

His expression is bemused. "Well, no. I suppose not. Of course you may stay if you'd like. As long as we stay put in the cave."

We move deeper and sit down by the waterfall. The sound of it soothes my overactive nerves.

"How is your arm feeling?" I ask.

"Well, it . . ." He seems about to tell me it feels fine but instead sheepishly admits, "It still hurts quite a bit."

"Can I take a look at it again? I can do another healing spell. It may not fix it completely, but it can't make it any worse."

"We'll see about that."

I stick my tongue out at him.

He removes his cloak and jacket and unbuttons his sleeve. I roll it up carefully and flinch at the sight of the wound, still deep despite my earlier attempt at healing it.

"You should have let me come back the next day," I admonish. "You shouldn't have made me wait."

His voice is tight and pained when he speaks. "That was for your sake more than mine. I wasn't sure how long it would take for them to notice my attempt to get into their system. It wouldn't look good for you to be gone at the same time all this was happening. But if you were at the school, nobody would have a reason to suspect you."

"But even if I wasn't at the school, their suspicion wouldn't automatically jump to me, would it? As far as they know, I don't have any connections to you, thanks to your memory spell."

"Yes, but memory spells aren't infallible. Sometimes certain events can trigger bits of recognition. It's a complicated process. An effective spell doesn't involve just replacing the memory, but also planting suggestions in case someone starts to remember. You want them to forget and have no desire to think about it again." I soak in this information, feeling like I should be taking notes.

Elm tenses as I place my fingertips on the edge of the

injured area, but he quickly relaxes again. "Anyway, I simply didn't want to take any risks. I would prefer you not get in trouble on my behalf, Miss Ava."

"I can take care of myself," I say. "But thank you." His concern is touching, if not unexpected. More and more I question how this man can be the enemy of the Benefactors and of Magus. If he's not, what does that mean?

"I'm going to start the healing spell now," I warn him, diverting my thoughts. "You'll feel some heat."

His brow furrows slightly as I increase the pressure of my fingers on his skin, but after a moment he leans his head back against the cave wall, eyes closed. He sighs.

"Are you alright?" I ask.

"That feels . . . immeasurably better."

"I'm glad."

By the time I'm done with the healing spell, all that's left is a faint red line running down his arm. It could have been no more than a scratch.

"Thank you, Miss Ava." He's much more at ease now.

Yet somehow, he looks vulnerable, sitting there in his shirtsleeves. He also looks tired. I wonder if the pain has kept him awake.

As if reading my mind, he says, "Forgive me that I won't be taking you out on an adventure today. Even if I felt it was safe to be out in the open, I'm not sure if I would be up for it just yet."

"That's all right," I reply. "I already had a bit of an adventure today." I give my hand a caress. "I played Zap Blaster for the first time in years. And won."

"Really?" he says, suddenly very interested. "As I recall, Zap Blaster requires at least two players. Who accompanied you?"

"Blake. He's been bugging me about it for a while now."

He shifts his position, leaning back with his arms folded behind his head. He isn't looking at me, but his face is clearly disapproving. "With that one, eh?"

"Why do you say it like that?"

"I don't believe his intentions are as innocent as they seem."

"He's harmless," I say dismissively.

"It appears we have differing definitions of harmless."

He's acting awfully moody. Almost as if he's jealous, but somehow that seems beneath him.

I decide to go out on a limb anyway. "Jealousy doesn't suit you."

"No, I suppose it wouldn't."

I blink. It's not exactly a confirmation, but he isn't denying it. For some reason, a nervous flutter goes through me.

I quickly change the subject. "So, since you're tired, I guess that means no lesson today?"

He doesn't reply right away. "That depends. What would you like to know?"

"Well, if it's an open invitation, a lot of things," I say. "How about a little question-and-answer session?" For the first time, I'm comfortable enough with him to feel he won't try something dubious if I pry into his background.

"The kitten's curiosity is piqued again, hmm?" He leans forward. "How about this . . . you can ask whatever you wish. I will not lie to you, but I might not give you an answer. At least, not yet. Perhaps someday. Just like your dear Benefactors do."

"I guess that's fair enough." I ignore his jab at the Benefactors, not ready to have that fight again right when he might potentially open up to me.

"Then ask away."

"First off," I say, voice serious. "Where did you get a new shirt?"

His eyes widen, and then he bursts out laughing. "That is not what I expected from you. I thought you had more perplexing things on your mind."

"I do," I say, embarrassed. "But it's been bothering me. I can't not think about things like that."

"It's just how your mind works."

"So, how?" I prod.

Now it's Elm's turn to look embarrassed. "Well . . . let's just say the day I met you wasn't the first time I've used that copy machine."

I raise my eyebrows. "Really? You just decided to make copies of your clothes one day?"

"Why not?"

I'm unsuccessful at suppressing my smile. The idea of Elm sneaking into the school to expand his wardrobe is incredibly funny to me.

He clears his throat. "Next question?"

"Why were you trying to get into the Benefactor's system?"

"Next question."

"Oh, come on," I protest. "You really can't answer that?"

He stares at the ceiling, avoiding eye contact. "Not now, no."

"All right," I acquiesce. "How about, where did you find a yellow flower to copy?"

"That's an easy one. As much as they try, the Benefactors are no match for Mother Nature. Even though they've tried to genetically manipulate yellow out of natural species, it still pops up on its own now and then. It's simply a matter of my finding it before they do."

"What did you plan on using them for before you drained them to help me?"

"I can't tell you that."

I huff in frustration and cross my arms.

"You agreed to this," he reminds me.

"Okay, okay. Um . . . you said that the Benefactors had some kind of spell on you to make it so that you can't approach others—they have to approach you. I've been trying to figure out what kind of magic would do that, but I can't seem to fit it into any color category. How did they do that?"

"The same way they formed the barrier around Magus. Protective magic, or White magic, as it's sometimes called."

"White magic?" I blurt, immediately thinking of the scarlet-haired woman on Chrysanthemum Street. "So, it really exists? Why don't they teach it or talk about it at Prism?"

Elm's expression darkens. "Probably because it requires all three magic types working together. You can't do it by yourself. Since yellow magic is no longer practiced at Prism, there's no reason to teach it."

"But . . . that spell was put on you recently, right? That would mean the Benefactors have access to Yellow magic. That doesn't make any sense."

He seems to grow distant, going to some dark place I can't reach. I sense another rejection if I press the subject any further. Although I'm dying to know more, I switch to a lighthearted topic to bring him back.

"What's your favorite color?"

"It varies. Right now it's blue, like those inquisitive eyes of yours."

I try my best to look nonchalant and hope that a telltale blush isn't betraying me again. "You know, you're really corny sometimes."

"Guilty."

Another burning question comes to me. "How do you make yourself invisible?"

"A device I made," he says, a touch of pride in his voice. "It's basically the magic equivalent of a mirror illusion." He reaches into his pocket and pulls out a rounded object resembling a gold pocket watch. The surface is etched with a Celtic knot-type pattern. He snaps it open to show me the round yellow stone seated inside. "When the device is activated, it projects a reflection of sorts to its surroundings to an area approximately my size. It's a little more complicated than that, since Yellow magic is involved in perfecting the illusion, but that's the gist."

Ah, so that's why he wanted to know how tall I was . . . he was tailoring the locket just for me.

I have a sudden prickle of irritation. "Why do you get an inconspicuous little charm and I get a big floofy dress?"

He grins. "Because I thought it would be funny."

This should annoy me, but my attempt to glare turns into a broad smile. I'm enjoying myself too much. There's something enchanting about talking to him like this, as though we are friends. And yet, I can't disregard the fact that there's so much Elm deliberately keeps from me. In spite of his playfulness and teasing and that devil-may-care facade of his, there are dark pieces he refuses to reveal. When I choose to overlook it, I drop my guard and begin to enjoy him. But the second I consider the situation more empirically, uncertainty works its way into my thoughts.

"Any more questions?" he asks.

"Last one for now." I look him directly in the eye. "Are you friend or foe?"

Something passes across his face, but I can't tell what it is. Hesitation? Fear?

"That, Miss Ava, is entirely up to you."

"Don't you have a less enigmatic answer than that?"

"I say it is up to you because it is. The things that make us decide friend versus foe depend on what path we choose in life." He reaches out and brushes a stray strand of hair away from my forehead. "I'm certain, with time, you'll know the answer."

I'm suddenly not sure I'm ready to know that answer yet. It would be nice to believe Elm is truly a good person, but what then? If Elm isn't bad, then what does that make the Benefactors? What does that make Selene? The leaders of Magus, who work tirelessly to keep us safe—they can't be bad people. I have to be prepared to accept the possibility that Elm is and always has been my enemy.

11

WANTED:
ELM RIDLEY
AGE: 19
HEIGHT: 6'2"
HAIR: BROWN
EYES: BROWN

I stare at the poster as though seeing it for the first time, despite every hallway bearing this persistent reminder of Elm. The way the poster describes him is so simplistic. His hair isn't just brown. It's more of a dark ash blond. Messy curls that the sunlight twists over. And his eyes. His eyes are most definitely hazel. Warm and inviting at some times, inquisitive and prying at others. As though he hides so many secrets but knows all of mine.

I force my attention from the poster and continue down the hall, suppressing the dizzy warmth that possesses me so often as of late. I'm supposed to be meeting Selene right now, so this is a horrible time for distractions. Especially Elm-related distractions.

The practice rooms are silent when I arrive, which means Selene closed them off for our private lesson today. My stomach tightens in a thick knot of worry. She only does that if she thinks there is some risk to what we're doing. What does she have planned?

"Shall we get right to it?" she asks.

I nod and follow her to one of the larger rooms. Resting at its center is a large pallet of bricks, secured tightly with wrap for transport. Will I be breaking them? Good. The stress release might be nice.

She is straight to business. "Lift it."

Is she serious? I haven't ever lifted anything close to that weight, especially without other magic sources to draw on. "Selene, you know I—"

"Just try."

I approach the pallet and fumble around the bottom edge, searching for a reasonable place to grip. This isn't going to work. Still, I begin my strengthening spell, focusing on my fingertips and spreading outward to my arms. I let the power build, waiting for the moment of plateau when I can't draw any more from my stone. I inhale deeply, and upon exhale, have another go at the pallet. It shifts, and one side moves just slightly off the ground. My arms shake and scream with pain. My fingers beg me to release my grip. I let go, panting heavily.

"Again," Selene commands.

"I can't."

Selene only sighs, reaches into her breast pocket, and produces a red stone and tosses it my way. I snatch it out of the air.

A ghost of a smile is on her lips. "Reflexes still sharp as ever. Try again."

This time I lift the side of the pallet off the ground, about a foot. But I can feel the strain. Even with the help of stones, an Augmentor has to take into account how much their body can handle. I let the pallet fall again and start a healing spell on my aching arms.

Selene tosses me another stone. "Lift it all the way this time."

"I don't think I can do that. Not without my arms breaking."

She stares me down, and I know she won't drop this until I at least try. I count to ten in my head, letting my nerves settle and forcing down my frustration. I begin a strengthening spell once more, amplifying my abilities with the stones. This time I'm able to tilt the pallet all the way up. I shift beneath it so I can lift the rest of the way, but balk at the intense pressure on my arms and my legs.

"Don't stop," Selene barks, sensing my impending defeat.

I can feel my bones splintering under the weight, and I scream in pain. My knees buckle.

"Help!" I cry. But Selene only watches. At once, I cast a healing spell on my arms to prevent further breakage while simultaneously holding the strengthening spell. I use the opportunity to heave the pallet away from me. It thuds to the floor, vibrating the space around us. I collapse to the ground as I release the strengthening spell to focus on fully healing my arms and legs.

I look up at Selene, wanting to lash out at her for not intervening before I reached such a desperate point, but the look on her face steals my rage and replaces it with bewilderment. Selene is looking at me with hunger. Her eyes are bright and fevered. I wanted her admiration, but the look there now is something beyond that. Something fearsome.

Her face quickly regains its composure. "Good," she says. "Well done."

"Thank you." My voice sounds too small. Why do I feel like a lab rat right now? Selene only pushed me to my limit for my benefit. To see what I can do. That's what a mentor is supposed to do, right? But my stomach turns.

Selene scrutinizes my uniform. "You had better go get

that fixed. We'll end today's lesson early so you can go to the recoloring center."

I glance down and take in the sight of my once burgundy skirt, now drained of color. I must have pulled from it in my panic. In any event, I'm grateful for the ready-made excuse to leave.

I'm surprised to find two Benefactors outside of the door of the coloring center, like black-clothed sentinels. They stand aside and let me in without saying a word, all the while scanning me and the surroundings with hard eyes.

A Shaper, Miss Ashford, greets me, surprise on her face. "Why, Ava. I don't often see you here." Shaper students are usually the ones needing color correction after a session.

"I drew on it by mistake while practicing." No need to give her details. I wasn't ever really in danger, right? Selene would have intervened. I try to ignore the slight ache still in my arms and the overall tiredness from exerting myself to that level.

Miss Ashford gives an emphatic nod. "I'm seeing more of that lately. I think everyone is extra nervous and distracted since that Yellow fellow broke loose." She lowers her voice. "And actually, I have had several Benefactors in here recently, too. Seems they're a bit jumpy, and they wind up drawing from their own uniforms." She seems bemused by this.

"Speaking of Benefactors," I say, "why are there two of them outside?"

She shakes her head again. "Oh, they think I can be controlled and forced to make yellow objects. I keep telling them I don't think I could even if anyone wanted me to. It's been so long. Take a seat, dear."

I sit down in a metal chair, which is peppered with blue stones. Shapers can alter the appearance of objects—traits such as size, shape, and color. But it typically takes a lot of energy, which is why the coloring center is equipped with extra stones in the event of back-to-back alterations.

Within a few seconds of sitting, I feel the familiar warmth of magic on my skirt, and its color begins to brighten. Observing Miss Ashford's lined face and graying hair, it occurs to me that she would have been around during the time Yellow magic was at Prism. Maybe she can tell me some of the things Elm won't.

"If you have changed objects to yellow before, you must have worked here a while."

"Going on thirty years."

"Then do you remember what it was like when the Benefactors were fighting against Mentalists?" I ask hopefully. "Where exactly did all the Yellows go?"

She thinks a moment. "You know, it really was such a long time ago. It must have filled the news back then, but I don't really remember."

Why doesn't anyone remember?

My skirt is back to normal. I press for more information. "What was it like? How were the Mentalists defeated?"

Her expression falls flat, and she looks vaguely confused. "I think you'd better get going now, dear."

"But—"

She holds up her hand. "No buts. Let's not discuss forbidden subjects. It gives me a bad feeling."

She steers me toward the hallway door and opens it briskly. I want to stay and try to persuade her to give me more information, but seeing the Benefactors outside seals my lips. I can't bring anything up while they're in earshot, in spite of my rampant curiosity.

As I slump through the hallway, petulant and unsatisfied, Elm's wanted poster beckons again. *I have your answers*, it seems to say. My eyes wander out the window toward the forest. Toward Elm. My heart rate increases. Going to visit him isn't even a conflicting choice anymore—it's my default option. And I can't help but feel that I'm getting increasingly in over my head each time. How close to the edge can I walk before I fall? Maybe I'm already clinging to the side of the cliff.

But something doesn't make sense around here, and I have to figure out exactly what it is. I push my principles and my inhibitions aside—deep down where they can't inconvenience me. It gets easier all the time.

Elm's artificial-sunlight spheres fully illuminate the cave when I step inside, so I know he must have been here recently. The rush of the waterfall echoes throughout the main chamber, but I don't hear anything else.

"Elm?" I call. No answer.

I tiptoe toward the whoosh of the water and stand against the cool stone wall, fidgeting. My intention is to wait for him here until he returns, but I can't sit still for long. Curiosity gets the best of me, and I peek around the cave, wandering away from my waiting place. I meander, thinking maybe I'll bump into him somewhere.

At first look, the cave is nothing unexpected: purple-gray formations, crumbled, rocky debris, and hints of a bat or two, who have since moved on. I stop short, nearly stumbling into a heavy black curtain strung across a large cavity. If Elm blocked it off like this, I probably shouldn't go inside, but the temptation is too great. My eyes dart around nervously. I'm such an intruder. Although, he *did* snoop around in my room after placing the flowers on the school grounds . . .

I pull back the curtain.

The small chamber of the cave appears to be a bedroom, lit dimly by another flickering yellow sphere. The soft light it emits reminds me of candlelight. A rough wooden bed rests on the opposite wall, along with a matching dresser. How did he get furniture in here? He has various other trinkets around the room: playing cards, marbles, gardening tools, newspapers, and various electronic components that look as though he salvaged them from broken devices.

I can't imagine what he's using them for. I smile wryly when I see he has taped one of his wanted posters to the wall. What an Elm thing to do.

My eyes stop short on a bookcase in the corner of the room, and I catch my breath. It's full of books on Yellow magic. They are agonizingly enticing. Forbidden fruit.

"Enjoying yourself?"

I jump and turn to see Elm leaning nonchalantly in the makeshift doorway. His arms are crossed, though he looks entertained rather than angry.

"You scared me," I gasp. "Don't sneak up on me like that."

"Well, you *are* intruding in my room," he remarks with a quirked smile.

"Yes, so now we're even."

"Fair enough."

He moves into the room, and I catch a whiff of his inviting cedarwood-and-orange-blossom scent as he walks past. It feels strange to be confined in this space in such close proximity to each other.

I pointedly look around at his belongings. "How did you get all this stuff?"

"I made most of it."

My eyes flit toward him, astonished. "I thought only Shapers were into woodworking."

"I don't know the first thing about carpentry. I made it with my mind." His tone makes it sound as though anyone could do it. He picks up a stack of playing cards from the dresser and absently shuffles them.

Made it with his mind. He must mean he created an illusion. "None of it is real?" I ask.

"No, it is. Every now and then, I create an illusion I'm able to turn into reality. I don't have a lot of control over it, but it seems to happen more in the cave than elsewhere."

I run my fingers over the wooden bed frame, astounded. "So Mentalists who are strong enough can create objects? Is that typical?"

He fans the cards out in front of him. "No, I don't think so. I can't really explain it myself. Pick a card."

"Hmm." I'm not sure what to think of this revelation. He doesn't act like it's extraordinary, but I would love to see how it's done. "Can you make me something?" I ask, drawing a card from the deck. My hand brushes against his momentarily, and even that quick touch sears my skin.

"No," he says cheerfully. "I can't make you anything."

"Oh. Well, I guess it was rude of me to ask." I glance at my card and hope the dim light hides the blush prickling my cheeks. The Queen of Spades.

"Not at all. It's not that I wouldn't like to make you something at will, Miss Ava. I simply lack control over it. I did make you the locket dress, and that was mostly luck. Card back in the deck, please, if you've memorized it."

I return the card. "What would you have done if it didn't work? The dress, that is."

"I would have used an illusion. But then I wouldn't have had any way of coercing you back to me."

"So you pretty much just took a gamble?" I can hardly believe it was only an accident. When he gave me the dress, he seemed to know exactly what he was doing.

"I did. And the gamble paid off." He shuffles the cards again.

I focus on his hands as they mix up the cards, my brow furrowed. "Honestly, this doesn't make sense to me. Are you sure you're not holding anything back?" There must be some trick he knows.

"I don't question it. It just is. Is this your card?" He flings the whole deck into the air. As they flutter past my face, I see the cards have all transformed into the Queen of Spades, but my face is there in place of the Queen.

"But . . . how?" My mind is grappling with his previous words. I haven't heard of anyone who can use their magic to create things. I sit down on the edge of his bed, frazzled.

"The card trick? Illusions, of course."

"No! Not that . . . although," I gape at the cards for a moment, only just now processing the trick, "that was amazing." But my focus shifts back to what is more perplexing: "I mean, how is it possible for you to create things out of thin air? Nobody can do that. Not even Shapers. They could turn a piece of cloth into clothing or wood into furniture, but not create something out of nothing. It makes zero sense."

"It's driving you mad, isn't it?" He laughs and takes a seat beside me. My heart plays its now-customary game of accelerating whenever he gets closer than I would like. "Sometimes, Miss Ava, we don't need to know the answers to everything. If you learn that, you'll be much more at ease in life."

I wish I could take his advice and let it go, but the desire to know persists in my head.

"Then I need something else to focus on," I tell him. "Otherwise, I'll keep trying to work it out, and I won't sleep for weeks."

"I could ask you how often you break into people's rooms."

"I didn't really break in," I grumble and glance at him. "You're not mad, are you?"

"No, of course not. I think it would be difficult to be mad at you, even if you had done something worth being mad about. And besides," he remarks, "I have decided to trust you."

This catches me off guard. For some reason, it never occurred to me that he wouldn't have trusted me to begin with. "Do I seem untrustworthy?" I ask.

He shakes his head. "Not really, no. But sometimes it's easy to be deceived."

I allow myself to fix my gaze on him instead of nervously glancing away. His eyes are looking forward rather than at me, which gives me a false sense of protection, as though if we don't make direct eye contact, he has no power over me. I study his face in the dim light. His eyes look distant, but his expression is calm. What could he be thinking about?

He continues, "And what about you? Do you trust me?"

"Oh. I . . . I don't know," I admit. I can't see the point in being dishonest about it. I want to trust him more than anything, but I know there must be valid reasons why he was imprisoned. Why would the Benefactors seek him out otherwise? And logic tells me someone with so many secrets can't be guiltless. "I'm not sure if I trust you, but I don't know if I distrust you either."

Elm doesn't appear too bothered by my uncertainty. But he does ask, "And what makes you hesitate in distrusting me?" He looks my way, and I quickly stare at my hands, twisting them.

"You just don't seem like you're, well . . . evil." I give a sheepish laugh. "Like when I first met you, you didn't break the monument in the school. You could have."

"I only wanted to have a little fun. I don't really have an interest in hurting anyone or being destructive."

"So that gives me some incentive to trust you," I insist, trying to validate my thoughts. I face him, and his eyes lock onto mine. Now, I can't look away.

"And how do you know I'm not just toying with you?" he says softly. "Drawing you in with my bag of tricks?"

His words should make me nervous. But instead, I can only gaze at him, transfixed, drawn by his voice and the way his eyes dance in the flickering light. I don't answer. I'm not sure how to answer. He tilts his head and continues to observe me. My cheeks heat.

Without saying anything, he reaches toward me and lightly grasps the locket. I jump slightly as his fingertips graze my neck. He studies the locket for a moment, looking puzzled, and then leans in closer to get a better look. I stiffen; the close proximity makes me nervous.

"That's odd," he muses. "I thought surely I would have to recharge it with my magic by now." He lets the locket slip from his fingers, and it falls once more around my neck. I relax, though my heartbeat will not slow.

"So, what is it that you want from me, Miss Ava?" he asks suddenly.

"What-what I want?" I stammer.

"Yes. I assume the reason you keep coming back here is because you want something."

I think carefully, wondering if he's looking for a specific answer. I'm afraid of saying the wrong thing. As far as I'm concerned, he's still unpredictable. "I want to learn more about Yellow magic." At least this is true.

I consider whether or not to tell him about my lesson with Selene earlier . . . and the strange way she behaved.

His eyes are intense on me, as though he could decipher everything about me by studying my face. Part of me wonders if he actually can.

"Is that all?" he says. "I've given you a lot of information. Not everything, of course. But more than you had. You could have turned me in to your Benefactor friends a long time ago."

Once more, I'm compelled to silence, unsure of how to respond.

He chuckles. "I think you are playing dangerous games, Miss Ava. But I'm happy to play along."

A shiver goes through me. He's right—I am playing dangerous games. My lines of reason are slowly blurring, and what began as an interest in Yellow magic has turned into an interest in Elm. And I'm no longer sure if it's objective.

I stare at him just a little too long. I obsess a little too much over the grace and confidence of his movements. His eyes pull me in just a little too deep.

Whether Elm detects it or not, he's gaining influence over me. But I get the feeling he does know. At once it feels like too much. I don't know how to need someone this way. All this time my emotions have been guarded by a stick house, and now a wildfire is outside my door.

I stand, suddenly and stiffly. "I need to go back now."

This has to be the end. I absolutely cannot see him again. And I can't tell him that, or he might try to persuade me to stay. And I might let him.

"Are you all right, Miss Ava?" Even the way he asks it, with that softness in his voice, feels like a manipulation.

"I'm fine. I'm just busy. Being a good student is hard, you know."

"Then back you must go. You mustn't be distracted."

It might be a trick of the light, but I'm certain his lips curve into a cunning smile.

12

"THIS IS US!" BLAKE SAYS AS THE HOVER
cart stops on a quiet platform outside his subdivision. We
unload our suitcases from the back and make our way to
the sidewalk. We're currently on a brief hiatus from school.
Normally, these are unwanted for me—nothing but a delay
in my studies and my goals. This is the first time the break
actually seems like, well . . . a break. Prism has begun to feel
stifling, and my self-imposed distance from Elm will be harder
to think about here. A change of scenery. Time for things
outside of school. This will be good for me.

"Remember when Mom used to always have those little red
and blue cookies waiting for us when we got home?" Blake
asks. "It used to embarrass me, but now I kind of miss them."

I laugh. "Your mom has always been so sweet. It's too bad
she thinks we've outgrown them."

Blake's neighborhood is upscale, with spacious houses
and lush landscaping. His parents do quite well on their
two Benefactor salaries. It's one of the reasons they have
the space and the means to take me in. We pass a large park
with fountains and a small lake. Blake used to beg me to go
play there with him, but I usually declined unless I could take
a textbook along. As I watch the glittering water droplets

spraying into the sunlit air, I'm not sure why I turned down the chance to enjoy it.

There is nothing I can do about the past . . . but I can treat Blake better now. Selene isn't here to watch me. I can spend time with him doing nothing, and she won't know.

"Hey, what are you thinking about?" Blake asks. "You've got this little smile."

I berate myself for the feelings that show so easily on my face. "Oh, I was just thinking it will be nice to actually hang out with you and your family for a change. It'll be good to take a break from studying."

He widens his eyes in exaggeration. "You want a study break? Is this Ava speaking?"

"Hey, people can change!" I swat at him. If he only knew how much I've changed recently.

We turn down Blake's street at last and make our way to his three-story home. It's clean and white with a pale-blue trim. As we stand outside the front double doors, the same shade of blue, an anxious knot forms in my stomach. I'm their obligation, according to Selene. I suddenly wonder what they think about having me here every time school is out.

The door swings open before Blake can even ring the bell. "Ava! Blake! Welcome home!"

Blake's mom, Olivia, sweeps us both into a hug that almost makes me cry. If she sees me as just an obligation, she doesn't make me feel that way.

"Matthew will be along shortly. I was just getting dinner ready, but let's get you settled. Blake, why don't you be a gentleman and help Ava with her suitcase."

"She's an Augmentor, Mom. If anything, she should be helping me with mine."

We all laugh, and Olivia shakes her head. "Fine, fine. This way, then."

Olivia leads me up to the guest level on the third floor to the room where I have stayed since I was a young child.

"Sorry if it's still a little dusty. We tried getting it tidied up, but things have been so busy with work." Olivia gestures apologetically at the room.

I smile at her, trying to ignore the sting of guilt from the role I play in the newly added stress on the Benefactors. "It's fine. Thank you so much for everything." Even if what Selene said was true, and I'm only here because she requested it, I still appreciate it.

Olivia smiles back, and after she leaves, I quickly check the inner pocket of my suitcase to be sure the locket is still tucked securely inside. It doesn't feel safe to wear it openly while staying in the home of two Benefactors, but leaving it at Prism didn't feel right either. I wrap it in a pair of socks and stash it away in the top drawer of the narrow dresser beside the bed.

Once everything is in order, I take a breath and make my way to the stairs, determined to be more social this visit.

I find Olivia in the kitchen, putting her Shaper skills to use. A wooden spoon stirs a sizzling skillet of chicken and vegetables on the stove while the table appears to set itself. Spice shakers add seasonings as a knife nearby sets to work dicing green onions on a chopping board. Limes squeeze into a pitcher of water while a tiny sugar spoon adds several scoops of sugar. Olivia stands in the middle of it all, murmuring over a cookbook with a drained Colorstick beside it.

She glances up as I enter. "Oh, Ava. I wasn't expecting you down so soon! We'll be ready in a few minutes."

Her magic doesn't waiver as she speaks to me, and I'm impressed at the level of focus it must take to coordinate everything like that. I guess that's to be expected from a Benefactor.

"Can I help with anything?"

"Well, you can see if the limeade is sweet enough, but I think I have everything else covered."

I take a sip of the pleasantly tart drink, and for a moment, I try to recall what fresh lemonade tastes like. I can't remember, and despite being such a small thing, it leaves me feeling hollow.

"Seems good to me," I say, even though the flavor has soured in my mouth.

"That smells amazing, Mom," Blake says as he enters the kitchen. "Are we waiting for Dad?"

"He said he'll be here soon," Olivia replies. "This is actually the first night in ages we've been able to get off work early since Selene knew you two would be home."

This sends a wave of unease through me. Blake and I are old enough to look after ourselves. The only reason I can think that Selene would tell Olivia to meet us at home is that she wants us watched. Wants *me* watched.

The door opens a moment later, and Blake's father, Matthew, steps in, still in his Benefactor uniform.

Olivia greets him with a quick kiss. "Perfect timing. Dinner's just now ready."

Matthew notices us and flashes a smile. "Blake and Ava, glad to see you."

Blake is the spitting image of his father, with the exception of the blue-rimmed glasses Matthew wears. But Matthew looks like he's aged since the last time I saw him. There are bags under his eyes, and he exudes an overall air of exhaustion.

He pulls out a chair at the table and sinks into it. "It's good to be home."

"Selene is working you all too hard," I say without thinking, as we all join him at the table.

Blake clears his throat, looking uncomfortable, and I inwardly flinch. Bad-mouthing Selene to two loyal Benefactors probably isn't the best idea.

"No, no," Matthew watches as the skillet hovers over and

begins spooning food onto our plates. "I'm happy to be part of the cause. Our schedules will go back to normal once Elm is safely locked up again."

I stare down at my plate. There's so much I want to say and ask. How much would be considered innocent curiosity, and how much would put them on alert?

"What was he locked up for in the first place?" I ask, feigning casual interest.

Blake's parents exchange a look before Olivia responds. "I'm not sure that's something we should discuss with students."

"Must have been something really terrible." Blake's voice has the sharp edge it always does when Elm is mentioned.

Matthew's face is somber. "Much of the crime committed by Mentalists was too terrible for most people to want to hear. When you're a Benefactor, Ava, you'll get the full scope of it. And Blake, too, hopefully, if that's what you choose."

"I've told you I don't want to be a Benefactor," Blake says, voice low. His hands are gripping the edge of the table. I rarely see him this tense, but this has been an argument between him and his parents for as long as I can remember.

"Regardless," Olivia interrupts, "we've had several years of peace on Magus once the issue with Mentalists was under control. None of us wants to see that disrupted. So if it means longer hours until Elm is captured, so be it."

The rest of the meal passes in near silence.

The light outside of the window tells me I slept longer than I should have. The faint sound of dishes clinking comes from the kitchen downstairs. Stretching, I get out of bed and exchange my pajamas for a comfortable red T-shirt and jeans.

Downstairs, I find Matthew seated with a cup of coffee, still in a robe, and Blake clearing dishes off the table.

"Good morning, Ava." Matthew is bleary-eyed but manages a smile.

"Morning, Ava," Blake says brightly. "I'll get some fresh pancakes going for you."

I take the plates from him. "I'll get them. Sorry I slept so late."

"You almost never sleep in. I figured you needed it." He goes to the stove where a bowl of pancake batter awaits, fresh blueberries nearby.

I turn to Matthew. "Did Olivia leave for work already?"

"Yes, early this morning. I'm off today."

"Oh, that's nice," I say, though my stomach twists again. I still can't shake the feeling that Selene wants them to keep an eye on me.

After breakfast, Matthew rises with a yawn. "Sorry to abandon you two, but while I've got the time off, I need to take a look at the watering system in the garden. Darn thing has been busted for too long."

"I can do that for you, Dad," Blake quickly says. "Want to join me, Ava?"

I nod. I'm eager to help in whatever way I can.

"Thanks, Blake." Matthew grins at his son. "You've always been better at that type of problem anyway."

The sight of the garden—or what remains of it—makes me

wince. In contrast to the perfect green lawn, the garden area is brown and crumbled.

"Wow," Blake says, surveying the husk of a plant. "I didn't know this had been neglected for so long."

I watch in fascination as Blake makes his way around the garden, checking the different plant boxes and unearthing water lines to examine. Like most Shapers, Blake has a natural knack for identifying the inner workings of objects and being able to solve their problems. He mutters to himself as he goes, his brow furrowed in concentration.

"Ah," he says, stopping at last. "This one is routed wrong. It's watering the dirt instead of bringing the flow through." He turns to me. "I'll need some connectors." He pops a piece off one of the other water lines. "They look like this. I think we have more in the basement along the wall with the tools. Could you go look for me?"

"Sure," I say, taking the piece so I can be sure to find the right one.

The basement is large but organized, thankfully. Blake and I have been down here many times for various projects over the years, so I know where to find all the tools and knickknacks. I begin sorting through the rows of tiny drawers in the large tool case along the wall. Nails, bolts, screws in every size imaginable. No water-line connectors, though. I glance up at the top row of drawers, just out of my reach. Where is that stepstool?

When I find the stepstool, it's underneath several other boxes that must have been temporarily put aside. Lifting them won't be a problem for me. My strengthening spell builds, but I overestimated their weight and lift too fast, sending the stack toppling over. A cluster of translucent spheres the size of large marbles roll across the floor. Pictorbs or dataspheres, probably.

I scramble to pick up the contents. I hope I didn't damage anything, especially since these probably have important family memories or data. My hand pauses over a pictorb with the words *Mentalist War Coverage* etched on it. I freeze. How much information might this contain? The temptation is too great. I go to the shelves where Blake's family keeps media devices and locate a dusty viewdrop. I hold my breath as the device turns on, and I pop the pictorb into the end of it.

An image projection flickers to life in front of me. A female reporter ducks out of the way of a crackle of sparks from a powerline. The footage is years old.

"Here on the scene, we have Olivia and Matthew Woods, responsible for the brilliant capture of a dangerous group of Mentalists."

Blake's parents? My heart falls as I consider what they might have done in the past, although I'm not sure why the potential violence during a time of war surprises me.

The camera pans to Matthew and Olivia as the reporter prepares to speak to them. They look so . . . young. They can't have been Benefactors for long at this point.

"What gave you the idea to use powerlines to take the Mentalists out of commission?" The reporter shoves her microphone in the flushed face of Matthew, who looks out of sorts.

I feel queasy as I process the reporter's words: Powerlines. Out of commission.

Matthew runs a hand through his hair. "Well, we really just acted with what was available to us. The only thought we had was to keep innocents in the area safe."

"Anything to add?" The reporter turns to Olivia, who looks shell-shocked.

"Oh . . . no. We're simply doing our duty as Benefactors. Protecting the people is what we signed up for."

"Has this been overwhelming for you both as rookie Benefactors?"

Olivia and Matthew glance at each other, seeming to consider how to answer.

"We're very honored to serve," Matthew says in a diplomatic way. "Very honored."

I jump as a hand reaches over my shoulder and takes the device.

"M-Mr. Woods!" I stammer in surprise. I'm really in for it now.

Matthew doesn't speak at first, giving me a quizzical look. "I didn't know this was still down here," he says at last. He ejects the pictorb from the viewdrop, and it begins to bubble and undulate, similar to what I saw my watch do when Blake fixed it. Only instead of the pictorb being repaired, it crumples into an unrecognizable mass. Matthew tosses it into a trash receptacle and turns to face me as I stand in stunned silence.

"Was there something you needed here?"

"I . . ." I can't find my words. What was I looking for? I glance down at the connector in my hand, and the answer comes back to me.

"Water-line connectors?" I say in a voice hardly more than a whisper.

My head spins with the ramifications of him finding me watching the video. Will he tell Selene? Will it matter? I can do nothing but stare at my feet, the words *Please don't tell Selene* chanting through my mind on repeat. I will it so hard my head aches.

Matthew walks to the tool shelf without another word and locates the connectors. He hands me a small package of them.

"Here. Thank you for helping Blake," he adds, almost mechanically. His expression is unreadable.

"It's no trouble." I clutch the connectors in my hand and retreat from the basement, attempting to process what just happened.

"There you are!" Blake says when I return to the garden. "I

was about to see if you got eaten by a giant rat or something."
He stops and examines my face. "What's wrong?"

I shake my head and hand the connectors to him. I think
I should tell him. "I accidentally found something I wasn't
supposed to see. It was my fault . . . I was curious."

He waits, eyebrows raised as I explain to him the recording.
I skip over the details in case Blake wasn't aware of the graphic
way his parents exterminated Mentalists. I know Blake isn't a
fan of Mentalists, but I can't imagine him approving of his
parents' violent methods either. A thought strikes me. Maybe
that's why he doesn't want to become a Benefactor himself.

"When your dad saw me with the pictorb, he destroyed it."

Blake furrows his brow, his expression thoughtful. "Well,"
he says slowly, "my dad has always kind of been like that. He
was probably embarrassed. He doesn't like a lot of attention,
and my guess is Mom saved the newscast without him
knowing."

"Maybe . . ."

"What's wrong? Why do you sound so suspicious? This
was all public. What is there to hide?"

"That's exactly what I want to know." I'm unable to stop my
reeling thoughts from pouring off my tongue. "What are the
Benefactors hiding? They say 'all questions will be answered,'
but when it comes to Yellow magic, they don't tell us anything.
Don't you find that odd?"

"Ava," Blake's tone sharpens. "You're trying to be a
Benefactor. My parents *are* Benefactors. We can't talk like
this here."

"We shouldn't be afraid to ask questions," I insist. "I
can't be the only one who wonders what happened to all the
Mentalists. And if Yellow magic is so dangerous, why don't
they teach us any kind of defense against it?"

Blake looks uncomfortable, but he humors me. "Well, all

the Mentalists were taken care of and imprisoned. Removed from society, right? So it doesn't matter."

"But *all* of them? Every single Mentalist was bad?"

He shrugs. "If they're controlling people, I don't see what can be good about that. It makes sense to protect people from that kind of power."

"So you think eliminating Mentalists is okay?"

He hesitates. "Well, yes. If it saves all the others."

I'm not sure why his opinion makes me so angry and distressed. As he said, his parents are Benefactors, and it seems most of Magus agrees with what happened to the Mentalists—otherwise it wouldn't have happened.

I'm the odd one.

"I'm going back inside, if that's okay with you," I say, fighting to keep my voice steady. "I have a headache."

"Sure. Thanks for getting the connectors." His eyes show concern, and he opens his mouth as if to say more, but instead turns back to the water lines as I rush away.

The contrast between last night's dinner and tonight's is painful. I can feel the weight of my emotions and everyone else's, pressing down on me and turning the taste of the food in my mouth dull and unpalatable. I can't look at Matthew, although he hasn't said a word about what transpired in the basement. Blake pokes at his food, shooting me furtive glances.

Olivia speaks. "Must have been a busy day for everyone. You all seem as tired as I feel."

"Blake got the garden watering again," Matthews remarks.

"Was an easy fix," Blake says with a small shrug. "How was work, Mom?"

"Oh, fine, I guess. It will all be better once that Yellow is found."

My fork hovers above a roasted brussels sprout. "He hasn't hurt anyone . . . has he?"

"Well, that's just it," Olivia's reply is swift. "How do we really know? How can we say any of the recent incidents of violence or suicide weren't caused by Elm?"

My hand stings from the tight grip I now hold on my fork. I force my fingers to relax before I damage the silverware. "But can they say for certain any of that was him?"

"I can guarantee you at least some of it has to be," Matthew states.

Do they really think that just because Elm is a Mentalist, he's out there causing people to commit violent and deadly acts? They have no proof. And whatever Elm's ultimate goals may be, I can't see him just senselessly hurting people. Nothing about him has ever led me to that conclusion.

Blake shoots a look in my direction, then asks, "Has there been an increase in violent crime since he escaped?"

Olivia gives a firm nod. "Yes. Just like before."

"Maybe it's just because people are more stressed and panicked?" Blake doesn't sound like he really believes that. Is he playing devil's advocate for my sake? I'm sure he can see the tension in my body, and he might be recalling our earlier conversation.

Olivia sighs, and she and Matthew exchange glances. "I know it's in your nature to try and see the best in people, Blake, but trust us on this one. Yellows are nothing but trouble."

My chair scrapes loudly across the hardwood floor as I make a sudden move to my feet. My entire body feels like it's aflame and about to explode. "May I please be excused?"

"Are you alright?" Olivia looks alarmed.

I need to be more careful. I'm being too obvious. "All this talk about Mentalists and how dangerous they are is making me anxious. I'm sorry, I just need some fresh air." I bolt away from the table before anyone can argue, and using a quick burst of speed, I'm out the door before Blake can think about coming after me.

I run down the sidewalk and out of Blake's subdivision, past the spacious houses and green parks. As I dash past, I earn several looks of surprise from people out on family walks, but I can't be bothered to worry about how I appear to them. I'm tiring fast, burning through my agility spell quicker than I should, thanks to my wild emotions. Selene would scoff at my lack of control. But I need space. Distance.

The houses thin out and shift from suburbs to agriculture, and somewhere in the back of my mind a voice of reason says I'm going to regret going much further because eventually I'll have to turn back. It won't do any good to allow myself to burn out completely. I force my legs to stop when I reach a large grassy field, neglected and dying. The plants here have dried and yellowed, though not to a point of concern for the Benefactors—their color is too dull to be used as a power source. I lean over, hands on my knees, and take in several deep breaths. I cast a long shadow as the sun works its way down.

Finally, I look up to better observe my surroundings, and the breath I just regained is taken from me again.

Yellow.

My world is tinted by it. No, *saturated* in it. The light of the setting sun bathes the field in vivid golds. It streaks through the tops of trees and cascades over every inch before me. The dust dancing through the air is like a parade of amber glitter. I look at my arms and see that I, too, am changed, aglow with flaxen light.

I fall to my knees and take in the sight, at last allowing this new reality to wash over me. This is everything now. The world of Mentalists and Yellow magic is an indisputable part of me. Call it destiny or the hand of a higher power. Whatever it is, this is the path I have been guided to. After meeting Elm and learning more about him and his magic, I know I can't continue to turn a blind eye to what the Benefactors have done. Meeting one good Mentalist means there had to have been more, and there may be more still. Now I have a responsibility. A duty. Selene might be looking out for the good of Magus, but she can't do that while completely ignoring an entire group. Who's looking out for them?

"I can," I say aloud, as the sun waves its last fading beams.

13

AFTER SPENDING THE REST OF THE TIME
off inwardly fretting at Blake's house, I find myself back in
Prism's library, puzzling out a way to help Mentalists without
breaking the law. There's no choice but to admit that this
forces Elm out of the equation. I have to do it the right way.
The honest way. Then I can still be a Benefactor and help the
people of Magus. *All* of them.

I'll do what Selene has always encouraged me to do—
make my point through research. If I can find enough solid
evidence to show Selene and the other Benefactors we need
Yellow magic, maybe that would be the first stepping-stone to
allowing Mentalists back into society. I have to try. It seems
cold to say we should treat Mentalists with worth again just
because we need them, but the change has to start somewhere.

My gut says the best starting point is finding out more about
White magic—now that Elm confirmed it exists. This would be
easier if I could just ask him about it, but that's breaking the
rules. Besides, I still don't know his crimes, and this keeps me
safe from him in case he's just been using me this whole time.

I yank a book off the shelf—a little rougher than intended—
that explains the protective barrier around Magus. This should
be a good place to start.

With the exception of Magus, the continents of the Earth were unable to sustain magic use. They quickly fell into disarray, and many lives were lost. Soon, the Earth became virtually uninhabitable. The Benefactors formed a protective barrier around all of Magus, so it might be kept pristine and livable while the rest of the world crumbled.

The barrier has existed since before I was alive and is just part of the world for those who grow up on Magus. But why haven't I ever questioned before how it was made? I don't know any Red or Blue magic-user capable of that kind of magic. And now that I've seen some of the things Elm can do, I know that it doesn't quite fit with Yellow magic either. So something else would have to come into play. The fact that all three types of magic are involved to create White magic gives a possible explanation. And that clarifies why White magic isn't taught at Prism—no point teaching something that can't be practiced. But if Yellow magic is banned, how does that barrier still exist? Even if it was put in place before Yellow magic was banned, it can't sustain itself forever without an occasional infusion of Yellow magic.

Somebody is lying, and I don't think it's Elm.

I'm getting that foggy feeling in my head again. That persuasive desire to think about something else. Through the haze, I struggle to remember something Elm told me: *Yellow magic involves not only replacing a memory, but planting a suggestion.*

That thought is growing dim and threatens to slip away, too. I feel like I'm suffocating. I scoop up my books and carelessly throw them on the return cart, ignoring the looks people give me as I burst free from the library doors. I need air. Thank goodness today is a free day.

Once outside on the grounds, my head feels clear again. I close my eyes and gather my thoughts.

Suggestion planting. Is that what's happening to me?

My heart sinks. If I've been under the effects of Yellow magic at any point, there is only one Mentalist I know. And he has plenty of secrets to steer me away from.

There has to be some other explanation. Maybe these thoughts are simply too complex for me to understand. Maybe my mind is trying to focus on what actually makes sense. Yes. There has to be another reason.

I can't sit still, and I won't go back inside. The last thing I want right now is the confinement of walls. I open the gate and start walking. I come to a crossroads where I can either continue toward the forest or take the path to the hover carts. I take one step in the direction of the woods but stop short. Even the possibility that Elm might be intruding in my head upsets me so much that the thought of being around him is painful. I had already determined not to see him again anyway. So to the hover carts it is.

The hover station is patrolled by Benefactors, checking students' IDs and permission cards to make sure nobody attempts to cheat the system. Two Saturdays and one weekday a month, students are allowed to go into the city. I present my permission card, which is easily accepted as it's signed by Selene.

"Have a good trip," the attending Benefactor says, ushering me onto the next available cart.

I keep my eyes fixed on the scenery outside the windows of the hover cart, but something about it seems dull. I'm suddenly aware of the lack of yellow in the landscape. It has been this way for most of my life, and I was used to it. But now, its absence is blatant. I miss it.

My last time traveling to the city I had Blake with me. I almost wish he were here now. Company wouldn't be so terrible. It would be better than leaving me with my own thoughts. Of course, Blake seems to think what the Benefactors did to Mentalists is justified.

When the cart finally docks and I gaze out over the blue-and-red city, I find myself questioning the way magic-users identify ourselves. It's ridiculous. Why do we have to define ourselves by our magic color? We have so many colors to choose from. I wish there were more variety. I wish I could wear blue without people assuming I'm a Shaper. I wish I could wear colors like green or purple without others seeing them as frivolous. I wish I could wear yellow.

Now that I'm here, I don't know what to do with myself. I didn't have a purpose for coming here other than to escape from something I can't even explain.

So I wander toward Violet City's library. Maybe there is more there than at Prism. Maybe the change in venue will allow me to think with a clearer head.

Thump.

"Ow!" I rub my cheek and grab whatever hit me out of the air. I blink at it in confusion. A yo-yo?

"Sooorry!" A young child dressed head-to-toe in blue runs up to me, a group of friends lagging behind. They all wear the same worried expressions on their faces.

"I guess you want this back?" I say.

The boy gives a little nod. "I was trying to make it do tricks by itself."

Probably too advanced for a Shaper this young, but I have to admire his gumption. I smile and hand him back the yo-yo. "Keep practicing, okay?"

He nods again, grasping the yo-yo, and runs back to his friends. I watch them scurry away.

And then my heart catches in my throat.

I rub my eyes and blink a few times to make sure I'm not seeing things. Standing just beyond where the group of boys disappeared, across the street from the library, is a figure in a gray cloak. Elm? Here now?

He paces back and forth, restless. Every now and then he glances at the library. He watches people who pass on the street, as though he is considering each one.

I've never really believed in fate, but perhaps there is something stronger at work here. I wrestle with the idea of approaching him or turning in the opposite direction. I know what the smarter choice is . . . but I have to find out what he's up to. Blasted curiosity!

I keep my steps casual and unhurried. At last he looks my direction, and he does the same double take I'm sure I did a moment ago.

"Well, Miss Ava! This is an unexpected pleasure."

I wish I didn't notice the way his face lit up when he saw me. Wish the sunlight over his curls didn't make me want to run my fingers through them. Wish that smile wasn't so distracting. I knew this was a bad idea.

"I'm surprised, too," I manage to say.

"I haven't seen you in a few weeks . . . I was beginning to think you were through with me."

He doesn't know how close to the truth that is. I was through, until about thirty seconds ago.

"What are you doing here? I didn't expect to see you in the city."

He shifts from one foot to the other, then sighs. "Well, I was trying to figure out how to accomplish the task I failed to do last time."

"Wait, you mean when your arm . . ."

"Yes."

I still don't understand the specifics of that last task, but it's clear he attempted a serious security breach. And now he's at it again. "Did you come up with a solution?" Do I even want to know?

"I've determined I can't do it alone." He seems vaguely uncomfortable. "I had thought perhaps I could simply . . . manipulate someone a bit."

I stare at him. "You mean control their mind?"

"Well, yes."

"Don't do that, please," I implore. "I really, really don't like that."

"I'm not terribly fond of it either, but there is really no other choice. Perhaps you should leave."

What did I expect? That he would drop this idea just because I asked him to? Whatever he's doing is important to him. Important enough to put himself at risk again. Important enough to take control of someone else—even if it's not what he wants to do.

I release a quivering laugh. "You're right. I should leave. I don't know what I'm doing here in the first place."

I turn away, and he catches my hand suddenly. "You're still conflicted. Is that it?" There's something in his voice that makes me ache.

Still, I pull my fingers free of his. "I've thought about a lot of things these past few weeks. I don't think what you're doing is right, but I don't know if the Benefactors are right either."

Elm watches me with great interest.

I continue, "I still think they want what's best for Magus, but I don't know if I agree with how they're doing it. I keep thinking about Mentalists, and I want to make things different. I don't know how to do that, but I know I can't do anything that would compromise my ability to help." I can't keep striving to be a Benefactor while working with an outlaw behind their backs. There has to be a better way to reconcile our goals.

"As I've said all along, you're completely free to do as you wish. If you don't want to be here—with me—I'll not force you a moment longer." He says this in a voice that's perfectly calm, but his eyes say something more. He looks vexed.

"I guess you're going to do whatever you came here for, no matter what I say?"

"I have to. Someone has to."

Elm is going to take control of someone's mind and be exactly what the Benefactors say he is. And yet, nothing about my time spent with him suggests he controls people just for the fun of it. Can I trust that? I pause. Wouldn't I behave just as desperately if I were fighting for something that mattered?

I know the way Mentalists are treated isn't right, and I can't ignore that. If I turn my back on him for good, what chance do I really have of changing things? I won't learn more about Mentalists and how to help them by shunning the only one I know.

I let out a frustrated growl.

"Are you all right, Miss Ava?"

"I'll do it," I say abruptly.

"Pardon?"

"I'll help you. Just, please, don't use your powers on anyone. Let me do whatever you need instead." This way nobody else gets involved.

"With all due respect, Miss Ava, I don't think you know what you're saying."

I bristle at him. "Look, I'm already digging myself into a pretty big hole just by hanging out with you. I may not know the reasons why I'm doing everything I'm doing, but I can make my own decisions, can't I?"

"Well, of course you can."

"Then let me do this. Whatever *this* is."

He contemplates me for a moment. His mouth slowly pulls into a small smile. "If that's truly what you want, I'll gladly accept your help."

My pulse quickens. Here we go.

"Before we get started, can I please keep your locket with me? If use of Yellow magic triggered the body-tearing spell, I think it would be better if you don't have it on you, since I'm not quite certain exactly how it works."

"Oh," I say, feeling awkward. "I don't have it with me." It's been stuffed away in the back of my drawer since I decided not to see him anymore.

"Ah. Well, that solves that, then."

The air is tense between us as we cross the street to the front of the library. I don't know if it's all imagined due to my own guilt or if Elm caught on that I planned to distance myself forever. A couple enters the library, and I pretend to be focused on a sign on the wall advertising upcoming events.

"So what are we doing here?" I lower my voice, aware of others in the area.

"I'm afraid I can't tell you the specifics. It would be much better for you if you were an unknowing accomplice." There is a slight trace of worry in his eyes. "I'm still not entirely convinced you should be doing this at all."

I'm not entirely convinced I should be doing this either. I'm sure I'm about to assist in something treacherous. I could still change my mind and tell him I can't do this. But instead I hear a stranger with my voice say, "Just tell me what to do."

Elm reaches tentatively into his front coat pocket and pulls out a datasphere. "Go to a workstation and insert the datasphere. Load the file and open it. It won't look like anything is happening, but it is. Take the datasphere out—we mustn't leave evidence. After that, look up a few books in the database and then mill around for about half an hour. Look busy. Browse through the books you looked up."

"Why half an hour?"

"I set up a timed system. The file won't do its work right away. I wanted to give you—or whoever I had doing this— enough time away from the workstation, so you wouldn't seem responsible."

I frown. "In that case, why don't I leave right after I put it in?"

"I don't think it would be wise for you to fiddle around for five seconds, leave, and then have something odd happen. That would definitely cause suspicion. You need to look like you just happened to be there."

Elm places a hand on my shoulder. "I'll ask you again, Miss Ava . . . are you sure you want to do this? You can say *no* at any time."

"I'm sure." It's not completely true, but I've made my decision. At the very least, if I'm acting of my own free will, I might be able to manipulate the situation in my favor if it goes sideways. And if Elm isn't as dubious as we've all been led to believe . . . well, it's better this way.

"If you feel anything strange, anything at all, leave immediately. You are not to put yourself in danger. I'll be waiting here to help you if anything goes awry."

I nod and clutch the datasphere tightly in my hand. "Got it."

After taking a moment to compose myself, I step inside the library and survey the row of workstations equipped with digidomes—small white domes with circular spots in the top for dataspheres and pictorbs. I recognize a handful of students from Prism. It's not uncommon to find Prism students at the town library—the digidomes at Prism are for research purposes rather than recreation. Thankfully, they all seem too absorbed in their various activities to notice me.

As I approach one of the library-catalog digidomes, I notice a problem—none of the catalog domes have a spot to insert a datasphere. They're basic models, designed for a single purpose. If I use one of the regular digidomes, it requires a login. I have one, of course, but if I use it, it will be easy to track who last used the device before Elm's file was implemented.

Just as I'm about to go back to Elm and explain our dilemma, I notice an open workstation, still logged into the library system. I take a quick look around to be sure nobody is watching, then stroll casually to the digidome and pop the datasphere in. I flick away the current image projection—some shooting game—and open the datasphere to reveal a singular file on the projected desktop space. I note the file name, which is simply "gotcha" and smile a little because it seems so characteristic of Elm.

I hesitate. I could still walk away. I could delete the file and act like I did what Elm asked. When nothing happens, it would be easy to brush it off as a technical difficulty. This could be my way out—I could still stay in good favor with Elm without doing something illegal. Still, I'm extremely curious as to what's on the file . . .

It's only after I swipe my finger through the file to open it that I remember Elm told me nothing would happen immediately. My stomach lurches. I'm officially involved. Whatever Elm has planned is instigated now, whether I want it to be or not. My fingers shake as I remove the datasphere and open the library's database program. I key in a few inconspicuous search terms on the workstation touch pad: Healing with Red magic, uses for Red magic, differences between Red and Blue magic—none of these should trigger any suspicions. Standard research for a student.

"Hey. That's my workstation!" an angry voice behind me calls out.

I turn to the owner of the voice, and my insides lurch. A boy, probably no more than eleven years old. I just involved an innocent kid.

"Oh, sorry!" I feign embarrassment while guilt devours me. "I needed to look up some books real fast, and I forgot my password. I didn't think anyone was still using this." Drat.

The boy gives me an annoyed look as I step aside. He promptly goes back to his game. *Please, don't let him get in trouble.*

As I go to pull books from the shelves, I do everything possible to appear calm. On the inside, however, nervousness bubbles up, threatening to spill out into my gestures and facial expressions. As I reach for a book, my hand quivers. I take a deep breath and cast a quick strengthening spell, hoping this might help. Instead, it makes me put an ugly crease in the cover of the book I'm holding.

I browse through pages with no real idea of what they say. Every now and then, I peek at the time. The half hour passes slowly, and I grow tenser by the minute. With five minutes to go, I return the books to their shelves and begin to navigate toward the main doors of the library at as natural a pace I can manage.

At half an hour exactly, I hear a loud, cheerful eight-bit tune echoing through the library. There are a few hisses of, "Shh!" which quickly morph into gasps. I would prefer to keep walking and get out as soon as possible, but any normal person would be looking for the source of excitement. Besides, I want to know, too. I turn, planting an intrigued expression on my face. The boy and several onlookers are staring wide-eyed at the projection before him, now taken over by a pixelated animation of bright yellow tulips, dancing.

I twitch. Really, Elm? All this for a prank?

But then, one by one, the remaining workstations flicker and surge to life with the same animation. It takes over the entire system. The cheerful eight-bit tune now sounds distorted and eerie, played at various points in the song on many projections at once.

The drone of chatter in the library turns to chaos, and I catch snippets of exclamations.

"Yellow."

"Forbidden."

I turn and continue to the door, banking on the fact that the distractions will disguise my exit. Just as the library doors close behind me, I hear several loud popping sounds and screams. I whirl around, ready to rush back in. Does anyone need healing? A strong hand grips my arm.

"Now would be a good time for you to leave, Miss Ava."

"Elm," I say frantically, whirling on him. "What did you do? Did you hurt them?" My voice is shrill and panicked.

He grips me by the shoulders, steadying me. "No, of course not, Miss Ava. Everyone is fine. I promise."

The inside of the building clouds with smoke. "I have to go back in there!" I struggle, but he won't release me. Traitor. I use a strengthening spell and shove away from him. He grabs me again, gentle but firm. He looks straight into my eyes.

"Listen to me, Miss Ava. The digidomes are damaged, but the people are fine. We do need to get away before the Benefactors show up. They mustn't find you here."

I hesitate; the urge to go inside is strong. But after a moment, I nod and let Elm steer me toward the hover cart station. The next cart is only for a single passenger. I want to wait for a larger one, but since I appear to everyone else as being alone, it might draw suspicion. We squeeze in and set Prism as the destination.

The hover cart's small size forces us to sit squished together. Earlier today, I might have been content with this situation, but right now it's like seeing a caterpillar turn into a poisonous moth; he's hardly the same creature I thought I knew. I would rather be anywhere but here.

"Miss Ava?" Elm says.

I keep silent and stare stone-faced ahead of us.

He sighs and refrains from speaking for a few minutes. When he talks again, he says, "I can see this was a mistake. I should not have gotten you involved."

"Well, I agreed to it," I say numbly.

He shakes his head. "You didn't really know what you

were agreeing to. Uninformed consent is hardly consent. It was wrong of me."

"Can you please just tell me what we did back there?" Yes. What *we* did. I'm officially an accomplice.

He lets out a slow breath. "I . . . can't tell you everything."

"Well, I think that's rotten." I turn away from him and slouch forward, resting my chin on my hand.

After another few minutes of silence, I steal a quick look at him. When I see the dull pallor on his face and the look of sheer devastation in his eyes, my heart softens, though he's not entirely off the hook.

I sit back with a loud sigh. "You swear to me that nobody got hurt?"

"Nobody," he assures. "The popping you heard was the digidome circuits frying. It was all internal."

I feel a little better. But only a little. "What was that program?"

"I guess you could call it a digital virus. Once in the system, it spreads to other devices on the library network."

"But what does it do?"

"Destroys them, as you saw. That's all."

"So we just committed vandalism."

"Or total destruction. Whichever term you prefer," he says.

I glower at him.

"Perhaps someday I can tell you why, but for now, you'll simply have to trust me. I hope you'll believe me when I say I wouldn't have done it without good reason."

"Good for who, though? Not the Benefactors."

"Don't you question anything they do, Miss Ava?"

"Don't deflect."

His face is unreadable, but I can tell he chooses his next words carefully. "Suppose the Benefactors made a . . . mistake." He practically spits out the word *mistake* as though it's not a strong enough description for his liking. "Perhaps they aren't working for the good of all. I was merely trying to correct that mistake. May we please leave it at that before I drag you in further?"

"Saying things like that just leaves me with more questions. I hate that." This is so frustrating.

"I apologize for that. Truly."

My anger dissipates as my inclination to trust him grows. I want to believe him so desperately. Everything is so confusing. But I'm terribly aware of how close we're pressed against one another. He sits with absolute stillness, as though afraid to move an inch closer or farther from me. There is something endearing about it, and I can't bring myself to torture him any longer. When it comes down to it, I know we need to work together.

"Hey," I say, nudging him and giving a slight smile.

He looks at me, simultaneously curious and cautious.

"You can relax. I'm not going to explode."

He lets out a laugh, and whatever apprehension he had leaves him. "Sometimes, Miss Ava, I'm not so sure."

The tension has broken, and we are friends again. Friends . . . when did I start thinking of him that way? We talk to each other effortlessly. I much prefer this to being angry with him.

"You know, it's funny," I say. "On the way over, I was thinking about how much I miss yellow. I've never really noticed it's absence before."

"When you depend on it, you notice very quickly," Elm says wryly. "So what do you miss the most?"

I think for a moment. "Hmm . . . sunflowers. When I was younger, the whole countryside was full of them. So bright and happy. You know what's weird, though? You can still get edible sunflower seeds at the store. Baked, of course, so they're useless for planting. But I have to wonder where they come from."

"I'm sure they're produced under strict regulation somewhere."

"Probably. They should be part of our world. Regulating sunflowers and keeping them hidden away doesn't make sense. It's a shame. I'd love to see one again."

"Sunflowers," he muses. "Interesting. I would have pegged you for a rose girl."

"Such stereotyping," I say in mock offense. Then, smiling sheepishly, I admit, "Though I do like roses, too. Red or otherwise. I'm guessing you must like tulips?"

He raises his eyebrows.

"The dancing tulips at the library. I figure you must like them. It's a bit random if not."

His smile is sardonic. "Oh. That. That was simply me being dramatic, I suppose. I was thinking about something at the time and chose them for their meaning."

"Which is?" I prod.

"The meaning of yellow tulips, specifically, is 'hopeless love.'"

A moment of awkward silence passes. Then another. My wheels spin, trying not to read too much into his statement. I can't make eye contact with him. I need to change the subject. "S-so, what is your favorite, then? Flower."

I hear amusement in his voice when he answers, but he politely ignores my fumbling. "I guess I've never really thought about it. I may just have to adopt the yellow tulip until I can figure it out."

We continue talking all the way back to the station, and I tell him other things I miss. Things like lemon cake and yellow birds. Old-fashioned yellow rain jackets that I used to see in pictures before the ban. I wonder if I'll ever experience these things again. I wonder if I could experience them with Elm. More racing heartbeats.

When we arrive at the station, he jumps out ahead of me

and extends his arm to help me down. I'm about to accept, but then remember and give a quick glance toward the station attendant. I still have to pretend Elm doesn't exist. We walk side-by-side down the path back to Prism as the light slips away.

"Promise me one thing?" he asks.

"What's that?"

"Don't come and see me for a while."

Oh. That wasn't what I expected.

"Miss Ava, this is going to cause a fuss. It's less dangerous for both of us if you don't give anyone a reason to question your actions."

"That's true . . ." I say, feeling awkward as we arrive back at the gates. "Then I guess I'll see you . . . sometime." I know I've crossed a threshold today. Now that I've helped him once— well, twice if counting the episodes with the yellow daisies— the wheel is set in motion for further escapades. I might not be as ready for this as I thought.

He smiles warmly and takes my hand in his, sending sparks through me, and I am momentarily distracted from my anxieties. "From the bottom of my heart, Miss Ava, thank you for today." He kisses my hand.

"A-Anytime."

He gives a quiet laugh and then goes on his way.

14

IT'S BEEN OVER A WEEK SINCE ELM AND
I invaded the library in Violet City, and I consume every image
and noise that flickers from the projection before me as I sit
in Prism's student lounge. The news overflows with reports
about the incident, but by now, the reporters monotonously
recycle the same information. Because it's a hot topic, the
media outlets have to hype it up as much as they can, but they
don't have anything new.

Each time the image shows flashes of the decimated
digidomes, guilt gnaws at my conscience regarding the
unsuspecting boy. But the Benefactors simply use him to
play up their angle, rather than accusing him of the crime. I
suspect he underwent rigorous interrogation prior to the news
reports, which makes me feel like a rat. I watch anxiously,
even though this recorded interview with Selene runs for the
third time today.

"We have no doubt that Elm is behind this. He has used his
clever tricks to manipulate the mind of an innocent youngster.
The things that we have been afraid of are starting to take
place. Now, more than ever, it's important that the public stay
vigilant. The sooner we catch Elm, the better."

The report cuts to an interview with the boy. "I don't
remember anything. I was just sitting at the workstation,

playing my favorite game. Then suddenly this really weird image came up." He talks rapidly, clearly excited. I'm sure the Benefactors reinforced the idea that Elm manipulated him often enough that he truly believes it by now. "I guess I was in some kind of trance. But I'm okay now." He grins happily. "I even have a cool bodyguard to watch out for me!"

Thankfully, nobody has asked me about it. In fact, not a single person seems to have noticed I was there at all. I find this particularly strange, since the library has security cameras. Surely I appeared on the footage at some point, and with the ongoing investigation, they're probably questioning any leads available. It's a little too convenient that Selene hasn't said anything. I have a feeling Elm was at work in the city again after we parted.

My gaze follows several Benefactors as they patrol the lounge area. They are only a small number of the recent influx now covering the inside of the school. They move through the halls like shadows, sharp eyes hunting for anything that might be amiss. They are everywhere now. I watch this group as they leave. When I'm sure they won't come back my way, I head toward my Blue-Magic Application class.

Since I don't practice Blue magic, this might as well be a throwaway class for me. It also forces me to be in close proximity with Blake, with whom things are still uncomfortable. I know he's been worried about me since my outburst at his house over the break, but I can't forget his view concerning Mentalists, nor do I trust that he wouldn't report me to Selene if he thinks it's the right thing to do. I stand as far from him as possible, while Mr. Dawson explains the intricacies of changing an object's color.

"You can't go with just any shade if you want to be good. It's an art. You have to understand how color works and blends. You can't turn a blue object purple without recognizing that there has to be some red involved."

Blake steals a fleeting glance at me after the word *red* but looks away again, sullenly. Guilt brings heat to my cheeks, and I'm grateful everyone else is paying attention to the lecture.

"Colors rely on one another," Mr. Dawson continues. "If you don't try to understand them all, then you'll be missing critical information."

My mind naturally drifts to the mysterious White magic Elm mentioned. By removing Yellow from Prism, we are definitely lacking something. There's a whole other classification of magic that we deprive ourselves of.

I have a sudden excited thought—Elm's books on Yellow magic might say something about White magic also. My mind salivates at the notion, and I don't process another word of Mr. Dawson's lecture as I consider the possibilities.

When class ends, I purposely slow my movements while gathering up my belongings, allowing Blake plenty of time to exit the room ahead of me. A stubborn insistence on finding answers today has filled me, and I certainly can't risk being observed.

I'm extra paranoid about how to get out of the school. If I use the locket in my room, would someone see the door opening of its own accord? Or perhaps see me go in but notice I don't come out? There are too many students and Benefactors hanging around the dormitories at any given time. Before, I would go invisible in the hallways when nobody was around and then slip out the door to the grounds either behind someone else or when the area was vacant. But now Benefactors have overtaken the hallways, intently observing students and searching for telltale signs of mind control. My chances of slipping away under these circumstances are slim.

And then I think about the old wing of the school. If the Benefactors are mainly here to protect the students and monitor for suspicious activity, would they focus on an area that rarely has students? I instantly head in that direction. Just as before, the hallways in this wing appear dark and vacant. I move cautiously into the shadows, grasping the locket.

"Hello, Ava."

The voice behind me makes me jump and spin around, eyes wide and heart pounding.

The face is not who I might expect—Jace. The Benefactor Selene introduced me to at the color-initiation ceremony. What is he doing here? More importantly, what is my explanation for being here?

"What brings you to this wing of the school?" His voice is even, but there's something that bothers me about his eyes. He looks almost smug.

"Inventory," I chirp. "I'm taking an inventory of supplies, and I realized we might save ourselves some trouble if I check the old classrooms first."

"How responsible of you." Then, catching me entirely off guard, he asks, "What's the latest on Elm?"

The world seems to shatter around me. I stare at him. Say something. My brain wills me to speak, but nothing comes out.

"I'm not sure what you're asking," I finally manage. I scrunch my eyebrows in a way that I hope conveys confusion.

"Sorry, I mean on the official reports. Selene has me running around a lot these days. I don't often see the reports."

My racing heart doesn't allow me to relax just yet. His question is still odd to me. "But you have insider information, don't you?"

He smiles. "Of course. But it's always interesting to see how it's portrayed in the public eye. I'm sure you're smart enough to realize the difference between public relations and the meat of the investigation."

"I try to know as much as I can." I flinch inwardly as soon as I say this. Probably the wrong answer.

He studies me for a moment more, and I can't shake the

feeling he's harboring a secret. Something about me. My insides turn to ice.

"Why don't you put the inventory check on hold?" he says finally. "It's not a good idea for you to wander like this alone. You wouldn't want anyone to get the wrong idea."

"That makes sense," I say slowly. "Since I'll be a Benefactor soon, I need to set a good example, right?"

"Right."

"Thank you," I say in as gracious a tone as I can conjure. "I'll be more careful." I hurry past him back into the main corridors of the school. My nerves are frayed, and I stop to take a few deep breaths.

Elm was right. It's too risky for me to chance seeing him now. Too many eyes watching every movement. Too much potential for mistakes. Mistakes that could be deadly to Elm if I'm not careful. But what do I do? Sitting around waiting for a few weeks until I can get to Elm's books is out of the question. Every day there could be more Mentalists suffering somewhere. Every day more secrets are getting buried. Where else can I go for information?

The scarlet-haired woman on Chrysanthemum Street comes to mind again. Maybe I could convince her to tell me more about White magic. But we don't have a free day for another week. The sense of urgency presses on me, making that week feel like an insurmountable obstacle. Things would be different if I could get a permission card . . .

My breath catches as I contemplate the thought. Could I get away with it? I hold Elm's locket in my trembling hands, waiting for the right moment. The instant I'm alone in the corridor, I whisper Elm's name and release my breath once the familiar sensation of the dress billowing out around me is complete. I never thought about using the locket to sneak around the school before. My heart hammers, and my hands continue to shake.

I walk the familiar path to Selene's office, taking care not to bump into anyone or land too heavy of a footfall. Once outside her office, I press my ear to the door and wait. There is a muffled sound of conversation. Fortunately, Selene is never in her office for long. It shouldn't be much of a wait before she's out and about again.

After about fifteen minutes, the door opens, and Selene gestures for one of the faculty members to exit.

"Are you headed to lunch now?" Selene asks.

"Yes, do you want to join?"

Selene shakes her head. "I don't have time, though I suppose I could grab something quick to eat at my desk. I'll walk with you."

Selene and the faculty member step into the hall, and I dart inside the office, sucking in my breath as though it will make it easier to slip in before the door closes. Wasting no time, I dash to Selene's desk and open the narrow drawer where I have seen her pull the permission card for me many times. I pocket the card and zip back to the door, listening for signs of anyone outside. Within seconds the deed is done, and I return to the hallway. I'm a little taken aback at myself. Did I really just steal a permission card from Selene? Not only that, but a permission card I'm planning to use to sneak into the city to find out about illegal magic.

Violet City is even more tense than the last time I was here. More Benefactors. More citizens moving quickly through the streets, avoiding any interaction with strangers. All of this because of one Mentalist?

"Do you have a permission card, miss?"

I start as a Benefactor steps in front of me, hand extended. Before leaving Prism, I made sure to dress in street clothes so as not to attract extra attention, but I guess even without my school uniform they're paying close attention to minors. *Act like you're supposed to be here.*

I produce the permission card and smile. "Of course, sir."

He examines the card and gives a stiff nod, handing it back to me. "Please complete your business and head home straightaway."

"I will. Thank you."

I hurry to Chrysanthemum Street as fast as I think I can go without drawing Benefactor eyes. When I reach the square, my heart sinks. Where the woman's cart once stood is only splintered pieces of wood and a few broken vials. Vandals? Or did Benefactors do it?

My shoulders slump. I shouldn't be too disappointed—it may be that she only mentioned White magic to sell more potions. She might not have known anything at all. Perhaps she was shut down for misleading people.

"You'd be better off not hanging around staring at the remains of Elsie's shop," says a gruff voice behind me. I whirl to see a middle-aged man with a beard just as scarlet as the hair of the woman I sought.

"Elsie . . . was that the woman who owned that cart?"

The man nods. "Benefactors didn't care for her business."

"But why?" I ask. "She wasn't doing anything illegal, was she?"

He shrugs and coughs. "Likely was her mouth that got her in trouble more than her merchandise. Talking too much about things the way they used to be."

I have to ask. "Do you know anything about White magic?" If he knows this Elsie, maybe he knows other things.

The man coughs again and looks around with a fearful

expression. "Are you mad, girl? You want to get locked up, too?"

"No! I just want to know—"

He cuts me off with a shooing motion. "Get back to your school. Stay away from this place."

"Is there a problem here?"

I freeze as two Benefactors appear in the square. The man's face smooths. "Girl was lost. Was giving her directions to the memorial museum."

The memorial museum? No. They'll make sure that's my destination. I don't want to go there. But I note the man's glance at me, eyebrows raised. Maybe he has a reason for bringing it up.

"Where did you say it was again?" I ask, though I already know—after making a point of avoiding it all these years.

"Corner of Poppy and Maple Leaf."

"Thank you."

One of the Benefactors gives me a long stare. Does she suspect something?

"Do you need an escort?" she asks.

"No, that's all right. I can find my way now." I turn quickly back to the man and add, "Thank you for the directions."

I walk to the museum as if I'm pulling a heavy cart burdened with my emotions. I don't have to go there just because the man suggested it. I'm no worse for wear if I simply go back to Prism, right?

The Canary War Memorial Museum was built around the site of one of the most horrific incidents during the war. I've never gone inside. Hearing about the war is one thing—being confronted with the slaughter directly is another. I would still have my parents if not for that war. Will going inside really do me any good?

C'mon, Ava, my inner voice urges. *Are you going to live with your head in the sand forever?*

I inhale and pull open the glass door to the museum. A rush of cool air greets me, adding to the goosebumps already forming on my skin. The museum is quiet. Hallowed. The kind of place you automatically whisper in.

A white-haired man in a brown suit and brown-rimmed glasses shuffles over to me. "Welcome to the Canary War Memorial. You are free to wander as you wish, but please be respectful. I encourage you to spend as long as you like visiting the memorial garden in the courtyard."

I say a quiet thank you and move timidly through the museum, not really seeing anything as I try to collect myself. I stop and force myself to focus on the objects in glass cases. Mostly personal artifacts from those who lost their lives. Heroes. But heroic for what? I shiver as I imagine Mentalists in electrical wires, screaming. I move on.

At last I come to the section of the museum surrounding the battle site—a simple gift shop. The museum has been built around it, the whole area cordoned off with glass. The placard on the outer wall reads:

> *On a calm spring morning in March, Shapers and Augmentors started their day as usual, some visiting a gift shop in preparation for a happy day with loved ones. Out of nowhere, a Mentalist attack began, shattering the serenity of what should have been an ordinary errand. Every magic-user in the shop lost their lives on that day. This site serves as a solemn reminder to hold your loved ones close and always be prepared.*

The shop is full of broken merchandise, battered walls and furniture. Every red, yellow, or blue object has been stripped of its color—evidence of the desperation of the battle. What was the point of it all? And did Mentalists really instigate it?

When I can't handle looking at it anymore, I move to the memorial courtyard. Beautiful plants adorn the space. Bluebells, roses, lavender. The walls of the courtyard are large dark stone panels, engraved with the names of those who died as a result of the Canary War. Well . . . all the Shapers and Augmentors. It doesn't seem right. I know there had to be innocent Mentalists who lost their lives, too.

In the center of the courtyard is a digital directory so people can find which panel has the names of their loved ones. My parents' names would be there somewhere. I can't avoid every unpleasant feeling. The respectful thing would be to see them before I leave.

I scroll through the directory to the *L*'s and furrow my brow. How odd . . . nothing under Locke. Could they have been alphabetized incorrectly by their first names? I check the *V*'s for my mother's name, Vivian. She's not there either. I return to the *L*'s and look for my father's name, Lucas. Nothing. I find the two names that should have my parents nestled between them. I go to the corresponding stone tablet. Nothing again. Confused, I return to the man who greeted me.

"Sir?" I ask. "Did you say the memorial garden has the names of ALL Augmentors and Shapers who died during the war?"

"Yes, I believe so. Did you lose someone?"

I shake my head. "No. I mean, yes, my parents, but I didn't see—"

"It's possible some names were mistakenly not recorded. We lost a great number of people."

"Of course. Thank you."

I leave the museum even more confused than when I entered. Once I'm back on a hover cart to Prism, panic starts to settle in. I take several breaths in an attempt to relax. I just stole a card and snuck into the city, and for what? More missing puzzle pieces. I didn't recognize any of the Benefactors as those who patrol Prism, but if any of them recognized me and word somehow got back to Selene, there would be all sorts of questions. Elm wouldn't be able to bail me out this time. All questions would be answered, at great cost to me . . . and eventually Elm.

But the desire to learn about White magic—or simply more about Yellow magic—presses, threatening to shatter me from within. Well, I've already snuck out of the school, so maybe this doesn't need to be a total waste. Now I can go to Elm and perhaps get the answers I need.

15

ON THE WAY TO ELM'S HIDEOUT, I MAKE up my mind not to tell Elm about Jace. I'm already going back on my promise not to see him for a while. If I tell Elm I had a run-in with a Benefactor on top of that, he'll become more adamant that I keep away. I'll just have to be ten times as cautious leaving Prism from now on.

A blinding flash of yellow light swallows me as I enter the cave.

I cry out, shielding my eyes. "Elm?"

The light stops immediately, and when the spots fade from my eyes, Elm gapes at me from a few inches away.

"Miss Ava! You were to stay away for several days."

"I decided to ignore that request."

His face changes. A strange mix of confusion, exasperation, and just a bit of delight. "You are your own agent," he says with a trace of a smile. "But I do worry about you disappearing from Prism so soon after our tryst at the library."

I dismiss his concerns. "I'm fine. I finished my classes for the day, and I made sure nobody noticed." The look on his face is skeptical, so I quickly continue, "What's the deal with that light?" As I look upward, I see one of his yellow spheres, now emitting its normal glow.

"It was a security measure. To alert me if anyone entered the cave. It utilizes basic motion detection technology. I apologize for its brightness," he adds. "I didn't know you would be here, or I'd have turned it off. The intention is to temporarily blind anyone, so I can send them away before they see me."

"You seem to have a knack for gadgets," I muse. "How did you learn to do all that?"

"It's nothing, really." He gives a dismissive wave of his hand. "So, Miss Ava, are there any new developments?" he asks, changing the subject.

He's less calm than usual. He keeps looking around, as though expecting something to jump out at him.

"Are you okay?" I ask.

"I've seen a lot of Benefactors around lately. In the forest."

"They're crawling all over Prism, too," I tell him. "But they can't see you though, right? Not when you're invisible."

"Theoretically, but I still worry. After all, I didn't think you would be able to see me in the beginning either. Yet here you are."

"That's true . . ." The idea that the Benefactors might be close to tracking Elm down makes me apprehensive. Considering his usual relaxed nature, the fact that he's visibly worried is even more concerning.

"There's nothing new on any reports," I assure him. "They don't seem to have any leads on you."

He gazes at me again in that way that makes me feel like he's reading my mind. For all I know, he can. "Are *you* okay, Miss Ava?"

The events of the day pummel me. Jace. Elsie. The museum. "I don't know," I confess. "That's why I'm here."

He tilts his head, waiting for me to continue.

"I'm ready to get to the truth. And if I'm going to help you, I need a favor."

"By all means. Anything within my abilities."

Why am I nervous? I'm asking to read a book, not plan an

invasion. "I need to see your books on Yellow magic. I think I have a better chance of getting the Benefactors in my corner if I actually know what I'm talking about."

He ponders for a moment and then replies, "I suppose you've earned it. You're already in fairly deep."

As if I needed a reminder of how deep I'm in . . .

We walk back to the chamber of the cave that serves as his bedroom. Eagerly, I move to the wooden bookcase full of forbidden knowledge. I'm reaching for the thickest volume I can see when Elm grasps my hand and gently pulls it away.

"Sorry," he says, looking me in the eyes. "I get to choose." His fingers linger on mine for a moment, and then he turns away and selects a less-weighty book from the shelf.

"Here we are. This is a good one for you to cut your teeth on."

I squint my eyes to read the title in the dim, flickering light of his room, *Yellow Magic and its Uses: An Overview.*

"Thank you." I am giddy with excitement. "I'm going to read it by the willow tree. The light is good there. Race you!" I cast an agility spell and fly out of the room without waiting for him to respond. I hear the echo of his amused laughter as he calls for me to slow down.

I'm already settled beneath the tree and reading with contentment when he catches up to me.

"Liking it so far?"

"I'm only on the intro," I say. A glow of elation fills me. "But I want to read it all. I don't want to miss anything."

To every good deception, there is an inkling of truth. The most skilled Mentalist knows how to read people, to form relationships, and learn the nuances of the human mind before ever tapping into it. The Mentalist also weighs the implications of every

*choice: Consider that an uplifted mind may do far
more benefit to the world than a controlled one.*

Interesting.

I read for a solid hour. To his credit, Elm doesn't say a word. He disappears deep into the cave, periodically returning and checking on me. Finally, his fingertips rest lightly on my back.

"Miss Ava," he says gently. "It's nearly dusk."

"It's okay," I say, still focused on the passage I'm reading. "Nobody will notice if I'm not there."

He kneels beside me and tugs at the book. I resist for a moment, but he raises his eyebrows at me, and I resentfully relax my grip, allowing him to pull it from my hands.

"The book will still be here for you next time. Now would be a terrible time for you to raise questions at your school."

"I guess you're right," I concede.

He pauses as he places the book beneath the tree and turns to me with a quizzical look. "Do you really suppose you could influence the Benefactors?"

I know the odds of that are slim to none. "It's worth a try, right? Bringing about honest change would be better than sneaking around."

He gives a laugh. "You still think you can have your cake and eat it too?"

"Yes," I insist.

He sees me out of the cave. "Well, I'm willing to watch you try."

16

EVENTUALLY, THE FLAMES OF THE incident at the library die down and smolder into nothing. Without any new information, the public becomes bored, and news stories move on. Elm is significantly more relaxed after learning the Benefactors don't have any clues as to his whereabouts.

I have seen Elm daily for a month now, taking every chance I can to sneak out to the cave. I'm more careful now when I leave, especially watching out for Blake and going invisible as soon as possible. I avoid eye contact with him when our mutual classes meet. He moodily ignores me. I have probably destroyed any chance we might have for friendship or keeping in contact once his parents are no longer my guardians, but I tell myself it's better this way. Less danger for both of us. So why does it sting?

Now that I know about Elm's security light, I shut my eyes tight before racing into the cave. I collide straight into him.

"Sorry," I laugh. "Good morning!"

Elm looks startled to see me. I'm here much earlier than normal, and I wonder if I caught him shortly after waking because his hair is extra messy, and he isn't yet wearing his vest or jacket. His disheveled appearance is . . . adorable.

"Oh! Good morning, Miss Ava." He stifles a yawn. Then he smiles sheepishly. "Sorry."

I smile back. "Wild, crazy night?"

"Something like that."

His gardening tools lie in a heap near one of the cave formations, covered in fresh soil. And grass. He doesn't have any actual grass in the cave that I'm aware of—only what he creates with his illusions. So where has he been using those tools?

"Have you been gardening?" I ask, pretending casual interest. Really, I'm dying to know what he has been up to.

His eyes flit to the tools, showing the dimmest trace of alarm, and then he looks quickly back to me, his face once again composed. "Yes, just standard upkeep. I should have cleaned up. I didn't expect you so soon."

I know he's hiding something. But I also know him well enough by now to know he won't tell me what it is.

He puts his hand lightly on the small of my back and steers me away from the tools. "Oh, I think I owe you another book, don't I?"

He's only doing this to distract me. He obviously didn't want me to notice the gardening tools, and he's almost certainly anticipating more questions. It's less trouble for him if he can just head them off. And yet, even knowing this, his tactic works.

"Actually," I say hesitantly, "I was hoping for a different form of instruction. But you're probably not going to like it."

"Try me."

I twirl my hair anxiously, but then drop my hands, hoping Elm doesn't notice my nervousness. "You've shown me a lot about what Yellow magic can do, but I want to learn . . . how to defend against it." Since I have been reading Elm's books, I understand more about what Yellow magic can do in theory, but I feel like I can't fully grasp it until I see it in action.

He is evidently not expecting this request. "But, Miss Ava, I can't teach you to defend without—"

"Fighting each other. I know."

"You're right. I don't like it."

"But I'm completely unprepared for dealing with Yellow magic. Wouldn't it be useful for me to know in case it ever causes me trouble?"

"It's not the easiest to defend against . . ."

He's obviously uncomfortable with the idea.

"I trust you not to hurt me too severely. And I can always heal."

"It's not so much physical harm I'm worried about," he replies gravely.

"Could I convince you if I told you it was for my overall well-being?" I ask hopefully.

"What Mentalist besides me are you in such desperate need of protection from? Although I won't argue that you might need protecting from me." His eyes hold a devious twinkle.

"You never know," I say stubbornly, trying to disregard his response. "Yellow magic might return to Magus one day. And if it does, I want to be prepared. Just in case."

"Very well, Miss Ava." He throws his hands up in exaggerated defeat. "It's nearly impossible to refuse you."

We are in the clearing where he first took me to show me the horses. It looks so empty and open with the herd's absence, although traces of them remain everywhere—hoofprints in the dust, a stray wisp from a mane.

I look at Elm. "Do you have any pointers for me before we get started?"

"You're dealing with illusions and the mind, so there isn't anything physical involved. The key is to decipher what's real from what isn't. If you can tell the difference, I can have no power over you. Matter over mind."

"How do I know the difference?"

He shrugs. "I believe it's probably just something that comes with experience and practice. No illusion is perfect. Are you ready to begin?"

"Ready when you are."

"If at any time you want me to stop," Elm says, "you need only ask."

I nod and prepare myself for his first move, keeping my senses sharp. At first nothing happens, but then something comes at me from the trees. An animal of some sort. It slinks toward me slowly, and I catch flashes of orange fur and stripes. A tiger.

"You're making this too easy," I protest. "I already know there aren't tigers around here, so that doesn't give me much to figure out."

He merely smiles.

The tiger continues its approach and then stops within inches of me. Without warning, it swats at me with one of its large paws, delivering a heavy thud and a twinge of pain. I swivel around and stare at Elm with surprise. "I felt that!"

He raises his eyebrows. "Didn't I tell you? I'm good at this. You won't experience any physical effects from my illusions, but I can make you think you do. Even knowing full well that the tiger was fake, you felt his blow."

Now, I see the danger. He could cause me pain if he wanted. My body would be fine, but my mind wouldn't know the difference. On the other hand, pain might be unpleasant and frightening, but it's the real physical effects that you have to worry about. Minus those, I'm sure I can handle it.

"Well," I say, "now that I know it can't hurt me, I'm not afraid. I can tough it out."

But suddenly I do feel afraid. An inexplicable terror creeps into me, causing my heart to race. I make an effort to shake it off, knowing nothing here can really harm me. Nevertheless, I take a step away from the tiger, trembling.

"Frightened, Miss Ava?" Elm asks, voice cocky.

"I . . . yes. But I don't know why."

"I can control your emotions as well. If I were being serious, you'd be screaming by now."

The fear feels genuine. How am I supposed to separate this imagined fear from real fear? *Because it's illogical*, I tell myself. There is no reason to be afraid. It can't hurt me. I close my eyes and repeat this in my mind over and over, but the quaking in my knees and the racing of my heart will not subside. Elm's magic is too strong, and I'm unequipped for dealing with it. What would I do to feel less afraid in a real situation? Strength. If I feel more powerful than the tiger, I won't be so afraid. But since the tiger is an illusion controlled by Elm, I might not be able to affect it with physical attacks. I'm not sure how it works. However, I can certainly dodge it.

I cast an agility spell followed by a strengthening spell, so I have power as well as speed. The tiger lunges toward me, and I dart out of its way without effort. It pounces. I jump higher. It runs. I run faster. Now, the fear replaces itself with confidence. There's no reason to be afraid when the thing I fear can't even touch me.

I grin at Elm as I continue to dodge the powerful animal. "This is easier than I thought," I say. "Once you know it's all tricks and illusions, Yellow magic is pretty harmless. This is almost like a game."

"A game? Well then," he remarks, "let's try something else, shall we?" I might be imagining it, but I think I hear a change in his voice, imperceptibly less jubilant than it was an instant ago.

"Okay," I reply, now feeling somewhat less assured. "I'm ready."

The tiger shimmers away. Elm reaches into his suit coat and produces something that glints in the sunlight. A dagger. Like most of Elm's belongings, it has yellow gemstones in its craftsmanship. In this case, the stones rest in the dagger's golden hilt. He tosses the weapon lightly at my feet.

"What's this for?" I ask, perplexed.

"I'd like you to take that in hand and give me your best shot."

"What?" I take a step back from the dagger. "I'm not coming at you with a knife."

"Oh? You don't think I can defend myself?"

I frown and hold my position, stubbornly leaving the dagger in the grass.

"I wouldn't attempt this if I were worried. Go on, give it a try." His voice is steady and persuasive.

"All right," I shrug, picking up the dagger carefully. At once, a strange feeling seeps in. My arms feel tingly and rubbery, like I don't have an ounce of control over them. They feel heavy and light all at once. Before I know it, I'm gripping the dagger in both hands and pointing it straight at my chest. Straight at my heart.

"Elm, what are you—"

"The mind is a funny thing, Miss Ava," he drawls. "You need your mind to control your body. I can control your mind, so . . ."

The dagger inches forward dangerously as he trails off. I don't need him to finish in order to grasp what he's saying.

I expect him to release his hold on me and stop the dagger's downward motion, but he doesn't. I have a new, sudden understanding of what I have been reading about in Elm's books. They all talk about mind control. Of course it follows that you could control a person's actions as well. This is what the Benefactors have always feared. What they're working tirelessly to prevent. And I have allowed it—begged for it—to happen to me.

My eyes widen, and I'm certain the fear within me now is entirely real and my own. Have I been wrong to trust Elm?

He moves close to me now, close enough that I can feel the heat from his body and his breath on my skin. My eyes lock with his, but I can't read his expression, can't decipher his intentions.

"I could end your life by your own hands right now, if I chose to. If I were that kind of person."

I can feel the pressure of the dagger through the delicate fabric of my dress, and my heart pounds. I hardly dare breathe for fear that the motion will cause the blade to pierce through.

"Elm," I whisper desperately. "Please stop."

The dagger falls at once to the ground with a dull clunk as my hands finally obey my will.

"But I'm not that kind of person."

Relief overtakes me, and my knees nearly give out, but straightaway Elm has his arms around my waist, bearing me up. He looks at me with fervent intensity. My lip quivers, and I bite down on it hard. But this only results in a tremor overtaking the rest of my body.

"Did you really think I would do it?" he asks. "Did you?"

"I didn't want to think so, but I wasn't sure," I whisper.

"Listen to me, Miss Ava. I need you to trust me. Will you ever do so? Is it possible?"

I can't guess what I must look like to him right now, but after searching my face for a moment, he looks alarmed, and he sinks to his knees, pulling me with him. He clasps my hands in his earnestly.

"I'm so terribly sorry. Truly I am. I will never intentionally hurt you. Ever. Please understand that." He's nearly begging. "Please believe it."

"I do," I say, and to my own astonishment, I mean it. I believe him. After all, I'm the one who asked him to show me his full power. And, true to his word, he stopped the moment I asked him to.

He gives a sigh and looks relieved. "You asked me not to go easy on you, and I thought it would be an insult to you if I did. I wanted you to understand exactly what it is you're dealing with. What Yellow magic is. This isn't a game."

"I get that now."

"I wouldn't have tried it if I thought any less of you," he says, gently touching my cheek, his tone soft. "I believe I've traumatized you enough for one day. I should take you back. But there's one more thing I have to do first . . ."

The clearing starts to shimmer and waver around me. "What's happening?" I ask, startled.

Before Elm can reply, we are back in the cave.

"How on earth . . . ?" I gape at him.

"Think, Miss Ava. Do you remember actually leaving the cave?"

I think hard. "No. I don't."

"We never left."

I stare at him, astounded. All I can manage to get out is "Amazing."

"You weren't so bad yourself. For your first try." He smiles. "Now, let me walk with you back to the school. I promise there will be no tricks this time."

He keeps his arm around me as we walk. Our difference in height makes this somewhat awkward, but if this bothers him, he doesn't show it.

Every now and then, I glance at him. How can someone with a face so gentle have so much power, so much potential to cause hurt? Physical hurt. Emotional turmoil. Power even to make a person believe they are somewhere they are not. The danger the Benefactors attribute to his abilities is not at all exaggerated. But he doesn't seem to get enjoyment from using his power that way. Especially not on me.

We reach the forest's edge, and I expect him to leave me there, but he insists on walking me all the way to the school's gate.

"I don't think you should keep getting this close to the school, even if we're invisible." The danger hanging over us casts a shadow every time we meet. I'm sure he feels it too.

"I have to make sure you're not broken, Miss Ava," he says. I laugh. "I'm fine." And I *am* fine. It would make more sense to fear him now that I know what he's capable of, but I'm convinced he doesn't want to harm me. He could have done it long ago and so easily.

I'm about to step inside the gates when he stops me again. "Wait, Miss Ava. Tomorrow is April 26th. Your birthday, isn't it?"

I blink. I had only mentioned it once in passing conversation a long while ago. "Yes, I guess it is." Birthdays usually pass quietly and quickly for me. I hadn't even thought about it until now.

"Can you meet me at the cave after classes tomorrow? Or do you have other plans?"

I shake my head wryly. "Nope. No other plans. I'm completely free."

"Wonderful. I think I can fill your day." He smiles. "I promise it will be much more enjoyable than today."

I smile back at him. "Today *was* enjoyable, Elm."

"Deceit? From Miss Ava? Oh my. I have corrupted you. They'll hang me for sure, now."

I force a laugh, trying not to think of what might actually happen to him if he's caught. "I'm serious. Okay, so the last part of your magic was awful. But before that, I enjoyed it.

I learned things. And I also got to see more of your skills. You're impressive."

"As are you," he says warmly. He looks at me, as if he's struggling inwardly with something I can't decipher. He begins to lean forward but then stops abruptly and clears his throat. "Until tomorrow, then."

I watch him until he disappears into the trees, a twinge of disappointment left in his place.

17

FOR THE FIRST TIME IN MY MEMORY, I feel expectation on my birthday. Previously, I only felt indifference. When class ends, I head for the door like an arrow toward a target.

I scan the hallways, searching for a good spot to use the locket. It's getting harder these days with so many Benefactors, but with patience, I can usually find the right kind of opening. Today's comes in the form of a tall library cart, waiting in the hallway with no students browsing. I duck behind it, turn the locket, and whisper, "Elm."

Nothing happens.

"Elm," I whisper again, more urgently.

Nothing.

I stand, feeling numb. What do I do if I can't see him again? His remark about charging the device comes to mind. Is that what's going on? Locket or not, I have to get back to him.

I stride down the path to the forest, textbooks under one arm and a notebook in the other. I just need to act like I know what I'm doing. The Benefactors dotting the path occasionally glance at me . . . and return to their conversations. I breathe a relieved sigh.

At least all these years of being a model student have been good for something—they don't suspect I'm up to anything but studying. Our stunt at the library also worked in my favor, as more efforts have been focused on the city, and the Benefactors near the woods have thinned out significantly.

I walk a few yards past the tree line and stop, listening and observing. No voices nearby. Nobody following me. Onward to Elm, at last. I relieve myself of the books and notebook so I can walk more freely.

The way is easy now, and I don't need to concentrate so hard as I go. I reach the sinkhole, poised to leap forward, when I hear a panicked voice behind me.

"Ava!"

Someone grabs my arm sharply, and I whirl around.

"Blake!" My heart stops. "What are you doing?"

"What are *you* doing?" he counters. "Were you about to jump in there? That looks dangerous."

"Oh, relax. I wasn't going to jump in. I thought I saw a . . . squirrel down there."

"A squirrel?"

"Yes, a squirrel," I say defiantly. "I like animals. A lot. But that's not the point. Why are you following me?"

"I tried to catch you after class to wish you a happy birthday, but you took off too fast. Then I saw you go out the gate. I was just worried. Wandering off into the forest again by yourself—so far in, too." He looks at me accusingly. "Why are you really here? What is it that makes you want to come out here so much?"

"It's not your job to babysit me," I retort, a maelstrom of emotions flowing through me. With Blake's memory, he's likely to remember the way back here much easier than I did. He could end everything. I fight the tears of fear and frustration threatening to appear. "If you wanted to know so badly, why didn't you just ask? Why are you sneaking around after me?"

"Because I wanted to know what you were up to." His tone is defensive. "I'm sorry, but you're not the same lately."

"I'm not up to anything." My stomach lurches. He's going to tell Selene. They'll find Elm.

I reach for anything that might change his mind. "Blake, I need to be by myself for a while. Birthdays remind me of what I don't have. My family." I let the weight of the words settle on him.

His face reddens. "Oh, I'm really sorry, Ava. I didn't mean to intrude. I never thought about that."

I have to soothe him. "But I would love to hang out again soon." I manufacture a smile. "I had a lot of fun with you in the city, and I really don't want us to fight." I mean that truthfully.

No sooner have I said this than a twig snaps near us. My heart races as I wonder who else could have followed us out here. Blake and I both turn toward the sound, but I see nothing.

Blake takes a defensive stance, edging protectively in front of me. "This is exactly why you shouldn't be out here."

Gradually, strange noises emerge from the forest. More breaking twigs and branches, followed by eccentric howls and eerie cackling. A shadow flashes through the trees on our left, and another in the area behind us.

"What's happening?" Blake asks with wide eyes, his voice shaking.

"I don't know," I say, although I think I have a pretty good idea. The way Blake shifted so suddenly from bravery to fear is too uncharacteristic.

All at once, a cluster of strange apparitions lurches through the trees. Dark, semi-transparent, distorted bodies stagger toward us with glowing, red eyes.

Blake loses it. He takes off at full speed through the forest, shouting and forgetting me entirely as the creatures pursue him. Seconds later, a smirking Elm appears, confirming my suspicions.

"We have to go after him! He's not going to find his way back in that state," I exclaim anxiously. "And what will happen when he goes back to Prism talking about ghosts in the forest?"

"I have thought this through, Miss Ava. My illusions will chase him in the right direction. By the time he gets back to Prism, he will have forgotten everything. He won't remember having followed you at all."

I give a sigh of relief. "If you could have done a memory spell on him to begin with, why did you have to mess with him like that?"

"I dislike him."

Well, at least Elm is honest. For the sake of avoiding contention, I don't press him.

"And why, my dear Miss Ava, for the love of daffodils, are you not invisible?"

"I tried," I say. "It didn't work."

His face pales. He leans in close to me and flips the locket open. "Oh dear . . . I can't believe I allowed that to happen. I'll set it right immediately."

Once he restores the locket to its full power, I say his name and feel the dress bloom instantly around me. I can breathe again.

"I'm so very sorry, Miss Ava. With everything going on, I—"

"Oh, hush up and tell me what's on the agenda today."

With a flourish, he produces a yellow blindfold. "Secret things," he says with a grin.

He's lucky I trust him. I wouldn't let just anybody blindfold me. I hold still as he carefully places it over my eyes and ties it in a tight knot at the back of my head. "Can you see anything?"

"Nope."

"Wonderful. We have a bit of walking to do, but I'll see to your direction." He steps behind me and places his hands on my shoulders, steering me forward.

We walk through the forest in pace with my slow, cautious

steps. I stumble now and then, but Elm makes sure I don't fall. After a few minutes, I hear the rush of a river. Elm scoops me up into his arms without warning.

I yelp in surprise as he lifts me. "I thought we were walking?"

"We could get there by walking, but it's faster and more exciting this way. Now, try not to wiggle too much, or you'll send us overboard."

He sets me down gingerly into a solid, concave object, which rocks and sways beneath me. "Are we on a boat?"

"If you could call it that. It's hardly seaworthy."

"You'd better be joking."

He merely laughs in response.

I feel a small jolt and then the sensation of movement. Because I can't see, the motion gives me a brief feeling of vertigo, and I grasp wildly for Elm's arm. Once I adjust, however, the movement becomes soothing. The air tickles past my face and through my hair. Occasionally, a cool mist of water sprinkles me.

After a few minutes, the motion of the boat steadies. I hear Elm rummaging around.

"What are you doing?" I ask.

He doesn't answer right away, but then says, "Open your mouth, if you please."

I crinkle my nose. "I don't like the idea of mystery food."

"Trust me!" He chuckles. "Surely you don't expect me to do anything mean-spirited, Miss Ava."

"Fine, fine." Reluctantly I part my lips, and my taste buds collide with a tangy sweetness I had all but forgotten.

"Lemon cake?" I ask in wonderment.

"How is it?"

"I want more."

Elm's hands work behind my head, and I blink at the bright sunlight as he removes the blindfold.

"You can peek for a little while," he says, "so you can nibble at your leisure."

He presents me a tiny plate with a perfect little slice of lemon cake, decorated with pink-frosting roses.

"How in the world did you get this?" I marvel. "Anything with lemon in it is hard to find. And expensive. And," I say, looking at the cake, "it's yellow. But everything with lemon in it is dyed a different color before hitting store shelves."

"I grew it."

"The cake?"

"The lemons, silly Miss Ava. But I did make the cake."

I'm astounded. "You have to show me where you're hiding a lemon tree. And an oven."

"The lemon tree is in the cave. I'll show you next time. It has actually been there for . . . a while."

"And the oven?"

He shifts uncomfortably. "I may have had to coerce someone into letting me use theirs."

"Hmm." My mouth is stuffed with more of the cake. I swallow. "I'll forgive you for that this time, because this is delicious." I savor every bite. I almost forgot what lemon tastes like. It pairs perfectly with the peaceful serenity of the river and the surrounding forest green. And, I freely admit to myself, the sweetness of Elm by my side.

After I finish my last bite of cake, Elm blindfolds me again. "We wouldn't want to spoil the surprise."

"I thought the cake was the surprise."

"That was just your birthday cake. Next, you get your present."

We rock down the river for perhaps five minutes more. I feel another small jolt, and we must have reached our destination. Elm guides me with great care onto the shore.

"Almost there."

The terrain feels different here. There is no longer the

crunch of dead pine needles, and my feet step upon softer ground. Grass? Instead of the scent of the pines from the start of our journey, a soft floral aroma reaches my nose. It's familiar and pleasant, but I can't place it.

"All right, Miss Ava," says Elm.

Once more, he removes the blindfold. It takes my eyes a moment to adjust to the sudden barrage of golden yellow before me.

"Sunflowers!" Stretched out before me is a whole field of them. Bright and beautiful and fluttering in the soft breeze. The afternoon sunlight beams through their petals, bathing them in a translucent glow.

"Are they real?" I ask, racing ahead and reaching to touch a petal.

"They are absolutely real," Elm states with pride. "It took some work to find them, but they grow marvelously."

"Where?" I ask breathlessly, gazing around in delight. "Where did you find them?"

"I tracked down the sunflower plant where the seeds come from. About two hundred miles from here."

"Two hundred miles?" I ask, stunned. "When did you find time to do that?"

"The distance wasn't a problem. The hover carts move fast enough. The hard part has been keeping them concealed all this time. Not just from the Benefactors, but I'm sure I planted a suggestion to ignore it in every horse from the herd. Apparently, they have a taste for sunflowers. It took a lot of diligence to keep them all safe."

"How are you able to keep them concealed?"

"Yellow stones," he says. "I placed them in the surrounding area, and they continue to transmit suggestions. Of course, I have to come back here to recharge them every two days. It's a lot of work, but it's—"

I interrupt him by standing on my tiptoes and tugging him

by his cloak to bring his head down. I give him a quick kiss on the cheek. I simply can't help myself. He freezes for a moment, and then smiles widely as he finishes, "worth it. Absolutely worth it."

I can't believe the amount of time and effort he put into this. The risk. And he did it all for me. Realization washes over me like a beam from the sun, resting in a snug place in my chest: the gardening tools, the hours spent outside of the cave. This is what it was all for.

"Elm," I say, my voice shaking with emotion. "Thank you. This is without a doubt the most thoughtful thing anyone has ever done for me. I love it."

"As long as you want them, Miss Ava, I will take good care of them."

I plop down on my back in the middle of the field and grin. "I think I want them forever."

He sits down beside me with his legs stretched out, reclining easily on one arm. We spend the rest of the afternoon this way, surrounded by bright yellow sunflowers, looking at the sky, and talking to one another. I breathe in the fragrant flowers, still in awe at the sight of them.

I wonder if anything could be more perfect. The world is beautiful, and I'm in the company of someone dear to me. Yes, he is dear to me. I can admit that readily now. To myself, at least. Could I ever say it to him? If I'm going to say it, will there be a better time than now?

I turn to look up at Elm, who appears content and happy as he reclines beside me. This is the most relaxed I have seen him in weeks. I slip my fingers into his, and he smiles and gives my hand a squeeze. This gives me encouragement—at least he doesn't shy away.

"Elm," I begin nervously, looking up at the calm blue sky in hopes that this will make it easier.

"Yes, Miss Ava?"

I don't know how to say it. I haven't ever done this before. "I'm glad I got to know you," I say, fumbling for the right words. "I . . . really, really like you." The word *like* feels inadequate on my tongue, but the thought of calling it something more is too terrifying.

"That's convenient," he says. "I find you satisfactory."

I stare at him, blushing furiously. I contemplate using a strengthening spell and then slugging him in the gut, but then I notice the mischief in his eyes and the smile quivering on his lips. He's teasing me again.

He leans over me and gently brushes a few strands of hair from my cheek, his eyes meeting mine. "I'm sorry, dear Miss Ava. I shouldn't tease you so much. I adore you."

My heart does a few giddy somersaults. That is a much more satisfying answer.

The evening air is cool as we go through the forest. I wish I could continue this moment with him instead of returning to Prism.

"Full moon," I note.

"The wolves may devour you."

I laugh. "I'm an Augmentor. A good strengthening spell would take care of a wolf."

"Wonderful. You are far too becoming in the moonlight. It would be a terrible waste."

"Whatever," I say, smiling shyly. "The wolf wouldn't care."

As we approach the forest's edge, I hear voices. I recognize one of them at once. "Selene," I whisper tensely. "You'd better go."

"She can't see me," he assures me. "I'm not worried."

The second voice, a vaguely familiar man's voice, speaks louder, and Elm stiffens. "On second thought, perhaps I shouldn't go any farther. You're fine in the dark?"

"If nothing can see me, then I have nothing to be afraid of."

He gives another uneasy look in the direction of the voices. "Don't linger. I would head straight back if I were you. Do forgive me, but I'll be making a quick exit now. Goodnight, Miss Ava."

"Goodnight."

He disappears into the trees, and I wonder what has him so suddenly on edge. Perhaps he decided to listen to my warnings for once?

I tiptoe quietly forward, unsure if the sounds of my feet on the crisp forest floor are still audible when I'm in the dress. As I get closer, I can just make out the faces in the moonlight. Selene, as I knew, and Jace. Neither of them sounds happy.

"What were you *really* doing out here?" Selene demands.

"I already told you. I thought I saw something strange, so I came out here to observe. But it appears to have been nothing."

They stare each other down for a moment. In the dim light, I can't be sure, but I think I see beads of sweat forming on Jace's face. He looks entirely different from the arrogant man I encountered in the old wing of the school.

Selene is the first to speak again. "I'm warning you, Jace. I don't want to see you put one toe out of line." She lowers her voice. "If you do, you know what happens to *them*."

Who is "them"? Selene is making threats?

I hear a slight tremor in Jace's voice. "How can you doubt I'm on your side? Haven't I given up everything?"

Selene points her finger at him. "If I detect anything even remotely suspicious, you will give up a lot more."

"I will always be loyal to the Benefactors. You know that."

"Let's hope that's the case." Her eyes scan the forest. "Let's get out of here. This place sends a chill up my spine."

As they head back toward Prism, I realize with a start that they will close the gate for the night if I don't get there before they do. Holding my breath in hope that I won't be noticed, I cast an agility spell and race ahead.

I'm not sure what that conversation was about, but if Selene is keeping an eye on Jace, perhaps I should too.

18

I READ OVER THE PAGE OF MY TEXTBOOK
for the tenth time, still unable to focus on the words. I sigh and
close the cover, wishing for the sun-dappled green shelter of the
forest instead of the sterile white of the lounge. Even if not to
see Elm, I could always study so much better there, but because
the end of the school year is so close, I promised him I'd keep
a low profile and stay at Prism as much as possible until after I
graduate.

After I graduate.

Every time I think of those words, a boulder forms in the pit
of my stomach. What am I going to do after I graduate? Since
childhood, I've prepared to become a Benefactor, but now that
goal is distorted. I don't know if I can begin my training while
at the same time fraternizing with the "enemy." Part of me still
has a strong desire to do everything I worked so hard for. If I
suddenly tell Selene that isn't what I want anymore, she's going
to be suspicious. But the other part of me knows losing Elm
and forsaking all other Mentalists is out of the question. If I'm
working with the people who are after Elm, how long will it be
before I unintentionally give him away? Or how long will it be
before I snap under the pressure of a double life?

Side with the Benefactors. Side with the Mentalists. There's
no way to do both.

Or is there? I still see the Benefactors as the peacekeepers of Magus, but through my association with Elm, I now know they are misguided in many ways. What if we could bring Yellow magic back into the world again? What if Mentalists weren't outlaws and could walk the streets like any other human being? Again, I ponder the idea that if I can work my way into a position of authority, I could have the power to change the entire organization. Even Magus itself. If only it were possible somehow.

But I still question myself. And sometimes, though I feel guilty for it, I still question Elm. I can't help it when I think about the past few months with him and knowing what his abilities are. There was the time in the library when my thoughts began to fog over. And when Elm used his power on me at my request. I didn't even realize what he was doing. There are all the irrational things I do for him—things I never would have done prior to meeting him. I keep telling myself I would know if he has been manipulating me this whole time, but I can't entirely eliminate the tendrils of suspicion creeping into my mind.

And if all is well with Elm, I have other things to consider. Like where do we go from here?

I glance up, across the circular tables full of students relaxing in red and blue chairs, and see Selene enter the lounge, in conversation with Jace. They both look my way, and I shiver. Jace gives me the creeps for reasons I can't explain.

He remains near the entry as Selene approaches me and calls over her shoulder, "I will just be a moment."

She turns back my direction. "Hello, Ava. You must be studying hard."

"Yes." Of course she has no idea my mind isn't on what my textbooks cover.

"I'm sorry to bother you at such a busy time of year, but I

wondered if you could join me in my office. There's something important I need to show you."

"Oh. Okay." In an instant, my nerves kick into overdrive.

What could she want to talk about? I follow her out of the lounge and cringe when Jace falls into step beside us. Is he in on this meeting too? He still has that unsettling "I know something" look on his face, and I find myself edging away from him. Not one of us says a word as we walk, and I can't decide if this is preferable or ominous.

"Have a seat," Selene says as we step inside her office. I sit across from her chair in my usual spot, while she and Jace seat themselves opposite me. This feels bad. Could this be where everything crashes down?

Instead of launching into accusations and beratement, however, Selene picks up a viewdrop from her desk, her face solemn. "You might find this disturbing, but I think you need to see it."

She clicks a button, and the projection coming into view shows a young woman, face gaunt, hair matted. Her eyes look hollow and haunted.

A voice off-image asks, "I know it's difficult, but please relay what happened. Be as accurate as you can."

The woman takes a shuddering breath. "I first met the Mentalist when I was training to be a Benefactor. I was young. No family in the area. He was charming, but I wasn't looking for a relationship then. He learned what time I finished with my training each day and would come to talk with me. And then one day . . ." She pauses and inhales, then continues in a strained voice, "I guess he just decided I was useful."

"What did he do?"

"He put me under his control. We started dating, so he could get information out of me without anyone questioning our closeness. It wasn't what I wanted, but I had no choice."

She stops and covers her face with her hands, sobbing. "Everyone I cared about became a target."

Horrified, I stare at the poor woman on the screen, imagining her plight. She lived her whole life chained to someone she didn't love. A prisoner in her own body. What was it like for her when she finally awoke?

The interviewer continues. "How long were you under his control?"

"Twelve years," the victim gulps. "He made me gather intel for him. Made me help him find my colleagues' weaknesses." Her voice becomes shrill, her eyes crazed. "I didn't want to hurt anyone!"

"Please, Selene. I think I've seen enough." I block out the frantic torrent of the victim's words, a chill breathing down my neck.

Selene blanks the image, her face bleak. "I need to be certain you really understand what we're up against," Selene says to me. "We may be headed for all-out war again. Are you ready for that?"

I swallow, remembering Blake's parents and the electrical wires. Would I do something like that if it came down to it? Could I kill a Mentalist? "All I've ever wanted is to help the people of Magus," I give the most honest answer I can.

She seems to find this answer satisfactory and slides a paper in front of me:

> *Height_____*
> *Weight_____*
> *Waist_____*
> *Pants length_____*
> *Sleeve length_____*

Confused, I look up. "What's this?"

"The required measurements for ordering your training uniform."

My training uniform. "Already? But I haven't graduated yet." I should feel more excited about this. At the very least, what I just saw should be motivating in protecting the people of Magus. "There's no guarantee—"

"I have complete confidence in you, and I believe this is a good morale boost for the rest of the student population. As top student and a soon-to-be Benefactor, many of the students look up to you. It would be good for them to see you advancing. But I need to know you're still fully committed."

This is all I have wanted for as long as I've been at Prism. So why does it feel like it's being forced on me now? It's happening too fast.

As I stare in silence at the paper in front of me, Selene continues, "When you go to work every day with a Mentalist on the streets, you have to be prepared. That woman on the video was just a taste of the depraved crimes a Mentalist will commit."

"But that was just an example of one criminal," I say carefully. "I'm sure there are recordings of horrible things Augmentors and Shapers have done, too."

Selene leans forward. "Yes, of course. But Mentalists are a whole different challenge. I showed you this because I sometimes wonder if you really understand. They're not good people, Ava. They have frightening abilities, and they delight in using them. Even I had my emotions manipulated once."

This startles me. "Really?"

Jace, who has been silent this whole time, chimes in, "Are you confident you would recognize if you yourself were ensnared?"

My heart seizes. Elm would never do that to me, would he? But if Yellow magic even fooled Selene once, then I'm certainly not invulnerable. Selene knows so much, and she even grew up in a world with exposure to Yellow magic and a familiarity with its capabilities. How could I, someone who is just beginning to scratch the surface, be less susceptible to deception than Selene?

Haven't I been getting little hints all along? Little telltale signs of manipulation?

No, I'm being stupid. If Elm just wanted to use me, why would he go out of his way for me all the time? He wouldn't betray me like that. Unless this was all part of a scheme to earn my trust and devotion. After all, he has been awfully charming.

How can I know for sure? How can I ever truly know? My heart wants to justify every action and begs me to believe he is being honest, but my intellect keeps flashing warning lights and asking questions. I want more than anything to trust him, but I wonder if I will ever fully be able to, knowing what he is capable of doing. The thought is intrusive, but I can't brush it off.

Selene's voice interrupts my thoughts. "Bring me that form when you can, Ava. I hope you'll make the right choice."

As I leave Selene's office, a vital desire to see Elm overwhelms me. I need reassurance. Something to tell me I can believe him and to convince me I haven't been another silly teenager who let her guard down because of a boy. Or, my heart sinks, something to convince me I have been wrong to trust him all along, and Elm really did catch me in snares of deception. If I can't make decisions for myself, perhaps inevitabilities will decide for me.

Elm raises his eyebrows at me as I stumble into the cave.

"Miss Ava. Why aren't you in class?"

"I skipped," I say tersely.

He gives me a disapproving look. "So close to the end of the year?"

"I'll be fine. I just needed to see you."

He looks as though he wants to say something more, but instead he shrugs. "I suppose I can't turn down extra time with the curious kitten. But I do worry about you jeopardizing your chances at becoming a Benefactor . . . if that's still what you want."

Yes, he would like that, wouldn't he? To have a Benefactor in his pocket. He hates them, so why else wouldn't he try to steer me away if not for his own purposes? "I said I'll be fine."

His brow furrows as he studies me. "You seem to be suffering a lot of stress. I could show you something to help with that if you'd like."

And what could he want to show me? Another trick? Another enticement? "What is it?" I ask warily.

"Well, you asked me a while ago how I power all of the illusions in the cave. I don't suppose you'd want to see that?"

Curiosity wins out over the suspicion biting at me—I do want to know how he does it. And I'm being unfair to him . . . aren't I? "Well, okay."

We go farther back into the cave than we have previously gone. The air feels heavy and damp here, and it's darker. My steps slow. Why is it that once a seed of mistrust is planted, everything seems dubious? Why am I worried he may be dragging me away to some trap when just this morning I would have followed without question? Elm conjures a ball of light with his cane, and I blink at its brightness. Whatever I'm feeling now, his illusion of light never ceases to amaze me.

He stops and I bump into him.

"So very pushy," he teases. "But I hope the spectacle improves your mood."

My eyes follow the ball of light as it moves to the center of a cavernous room. The walls sparkle in a cascade of vivid color. Purple, red, blue, green, orange. And yellow. Especially yellow.

"What is it?" I ask. I can't help but be awed by the sight.

"Fluorite," he replies. "In just about any color you could imagine. But the cave is partial to yellow, as I'm sure you've noticed."

"So that's where you got all those stones on your cane. I'm surprised you don't carry more."

He makes a face. "Tried it. Last time I about collapsed the cave on myself. I don't really have the knowledge or the resources, but I managed to chip a few pieces out."

As he says this, I notice a large pile of fallen boulders and guess that must have been where he had tried to extract the fluorite.

"But as long as I'm here," he says, "I have plenty of power."

Now I understand why Elm prefers it in the cave. It may be the only place where he truly feels strong.

Power to control, says a little voice in my mind.

"Do you mind if I try some of the red fluorite out?" I ask, shaking away my unease. After all, he has power here, but so do I. This much energy at my fingertips is too much of a temptation to resist.

"By all means."

A strengthening spell decidedly isn't a good idea in such a delicate place. Instead, I focus on agility. The second I close my eyes, heat surges through me. The force hits like a tidal wave, and the intensity of the power is almost painful until my body adjusts. As it courses through me, it's as though I can take on anything and everything. I open my eyes, alive with energy, a smile bursting on my face.

"The feeling is a bit addicting, isn't it?" Elm's eyes twinkle.

"It's unreal. I've never felt anything like it."

"Are you going to try it out?"

"Maybe." I snatch his cane out of his hands.

His eyes widen in surprise, but he laughs. "Oh, now that wasn't sporting. I wasn't quite prepared."

I toss the cane back to him and flash to the other side of the room in less than a second. "Well then, prepare yourself."

He smiles and grasps his cane tightly, holding eye contact with me. "Okay. Go at it, Miss—"

Before he can finish, I take his cane again and return to my original starting point.

"Very impressive, Miss Ava." He nods.

We repeat this two more times, and my confidence billows. "Ready to give up yet?"

"Let's try one more time." His eyes glimmer with mischief.

We stand on opposite sides of the cave room once more. I plunge for the cane, but instead of being able to grasp the hilt, I fall right through it and land on the floor.

"Huh?" I get to my feet and look around. Elm waves at me from the other end of the room. I zoom toward him, hoping to catch him before he can react. Once again, I go right through him. I chase phantom after phantom around the room, until I suddenly look up and see multiple Elms all around me.

"Not fair," I protest. "How am I supposed to know which one is really you?"

The Elms laugh simultaneously and wave their canes. Suddenly I feel arms around my waist.

"Gotcha," he whispers, pulling me close to him. The other Elms vanish, leaving us alone in the shimmering room.

"Sneaky," I breathe, my heart racing with a mix of emotions. I can't believe he got me to let my guard down. Again. "I think that was breaking the rules."

"Oh? You used your talents, I used mine. I'd say it was fair."

"Yes . . ." How often has he used his talents on me, I wonder? I slip out of his grasp. "Elm, can I ask you about something?"

"Of course. Anything."

"Before we met in the copy room at Prism, I kept dreaming about you. Did that have something to do with you and your magic?"

He looks uncomfortable by the question. "Ah, yes, that."

"So, yes?" That means he used his power on me at least one other time. Am I imagining the guilt on his face?

"Yellows have the power to enter other people's dreams. Highly accomplished Mentalists can make sure nobody dreams about us unless we're entering a dream. It's all part of the mind-aspect of our magic."

Slowly, wheels click in place. I want to smother the dawning realization down, back into the deep midnight of my consciousness, but I force myself to keep it on the surface for once. "Do you . . . do that often?"

"I don't like to, no. When we're in another person's dream, it's their world, their rules. Anything that happens to us in a dream happens to us for real. It can be dangerous, and it can leave us vulnerable to that person. I only use it as a means to an end." He gives a slight shrug. "But that's unimportant. Would you like to choose another book today?"

I look him straight in the face, ignoring his attempt to distract me.

"Is that what I was? A 'means to an end'?"

He looks genuinely startled. "Of course not, Miss Ava. What are you talking about?"

My fists clench. "This was all one of your games, wasn't it? And I played right into it like a fool."

"Miss Ava, I don't understand you." He tries to take my hand, but I jerk it away.

"Don't you 'Miss Ava' me! You know exactly what I'm talking about." Now hot, angry tears pool in my eyes. "I dreamed about you. Before we met. Over and over!" I throw my hands around in frustration. "And you got inside my head! Why would you do that?" From the beginning, he targeted me, slipping inside my dreams to get my interest. And I took the bait.

"Miss Ava, I swear that I have never lied to you. Manipulating you was never my intent."

I give a harsh laugh. "Oh, it's exactly what the Benefactors warned us about all these years. Yellows controlling people's feelings and their minds. And I fell for it. What was I to you? Your pawn to get closer to the Benefactors?"

"Miss Ava, please. I need you to listen to me." His voice takes on the calm, persuasive tone I have heard so many times before. I can't allow him to coerce me again. I know that if I give him the chance, I'm liable to fall once more under his spell. I need to get away, and fast.

He comes up to me, and I shove him roughly away. "I'm done listening to you. Goodbye, Elm."

I spin away from him and take off at a run. As I flee toward the cave entrance, he calls after me, "Wait! Wait! AVA!"

I halt for the smallest moment. It is the first time I have ever heard him say just *Ava*. I listen to his shout die on the cave walls. No. I can't let him see an ounce of hesitation. If I do, he'll use it against me. Without looking back at him, I continue to run. I run into the yellow sunlight, which suddenly burns searing and ruthless. I run from the illusions that I fell so deeply into. I run from all the good memories that we shared, knowing that they bloomed out of deceit.

Frantically, almost desperately, I cast an agility spell, so I can get away from him that much faster. I hardly notice when the trees thin. I reach the end of the forest, and soon I'm back at Prism's gate, rasping for air. As I fling open the doors of the school, I don't even care that people are in my path. I simply keep running, pushing whomever out of the way, and I don't stop until I'm back in my room.

Let them try to figure out what mysterious, invisible force knocked them down.

Breathless and sobbing, I struggle out of the dress, hardly caring whether it's damaged or not in the process. I want to be rid of it forever. I rip the locket off my neck the instant it appears and shove it into the back of one of my drawers. I collapse onto the bed and muffle my cries with my pillow.

Stupid, stupid, stupid! Some Elite student I am. I didn't even know I was being controlled. Why didn't I ever make the dream connection before? Hadn't the suspicions and warnings been lingering in the back of my mind the whole time? But I chose to ignore them, because the illusions were so much more tantalizing than reality. Now—because of my ignorance—Magus is likely much closer to falling victim to Elm's desires. Just one small step closer to mind control of the entire population. But that isn't what bothers me the most.

My chest feels tight and pained as I think about these past few months with Elm. It doesn't matter if the feelings I had were the product of illusions; the pain is undeniably real. And what does it mean for Mentalists as a whole? I really don't want to believe there could be an entire class of magic-users who were innately bad. If there was just one good Mentalist, there was hope for others, but Selene was right.

I lift my hot, tear-stained face from my pillow and force myself up, taking several deep breaths to regain my composure. This is no time for me to give way to self-pity. The more time I waste crying, the more danger we are in. I know now what I have to do.

I tap softly on Selene's door, and she opens it and stares at me. I'm sure my hair is a tangled mess from running through the forest, and my eyes are probably still red and swollen.

"My dear child, what has happened to you?"

"I've been tricked," I say numbly. "By Elm."

She gives a quick look around the hallway to make sure we're alone and then puts her arm around me, steering me into her office. "You'd better come in."

I give a weak nod and follow her. She directs me into the chair across from her desk and seats herself somberly opposite me.

She places her fingertips together. "Well, I suspected that this might have been the case. You haven't been yourself. Tell me what's going on."

Her voice is warmer than I expect, and the almost unbearable kindness in the face of my treachery breaks me down. Tearfully, I recount the story to her, telling her about the dreams, about meeting Elm, day after day, in the forest. I leave out the part about helping him with the library, though I suspect she'll deduce that on her own. She nods and listens to my story without interrupting, sympathy and concern in her eyes.

"I believed he was a good person," I say bitterly. "I'm not sure what came over me."

"Mind control is a powerful thing, particularly when the heart gets tangled into the equation," Selene says gravely. "I'm sure this was all his doing and had little to do with you. You're lucky you were strong enough to recognize it before it was too late."

"I'm so sorry, Selene. I'm so ashamed." A fresh reservoir of tears opens.

"Don't worry about that. People with more experience than you have been tricked by the likes of him. The question now is what will we do about it?"

"Am I being kicked out?"

She smiles at me. "Of course not. You're not to blame for this. It could have happened to anyone. Even me."

The relief nearly crushes me. I don't know how I could have kept information from Selene all of this time. Hasn't she always looked out for me? I glance at her, hope in my heart. "So then, I could still become a Benefactor?"

"Absolutely. As far as I'm concerned, nothing has changed. The fact that you are back here, telling me all this, just proves your strength. And your association with Elm may even be useful to us. You have a unique insight into his dealings." She looks at me intently. "Now, can you tell me where he is?"

"I . . ." I know I should tell her. After all this time helping him, I should at least divulge his whereabouts. But I can't make myself do it. Shame floods through me, but my heart is too weak. I'm not ready to expose him yet. "I'm sorry. I don't know."

Selene leans forward, uncomfortably close. "Surely you've gone somewhere with him all this time?"

"Yes, I guess I must have. But I don't . . . remember. I could never remember where I had been once I got back to the school." After everything, I'm still lying for him. My heart aches, and I hate myself for it.

I know I can never go into that forest again. I should stay in the safety of the school, where he is out of my reach, and I'm out of his. I'm sure he won't try to approach me here, especially with the Benefactors on high alert. But as long as I'm not seeking him out, the Benefactors' protection spell should keep me safe anyway. Then a thought strikes me: he has another way to get to me.

"Selene," I implore. "I don't want him to use me again. At all. Is there anything I can do, a spell or something that can keep him out of my dreams?"

She considers me for a moment. "Well, there is one thing you can do. But I'm not sure if you'll like it."

"Please, Selene," I am desperate. I can't bear the thought of having him in my dreams again.

She stands and goes to a cabinet on the other end of the room. She opens it and pulls out a tennis-ball sized orb made out of translucent white stone.

I gaze at it. "What is that?"

"I'm sure you recall learning that magic requires other magic to act?"

"Yes." I nod. "Magic can't be used on non-magical people." Suddenly, it dawns on me what she's getting at. "Are you saying the only way to keep him out of my head is to lose my powers?"

"Not permanently," she points out quickly. "It can be reversed at any time. And you won't feel any different."

What? No. I'm so dependent on my magic. It is so much of who we are on Magus. How can I give it away?

"I think it's for the best," Selene says decisively. "Not just for you, but for all of Magus. I know it's not your fault, but we don't know exactly what has been compromised or how big of a hold he has on you. Keeping him out of your mind would be wise, and this is the only sure way to do it. And," she adds, concern in her eyes and tone softened, "I want to make sure you're safe, Ava. You have been through a sordid ordeal."

My heart drops. She's right. If Elm controlled me once, who's to say he can't and won't do it again? After all the harm I've let in, this is the least I can do. Perhaps it can repair the damage in some small way.

"Okay," I hear myself saying. "Tell me what I have to do."

Selene nods in approval and hands the orb to me. "Concentrate on this as though you are healing it. Keep going until you are completely unable to do so."

I place my hands on the orb and focus. Warmth spreads from my body, down my arms and onto its surface, but my insides feel cold with terror. The orb lights up, bright and red. I shiver, feeling more chilled as my powers leave me. I keep going until the last of the heat fades from my body. Any lights left inside me have been turned off.

"I should hold onto that," Selene says, taking the orb gently from me.

A tremor of panic ripples through me. "Can't I keep it?"

Selene rests her hand on my shoulder. "Don't worry, Ava. I will take good care of it. I understand why it would make you nervous, but I think it's better if you leave it to me. The last thing we want is for it to fall into the wrong hands."

"Oh. Okay," I reply hesitantly. I suppose she is right, but I feel so insubstantial, like I'm made of tissue paper. She holds my very essence in her hands.

Her smile is kind. "I know this is a sacrifice for you—trust me, I do. But you're doing the right thing."

Another thought occurs to me. "What about school? I can't finish out the year if I can't use my powers." My voice is frenzied. After losing Elm and my magic, school is, once again, all I have.

"Don't worry about that. I will speak with all your teachers. Your goal is to be a Benefactor anyway, isn't it? You're skilled enough that I think we can safely advance you." She pauses. "We'll wait a few weeks to let you get your head together after this awful experience. Then we can restore your magic and begin your training."

"Thank you, Selene." I'm not sure if I'm relieved or disappointed. I won't get to finish my schooling formally, but at the same time, I get to begin Benefactor training. It's what I always wanted, isn't it?

Selene's face grows more serious. "I'm sure this doesn't need saying, but I'd like you to stay on school grounds for the time being. Elm is likely still targeting you, and you would be defenseless against him."

I wonder what I would need to defend against without my powers. He won't be able to use his mind abilities on me. But

I suppose if he wanted to harm me, that wouldn't stop him. People were hurting each other long before magic came into the picture.

"And once your mind is cleared," she continues, "I would like to ask you some questions about Elm. Maybe once you are free from his influence, you'll be able to assist us with information?"

I nod, not trusting my voice. I still feel so defensive of him. Maybe it really is just lingering effects of his power, and in a few days, I'll be fine.

"Lastly, I think it might be best if you keep to yourself as much as possible. We don't want the other students knowing about this. If Elm gets into another student's mind, it's better if he can't get any additional information or set them against you while knowing you are powerless. The fewer who know about it, the better. Understand?"

"Yes." Well, being alone won't be a problem. I have lost Elm and alienated Blake. I don't have anyone else.

I return to my room, unsure of what to do with myself now that the responsibility of school is off my shoulders. The last thing I want to do is think about Elm. The wound is far too fresh.

Curious of whether my powers are really gone, I try to cast a strengthening spell. Nothing happens. I feel empty in so many ways, like some unseen force stripped me of everything I valued. Except being a Benefactor, I suppose. I still have that road in front of me. But somehow, it feels hollow and meaningless.

Flinging myself across my bed, I stare at the ceiling, trying to empty my head of any and all thought.

I'm in a field of sunflowers. Beautiful, bright sunflowers. Elm is there, smiling. He reaches out to me, but I don't go to him. I can't. I know it's a trap. His smile fades, and his hand falls limply to his side. His eyes fill with pain . . .

I blink open my eyes, full of fresh tears. Even now, I can't escape him. I know it all came from my own mind, but the effect is the same.

I'm not sure how long I sleep, but the light from the window fades. I get up stiffly and decide to take a walk around the school. Anything to keep busy.

After a few moments of walking, my eyes inexplicably start to water again. Darn it. This is going to be a struggle. All along he has been scheming to overthrow the Benefactors, and I have been his happy little pawn in the process. Well, once this haze of his power leaves me, I'll do whatever I need to do to make sure he doesn't use anyone ever again.

19

ADJUSTING TO LIFE WITHOUT MY POWERS
is even harder than I expected. I'm used to healing myself
at the slightest scratch or bruise. Now I can't. I'm exposed.
Delicate. I know if I get hurt or sick, I won't be able to go to a
Healer. I will have to let my body heal itself. How did people
manage to live this way before having magic?

Aside from feeling so breakable on the outside, my mental
state is perilously close to shattering. I can't think straight
anymore. I remember things that didn't really happen . . . or
did they?

Although Selene told me I wouldn't feel any different after
she removed my powers, I do. I'm sure these strange scenes
that surface can't be my own, yet somehow, they come to
me more clearly than the memories I clung to my whole life.
Memories of my childhood, my parents. And yellow. There is
so much yellow. It pollutes my mind.

In my thoughts, I see flashes of my parents with yellow
pendants, but I know this isn't possible, since they were
Augmentors. My childhood home appears with a door painted
the color of a canary rather than the farmhouse red I once
knew. I think I'm going mad. I fear that Elm has damaged my
mind permanently.

Not being able to attend my classes anymore doesn't help.

Most of my time is spent alone, and without distractions or company, there is nothing to keep the strange, yet newly familiar, mental invasions away.

I find myself wandering outside on Prism's grounds often. Being inside feels claustrophobic, but being outside, I struggle with the desire to fling the gates open and run.

I ramble through Prism's flower garden for the third time today. Under better circumstances, the colorful blossoms would cheer me, but now I am catching occasional whiffs of floral perfume on the breeze, which send me into painful reminiscences of the sunflower field with Elm. I don't know why I torture myself by staying here and recalling things that would be easier to forget if I were elsewhere.

"Ouch!" I cry out and jump back as a thorn from a rose bush slashes into my arm, leaving a long trail of crimson. The harsh red line stands out dramatically against my skin, and now I worry that other students will notice. Surely someone will observe the scratch and wonder why I haven't healed myself by now. My uniform jacket was carelessly slung over my shoulder, and now I hastily grab it and tug it on over my shirt.

My arm stings, and I find myself overwhelmed. The scratch is such a small thing, but I'm emotionally drained, physically and mentally exhausted from days with little sleep, and utterly powerless. I move out of reach of the rose bushes and sink down on the grass, my back against Prism's wrought iron fence, closing my eyes tight to the world.

"Ava?"

Blake. I choke back a lump in my throat. His tone is genuinely kind. I treated him so badly after the stay with his parents, even though they were all just trying to protect Magus. To protect me.

"Do you mind if I sit down? I was taking a break between classes and saw you here."

"Sure," I say, listlessly.

He sits beside me. "It's getting hot. I can't believe you're still wearing your jacket."

In a quick moment of panic, I tug down on my jacket sleeve, hoping no trace of the scratch is visible. "It doesn't bother me," I lie.

He looks me over, and his brow puckers slightly. "You don't look well lately, and I haven't seen you in class. Are you okay?"

Of course he would notice I haven't been there. This shouldn't surprise me at all. I look at him, trying to think of some fabrication or excuse to explain my absence. But I'm just so tired. I'm tired of lying and coming up with reasons to explain myself. "I . . . I don't know."

He is still for a moment, then takes my hand. To support me, to let me know I'm not alone. I might have rejected this gesture just a week ago, but now it's comforting. All I want is to cling to any comfort.

I wonder what it would have been like if I were more open to Blake when he first started talking to me. I probably wouldn't feel so miserable now. My life would have been more ordinary, but it probably would have been happy. We could have been good friends. Or more.

I would still be on track to graduate, and perhaps we would have begun Benefactor training together. Blake is a nice person. If I had given him a chance, my choices might never have entangled me with Elm. Now, even just thinking of Elm sends a surge of pain through me, as though the rosebush's thorny branches somehow worked their way into my heart.

"Do you want to talk about it?" he asks.

I want to talk about it desperately, but I can't. Even if I hadn't promised Selene, knowing Blake, he would go rushing off himself to find Elm if I told him the truth. But maybe I can find a way to talk without revealing anything.

I'm barely holding myself together and can only respond,

"Do you ever feel like you don't know anything anymore? Like your world is falling apart?"

He frowns. "Not really. Well, not all at once, anyway. I have had times where it's like little pieces of my world are falling apart, I guess." He looks at me. "Why? Do you feel that way? Do you need help?"

"I can't finish school." The words tumble out. I don't see the harm in telling Blake this. "But please don't tell anyone. I'm devastated about it."

"I won't tell. What happened?"

"I fell behind. Too far behind to finish out the year."

He cocks his head, processing this. "So, what, you have to repeat the year or something?"

"Maybe," I say. "The details haven't been worked out."

"Well," he says carefully, "it'll work out somehow. You've always been a great student. I'm sure they aren't going to just let you go that easily."

Another puzzling memory comes suddenly to mind: My father, again wearing that yellow pendant, saying, *We're going to have to be extra careful now. Selene isn't going to let her go that easily.*

I shake back to the present and find Blake staring at me with apprehension. I return his look uneasily, teetering on the edge of a meltdown.

"Hey, I'm serious. You don't look well. Maybe you're sick."

"Maybe," I say, my eyes watering with tears. Sick or crazy.

He gets to his feet and grabs my arm, pulling me up. I let him, too fatigued to fight it.

"I'm taking you to Dr. Iris," he says. "I'm sure she can help you."

No, she can't. But I can't possibly tell Blake that. My insides sink as I realize I'll have to find some way to explain myself to Dr. Iris now.

The instant Dr. Iris sees me, with my pale face and

shadowed eyes, she quickly ushers me into her office. "I'll take it from here, Blake. Thank you."

Blake looks hesitant to leave but finally nods. "I hope you feel better, Ava. Let's talk soon."

As soon as he is gone, I avoid looking at Dr. Iris, unsure of how to begin.

She closes the office door and says gently, "Selene already informed me of your situation. All of it. You don't need to worry."

"She did?" I look at her now, overwhelmed with relief. "Who else knows?"

"I'm not quite sure. She didn't say. But I think she realized I'd probably find out at some point."

I break down into full-on sobs, grateful to have someone I don't have to hide from. The only other person I'm aware of who knows is Selene, and I'm too afraid to show her how difficult this is. Dr. Iris steers me to the exam table and forces me to have a seat. She sits next to me and puts a comforting hand on my back, letting me cry as long as I need to.

"You're having a rough time," she says, once my tears slow.

I nod, not quite trusting my voice yet.

"It's a lot to take on all at once," she says compassionately.

"I'm afraid I'm going to give myself away," I say, pushing up my sleeve. "Things like this happen, and I can't fix it."

She examines my arm thoughtfully, then walks to the clean-white medical-supply cupboard. She pulls out some cotton balls and a bottle of clear liquid and then returns to me.

"This will sting a little," she says, preparing the cotton ball. I feel coolness on my arm when she presses it to my wound, followed by a quick, prickling sting. She dabs away at the scratch, wiping up the dried blood. Even though it hurts a little, there is comfort in the gesture. It feels nice to have someone take care of me.

"My sister used to do this, before I got good at healing.

She's a Shaper. She used to tell me that anything I could do she could do some other way." She smiles at me, and I smile lightly back.

"Will it heal the scratch?" I ask. I'm unfamiliar with how non-magic healing works.

"No, but it will keep it from getting worse. Until it heals itself, you may want to cover it with a little makeup, so it's not so conspicuous."

"I'll do that," I say. "I'll do whatever you think will help. Whatever avoids causing any more trouble."

She studies me. "You need something to keep yourself busy," she observes in her wise way. "A distraction."

I release a heavy sigh. "I can't go to class, and I'm afraid to do much without my powers."

She throws away the cotton ball and returns the bottle of liquid to the cupboard. "Try writing. I find it therapeutic, personally. You might try writing down happy moments."

I can't think of any happy moments that I would want to write about. All my happiest moments have been spoiled.

Dr. Iris must guess what I'm thinking because she says, "It doesn't have to be anything recent. It could be from your past. You like the color-initiation ceremonies, right? Maybe write about yours."

"Okay." I force myself to sound more cheerful. "Maybe I'll try that."

The way I stare at the blank notebook on my desk in front of me, you would think it held all the mysteries of life. But in reality, I'm just struggling to get started. I want to follow Dr.

Iris's suggestion, but I'm afraid thinking too hard will drag my mind to dark places.

"Okay, my color-initiation ceremony," I say aloud. I twirl my pen between my fingers and close my eyes to remember that day.

I was five. I was—

A floodgate opens, and all at once vivid images come rushing in, too swiftly for me to suppress them.

I am five, and I'm at my color-initiation ceremony. The room feels so big. Selene is here with two other Benefactors I don't recognize. And . . . Jace? My parents are also here, yellow pendants displayed around both of their necks. The Benefactors watch them closely, almost as though guarding them, though I can't understand why.

"We should begin now," Selene says, motioning me to step up to the pedestals.

I look nervously back and forth between the unlit blue and red cubes in the center of the room. With a start, I realize I'm wringing the bottom of my white dress in my hands, and I let go at once so I don't ruin it. I twist my hair instead, unable to relax.

My mother gives me an encouraging smile. "It's okay, Ava. There is no wrong color. You don't have to be afraid."

"Just concentrate, and it will happen naturally," my father encourages.

I close my eyes and focus all my energy on the cubes. I imagine warmth flowing from me, illuminating them. I jump as a tiny spark of power shoots through my head, but I keep my eyes shut tight. I don't want to make a mistake. Behind my eyelids, I see a flash of light, and I hear gasps around the room.

I pop my eyes open, and I can instantly see a problem: The red cube is shining brightly, but it is not red. It's orange. It's not supposed to be orange.

"Did I do something wrong?" I ask in a shaky voice.

"What does it mean?" my mother asks, stepping forward to calm me.

Selene approaches the cube for a closer look, as Jace and the other Benefactors whisper amongst themselves. "I haven't personally seen this happen before, but I've heard of it. It means she could be equally skilled at either Red or Yellow, with the proper training. Dual-magic use is a rare gift."

My parents look at each other and then back at Selene.

"Bright no longer teaches Yellow magic. Where is she supposed to get this 'proper training'?" Dad sounds the way he does at home when he's trying not to get mad at me for something.

My insides tighten with worry.

Selene seems to choose her words carefully. "You're correct, Yellow magic is banned at Bright, and the ban has extended to Prism, of course. The way things are going, I don't think it will be long before the practice of Yellow magic is forbidden to all of Magus. I would strongly advise you to choose Red, in the interest of Ava reaching her full potential."

My father's eyes darken, and he puts his hands on my shoulders protectively. "Perhaps your institutions aren't the place for us any longer, and we should let our daughter 'reach her potential' elsewhere. There are other schools or even private study."

Selene's face turns cold, but her voice remains controlled. "We would love to have Ava at Bright, and of course, Prism, in the future. I could teach her personally. I believe she could do great things."

My father is already steering me toward the door, and I look back at the glowing orange cube, wishing I could fix it. If I could just make it turn red, nobody would be fighting.

My mother looks uncomfortable as my father makes his exit with me. "I'm so sorry. We'll think about it."

As we travel back to our home in the hover cart, my parents

argue. I wish I could block them out, but their voices seem ten-times louder than normal to my small ears.

"We'll have to be extra careful now. Selene isn't going to let her go that easily," my father says. "I knew we shouldn't have taken her there at all."

My mother sighs. "So this is my fault? You know I just want the best for her. Prism is still the top-ranked school, and she has a much better chance of getting there if she starts at Bright."

"Yes, the best school if you practice Red or Blue."

"If she can do well with Red magic, then why don't we just let her? It will make her life so much easier." My mother's voice sounds tight and anxious.

"Because it's not who she is, Vivian!" my father says angrily. "If a yellow cube had been in the room, would that red cube have lit up at all? Doesn't she deserve a choice?"

"I don't want her to go through what we go through. People are afraid of Mentalists, and it's getting worse every day. I can't even walk down the street without getting looks. I feel like I have to hide anything that's yellow before I go out in public, especially since raids on Yellow homes are getting more common. Don't you think she would be safer if—"

"If she hides behind the more acceptable color? This is wrong. Can't you see that? Mentalists are no more evil than Reds or Blues. We've been demonized. Are we just going to accept it? Are we just going to let the Benefactors win?"

My mother sounds close to tears. "This isn't about winning or losing. It's about our daughter's safety. Her life." She pauses, then adds, "I want her to have as many opportunities available to her as possible. If she becomes a dual-magic Benefactor, she could unite us again."

"Or she'll be brainwashed by Selene and renounce Yellow magic altogether," my father snaps.

Oh no. This is awful. They fight so rarely, but now they're

yelling, and it's my fault. I start to wail loudly, a torrent of tears breaking free. They turn to look at me in alarm. I think they forgot I was there.

"Lucas," my mother whispers sharply, "we'll talk about this later."

The remainder of the ride home is silent but for the hum of the cart and my occasional sniffles.

That night my mother tucks me into bed, and I fall into an uneasy sleep. I awake to shouts and thuds in the next room. I listen, petrified, to the commotion. Soon I hear familiar voices, but they sound very afraid.

"What do you think you're doing?" my father shouts.

"Stop!" screams my mother. "Please! Stop!"

My parents are in trouble. I don't know what else to do, so I run to their room as fast as I can.

A cluster of Benefactors are here. Why? Several of them hold tight onto my parents and remove the pendants from their necks. Selene is also here.

"Do it quickly," she directs, turning to look out the window. "Before they can use their tricks."

Suddenly, my parents glow with red light. They scream. Agonizing screams of pain. I scream with them as I watch their bodies torn apart by Red magic. Then my parent's tortured voices are silent. Gone forever.

My own screams stop in my throat. I want to run, to escape these demons who pretend to be human. But I am frozen. No one has yet noticed I'm here. My previous shrieks must have been drowned out by my parents' cries.

"That was a little excessive, don't you think?" Selene says, her voice cold. She refuses to look in the direction of my parents' bodies. Mercifully, the crowd in the room prevents me from seeing them.

A Benefactor responds, "That was the fastest way."

"Well, we need to secure the child, and then we need a

team to dispose of the remains. Burning the house is probably best." Selene says callously as she turns, and then she sees me.

I stare at her with horrified eyes, and I'm sure she knows that I saw everything. She takes a step and reaches out to me. No! I can't let her take me. She's a bad person. A monster. I want to run, but in my attempt, I fall down, overcome by shock and terror. My legs won't work. I wail and tremble on the floor. Everyone in the room stares at me, waiting for orders.

"Jace," Selene commands. "Do something for the girl. Quickly."

Jace steps forward and grasps my arm. I feel sudden warmth, and my terror slips out of my body. I'm calm. At peace. The memory of my parents' slaughter fades . . .

I'm not sure how long these wracking sobs have been tearing through my body. It feels like hours. I clutch my head, gasping and willing these horrid images to leave my brain. It's not real. It can't be real!

But even as I try so desperately to deny it, the truth mercilessly seeps its way in. I thought deception only molded me the last few months, but it's so much worse than that. Nearly my entire life rests on fabrications. Nothing more than false memories and ideas planted into my head to mask the atrocious truth. This whole time my life has been in the blood-stained hands of the very one who demanded my parents' execution.

There is new clarity. That's why I can never get answers to my questions about Yellow magic—the Benefactors control everyone, inventing a new history and ensuring nobody remembers. The only reason I have been able to think about it at all is likely because I have some sort of resistance due to my Yellow magic abilities. The Benefactors were able to create the barrier around Magus using Jace's help, since they required all three types of magic.

I continue to tremble as I try to process the betrayal and

the lies. Selene, the person I have trusted for so many years, is responsible for the eradication of an innocent people. Responsible for the murder of my parents. I rush into my bathroom and retch.

I splash cold water on my face again and again, as though doing so could wash away everything I now know. I grip the ceramic sides of the sink in an effort to steady myself.

Another realization deepens in me. I'm a dual magic-user. No wonder Selene wanted me so badly. She hoped I could add power to the Augmentors while at the same time using my Yellow abilities to control the population. But she wanted me securely in her pocket before daring to develop my Yellow magic.

Now that I know this, I have no idea what I should do. I don't know how many others are in on it, so I can't trust anyone within these walls. I'm absolutely sure I can't trust the Benefactors. But I'm also certain they don't realize I have any clue about my past. The Benefactors knew that Elm couldn't use new tricks on me if I was powerless, but they hadn't counted on their own manipulations ceasing to work. All this time, they have been doing the very things they accuse Elm of.

Elm.

Time stops for an instant and then moves doubly fast. Adrenaline gives me a renewed surge of energy, bringing me back to life.

I need to go to him. I need to find him and apologize for this horrible mistake. Will he ever forgive me? After all the times he looked out for me and all the kindness he has shown me, how could I have so easily believed he was using me? I chose a lifetime of lies over possibly the one person who has most likely been telling me the truth. But something dawns on me. This whole time I have wondered if Elm ever tried to come to me, but because I have no magic, the Benefactors' protection spell would no longer affect me. This means he hasn't been trying to come to me at all. Tears spring to my eyes. I've probably lost him forever.

I must get to him, but I don't know how. Selene instructed me to stay on school grounds, and I know she's sure to notice if I leave. If only I could be invisible . . .

Although I don't have much hope of it working, I feverishly search through my drawers and find the locket so angrily discarded there. I cling to it like it's my own beating heart instead of a silver imitation. Maybe the magic of the locket works differently from regular magic. I'm grasping at straws, but I have to try.

"Elm," I say. Nothing happens. "Elm!" I call again, hoping frantically that the dress will appear.

The locket lies cold in my hands.

Fine then. Invisible or not, I will find him. With extra caution, I work my way through the halls of the school, which seem longer and more cavernous than normal. I'm paranoid, my eyes darting wildly around, my heart jumping at every noise. I definitely took for granted how easy it was to sneak out before.

Once I'm sure nobody will see me, I bolt for the forest. I know the way to Elm's cave so well that I could probably make it there with my eyes closed. I power forward, not daring to stop for anything. What I see in the space where the sinkhole should be catches me off guard. Now that I'm immune to magic, the opening of the cave is clearly visible. I step inside and find that most of Elm's illusions have disappeared. It takes me a moment to realize it is actually bright in the cave. The round spheres of artificial sunlight still glow warmly above me. I squint at them, confused. They are real?

"Elm," I call. Then louder. "Elm, are you here?" There is no response, and my heart sinks. What if I can't find him? Or what if he feels nothing but hatred at the sight of me? I was so blind and hasty with judgment. I wouldn't blame him if he never wanted to see me again. Maybe he has disappeared to some unknown place, fearing that I would turn him in. He's so elusive, I may never find him. Or the Benefactors may find him before I do. The thought constricts my lungs. A sob catches my throat.

I wait anxiously in the cave for a few minutes, hoping he might return, smiling like he always does. But every second spent waiting feels like I'm growing closer to disaster. I have to do something more proactive, so I leave again to continue searching. I try the clearing, but he isn't there. Finally I search the riverbank where he took me on my birthday and many times after.

His boat is gone.

Gasping for breath, I follow the river, running as swiftly as my legs will take me. How I wish I could cast strength and agility spells to get me there faster! I have never felt so exhausted, but I force myself to keep going. I understand now why Elm thought it was better to go down the river. The forest here is thick and tangled, clawing through my hair and scratching my skin. I ignore the stinging and tugging of the overgrowth and push ahead.

I reach the point where the pine needles turn to soft, lush grass. And there I see him, his back toward me at the edge of the sunflower field. He is watering them. After everything, and the way I have hurt him, he still takes care of this gift to me. My heart flies to my throat.

Relieved and overwhelmed, I stop for a moment, leaning against a tree to catch my breath. He still hasn't noticed me. I approach him slowly, so as to not startle him.

Suddenly he turns, as though sensing my presence. Amazement fills his beautiful hazel eyes. Those eyes that feel like home.

"Miss . . . Ava?"

"Elm," I say, my voice choked with emotion.

He puts down the watering can and just continues to look at me, as though unsure how to react. Like a birdwatcher, afraid I might flutter away if he makes a sudden move. I decide to act for him and rush forward, throwing myself at him, unabashed.

"I'm sorry," I squeak through my tears as I hug him. "I'm so, so sorry."

After a moment of surprised hesitation, his warm arms wrap tightly around me. We don't say anything else right away. We merely cling to each other, and in a moment of clarity, I realize this is real. There are no illusions that can affect me, no intrusions in my mind. Everything I feel now is my own.

"Why did you come back, Miss Ava?" Elm finally asks, in a voice barely more than a whisper. He holds my shoulders gently and leans slightly back. As he surveys my appearance and takes in my wretched state, his grip tightens. "What have they done to you?"

"I was wrong," I say through tears. "I know everything now. About the Benefactors. About what they did to Mentalists. To . . . my parents." I steady myself. "Elm, I know about Jace."

"How?"

I take a deep breath. "Selene took my magic. No . . . that's not quite true. I gave it to her. Before I knew anything."

His eyes darken. "Your magic? But why?"

I look away, ashamed. "I didn't want you inside my head. She said that was the only way to keep you out. But after a while—"

"The effects of Jace's magic wore off," he finishes. "Apparently they didn't take that into consideration. Fools."

I look at him again, and I can see the anguish in his eyes. I betrayed him so deeply. So carelessly. "I'm sorry," I say again, knowing it will never be enough. "I'm so sorry I believed them instead of you. After everything you've done, I never should have given up on you so easily."

He's quiet a moment. "I'll admit I never expected you to reject me like that. But I suppose that's the price of secrets."

"But why did you have to keep all of this a secret from me?" I ask. "Why couldn't you just tell me from the beginning?"

He tips my chin up gently and looks me in the eyes. When he speaks, his voice is tender and warm. "Please forgive me for that indiscretion. I was unwise, and I acted selfishly." He looks briefly pained. "In the beginning, I didn't tell you because I didn't trust you. And"—shame colors his features—"I had plans that I didn't want you to muddle. But once I began to trust you, I kept secrets because I saw only two possible outcomes. One, I tell you and you don't believe me. You go back to the Benefactors, and we become enemies. I didn't favor that. And two, I tell you and you do believe me. You challenge the Benefactors and end up exiled like me . . . or worse." He smiles at me and clasps my hands tightly in his. "Either outcome would result in a world without Ava. And who, dear Ava, could ever possibly want that?"

Sniffling and overcome with emotion, I try to keep myself from sobbing, but it all comes out anyway. Ugly and unrestrained. After I have treated him so poorly, he can forgive me so readily, and this makes me feel all the more wretched. He doesn't say anything, but merely holds me, his hand resting on the back of my head until I have worked the tears out of my system.

"I'll keep no more secrets from you," Elm says when I have calmed down. "But rather than stay out in the open like this while you're visible, let's return to the cave. Once we're back there, I will tell you everything."

20

WE NESTLE CLOSE TO EACH OTHER BY the waterfall, safe in the cave. "In order to properly explain everything," Elm says. "I have to start a ways back.

"Jace was my mentor, from the time I was four years old, before I was even school age."

I gasp.

He nods and continues. "Since I already showed a strong disposition toward Yellow magic, my parents didn't feel the need to hold an initiation ceremony. Selene was interested in taking me on as a student, but at that time, the Benefactors were already spreading prejudice against Mentalists. My parents didn't want me to go to Bright or Prism. Instead, Jace took me on and became my private tutor.

"We became more secluded over the years as the hatred for Mentalists grew. Rumors spread. There were Mentalists who committed crimes, of course, just as there were Augmentors and Shapers who committed crimes. But crimes committed by Yellows were highly publicized in order to perpetuate the idea that we were dangerous. It didn't take long for that idea to root itself into the mind of the public.

"At the time, there were groups of Mentalists who would meet and discuss the possibility of using our powers to change the people's way of thinking, so we could be at peace again.

While it seemed like a favorable alternative to some, the majority of Yellows were against it, arguing that doing that would make us exactly what the Benefactors claimed we were.

"My parents were strong advocates for Yellow-magic-user rights. They spoke out against the Augmentors and the Benefactors, calling them out on their tyranny. They were soon considered radicals and kept under close watch. By the time I was eight, the negative feelings toward Yellows had escalated dramatically. My parents were highly scorned in the public eye, and our house was often surrounded by angry, ignorant mobs."

"Weren't you scared?" I ask, trying to imagine what that must have been like.

"I was. We all were. This fear is why my parents sent me away with Jace, honestly believing that it would be a safer environment for me. Not long after that, my parents were killed in the middle of a protest. If they hadn't sent me away, I likely would have been killed along with them."

I think of the horror of my parent's death and am sickened once more.

Elm's eyes look far away. "It all took a toll on Jace. He became scared. He continued to train me as intensely as possible, but we were always in hiding. As for me, my parents' deaths set off a passionate fury. My goal was to become as strong as possible and take my revenge on those responsible for murdering them. I learned as much as I could with Jace and studied independently when he wasn't with me. I practiced on my own and tried new spells. It was actually during this time that I found this cave. It was a treasure trove of untapped power. I grew stronger here, capable of doing things that even Jace couldn't. I started experimenting with the artificial sun devices I invented, and that's when I planted the lemon tree, to see if it would actually grow. I had crazy delusions of making unlimited sources of power. Foolish, childish notions. I mostly kept my experiments secret from Jace.

"During the next year, the massacre of Yellows became a daily occurrence. The Benefactors were wiping us out. It was then that Jace came to me and told me what he wanted to do.

"'We're on the losing side, Elm,' he told me. 'There's only one way we come out of this on top.' He wanted to join up with the Benefactors and take me with him. He wanted us to betray the Yellows and fight against them instead of with them."

"Obviously you refused," I say quietly.

"Obviously. He tried to force me into compliance, but he didn't know how strong I had become. I was able to resist and get away and hide.

"What I didn't know was that Jace had already been working with Selene in secret for nearly three years—even before my parents died. With his help, the Benefactors could complete the task they had set out to do—turn everyone against the Yellows for good. Jace began using his mind control to force more and more of the people of Magus to hate and fear Yellows. With Jace's help, the Benefactors created the barrier around Magus with White magic. They sustained the barrier with stones, placed all over Magus, which they periodically recharge. But before long, assisting in maintaining the barrier and controlling the minds became too much for Jace to do alone. They began to seek me out more aggressively, knowing how much power I could bring.

"I was young—only twelve at the time—and foolish. I thought that I could bring Jace down on my own. Revenge blinded me and stole my reasoning. I sought out Jace one night, but he quickly overpowered me with the assistance of his band of Benefactors.

"They left me bound and in a weakened state. They hooked me to machines that drained my power for their use. Against my will, I powered many of the mind-control devices placed in Magus. They sustained me with machines and IVs and had a regime of certain foods and a secured area for exercise to prevent atrophy by using my dream state. But eventually my strength began to diminish, and with it, the power I produced. They realized they had to do something more to keep me strong as well as alive.

"Because I had been so weakened, it was easy at that point for Jace to take control of my mind. The Benefactors still had hopes that I would willingly comply. So they had Jace get inside my head and my dreams. He planted the illusion there that I agreed with the cause of the Benefactors and was on their side. He also continued to train me, because the Benefactors wanted me to grow as strong as possible if I was to join them. Because of the close connection Mentalists have to the dream world, I became stronger in reality, too." He looks at me thoughtfully. "I suppose you and I are alike in that way—believing the Benefactors were good until we woke up."

"I wish I had opened my eyes sooner," I say bitterly, thinking of Selene. "But how did you finally escape?"

"Periodically, Jace and Selene would wake me to see if the illusion took. But it never did. As soon as I awakened, my mind rebelled, and I made attempts to break free. Under the power of their devices, however, they always imprisoned me again quickly. You cannot imagine the agony each time I awoke, realizing that I had been living for days, weeks, months, years, in a world that wasn't real. I was passing my whole life by as a slave, living in a lie. I wanted to end my life so many times, but never had the power to succeed. But whenever I was lucid, I looked for ways to escape."

"I can understand it a little," I say, thinking of the years I dedicated to lies, a slave to an ideology that was aggressive and wrong.

"Yes, I suppose you can," Elm says. He continues, "One day, not too long ago, something happened out of nowhere.

A power surge of sorts. It disabled the device that held me and drained my power. The surge only lasted for a few seconds, but that was enough. As soon as I came to, I quickly seized the opportunity. I took control of the mind of my captors and had them release me. That's when I bumped into you. I went immediately to the cave, grateful to find it still existing, undiscovered after those years. It was something safe and familiar.

"The world had changed so much, and the ban on Yellow left me feeling vulnerable and alone, especially with the absence of other Mentalists. And you can't imagine the time I spent doubting whether or not my freedom was real. Was it just another trick of the Benefactors? Was I still in prison? Eventually, I was able to sort things out and understand it was real. From there it didn't take long before the idea of revenge again possessed me. The Benefactors had taken everything from me. My parents, my freedom, the last few years of my life. There was a time where all I wanted was to destroy them and anyone loyal to them, no matter the cost."

I squeeze his hand, my heart aching. It's unthinkable—the pain he must have felt when he first escaped, grieving the loss of all the years of his life spent as a prisoner, trapped in illusion after illusion.

He circles his fingers around my hand more firmly in response. "When I first saw you in the forest on the day I escaped, you may recall we had some brief physical contact."

"I remember you flicked me on the forehead."

He nods. "That was to gain access to your dreams. I had to use someone at Prism as an entry point of sorts. Mentalists can hop from dream to dream, but we have to start somewhere. You were most conveniently available . . ." his voice trails off for a moment. "It's safer to use students as a jump than it is to enter the dreams of the Benefactors directly. From your dreams, I began sneaking into the dreams of Benefactors to try and find weaknesses. I just didn't count on you being so . . . present. In every other case, the students never recalled seeing me. But you did. You were there every night. I couldn't figure it out. Your presence felt so real. More than consciousness. It was like you were there in the same way a Mentalist could be, but that shouldn't have been possible. And then you showed up in the supply room, able to see me when nobody else could. Probably because I was careless—entering someone's dreams opens you up to vulnerabilities, and I was fascinated with you, Miss Ava." He flashes a smile at me. "Seeing you night after night must have linked us in a way that allowed you to see through my invisibility. I thought I had things more or less figured out, but you uprooted my reality again. You sought me out and didn't seem afraid. You were brilliant and strong and also kind-hearted. But I started to doubt everything again, believing the Benefactors had sent a pretty, charming girl to ensnare me."

My cheeks are hot from hearing him describe me that way. He must notice my blush because he pokes my cheek. "Warm in here, Miss Ava?"

"Keep talking," I mutter, flustered.

He laughs. "Very well. It took a while before I was fully able to trust you. The fact that you kept coming back and weren't afraid of me made me wonder again if I was still trapped in an illusion."

It strikes me now why Elm was so prone to casual touch—a stroke of my cheek, a touch of my hair . . . and the way he always watched me so carefully, staring at me as though he'd never seen anything quite like me. How difficult was it for him to convince himself that I was actually there and that he was awake? I nestle against him as he goes on.

"Once I felt more confident you were real, and you were here of your own curiosity, and not because you were sent to destroy me, I started to see possibilities." His expression falters. "I am not proud of this, but in the beginning, you were nothing more than another element in my desire for revenge. What better way to anger the Benefactors than to claim their prize student as my ally? Aside from that, you . . . well, you were amusing. I thought that if nothing else, you would keep my days entertaining." He shrugs, expression sheepish.

I stick my lower lip out at him. "Oh, thanks."

"But don't fret. That soon changed." His voice is warm again. "It wasn't hard for me to care for you, and soon my entire outlook began to evolve. Spending time with you helped me to see that I didn't just want revenge—I wanted a future. What I was working toward became about more than my personal vendetta—I now had a desire to fight for a new Magus. One where I could walk down the street in full view, hand in hand with . . . with someone like you."

Words fail me. It never occurred to me that he might be imagining a future with me or, at least, with someone like me. Or if he's referring to the idea that a Red and a Yellow magic-user could be together. Maybe both.

"Well," I say, suddenly feeling awkward, "I wouldn't mind a future with someone like you either."

"Someone like me . . . For the past few years, I constructed my whole persona inside a false reality. How much of who I am now is real?" He shakes his head. "I sometimes feel like I am simply their puppet, and even if I'm off of their stage, they still pull the strings."

"If you're a puppet," I counter, "then what am I? I've been living in their lies since I was five years old." I grasp his hands firmly. "You are yourself, Elm. You have your principles and your morals, regardless of how you formed them. You never stopped fighting back that whole time, and you reclaimed your freedom as soon as that magic surge gave you the chance."

My eyes widen. The day I was practicing in the forest was

the same day Elm escaped. The day I experienced the strange, erratic swell of magic for the first time.

"It was me," I blurt.

"Pardon?"

I never told him all the discoveries that came with regaining my memories. "You escaped because of a magic surge, right?"

He tilts his head, thinking. "Yes. Or at least, that's the best way I can describe it. Something caused a ripple in the flow of Yellow magic that I was being controlled with."

"I'm almost certain that was me."

"What?" His voice is incredulous.

My words rush out. "When I got my memories back, I learned that at my initiation ceremony, the cube turned orange, and Selene said that meant I could use both Red and Yellow magic."

Elm is staring at me. "That would be remarkable. But I have never seen you use Yellow magic."

"But I don't really know how," I say. "All these years, I've only had Red magic as a focus. But I think I could do it with practice, now that I know I'm capable of it."

"This would certainly explain how you were able to see me when I was traveling through dreams and when I was invisible. And now I see why I didn't need to charge up your necklace as much as I had thought I would—it was gaining some energy from you. It also explains why you were able to catch onto some things that the rest of Magus missed. But it's curious that it never manifested in other ways."

"But I think it did. I did something with it on the day you escaped."

"How?"

"Well, I was . . . I guess it sounds silly now, but I was testing a theory. I thought that maybe an Augmentor could use strengthening powers to gain control over the mind, because you know . . . the head is sort of like the mind . . ."

I trail off, embarrassed at explaining this to him. He looks amused as I continue, "Anyway, I was trying to strengthen my head, and something weird happened. I felt a strange surge of power, and then my head was killing me. The pain was awful. I didn't know what it was. But it happened on the same day the Benefactors announced your escape."

He considers this for a moment. "That actually would make sense. If you didn't know what you were doing and were trying to use Red magic where Yellow would have been more effective, I could see it causing a strange disruptive emission. Especially being inexperienced with Yellow magic." He regards me solemnly. "That was fairly dangerous, Miss Ava. You're lucky your pretty head didn't explode."

"I didn't know," I protest. "But for what it's worth, I haven't tried it again." I bite my tongue, suddenly remembering the other occasion in the practice room. No need for him to know there was another time.

"I'm grateful you tried it once," Elm says. "On top of everything else, it appears I owe you my freedom." He grins at me playfully. "Your theory, however flawed, gave me back my life."

"I have another theory, actually."

"Oh?"

"I think you're also a dual magic-user."

He laughs. "I think not. If I could have used Red magic against the Benefactors, I'd have tried that trick a long time ago."

"Not Red," I tell him. "Blue. I think you can create objects because you can imagine things up with your Yellow magic and then use Blue's power over material objects to make the objects of your illusions reality."

"Poor, misguided child. She's gone mad."

"It's not that crazy," I insist. "Maybe you want to believe you're so skilled you can do things no Mentalist has ever done, but I think it's different than that. I think you can do what you do because you're predisposed to more than one form of magic. But, like me, it's untrained. And without a pendant, it's weakened."

"Hmmm . . ." He ruminates on this. "We shall have to think of ways to test your theory. I suppose it's possible."

"I'm right," I say confidently. "You'll see."

"Perhaps." He still doesn't seem entirely convinced of the idea. He shifts. "Now, are there any other questions I can answer for you?"

"Yes, actually." Since we're letting everything out in the open now, I have nothing to lose. I glance up at him. "Why didn't you kiss me that time?"

His eyes widen and for the first time since I have met him, Elm blushes. "I didn't know if you wanted that. I wasn't sure whether you would think I was just . . . manipulating you."

At once I'm shy again. "Of course, if that's not what *you* want, I don't—"

His lips upon mine cut off my nervous rambling.

When he pulls away gently, I search his eyes, as they gaze at me, for any signs of unease. Finding none, I take him by the shirt and pull him back in for another kiss.

21

THE NEW OPENNESS BETWEEN ELM AND me, with his hand tightly grasping mine as we walk toward the school, is almost enough to make the task before me less frightening. The idea of going back to Prism is about as appealing as eating slugs, but we both know it's best I return for now. Selene has my magic literally locked away, so the longer we can hold off her suspicion, the better.

"I do wish I could see Selene's face when she learns I corrupted her best student," Elm says cheerfully. "But for now, you have to play nice with her until your powers are returned."

"I don't know how I'm supposed to do that." Molten fury rises in me at the mention of her name. "Not when I know what I know."

"Just think of the end goal. And be patient. Don't make the same mistakes I did. We need something solid in place before we act."

The trees start to thin, and I know I can't walk with him any further. Not while I'm visible. "Well then," I say with a sigh. "I guess I do need to get back there. I'll meet up with you again tomorrow as soon as I can, and we'll brainstorm." I don't let go of his hand.

"Yes. Please don't do anything rash, Miss Ava. We'll formulate a careful plan. You'll be outing the Benefactors to all of Magus in no time."

"Until tomorrow, then," I say.

"Until tomorrow, Miss Ava."

He releases my hand, planting a gentle kiss on each finger as he does so. He's not making it any easier to leave. I give him a wistful smile and turn away toward the path to Prism.

I force myself not to look back, just in case someone is watching, and slip through the main entrance and walk down the hall toward the dormitories. Did I really get away with this? The halls are busy with students, and I blend with the crowd. Almost there. Almost back to my room.

"Ava."

At once I'm face-to-face with the woman who choked me with lies. Who assisted in killing my parents and then pretended to care about my well-being. Who enslaved Elm. I would like nothing more than to deliver a Red-enhanced slap to her face, but I can't. Even if I had my powers, I have to control myself and pretend that everything is as it was.

"Hello, Selene," I say calmly.

"Where were you?" she asks bluntly.

"Where was I?" I throw the question back at her, hoping my face looks sufficiently surprised. "Reading. I know I'm not supposed to worry about school, but I can't help it. I needed something to focus on."

"And you had to do this in the forest?" The edge to her voice sends a chill down my spine.

"Yes," I say, as casually as I can. "It's my favorite spot. I just needed a break from everything."

She studies me, and I continue to keep steady eye contact with her. I can't imagine what she must be thinking as she surveys me, my hair tangled from thrashing through the woods. Stray scratches on my arms and face. I wish I'd had a chance to clean up before seeing her.

"I'm sorry, Ava," Selene finally says. "I don't need to keep tabs on you. You're entitled to leave the school at any time you want to. However . . ." She grips my shoulder. "If you're going to be wandering around, we'd certainly hate to leave you unarmed. Perhaps it's time we returned your power to you. I've been thinking about it, and we may have been rash. Do you think you're ready?"

Her voice is just a little too friendly, and her eyes just a little too hard. I'm not sure what she's thinking now. "You're going to give me my powers back?"

"I think you've cleared your head enough by now. If Elm gets into your dreams again, I trust you'll come to me. Come on." She guides me to her office and shuts the door securely once I'm inside. I would rather be anywhere but here. I wanted my magic back desperately, moments before entering the school, but now something doesn't feel right. This is too fast. Too easy.

Selene goes to the large cupboard once more and opens it with the key around her neck. The tiny orb shines brightly inside. And it's orange. Suddenly, it occurs to me that it always was orange, and Jace must have created the illusion of its red color before. It probably still hasn't occurred to Selene that his previous spells have no effect on me while I'm powerless.

"Is something wrong?" Selene asks in a syrupy voice.

"Oh, no," I interject. "I just think it's beautiful. So . . . red," I say.

She smiles widely. "Red magic is a beautiful thing, isn't it? Go on, take it back. I'm sure you've missed it."

I hesitate. She's not asking enough questions. Selene is many things, but dumb isn't one of them. She has more reasons for doing this than she lets on. But what do I do? If I don't take back my magic, she'll definitely suspect something, and I might lose my chance of getting my powers back forever. No sane person on Magus would choose to remain powerless. Whatever her intentions, I'm sure I have a better chance of fighting her if I can use magic again.

I gingerly take the orb in my hands and feel the warmth spreading through me from my fingertips and outward. It does feel good to have it back, like a security blanket. The orb gradually loses its light and fades to its original colorless gray.

"Now," Selene says sharply.

The next thing I feel is a thud to the back of my head.

My head hurts.

I try to reach up and touch the throbbing spot on the back of my head, but I can't. My wrists are bound. My eyes pop open, and I'm in a small dark room, sitting in a metal chair with red stone shackles on my wrists. I struggle against them, but I can't budge. I try a strengthening spell. The shackles light up and surge with heat, and then dim again. I'm not any stronger.

"I'm glad you're awake." Selene steps out from a shadowed corner of the room along with another Benefactor. I recognize her icy blue eyes at once. She was the other Benefactor with Selene on the day Elm escaped. Selene gestures toward her. "This is Veronica."

Veronica says nothing. She merely looks at me with a cold, cunning stare.

"Selene, what's going on?" I try to steady the shaking in my voice.

Selene approaches and bends down to look me in the eyes. "Believe me when I say I didn't want it to come to this. You were my star pupil, after all. I had the highest of hopes for you."

"I've done everything you've ever asked!"

She lets out a sudden, harsh laugh. "Oh, yes. You've done everything I asked, all right. And then some. You have actually been helping Elm." Her voice lowers. "You are a traitor. A traitor to me, a traitor to the school, and a traitor to all of Magus."

I tremble as anger lashes through me. No need to keep up the good-student act anymore. "You're the last person who should be calling me a traitor. I know what you did to my parents. What you and the Benefactors did to Magus. I know everything." I despise her. And now that she knows I'm against her, all bets are off. I am free to challenge her.

She narrows her eyes and stands, taking a step back from me. "Yes," she says bitterly. "I realized my mistake a little too late. It hadn't occurred to me that removing your powers would reset your memories. I had thought that once a memory was altered, it stayed altered."

"If your school studied Yellow magic, maybe you would have known better," I mock.

"Don't test me," she snaps. "Now, don't think that I'm without feeling. I put a lot of time and effort into you over the years. Watched you grow. Thrived on your success. You may not believe it, but I did—do—care for you. I could never let myself get too involved, as it wouldn't have been appropriate for me to show excessive favoritism in my position. But you were so good and so loyal, and I hoped we could work together and you could eventually take my place someday. You were my protégée." For a moment, her voice sounds choked up. "And then that fool had to ruin everything, the way their kind always does."

"I think you're the one who ruined everything by murdering my parents and lying all these years." I try to control the rage building inside me, but it manifests in furious tremors.

"I regret that. I always have. But I had no choice." She shakes her head. "You're too young to understand."

I open my mouth to fling some insult at her, but I have no chance because she continues, "I did what I did for the greater good. Your parents wouldn't volunteer you for the benefit of Magus on their own, so drastic measures had to be taken. It would have been a waste of your gift. Besides, even with you out of the picture, their very existence was a threat. If they hadn't died then, they would have died later on, fighting for that ridiculous cause."

"I'm pretty sure they just wanted normal lives," I throw back at her. "To raise their daughter in peace."

Selene shakes her head again. "People get so touchy if anyone tries to say that a specific group of people could be innately dangerous. But the human mind was meant to be free. An entire body of people who can control and manipulate it should never have a place in this world."

"Amazing," I laugh. "You can't see the hypocrisy in that statement? As we speak, you're controlling the minds of an entire nation for the sake of your cause."

"Temporarily. And it's not just *my* cause. It's different, and it's only to spare the tender-hearted the discomfort of doing what has to be done. Soon, the younger generations will know no other way, and there will be no further need for force."

"Try to justify it all you want," I say coldly. "You're wrong."

The way she looks at me is frightening—her eyes look dead, as though she is separating herself from any emotion. "I can see it's too late for you to join the Benefactors—your mind has been too polluted. What a waste." Her voice sounds truly pained at that remark, but her hardened tone takes control again. "Still, I'm determined to find out everything you know about Elm, and we can either do it the easy way, or"—she glances at Veronica—"we can do it her way."

I had almost forgotten Veronica was here at all. She steps forward, smiling face filled with smug satisfaction now that her moment has come.

Selene continues, "Veronica is trained in a very specific

area of Red magic. Her specialty is pain. Last chance, Ava. Tell me what you know."

I want to be brave, but I'm terrified. The memory of my parents' deaths infiltrates my mind, and I have no doubt Veronica could do the same thing to me. It's clear why Selene wanted to give me back my magic; she needed Veronica to be able to hurt me. Of course, she could hurt me physically even without magic, but normal human pain wouldn't be enough. She wants the terror. She wants me to know she has the power to rip me apart from the inside out. But I can't give in, no matter what. For my parents. And Elm's. For Elm himself. And most importantly of all, for the future of Mentalists and Magus. This is much bigger than me.

"I don't have any information for you," I say.

Selene studies me, her face impassive. Finally, she says, "Have it your way." She addresses Veronica. "Do what you have to do." A slight waver comes into her voice. "But wait until I'm out of earshot. It's not as though I'll get any pleasure out of this."

"Understood," Veronica replies crisply.

Selene removes a sleek red key from around her neck, different from the one she used to lock up my powers. It must belong to my shackles because she hands it to Veronica. "If she changes her tune, bring her back to me. But if you can't get her to talk, well, it's obvious she's too much of a threat to be kept alive."

Veronica gives a sharp nod and I shiver.

Selene meets my eyes one last time, full of heavy disappointment. There was a time where a look like that from her would have devastated me, but not now. Now that I recognize what she has done, I can wear her disappointment like a badge of honor. She pivots and exits the room, the heavy thud of the door echoing as she goes. For several long, intense seconds I hear Selene's footsteps grow softer and eventually fade. Veronica turns back to me, her face twisted into a sinister smile.

"You seem to be looking forward to this," I say. "I thought the Benefactors were all about peace."

"Oh? I'm not a monster," she replies with a small laugh. "But if there's one thing I do enjoy, it's punishing a traitor. And you, Ava, are a traitor of the worst kind. The Mentalists can't help who they are, so I might feel some sympathy for them. But you . . . you willingly allied yourself with *them*."

At first, I feel nothing, but then a prickling heat begins within me, followed by an uncomfortable tightening sensation. I resist the urge to react and instead keep my eyes fixed on Veronica.

She looks at me straight on. "As Selene said, it's not too late to redeem yourself. All we need is information."

"I have nothing to tell you."

Sharp pain spasms through me, causing me to arch my back and cry out.

"Oh, I'm sorry," Veronica says mockingly. "Did that hurt? Selene was reluctant to damage you, but I won't hesitate in doing whatever it takes."

Another spasm begins, extending for several agonizing seconds. My nails dig into the arms of the chair imprisoning me. I try not to scream, and my teeth clench together so hard my jaw hurts. When the pain at last ebbs, my body remains on edge and won't relax. My heart hammers in my chest, and my skin shimmers with beads of sweat. I breathe in shuddering, heaving gasps.

She leans her face in close to mine. "Did that loosen your tongue at all?"

I spit at her.

"Brat!" she screams, leaping back and wiping her face with her sleeve. Another wave of pain, more intense this time. It pulls and tugs at my body, both inside and out, as though I'm on the verge of being ripped in two. Spots flash in front of my eyes, and my head feels like it's going to rupture. Was this how my parents felt just before they died? Unable to suppress it any longer, I scream. I scream until my throat is raw, but the pain does not stop.

I black out.

I'm not sure how much time has passed. Maybe ten minutes. Maybe an hour.

I pass out several more times, fading in and out each time, barely registering what's happening to me. I can't understand what Veronica is saying anymore. Gashes cover my body where she used her magic to pull apart my flesh. Initially I tried in vain to heal them, but I rapidly learned that the stone shackles absorb any magic attempts and serve to give Veronica more power.

I don't scream anymore. I no longer have the strength. Each burst of agony shocks my wilted body back into writhing, twitching motions, and then I fall limp again, unable to carry myself.

"I'm getting bored," Veronica warns. Her words sound distant, and I'm surprised when she appears right in front of me. She grips my chin and forces my face upward to look at her. Her touch is agonizing.

She contemplates me. "Here's what I'm going to do. You have a few seconds to start talking. If you don't, I'm going to start draining all of the color from your blood. And I think you know what will happen if I do that."

As she says this, multiple gashes blossom over my body, causing fresh crimson to flow from each wound. I scream weakly, terrified and raw with pain. I'm already so depleted. But my resolve hasn't changed. I can't tell her anything.

"Fine then," Veronica says. "Enjoy your last moments."

I stare through blurred eyes at the blood pooling around me and see its brightness dulling. The gray spreads, moving in upward streaks. Suddenly, I feel lightheaded and strange, as if the life is being sucked out of me. This is an entirely different feeling from the pain inflicted—a helpless feeling of death, swallowing up the little vitality I have left.

This is it. I slump in the chair, surrounded by my now-colorless blood. This is how my life ends. My goals of bringing justice to the Mentalists are gone nearly before they started. I just hope Elm can do alone what I couldn't help him do.

Elm, who has brought more vibrancy to me in these past few months than in the entirety of my existence. I won't even get to say goodbye to him. Half-delirious, my mind wanders, slipping away somewhere else. I'm walking down the forest path, searching for him as I have done so many times before. I cannot find him.

"Elm. Where are you?"

"What's that?" Veronica jerks up. "What about Elm?"

I blink at her, gradually remembering where I am and what is happening. I clamp my aching lips firmly shut. I hadn't realized my words were spoken aloud. I must not tell her anything. I must not.

A look of discomfort crosses Veronica's face. Her eyes grow wide, frozen with a look of sheer terror. She clutches and scratches at the sides of her head and suddenly begins to laugh insanely, shrill and disjointed.

In spite of the debilitating pain, I'm still able to register new fear. What is happening?

Then, out of the shadows, steps Elm. His face is hard and cold, his eyes dark with loathing. I have never seen him look this way. Even his wanted posters, which made every effort to make him look menacing, could not compete with what I see now. He walks slowly and deliberately toward Veronica, whose mad laughter becomes progressively more erratic. When Elm reaches her, he rips the key away from her neck and swiftly frees me from my bonds. Without saying a word, he tenderly gathers my damaged body into his arms. In spite of his gentleness, the new wave of pain at being moved is excruciating.

He carries me to the door, and I glance back to see Veronica writhing on the floor. Her cackling becomes mind-shattering screams, wracked with horror and lunacy.

"Look away, Miss Ava," Elm says in my ear.

I bury my face into his chest just as Veronica vomits. She chokes and gurgles through her screams. I faint. And come to again, still in Elm's arms.

22

ELM MANAGES TO CONCEAL US BOTH
as we escape from Prism. Back in the cave, he gently places
me down.

"Are you able to heal, Miss Ava?"

My voice is barely above a whisper. "I think so."

I begin the healing spell, but in an instant, I'm drained, and
the heat fades. "I can't . . ."

But suddenly, I begin to feel stronger, and pain gently eases
out of my body. But that shouldn't be happening. Not after the
torture I've gone through. Unless . . .

My eyelids flutter. "Hey," I mumble weakly, "get out
of my mind."

"I apologize, Miss Ava," Elm says. "But this is one instance
where I must ignore your wishes. Please try the healing once
again, if you can."

"Considering the circumstances," I give a faint smile. "I'll
forgive you." I can't deny that my wounds feel much better.

"Elm," I ask tentatively, as the healing continues to
strengthen me. "What exactly did you do to her?"

He stiffens. "I did not want to do what I did. I really didn't.
I simply lost control." He is silent too long. I can only think
he isn't going to say anymore. His voice is dull when he does
speak. "Essentially, I destroyed her mind. She won't recover."

We are both quiet now. The idea that Yellow magic is capable of doing something like that rattles me. Then again, I suppose it isn't any more brutal than what I have seen Red magic do. Once again, I'm astounded by the sheer amount of power Elm possesses.

It is Elm who breaks the silence first. He brushes back my hair. "I'm sorry, Miss Ava."

"For what? You saved my life!"

He shakes his head. "I'm sorry I couldn't save you any sooner, and I'm furious with myself for letting you go back there to begin with. What on earth did I expect?" He gestures, obviously upset. "I just had an intense feeling that I should go back to the school. I was invisible, of course, and went in determined to find you. That's when I saw you with Selene. I should have done something then, but I didn't. I thought it would put you in danger if she realized I was there." He shakes his head. "Idiotic. I didn't follow into Selene's office because there was no way for me to open the door without attracting attention. Next thing I knew, they were dragging you out, unconscious."

"How did they do that without any of the other students noticing?"

"Jace." His voice is bitter. "He masked you with an illusion while they took you to that room where—" his voice chokes, and he clenches his fists. "I couldn't go in with you. Because of the Benefactor's protective spell, I couldn't approach you. No matter how many times I tried, I couldn't get to you. I saw everything that woman did to you."

His head drops. I can't imagine what he went through, unable to do anything except watch.

He raises his head, eyes glistening. "I kept trying, though. The whole time we were there, I kept trying. I'm not sure what happened, but suddenly I was able to get through. By that point, all I wanted was to destroy that vile woman so I just . . . acted."

He looks at me. "I haven't ever done something like that before, and I'm not proud of it, Miss Ava."

"But I understand why you did." I try to assure him. "And Elm, I think I know how you got through. Just before I saw you, I started hallucinating. I thought I was in the forest looking for you."

His eyes light up. "That makes sense. You were making an effort to find me, so I was able to approach. Oh, Miss Ava, thank goodness for that." He embraces me, but quickly stops, looking me over in alarm.

"It's okay," I say, smiling at him. "I feel much better now. You aren't hurting me."

He pulls me close, gentler this time.

I wish that I could just stay this way, huddled up against him with nothing else to worry about. But I know there are crucial matters to deal with, and every second counts. "So what are we going to do now? Obviously, I can't call Prism my home anymore."

"Stay with me," he says.

"Of course. I really have no choice. But that's not what I mean. Now that the truth is clear, I don't see how we can just sit by and do nothing. And," I add, "I highly doubt your intention was just to stand by, anyway. Do you really think there are other Mentalists out there?"

"Almost definitely."

"Can you tell me about what we did at the library?" I'm amazed at how much stronger I feel now. With the assistance of Elm buoying up my emotions, most of my wounds have healed.

"Certainly. The digidomes there were utilized to continue planting thoughts in people's heads and making sure old memories didn't creep in. Since people often go to libraries seeking answers, this was a natural spot for the Benefactors to plant devices, since they could stop any unwanted thoughts almost as soon as they occurred. Each one was powered by

Yellow magic. Destroying those hopefully put a big dent in their power source."

"But then, shouldn't other people in Magus be getting their memories back?"

He puzzles over that for a moment. "I would like to think some people have started to. But, as you discovered, even when you were completely immune to the effects of magic, it took some time before your head fully cleared. Besides that, the Benefactors have other devices set in place, so it would take even more time before people start to realize they've been duped. And even then, they may not really understand what is happening or be able to separate memory from errant thoughts."

"There must be devices in place all over Prism," I say. "Definitely in the school library. I was trying to figure some things out a while back, and my mind just couldn't focus."

"Suggestion planting," Elm confirms. "I'm sure Prism is a particular focus point for the Benefactors. If they can train their upcoming students in their views, they have a greater hold on the future of Magus."

"Well then," I declare, "let's go back to the school and do some damage. If we're ever going to bring Yellow magic back to Magus, we're going to need a lot more people on our side."

My determination brings a slight smile to his face. "This isn't going to be easy, Miss Ava. Or safe. We're perilously outnumbered."

"I know. But we have to start somewhere. We can't just let them lie to people like this. You said you wanted a future, right?"

His smile becomes a slow grin, and his eyes sparkle at me. "Yes. You're right. I suppose we need a plan."

Prism is quiet the next morning as Elm and I stand just outside the gate. One thing we have been able to count on is that the Benefactors don't want anyone else to know what's going on. I'm sure the rest of the school has no idea something is amiss or that I'm nowhere to be found.

I wear the yellow dress again, and Elm, of course, is also invisible. The fact that the Benefactors aren't yet aware of this ability is our wildcard.

"The gate's locked," I say, giving it a soft tug. "They won't open it for another hour."

"We'll just have to go over it, then," Elm says.

"It's pretty big. And I don't like the look of those spikes." The elegant, pointed tops of the gate's bars look as though they could impale us with no trouble if we slipped the wrong way.

Elm seems to struggle with something. Finally, he says, "I know another way in. Come with me."

He's jittery and nervous, and it's strange he's this anxious over what we are about to do. He seemed so confident when sneaking around before. He leads me back to the forest, and we stop under the large oak tree.

"This is my study spot!" I tell him.

"Is it?" Elm's voice is flat. "I know it as something else."

He steps around to the back of the tree and motions for me to join him. He reaches up and gives a sharp twist to one of the branches, then pulls down on it. My mouth gapes as a hole opens in the back of the tree.

"We have thirty seconds, so move fast. Better let me go first." He slips into the hole and out of sight. I follow with haste and slide roughly down the weathered tunnel leading below the tree.

"Sorry," I say, as I crash into Elm at the bottom.

"No apology needed." I wait for him to make some kind of joke, but he is all seriousness.

I stand and look around at the dimly lit room we're now in. Goosebumps crawl up my skin as the chilly, musky air hits me. As my eyes adjust to the darkness, I can just make out some sort of gurney in the center. I go closer for a better look, and notice stone shackles, eerily similar to the ones used on me by Veronica. But these are yellow. Coming out from the shackles are several yellow tubes that go up to the ceiling.

I gasp. "Elm, is this where . . . "

He doesn't answer, but he doesn't need to. His pale face and the look in his eyes say enough. This is where Jace and the Benefactors held Elm captive for those lost years of his life.

"How can this entrance be here?" I ask, bewildered. "I've been going to this tree for years and never see anyone else here."

"Jace built that entrance as another way of covering his own hide. Even the Benefactors don't know about it."

"What do you mean?"

"Think about it," His voice is bitter. "He saw what they were doing to me. What they did to the other Mentalists. I'm sure he figured if his alliance with them ever backfired, he wanted a quick way out. It wouldn't surprise me if he's used his magic to steer people away from this area as well."

It makes perfect sense. Seeing a Mentalist imprisoned the way Elm was would have triggered Jace's strong sense of self-preservation. His magic ability to create aversion and diversion explains why I never saw Benefactors around this area.

"I'm sure Jace preferred me ignorant about the entrance, also," Elm continues. "But when you get inside another

Mentalist's head, there is a risk of revealing more information than intended."

He looks ill, his eyes fixating on the shackles. I grasp his hand and tug on it. "Let's get out of here."

The small room connects to a long, narrow corridor. We go down it until we reach a hefty door at the end. I press my ear against it and listen while holding my breath.

"I don't hear anything."

We push the door open just enough to peek outside and verify that nobody is around. I can see now that we're in the administrative corridor, where all of the faculty and Benefactors' offices are. I'm amazed that this door has been here all along. I just assumed it was another office.

As we pass the door to Selene's office, we hear muffled voices inside.

"Selene and Jace," I whisper. "They don't sound happy."

"Good," Elm whispers grimly.

We creep through the halls to the dormitories, taking the lightest steps we can manage. Just as we round the corner to get to my room, we stop short. A Benefactor waits outside, probably instructed to keep watch in case I return. I'm about to pull Elm aside to ask what we should do when the Benefactor's eyes glaze over.

"Go quickly," Elm tells me. "For the moment, he thinks all is clear."

I slip inside, keeping a close eye on the Benefactor to make sure he doesn't notice anything odd about the door opening. He doesn't react. I stop momentarily, taken aback at seeing my ransacked room. I guess it shouldn't surprise me—they must have been looking for information. My school bag lies with its contents dumped all over the floor. Fortunately for me, the key to the supply room is still there, buried in the pile. I clasp it securely in my hand and grab my bag. As an afterthought, I go to my closet and search behind my clothes and am relieved to find the spot where Elm's hat still hangs. I return back to the hallway, softly closing the door behind me. As soon as I'm back by his side, Elm breaks his spell on the Benefactor to avoid using up any more power than necessary.

When we are out of earshot, I give Elm a quirky grin and place his hat on his head. "We might as well do this in style." The warmth of his broad smile makes my heart skip a beat. We continue to the supply room.

"Phase one—diversion," Elm is almost gleeful as we enter. He reaches into his pocket and pulls out a lemon. "When life gives you lemons—"

"You make thousands of copies and run," I finish with a laugh.

He places the lemon on the copy machine's surface, and I punch in 50,000 copies. Just before hitting start, I grab a pair of scissors and use them to pry off the *stop* button on the machine.

"That should keep them busy for a while," I say with satisfaction. As the lemons begin to pile up, I grab several and stuff them into my bag. I glance at Elm. "Just in case you need them."

"Thoughtful," he says with a wink.

We exit the supply room without bothering to lock up again; we want this noticed. We run down the hallways to the library. Nobody but the librarian is inside at this hour. She looks up as the door swings open. Suddenly her eyes grow wide, and she retreats from her desk and flees squealing from the room.

"What did you make her see?" I ask Elm.

"A very large and very diseased-looking rat. I suspect we have just a minute or two before she returns with someone or something to exterminate it."

"Well then," I say, "we'd better hurry up with phase two. Destruction."

We go to the row of library workstations, and I do a strengthening spell and deliver a powerful punch to the nearest digidome. Elm takes his cane and begins smashing. Before long, we decimate the entire row. If we're correct about the devices implanted there, this will be a major blow to the Benefactors.

"Miss Ava," Elm says, "look up there."

He indicates a black dome attached to the ceiling. "The security camera?" I ask. "I'm not worried about it. They can't see us, but they will see the digidomes exploding. We just have to get out fast."

"No, that's not it. You haven't noticed? It's yellow."

"Another device?" I ask. Eventually I'll learn how to see through these illusions, too.

"Probably."

"Lift me up."

Elm boosts me up on his shoulders so that I can reach the camera. I build up my strength again, just as we hear footsteps echoing down the hall.

"Better hurry," he warns.

I deliver another punch, shattering the dome into tiny shards. And not a moment too soon. The librarian comes back with another member of the staff. They look at the destruction in the room, and then at each other, with frightened eyes.

"Get Selene!" the librarian shouts.

Elm and I slip out the door behind the panicked staff member.

Next stop is the auditorium. As we move past the corridor where the supply room is, we hear a loud commotion. I glance sideways and have to suppress laughter at the sight of lemons tumbling out of the supply room door. Selene is there, along with a small crowd of hysterical faculty.

"It won't stop!" I recognize Mr. Dawson's voice. They must have been hoping he would know how to stop the copier since he recharges its stone.

"Well, figure something out," Selene's order is nearly a shriek. "It gives *him* more power!"

I'm filled with almost delirious vindication. I glance at Elm, who has a satisfied smirk on his face.

We continue toward our destination—the auditorium— which is also connected to the media room. Now that we have successfully disabled several of the mind-altering devices in Prism, our goal is to broadcast a message throughout the school. I hope, with so many devices out of commission, the message will take. It's a long shot, but we have to try.

Almost there. We're really going to make it. I'm sure we initiated enough distractions with the copy machine and the library that nobody will think twice about the auditorium. And since we're invisible, we can pass by unnoticed.

Elm pushes open the heavy auditorium door, and we cross the threshold into the vast red-and-blue room. I dash toward the doors of the media center, fixed on that and nothing else. It's a wide-open shot. Maybe this is why it comes as such a shock when something trips me.

My knees skid on the wooden auditorium floor, stinging sharply. I look up and see Elm standing over me smugly, cane held outward.

I blink up at him from the floor in confusion. Is he playing games? I know he's one for mischief, but he couldn't have picked a worse time to joke around. But his face doesn't look playful. It's full of nothing but malicious intent.

"Elm," I say, voice shaky. "What are you doing?"

"It's time to put an end to all of this, Ava. You've gotten me where I need to be. I no longer have any use for you."

I gape at him. "What are you talking about? I'm on your side! After all the lies the Benefactors have planted . . . aren't we working together to stop all that?"

"I had a feeling you would buy that story." He laughs. "So gullible. You played into my plans perfectly."

This can't be happening. Elm wouldn't turn on me now. He can't have been lying to me all this time. A tight feeling of panic squeezes my chest.

"Elm," I say, voice low, "this isn't funny."

"Sorry, Ava. It's time to face the facts. Your mind belongs to me. It seems Selene was right about me all along. "

Wait. Why is he calling me just Ava now? I have been Miss Ava to him from the beginning. Except that one time when I ran away from him. And Elm couldn't have implanted the recently recalled memories of my parents and my childhood—not when I didn't have my powers at the time. This is not right. But if this isn't Elm in front of me, who else could pull off such an illusion?

And then it clicks.

"You almost got me, Jace," I say, trying to keep my voice even.

The fake Elm sneers, and the illusion distorts, no longer having power over me. It shimmers away, and I'm met with Elm—the real Elm—standing eerily still. Jace stands a few feet behind him, looking calmer than I would expect.

"Very good, Ava. But it's not going to help you much." He utters a laugh. "Not when the real Elm turns against you."

What is he talking about? "Elm!" I shout, but Elm doesn't hear me.

He's trapped. He doesn't know what's real, and I can't imagine what Jace is putting in his mind.

I run over and reach out to Elm. He turns and swats at me. I jump back. His eyes show no sign of recognition as he lunges, in almost wild pursuit. He flicks his cane at me, sending a jolt of pain through my body.

Not real, I tell myself, gritting my teeth. The pain is not real. You're not being hurt. I pull myself together and cast an agility spell to stay beyond his reach.

"Snap out of it, Elm!" I shout. "Whatever you're seeing, it's not real!"

I steal a glance at Jace, but he merely watches, amusement on his face. "Well, this is easy. I can simply let him finish you off."

Because of the momentary focus on Jace, I don't notice Elm approaching me again. I feel a sharp jab in my side and clutch at my ribs. I leap backward as he moves to strike again, but he grazes my leg. One of the stones on his cane scrapes across my skin, tearing as it goes. This time the pain is real.

Soon I'll have no choice but to start using physical force. If he's no longer only using illusions to fight me, I can't just use willpower to stick it out. I want to heal the cut on my leg, but I can't do that and use agility to evade him at the same time. I dart across the room from him and begin healing while there is space between us.

Suddenly, a tight pinching compresses my skull. Elm is still across the room but staring at me intensely. Horrified, I recall flashes of Veronica, driven to madness, her mind utterly destroyed. He could do this to me too. My bones turn to ice. I'm going to have to fight back, and fast.

"Don't make me do this, Elm," I plead. "I don't want to hurt you."

The strange clenching in my head grows more intense, and I panic. I give myself a quick boost of speed and dash straight toward Elm, kicking him hard in the side. He cries out and clutches where I hit, which brings remorseful tears to my eyes. I succeeded in one thing, however; my head feels normal again. Unfortunately, it doesn't take Elm long to get his wits about him, and I can tell by the look on his face that he's preparing another attack.

What can I do? I don't know anything about how to break someone else out of a Yellow-magic spell. I hardly know how to defend against it myself. But if I can't bring Elm back to reality, we will both die here. I almost wish it were me under Jace's control instead because Elm would have the abilities for greater advantages than I have.

But I have Yellow-magic abilities, too, don't I?

I don't know anything about using them, and Elm had warned me not to try. That it could be dangerous and unpredictable if I didn't train properly. But what other choice do I have now? My Red magic is useless in this situation for anything other than dodging and physical attacks. And that isn't enough to jolt Elm back to himself. To the real world.

I put as much distance between myself and Elm as I can to buy some time. Unsure of where to start, I focus once again on my mind. I try to bring energy to it and push it outward. The heat and pressure build.

My head snaps back, and that strange surge of power breaks forth once again. When I open my eyes, both Elm and Jace are on the floor, clutching their heads.

"Elm!" I shout once more, staggering toward him, trying to right myself after the intense surge.

Elm looks up, and relief floods me as his eyes come into focus. "Miss Ava!" Realization dawning on him, he glances to his side at Jace and jumps to his feet. He quickly crosses the room to stand in front of me protectively.

Jace has risen shakily to his feet, chuckling dryly. "Interesting trick you have there, Ava. But it won't work again." He makes eye contact with Elm. "And you, Elm. It will be easy to have you back under my control—and believe me, I will. I'll have to find out how you made those invisibility devices. Very, very clever. A device-formed illusion was something I never expected, so they even had me fooled for a while. I'm sure the Benefactors would love to get a hold of one."

We should have been more careful. The invisibility devices have been practically flawless for disguising us from Augmenters and Shapers, but when it comes down to it, it's just another Yellow illusion. Something a powerful Mentalist would learn to recognize.

Elm doesn't flinch or shift his attention from his former mentor.

"You can't win, Elm," Jace says. "Once the Benefactors catch on and show up here, you'll be outnumbered. You'll be back in chains before you know it. And in the meantime, I'm not too concerned about battling with my former pupil and his little girlfriend."

"I'm stronger than you remember," Elm says sharply. "I wouldn't underestimate either one of us." He nods over his shoulder at me.

Jace guffaws loudly. "I'm to be worried about a dual-magic student who doesn't even have a good grasp of her power? I don't think so." He smirks. "Besides, her mind is weak. Do you recall how quickly she turned on you? A few suggestive words from Selene and some playing up of her own insecurities was all it took."

What? Jace used his power on me? Anger grips me. It should be a relief knowing my treachery toward Elm wasn't all my own, but I'm too disgusted thinking of being manipulated by Selene's cowardly accomplice. Elm's stance is full of tension.

Jace laughs again. "Didn't even know it, did you? But it doesn't have to be that way." He circles us slowly, still keeping a safe distance, his eyes on me. His voice is persuasive. "I can help you become stronger. You're already gifted with Red magic. Imagine if you could become equally skilled with Yellow. I can teach you. Look at what I've done for Elm."

"I know what you did to him," I snap. "You're just a coward. You always have been."

Jace's eyes harden. "Don't choose the wrong side, Ava."

As he says my name, his voice fades out into an eerie echo. The room grows dark. Pitch black.

23

"WHAT'S HAPPENING?" I ASK. BUT THERE is no reply. Elm is gone. I float alone in black nothingness.

"Elm, where are you? Elm. Elm!" I call his name in panic over and over again, but nothing calls back but my own echo.

Where is he? And where is Jace?

I turn frantically in all directions, wondering where and when he might strike. I look for a sign of something, anything outside of this darkness. But on every side, I'm surrounded by the oppressive shadows. Hopelessness and despair seize me. I am alone. Just like I have been for most of my life. No friends. No family. And Selene, the one person I thought was always there for me, lied to me all along.

All of my faults come to the forefront of my mind. What was it Elm had called me? An academy robot. I'm no more than that, and I doubt my abilities and my motives. Do I care about Magus, or am I just looking for adulation? Maybe all I wanted was a reason to be better than everyone else, to have power. I'm no better than Selene. What reason do I have to continue? I'm worthless and boring. I have books, but no passion. Studies, but no experience. My life is influenced by whoever shouts the loudest at the time.

Something flickers within me.

But that's not true, is it?

During these past several months, I learned there is an Ava who exists outside of textbooks. An Ava who can fall in love and fight for someone. I really do want to protect Magus, and I'm willing to risk everything to do it, even if it means tearing down the walls of the reality I grew up with. Where has that Ava been hiding for so many years? I probably have always had access to the power in me to make tough decisions for what is right. But could I have done the same a year ago?

As Elm says, I'm my own agent. But this doesn't mean I have to operate alone.

I am not alone.

Even as this darkness swallows me, I know it's not the reality of my situation. My heart swells with sudden heat. I think of riding horses through the forest. I think of huddling with someone by a waterfall in a cave. I think of earnest conversations and laughter and a pleasant smell. I think of sweet lemon cake. Of sunflowers. Of eyes filled with warmth. These things are part of me, too.

This darkness is the lie.

My eyes blink open, free of the shadows, and stare into rich, warm hazel.

Elm smiles at me and places his hand on my cheek. "So glad to have you back, Miss Ava. I knew you'd come through."

I look around in new awareness. "Where's Jace?"

Elm looks over his shoulder, and I follow his gaze to where Jace stands, hands on his hips, laughing in triumph.

"He thinks he won," Elm says. Jace's cloak has been drained of its color, and so has all of the yellow on Elm's clothing. My own yellow dress is a dull gray as well.

"A shame," Elm says, toying with one of the colorless ribbons. "I'll have to make you a new one. And I'm afraid we're not invisible anymore either, as I had to draw on my devices as well. I'll recharge them back at the cave."

My school bag lies a few feet away, colorless lemons spilled all over the floor. Securing Jace in this illusion required Elm to draw on every source of power available to him.

Elm watches Jace. "I'm actually not too sure how long he'll be that way. He's strong and knows his abilities well."

I tug Elm's cane gently out of his hands. "Can I borrow this?"

I approach Jace, feeling warmth run through me as I cast my strengthening spell. I step behind him, and with a quick tap of the cane to the back of his head, he slumps forward, face flat on the ground.

"I'm assuming you didn't kill him, Miss Ava," he says wryly.

"Of course not," I say, but then I frantically second-guess myself, and I have to check. I scramble to find a pulse. I proclaim more confidently, "No."

"I'm not sure whether or not I'm relieved about that," Elm remarks.

"Me either. But let's think about that later." As an afterthought, I reach down and pull the yellow pendant from around Jace's neck. Now at least if he wakes up, his power will be severely limited.

It happens in an instant—a red blur, and Elm crashes to the ground.

It takes me a moment to register what happened, but then I see Selene, her hands around Elm's neck. Her lean, powerful body quivers with wrath.

"No!" I scream and lunge at her, imagining how swiftly and easily she could snap his neck. I drain the stripes on Selene's uniform of their color, drawing on whatever power I can, and wrench her away from Elm, who clutches his throat and gasps. I throw Selene across the room. She slams against the wall and stares at me, wide-eyed and surprised. She barks a laugh.

"I have to admit, I wouldn't have expected that from you. Oh, Ava. It's such a shame we're no longer on the same side."

She's right in my face again. She's so fast! I throw up my arms instinctively, but she pushes back with no trouble and gets me in a headlock. Elm grabs her arm to pull her away from me, but Selene only releases me to deliver a blow to his stomach that sends him straight to the floor.

"Filthy Yellow," she hisses.

"Don't touch him!" I grab her wrist as she pulls her arm back to attack him again. She flings me across the room, and my back jolts with pain as I hit the wall.

"Miss Ava!" Elm springs to his feet and goes at Selene with his cane. She snaps it in two, ripping the stones free and crushing them to dust. My blood ices over. We're no match for this.

I get to my feet, desperate to reach Elm at any cost. He's weakened from draining all the Yellow, and I have Jace's pendant. I lunge and pull Selene by the hair. She growls and claws at me, but again I fling her as far from Elm as I can and move to shield him. Any moment she will attack again, and all I can think about is keeping him safe, no matter what happens to me. Just then, Elm grabs me and pulls me behind him.

"Don't," I snap, hot tears coming to my eyes. "I can't let her hurt you."

He shakes his head firmly. "I'm not about to let her hurt you again, Miss Ava."

Selene advances and I don't think. I simply react. I'm determined to protect Elm with every aspect of my being, as though I exist for that one purpose.

There is a surge of heat and a blinding white flash. Through my squinting eyes, I see a wide dome of light around Elm and me. The force throws Selene back against the wall. It becomes clear to me what this is. *White magic.* I glance at Elm, who looks equally astounded.

The once-blue walls now stand colorless and drab, and comprehension hits me.

"Ha," I boast. "I was right."

"Right about what?" Elm asks, baffled.

I grin at him and gesture toward the wall. "You said all three magic types are needed to use white magic, right? So you *are* a dual magic-user. Between the two of us, we have all three colors."

Astonishment registers on his face, and then he grins back at me. "Well then, I have no choice but to concede and admit to your rightness."

I hear a wail of fury and turn to see Selene coming at us again. The barrier throws her back once more. Livid, she tries to strengthen herself and break through. Her efforts do her no good.

"Let's hurry," Elm says. "We have no idea how long this barrier will last."

He's right. The fact that the barrier is here at all was essentially an accident. I'm not sure we could replicate it again if we tried. I grab his hand, and we run toward the media room.

"No," I hear Selene hiss.

I look back at her, seeing realization dawn in her eyes. She glances at Jace, still unconscious on the floor, and rushes to him. She places her hands on the back of his head.

"She's trying to heal him," I say, worried. "You don't think he can get through here, do you?"

"Let's hope not."

We enter the media room, and I flick on the main camera while Elm connects to different areas of the school. He wires into the viewdrops in the lounge, the lobby, and the classrooms, and hooks into the PA system. I'm now especially grateful for his aptitude with objects and inventions.

He gives me a thumbs up. "Ready!"

I push the *record* button on the camera, and the test projection in the media room flickers to life with Elm's smiling face.

He looks right into the camera. "Hello," he says cheerfully, and his voice echoes throughout the school.

I hear Selene wail from the auditorium, but with Jace out cold and our barrier in place, there is nothing she can do.

"By now, some of you may be feeling strange," Elm says. "And you undoubtedly have a lot of questions. Well," he pauses, and then says in mock solemnity, "all questions will be answered. The truth is, you've been fooled into thinking all Mentalists, like myself, are evil. Most of us are not. The Benefactors have tricked you and slaughtered the majority of Yellows. Perhaps some of you are starting to remember."

Elm pulls me to his side. "This is Miss Ava. Most of you know her as Prism's top student."

I glance awkwardly into the camera.

"The two of us are putting a stop to this. You can expect a lot more where this came from. If you're tired of being duped, you can fight back."

"You're smarter than this," I interject. "Think about it hard, and you'll know something isn't right. Fight it."

Outside the media room, the dome fades in brightness. "Time for us to go," I say. "Make sure you choose the right side."

"Ta-ta!" Elm waves and pulls us both off camera.

As the dome flickers, crowds of people push their way into the auditorium. Students, teachers, and Benefactors, all shouting and pointing.

"What are we going to do?" I ask.

"A valid question."

As I stare at the growing crowd, I notice flashes of yellow in some of the students' hands. I strain my eyes for a better look.

Lemons.

In the crowd, Blake gives me a pointed stare and then glances at the pile of lemons he's carrying. Several other students also have their arms loaded with them.

"Elm," I grab his arm. "Look!"

He throws his hand to his head in disbelief. Joy spreads across his face. As the barrier rapidly diminishes, Elm wastes no time drawing from this new, unexpected power source. One by one, the bright yellow lemons, scattered around the auditorium, dull.

The dome vanishes at once, and I expect a surge of people to rush and attack, but they don't move. I catch the same vacant expression on all of their faces—the expression that tells me they are being controlled by Yellow magic.

"Quickly," says Elm, grasping my hand. "They believe we're still behind the dome."

"All of them? Even the ones who helped us?"

Elm nods as he pulls me forward. "I don't know for certain who is on our side at the moment. I couldn't pick and choose."

As we leave, pushing our way unnoticed through the crowd, I look over my shoulder and see one person who does not appear to be in a trance like the rest. He stares at us coldly.

"Jace," I whisper to Elm.

"Don't worry," he says. "Without his pendant, he isn't much of a match for us. Like you said, he's a coward. He isn't going to go after us now with weakened powers and nobody else with him. Jace won't fight unless he believes he can win."

Elm is right. Jace holds his ground, fury distorting his face.

As we head back toward the forest, I can't help but wonder about the fate of the rest of the students. Will they be punished? Or will the Benefactors simply entrap them all under Jace's spell again?

"Will the rest of the students be okay?" I ask.

"Along with the illusion, I planted a strong suggestion that nobody else was aware of what was going on," Elm says. "At the least, they won't be blamed for our escape. And if we're lucky, some of them might still remember the message. With so many of the mind-altering devices destroyed, we can only hope it's enough to raise questions."

"But Jace knows what really happened," I point out.

Elm shakes his head. "That skunk isn't going to say anything. That would mean openly admitting to the Benefactors that he let us walk right out the door. He'll likely pretend he saw the same thing as everyone else." He senses I'm still troubled. "I'm sorry, Miss Ava. That's the best I can offer right now."

I lift a hand. "Don't be sorry. I think we made a great start. "

As we enter the forest, I take one last look at Prism, my home for so many years. It's no longer the haven I once felt it was. Any positive memory I had of Prism has crumbled with the knowledge of its deceitful foundations. I never imagined the place I once looked to for all of the answers would require my leaving it in order to find them.

"Goodbye," I whisper.

24

WE SIT SIDE BY SIDE IN THE CAVE, absorbing what has happened today. I rest my head against Elm's chest. His heartbeat still hasn't entirely slowed. We are both edgy from the catalyst of our rebellion. I place my fingertips on his vest and absently trace its light paisley pattern. The vest is gray now because Elm had to absorb its color.

"So, where do we go from here?" I ask. "We had a victory today, but we're far from winning."

He ponders this for a moment. "Most Mentalists were killed off. But that means some weren't. We have to find them. Jace couldn't possibly be doing what he does alone," he adds.

This idea sends a wave of mixed emotions through me. On the one hand, the idea that there are still more Mentalists out there is exciting—unless they're like Jace. On the other hand, it means they are most likely imprisoned and have been for who knows how long. Elm must be right. How else would the Benefactors continue to obtain so much Yellow energy?

"Well, of course," I say, "if there are more Mentalists out there, then obviously we have to find them."

"Obviously," His smile is weary. "There is a lot of ground to cover. Unless we can discover where the Benefactors are getting Yellow magic, we won't be able to completely end their control of Magus. And things are a little more complicated due to the fact that we have no idea who might be on our side."

"That's true, but if nothing else, we have a handful of people we know for sure we *can't* trust." I notice a small scratch on his forehead and trace my fingers along it gently. "Let me take care of that."

My spell completes, and I let my hand linger on his face. His eyes meet mine and wear that same disbelieving look I have seen on him so many times before. He reaches out to mirror my gesture, touching my cheek with a careful softness.

"I'm really here," I breathe.

He smiles, a touch of sadness in his eyes. "I know it. I knew it without a doubt for the first time as soon as you left me."

Tears come to my eyes at his words, and I wonder what I must have put him through.

"The Benefactors wanted me to feel secure and happy in my illusions. The fact that you left sealed it for me that you were real, and you would only stay if you wanted to."

I look directly into his eyes. "I want to," I say and lean in closer.

Just as I think we'll share another kiss, my ears pick up a sound. I bolt upright.

"What's that?"

Elm stands, alert. There is a definite murmur of voices coming closer.

"Do you think we've been followed?" I whisper and begin preparing myself for an ambush.

Elm listens for a moment, and his face relaxes somewhat. "They sound like . . . students."

Suddenly, a familiar voice calls, "Ava? Are you around somewhere?"

Elm frowns. "Your boyfriend."

I roll my eyes at him. "You know that isn't the case." I'm

relieved to hear Blake's voice. It means he's okay. "Do you think it's safe?"

Elm takes my locket and holds it for a few moments. "There. Should be charged up now. See who else is with him."

"Elm," I utter softly, turning the locket in my hands. It feels pleasantly warm with its new energy. My dress bursts back into yellow.

"I'll be right behind you," Elm says, as he toys with his own invisibility device.

I step unseen out of the cave, where a group of about thirty Prism students cluster around the sinkhole, Blake at the lead. They all look anxious, many of them darting their eyes around suspiciously. I don't see any Benefactors or teachers among them.

"Ava!" Blake calls out again. "If you're here, we're on your side."

The assortment is so random that I can't see it as being contrived by the Benefactors as a trap. I remove the locket, and several students jump back as I seemingly appear out of nowhere. Their astonished looks become smiles, some warm, some reluctant.

"Hey, Blake," I say. "How did you know to come here?"

"I . . ." Blake looks around at the rest of the students and corrects himself. "*We* started to remember things. It's not all clear, but what you and the Yellow said in the broadcast . . . we believe you."

Elm appears behind me, and Blake's mouth drops open, then he frowns. "And I remembered other things, too. Like following you out to this sinkhole."

"Spooky place, isn't it?" Elm says cheerfully.

Blake glares at him, and Elm grins back. I glance nervously between them, sensing a clear clash in personality.

"Anyway," Blake continues, expression mildly annoyed, "I

figured if I had any chance at tracking you down, this might be my shot."

"So you're with us then?" I ask, looking over the group of students. "All of you?"

There are several enthusiastic nods and a few murmurs of assent.

"Very well then." Elm gestures to the sinkhole. "Come on in."

The students pile down into the sinkhole, a blend of anxious excitement. I hear several surprised gasps as they enter the cave. Elm also attracts a fair amount of attention—I'm sure everyone is curious about the young man who has stared at them from wanted posters for so long. A few of the students give him an extra wide berth as they pass, and I get the sense that it might take some time before their skepticism and prejudices fully subside.

Once everyone is secure in the cave, Elm steps through to guide them.

As I follow him, I laugh to myself in amazement at our little group. This morning it was just Elm and me, and now the number on our side has multiplied. We have a long way to go, but it's a start.

"Nicely done, Miss Ava," Elm says beside me.

I smile wryly at him. "Why is it always 'Miss Ava' with you? After everything we've been through, must we be so formal?" Truthfully, I don't mind.

He kisses my hand and says, "Dear Ava. Wonderful Ava. *My* Ava."

My smile broadens, and my heart swells. The excitement in the cave as the students explore is contagious. I don't know what is ahead for us, or how successful we may be. And as I look at our mixed lot, full of everything from first-year students to Prism's Elite, I know experience is not on our side. We are a newly born phoenix, fragile, but with untapped power. I don't know if we can reach that power without having our flame extinguished. But what I do know is that we have started a movement in Magus. We are taking back our world, and I'm beginning to think that the future Elm wants might actually be possible. This hopeless love might not be so hopeless.

The colors of Magus are changing.

Acknowledgments

FIRST AND FOREMOST, INFINITE THANKS go to my Heavenly Father for putting me on this path and sending the right people to guide me. Thank you for all the "no's" along the way because you knew there was a better "yes" out there. God is good.

Thanks to Steve Laube for taking a chance on me and providing such brilliant insight, and to Lisa for helping *Vivid* shine. Many thanks to Jamie, Trissina, and the entire Enclave team! You have been amazing to work with, and I'm so blessed to have my book baby in such talented and capable hands.

To my dear husband, Chris, for riding this crazy wave with me. Thanks for kicking around ideas with me, letting me whine, being honest when something wasn't working, having brilliant ideas, and just being silly with me. I love you with all my heart. To my kiddos, Elly, Constantine, and Quinn, for bringing more joy to the journey. Elly, your excitement over the book (and crushing on Elm) makes me smile.

To my parents, Marlene and Trace, for believing in me from day one and being so proud of me. Thank you for always reading my words over the years, from the very first time I could put pencil to paper. I'm lucky to have such support! To my in-laws, Rudy and Denise, for giving me a place to write and encouraging me to grow my talent. Thank you to all of my grandparents for instilling in me a love of learning and storytelling.

To my siblings/their spouses, Theron, Cade & Valerie, Zane, and Rayanna. Thanks for laughing with me, giving me space to vent, and always supporting me. Special thanks to Zane for reading multiple drafts and commiserating with me over rejection. To my sister-in-law Bethany for providing valuable feedback early on and for wanting more Ava and Elm. :)

To the Writers of the Round Table, especially Hannah, Chantel, and Sara. Thanks for all the great advice and support! You are an amazing bunch! (Purple mafia forever!)

To author friends: Jessica Arnold for telling me it's not over until I say so. Sara Ella for being empathetic and encouraging and pointing me in the right direction. Lisa Mangum for reading it and liking it! To Rebecca Jaycox (Slayer of Adverbs!) for helping Ava be a better person. To all my ANWA peeps— you guys are the awesomeness. I love you.

And last but certainly not least, thank you so very much to my readers! Thank you for surfing through the vast ocean of books out there and picking mine. I hope you liked it, but even if you didn't, just knowing you read it means so much to me. Thank you.

ABOUT THE AUTHOR

ASHLEY BUSTAMANTE (AUTHOR OF *A Lamb and a Llama*) has been creating stories from almost the moment she could write. She never considered writing as a profession when she was young because it was just something that was always there.

Ashley strives to create stories with positive messages that encourage others to come together. She enjoys participating in the writing community and hopes to nurture other writers in the way she was nurtured by so many throughout her youth.

When not running through lines of dialogue in her mind, Ashley enjoys taking photographs and spending time with her husband, three children, and any furry, feathered, or scaly creature she can find. She is happy to connect with other writers and readers at ashleybustamante.com.